I0556542

UNTRUST

UNTRUST Deszion Nasir

Also by Deszion Nasir

Wicked Blues

un.trust- to undo one's faith in a person or situation that had previously been established. Not to be confused with "distrust"-from the dictionary of Nasir

Where there is God, there is love;
Where there is no God, there is chaos;
Where there is chaos, there is the Devil;
Where the Devil is, Blue follows...
With twin Desert Eagles....

UNTRUST Deszion Nasir

PROLOGUE

Jerry snapped awake, panting. He blinked, and panicked when he realized he couldn't see. Then he remembered. He was in his closet. He'd passed out in his closet. He told himself it was time to stop getting fucked up. Getting skied and falling out was one thing... but passing out in a closet? Too much.

Jerry felt around for a door knob. When he gripped it, all of a sudden he heard DMX blasting. He frowned, wondering who was leftover from his party last night. If he found some random niggas tryna steal his new shit, man...

He turned the knob and pushed the door open, ready to fuck somebody up. He widened his eyes and froze.

"Oh... whassup, man?" he asked the man playing with his stereo.

"Chillin, man, looking for you." the guy told him, his green eyes flashing. "Was you in the *closet*, yo?"

Jerry laughed nervously. "Looks like it."

The man shook his head. "Cocaine is a hell of a drug."

Jerry laughed. "I'm a quit, man... my girl already done told me she leavin' and shit,"

The man shrugged. "*Fuck* that bitch, man." he said, wandering around and looking at Jerry's 42" flat screen plasma HD TV.

"Ay, this is tight. I thought MY shit was big... *damn*, this musta set a nigga *back*..." Traffic light eyes bounced around the room, taking in all the new upgrades Jerry'd made since he had visited him last.

Jerry scratched his head, trying to put puzzle pieces together. His mind was just too jumbled to make them fit where they needed to go.

"Was... was you here last night?" he asked.

"Nah, you know I don't get down like that no more."

"Right, right..." Jerry frowned as the man continued to fool with his new TV. He put a small hand on the top of it

5

and shook it back and forth.

"Ay, ay... come on, man, that shit was mad expensive." Jerry had to keep his tone from being disrespectful. At 5'7", the young man in front him didn't tolerate disrespect too well.

The guy turned to him, then kicked the TV and the stand on the floor. Jerry jumped back out of the way, shocked.

"What the *fuck*, man?!" he screamed. "How you just gon' *fuck* my shit up?"

"Oh, that ain't your TV," the guy laughed. "Don't worry 'bout it."

"Why it ain't mine? My girl trippin again?" Every time he and his girl got in a fight, she started threatening to take everything in the house while he was at work.

"Oh, naw, naw," the guy frowned and shook his head, walking over to the front door, where Jerry noticed a wooden bat was leaning up against his door.

Jerry watched in horror as the man carefully stepped around the TV. He stared down at it. If this muthafucka smashed his shit anymore, he'd never be able to get it fixed.

"Don't sweat that shit man," the guy said. "It's Blue's TV. And he said he don't want it."

All the color drained from Jerry's face at the mention of Blue's name.

"Ain't this Blue's TV?" the guy asked. "Didn't you buy this with the money you stole from him?"

"Aw, man... look..." Jerry began to back away. "It ain't-it won't even like that... let me tell you what happened!"

The man shook his head. "Ain't my business what happened, man. Talk to my boss. I don't do claims. I'm just the Repo man-"

With that, the man raised his bat and swung it so hard the air cracked. Jerry felt the whole side of his face shatter as the impact swung him around. As he hit the ground, the only thing he regretted was that that swing hadn't killed him. As blood leaked onto his carpet, Jerry closed his eyes, praying when he opened *his* eyes again he wasn't looking into a pair of blue ones...

UNTRUST Deszion Nasir

PART I
BAY DAYS

12 hours ago…

"Oh, *hell* no. Mikell, this shit ain't even close to workin, nigga. Get off me."

"C'mon, Patrice, quit trippin. You know this the best dick you done ever had."

"You mean today? Cuz if you did you'd *still* be wrong you limp-dick muthafucka."

Mikell sat up and shoved Patrice off him and onto the floor. "You won't talkin all that shit yesterday," he snapped.

Patrice rolled her hazel eyes as she popped up off the bed. "Your credit card ain't get *declined* yesterday, neither," she snapped, snatching her dress off the floor and wiggling back in it.

"Whatever, hoe." Mikell waved her off. "I got ten more of you."

Patrice laughed. "So, you ruined sex for 10 other bitches?" she snapped, heading for the door. "I 'on know, boo-boo, you might wanna watch your back behind that. Someone might fuck around and kill your ass like that."

"Bitch suck my dick!"

"Every time I do, I feel like I'm a pedophile, you mini-dick nucca-" Patrice snatched open the front door, laughing. Her laughs turned to silence as a hollow-tipped bullet pierced the flawless skin on her forehead and forced its way out of the back of her head. She hit the ground without making a sound.

Mikell heard her body fall against the hardwood floor and stuck his head around the corner. When he saw Patrice's hair spread out on the carpet, he frowned and took a few steps in that direction. He froze when a set of Timbs the size of his head stepped into view. Attached to those feet was the body of a tall man with auburn red hair and a fitted cap over waves. Behind him was a short Hispanic male with a crazy look in his eye, holding a smoking Glock.

7

UNTRUST Deszion Nasir

"What the *fuck*?!" Mikell yelled. He backed up into a table, horrified.

"Mikell Pearson?" the tall guy asked, reading off an index card. He raised an eyebrow at Mikell's stricken expression.

"Huh..?" Mikell stammered.

The tall guy stuffed the card in his pocket. Then he looked down at Patrice's body and shook his head. "You fuckin ya girl's sister, man?" he asked.

"She-uh-No-" Mikell kept his eyes on the silent Hispanic, who was pulling on a pair of gloves. "Aw, *shit*, man, don't shoot me."

"Nigga, please. Ain't nobody gonna shoot your dumb ass. We just supposed to shoot *her*," he nodded at the body.

Mikell relaxed. "Damn, man. How did my girl find out? She sent ya'll to kill her?"

"Yep. I believe her exact words were 'Blast that bitch's brains out.'"

Mikell was so relieved he didn't notice the other man walking behind him. He didn't see him, but a second later, he felt a sharp stabbing sensation and pain flowed through his body. He looked down and saw the end of a long hunting knife sticking out of his stomach. He heard a grunt and the knife was snatched upwards, slicing through his body. Then the blade disappeared and Mikell watched his insides spill onto the carpet. Stunned and paralyzed, he fell to his knees, then face down, his body damn near inside out.

"Oh yeah," the tall guy said, snapping his fingers. "She *also* said to rip your shit out your back," he laughed. "My bad, my nigga." Mikell couldn't see or speak, but he could feel something being ripped from the back of him. If he could have turned around, he would have seen the Hispanic guy pulling out his intestines and other organs and tossing them around the room. When he was done, it looked like Mikell had been attacked by a wild animal. In essence, he had.

The two men stood next to each other and examined the

8

shorter man's work. The tall one nodded, and the other one was panting, covered in blood, his eyes wild.

"Aight. Clean this shit up and let's go. I gotta pick these twins up for this shit you got us coming to tonight. You still performing?"

The shorter man nodded and wiped sweat off his forehead, leaving a bloody streak. Then he picked up a gas can he'd sat by the door. "You get back in the car. I'll be out in a minute."

"Bet."

The tall guy calmly walked outside, done with his assignment, 25,000 richer without even breaking a sweat. Life was good.

9

LUCKY

Hampton, Virginia

"Ayo, nigga, put that fuckin' gun down!"

"My dude! Are you serious right now? You gon carry shit like that right in your people's house like that?!"

"Shut the fuck up, you pussy-ass nigga! Matter-of-fact, since you wanna talk so gatdamn much give me one good reason-just one-why I shouldn't *body* yo ass right now, nigga."

Silence.

"Oh, now nobody ain't got shit to say? Ain't that what got you bitches in this situation in the first place?!"

"Lucky Lucky Lucky hold up-"

"BANG!"

I jerked and sat straight up, sweating my ass off. Again. My chest was going in and out so hard I felt like I was having an asthma attack. I rubbed sweat out of my eyes, tried to wipe the salty taste from my mouth with the sleeve of my shirt. I leaned over the edge of the bed and tried to get my head together before I went downstairs. Cain't let the niggaz I stay with see me knocked off my square. I lived in a big-ass house off Washington Ave. with five other niggaz who all went to Hampton University. As you can probably tell, *I* won't no college boy. On some real shit? I was just staying here until it was time for me to move into my own spot. I mean, *technically* I got the money to buy a fuckin' house like yesterday, but a smart nigga cain't be doin reckless shit like that and draw a lot of unwanted attention to himself from police and jealous, bitch-ass niggaz. Man, I had to catch rides and buses and shit for *two* years before I could look right walking onto the car lot and buying my 2009 Suburban cash. It had the gold rims and grill and all that shit, but I ain't put like, 23 televisions and speakers bigger than *my* little ass in the back. I already caught enough hell behind me being 5'6" and driving a truck. The niggaz I fuck with do that shit cuz they own businesses and all that. But a nigga gotta carry it like I'm doing what the hell I'm 'posed to be doing: managing one of my man Blue's auto detailing businesses. My real "job" is a story for another time. And no, I don't sell no damn rocks.

So anyway, I get up because I know I'm not going back to sleep. I get in the shower right quick to get myself right. It wakes me up and now I feel more alert, more like myself. I get out the shower and stare at myself in the mirror; I stare at my mom's green eyes that people have always said look like traffic lights, and at the black hair starting to spin out of control growing out of my head. I had weird hair. It wasn't "kinky"-that's what my mom used to tell me to say instead of "nappy"- and it won't curly. My hair grew stiff and straight. It looked good when it was cut, but when it grew out it stood straight up and made me look like a damn cartoon. I'd be at the barber shop in the morning.

I threw on some clothes and went downstairs, stepping over naked bitches left over from the 32nd party these niggaz have had this semester. The party had ended yesterday night, but cats were still drunk, passed out, or sleep from smoking some trash weed. It was now after 9p.m. the next day. I don't really fuck with them, and they don't really fuck with me like that so even though they invited me, I stayed up in my room last night. They ain't complain; they ain't really want me there no way.

I looked at the clock and left out the back door. I went across our yard, hopped the little bullshit fence and walked up to the window of my neighbors' house with the purple curtains. I hesitated at that window. Every time I came here, I wondered if it'd be my last visit. Every time I came here, I wondered if she'd cuss me out. I didn't have no right to speak to her. She was the first girl I loved. She didn't know it. I was the first guy she loved. She didn't know that either.

I snapped to and knocked on her window. I had to bang on that shit like 5 times before the lamp by the bed went on.

11

She was slippin'.

ANGEL

Tap, tap, tap.

I *know* ain't nobody at my window. But I heard the noise again. And sure enough, when I looked out the window a pair of bright eyes-as green as traffic lights-were staring back at me. It took me a minute to get myself together. Whenever I looked into his eyes something shot through my body. Some kind of emotion I couldn't explain. It was kind of like… tragic irony- my teacher put that in my head back in high school at Phoebus High-and it only hit me when I was around him.

I met Lucky a few years ago when he was walking his dog. I was getting the mail and he was waiting for his Jack Russell terrier to finish peeing. He looked up at me, I looked at him and we just stood there. It was the 1st time I had the feeling I'm having now.

"No pit bull? " I joked, cuz we were both just standing there.

He laughed. "Naw, not for me…I don't need no dog bigger than me."

I laughed, but that's all he said. But every time he saw me from that point on, he made sure he spoke to me until we ended up being friends.

I pulled my hair back off my face, went to the hallway and made sure I could hear my mother snoring, then closed my door and slid the window up.

"Hey, baby girl, "Lucky said, peeking in the room. "What you doin' sleep at 9:00?"

"*Sleepin'*."I said, giving him a look that told him he'd asked a stupid question.

"Naw you got to get up and come with me."

"What? Go with you where?!"

"Bay Days. "

Bay Days was an event that went on at the end of the summer a few blocks from our house. It was like a little

13

carnival-type thing that lasted the weekend, but for the people that lived around here the shit was basically just irritating because nobody never had no place to park. It was pretty rowdy at this time of night because all the college boys were drunk and since I lived on this corner they spent a lot of time drunk on our grass and my mom spent a lot of time calling tow trucks. I didn't usually mess with it.

"It's over in an hour and it's cold." I complained, wrapping my arms around myself as a chill from the night wind hit my bare arms. Thick as I was, I didn't do cold weather. Like *ever.*

"It's over in two and put some pants and a jacket on or something."

I guess I was taking too long, so he disappeared from my window and a few seconds later I heard him knocking on my brother Jay's window. Jay was 16, two years under me, and everybody thought he was older because of his height and demeanor. I waited for him to curse Lucky out, but I only heard mumbling, then a few minutes later Jay was in my room, fully dressed.

"Why are you still wearing that shit? You always got people waiting on you, girl, damn!" Jay looked at me with those gold-tinted eyes that we both got from my mother and then I looked out the window and saw Lucky grinning at me. I shook my head and sighed.

"Okay, I'm coming; get out so I can change." I pushed Jay out of the room and closed the door.

"Aw, we all friends!" Lucky protested as I slid my curtains closed.

Ten minutes later we were climbing out of my window and crossing Pembroke Ave. towards the sound of the reggae band that played at Bay Days every year. Once we walked into the thick of the crowd, Lucky grabbed my hand and drug me past all the rides and games to the back of the event where a huge crowd was gathered.

"Why are we passing all the good shit?" I demanded. Lucky knew good and damn well I was a roller coaster

14

fanatic. I tried to pull my hand from his, but he squeezed it tighter.

"Chill. I want you to meet somebody. Stop bitchin."

"Only bitches bitch. You calling me a bitch?"

"Stop bitchin." he repeated.

We walked up to the crowd and I could hear somebody freestyling in Spanish. Then he switched to English and back again. The crowd was loving him and by the time we made it to the front of the crowd I saw this little Dominican cat standing on a bench yelling his ass off and the people around him were acting like he was Kanye' West or something. Can't even lie, dude was nice. I looked at my brother Jay, who was always doing music for some local little boys' tracks and whatever, and he was paying attention; his musical antennae were up. He'd had a brief internship with Timbaland a summer or so ago, and was very good at what he did. Not every 16 year old has Timbo on speed dial. I could already tell that he was planning on cashing in on dude's talent. And what Jay wants, Jay gets.

So Lucky introduced us to the guy, Jai Cruz. He nodded at us politely, then turned back to Lucky, who was texting someone on his phone. He waited a minute until he got a reply from someone and he looked at Jai. "Let's go meet this nigga."

"Oh, you want me to meet another one of your friends?" I asked, wondering what this was all about. Me and Lucky were always cool, but we never really hung out like that, although Lucky always made it a habit to speak to me frequently and ask how I was and check up on me when he hadn't seen me in a day or so. He'd never tried to push up on me, so I figured he saw me as a little sister or something, even though his eyes read something different.

Lucky smirked. "We ain't friends."

BLUE

"**B**lue, can you put that phone down for two seconds and listen to me?"

That damn girl was talking to me again. I'd forgotten her name a long time ago, but it ain't seem to matter to her cuz she wouldn't stop talking to me noway.

"What?" I asked, irritated.

"I said that I gotta be home at ten."

"So?" I asked. Was I supposed to give a shit about that?

"So... it's like, 9:00. I live all the way in Denbigh."

"I know where you live; I picked you up. I know where the hell you live."

"So... I'm sayin... I *know* that but you gotta take me home before my curfew."

I laughed. "No I don't. I said I was gonna *pick you up*. I neva said I was gonna *take you home*. I'm not ready to go yet. Look, here, take this ..." –I gave her a hundred dollar bill-"Catch a cab."

She stalled. "But... I wanted you to take me back to your spot so we could, you know baby, get closer," she said, standing close to me. Hoes was always tryna get in my spot. I *never* brought bitches home. Not na'er one of 'em.

I pushed her off me. "Bitch, I ain't on your time. I just said I won't ready to go and we fucked yesterday *and* today so *I'm* good as far ass and all that getting' close business."

"Damn!" that was my right hand, Doe. Dumb ass. I would've laughed too if I wasn't irritated.

"Hold up, *we* never had sex yesterday!" the girl snapped, rolling her neck and shit.

I just shrugged. "Whatever, ma. Must've been someone else. Either way I'm *still* good."

She kept whining and I got pissed off and snatched the bill back. Then I gave her 6 quarters. "Catch the fuckin bus and lose my gatdamn number. You just fucked up your ride home. Bye." I turned my back to her and never looked back.

16

Doe was just laughing at the shit as usual. All that nigga did was laugh and fuck. Red nigga.

Doe's simple ass was laughing at the girl so loud I had to hide my smile. Armando Creighton was almost as tall as me at 6'6", with red skin and red hair that was always Steve Harvey sharp; but you never saw it because he had a du-rag and a fitted on at all times 24-7, 365 days a year. I bet he wore them shits in the shower. White people always thought he was a rapper and I was his manager or something cause I always had on a suit or something non-stereo-typical. Others thought he was my security. That was just the type of niggas we were, I guess.

Just then, my twin sister Jasmine Knight came flying past me. I only knew it was her because of her Dolce and Gabanna perfume. Jas was 6 feet even, with 2 feet of wild black hair trailing behind her. She got into a fight about her hair more than once cuz some broad would say it was fake. One girl even tried to snatch what she *thought* was a wig off Jas' head. Since it wasn't, Jas fell and she jumped up and beat the cowboy shit out that girl. Jasmine beat her ass, *then* sat on her after she went unconscious and cut all that bitch's hair off with a box cutter. Jas had a real shitty-ass temper, she thought she was better than everyone and would tell them that to their face, rolling those blue eyes just to be dramatic. Fuckin drama queen. It was my fault, though. I don't got no other family- other than my son- and I spoiled her like she was my daughter.

As usual, some nigga was running behind her, trying to get his number and she was ignoring him.

"Blue, handle that," she called to me, not looking at me.

"You got *me* fucked up. I'm not your damn attack dog."

"Yo, ma, I just got a new job, I'm *telling* you I *got* you." the dude was saying. "I mean, I ain't gonna get my first check for like 3 weeks-but whatever you spent on us you know I GOT YOU, RIGHT? RIGHT?!"

"Blue!" Jasmine yelled. "*Seriously*? Please?!"

I sighed, flicked my Newport on the ground and

17

scratched my stomach.

"Aight, man, beat it nigga," I told him.

"*Fuck* you, man," they guy spat, so frustrated that he never turned around to see who was talking to him.

Everybody around us stopped talking and stopped moving.

I laughed. "What did you say to me?"

"Nigga I SAID-" he spun around and was eye-to-chest with me. He stopped talking. When he looked up and saw the dark blue eyes that matched my twin sister's , the dark blue eyes that niggas whispered about amongst themselves, wondering if I was real, if I was a demon or just a fucked-up nigga, he froze.

"Oh shit-Blue! Aw man, I didn't know that was –"

I just grinned and took a step toward him as Jas's phone rang.

"Hello… nothing, girl, just watchin' Blue bout to beat the brakes of this nigga… guuurrrl told him 'fuck you' and *all* that good shit… of course he didn't… I know right? *Real* good insurance…" Jas's loud laughter and conversation made the dude's face turn pale. But the reaper wasn't in no life-sparing mood.

I guess the cat decided if he was gonna go down he was gonna at least go out like a soldier so he swung at me. I saw it coming but I let him hit me. I let him get that one off. Cuz I let him have his balls. He hadn't really done anything *personally* to me; I just had to beat his ass cuz he was getting on my sister's nerves. I went through this shit all the time.

So after he hit me and I didn't blink his face changed. Oh, dude was scared, now. Doe's stupid ass never stopped laughing and I was getting tired of the whole thing real quick so I said fuck it and hit the nigga with my ham-sized fist. That nigga flew off his feet and into a ring toss ride like he was shot out of a cannon.

Females started screaming and Doe screamed "Dayum!! Why you have to *do* that boy like that?!" He was laughing so hard he was crying.

UNTRUST Deszion Nasir

Dude *actually* tried to get back up and that could hurt my rep, so I bent down, picked him up and tossed his ass over people's heads and he landed in the rigged basketball toss game. He laid down like a good little bitch after that. I brushed the wrinkles off my brand new white Coogi suit-I loved white-and pulled a knot of money out of my pocket. I peeled off three g's or so, and handed it to the guy behind the basketball counter. "My bad, man. Can you keep security off my ass?"

"Shit, what security? You good..." the guy said, smiling. He used his foot to roll the now unconscious man off his stand and Doe poured some beer on him, then threw the empty bottle at the guy's head. The fallen idiot didn't even move as the glass bounced off of his head.

We walked past the stunned people who didn't know me and the scared people who did and went and got a funnel cake. Jasmine had grabbed her diva squad and left the area as soon as dude went airborne.

I was just about to take a big nigger-sized bite of my funnel cake when something scented sweeter crept into my nose. It was some kind of sweet smell, like... cookies and something else. I turned around and froze. The nigga Lucky was walking toward me with crazy-ass Cruz and some nigga I ain't know; some Pharrell-looking kid with them funny-looking eyes. You know, the kind that looked hazel and gold and green all at the same time. Then I seen the girl walking almost behind Lucky. She had the same funny eyes, but she was dark chocolate and had a body Buffy would stab a bitch for. She didn't look real. I had a thing for dark girls, always had. She had wavy, not curly, blue-black silky hair pulled off her face so I could see the deep dimples she had that popped up even when she won't smiling. I cain't even lie. *I'm* that nigga but *this* chick was the baddest broad I'd ever seen. I hoped Lucky wasn't claiming her cuz I was gonna have to break my boy's heart.

Since I was just standing there looking retarded, Lucky kinda grinned. "Blue, this is my stick girl Angel and her brother Jay. Ya'll, this is my nigga Blue, and that's Doe."

I glanced at Doe to make sure he was seeing the same thing I was. He was grinning so hard his twin nut-lickers-for-the-night were frowning, looking back and forth from him to Angel. I got myself together instantly. "What did Lucky have to do to get you to go out with him?" I joked. Truth be told, the females stayed on Lucky, but that cat was so quiet and kept to himself so much they probably thought he was weird as hell. He WAS weird as hell, but he was sharp as shit and loyal. I had trusted that man with my life several times and I was still here. Excellent aim. Strong as fuck to be so short. Never ran his mouth like a bitch.

Angel smiled back at me, locking eyes with me. "He woke me up," she said smoothly. "Figured I might as well come out and get a snack," she said, eyeing my funnel cake. My dick got hard just listening to her voice. *That* shit was crazy.

"Is that right?" I asked, grinning. Doe stopped laughing. I didn't smile that much so he knew this shit was serious, I guess.

"Are you serious or are you just being sarcastic?" she asked me, reaching up and pulling off a huge chunk of my funnel cake.

"Are you crazy? How you just gonna take my shit off my plate and I don't even *know* you?" I asked her.

"Lucky already told you my name," she laughed.

"That don't mean I *know* you. Your hands might not even be clean, yo."

She stepped up to me and stuck her muthafuckin finger in my mouth. It had powdered sugar all over it. "Well... now whatever I got, *you* got too," she said, sliding her finger out of my mouth and into hers, smiling at me. I couldn't do shit but smile. Time waits for no man so I go "Look, my man is coming home from upstate tomorrow. You should come and come see me." I glanced at Lucky. He didn't look mad, though. If I didn't know better, I'd say that nigga looked relieved. And there was something else going on with him-I

20

could see it in his eyes- but there was always something going on with him so I let it go, but I filed it away in my mind's Rolodex cuz I don't miss nothing.

"What makes you think I want to come to your party? You're probably crazy and just looking for new pussy." Angel said, free hand on her hip. I stared at her a second with narrowed eyes. I wasn't used to a female talking shit to me like that. She probably didn't know who I was, but I was cool with that. If she *did* know she was a bold bitch. Either way I had to give it to her, but I'm still me and I cain't be talked down to by no broad, no matter how bad she was.

"You think I need your pussy?" I asked her, taking a step toward her.

I expected her to say some shit like "Naw, but you want it." She didn't. She took a step into my space, leaned up to my ear, and said "You will." Then she turned around, took the rest of my funnel cake right out of my hands and walked off, calling to Lucky and telling him she'd get up with him later and she was going home. And damn if she didn't leave. No glance back or nothing. She walked over to the lemonade stand near us and got in line, tearing my jacked funnel cake up.

"Close your mouth," Lucky said to me, smirking while Doe was yelling "DAAAYYUUMMM!" Fuck that nigga. My mouth won't open ...I don't think it was. Naw, not the kid.

I noticed Cruz studying Jay, smirking.

"*Que*?" I asked, wanting to know what was so funny.

Cruz smirked. "*Este tipo es probablemente un maricón.* The nigga probably a faggot," he said to me in Spanish, nodding in Jay's direction. He didn't whisper, as he felt he didn't need to. I shook my head, then something in the corner of my eyes got my attention. When Cruz said the word "faggot," Angel, a couple dozen feet away, cringed. Jay's fist balled up and a half of a second after I figured out that Jay and Angel spoke Spanish, Cruz was stretched out on his back, stunned. Now, don't get it twisted. Cruz was a psycho.

21

Little guys always had to be crazy. I haven't seen anybody land a blow on Cruz for 3 years, so I was as surprised as Cruz.

"*Chúpame el pito ¡maldita sea!* Suck my damn dick! *Call* me a faggot again, Fuck Boy!" Jay yelled, enraged. Angel ran back and grabbed Jay as Cruz got to his feet, pissed off and embarrassed.

"He's a little homophobic," Angel offered, shaking Jay's arm and shoving him off to the side to calm down. He started pacing back and forth like until the madness left his eyes.

"A *little*? What the FUCK?!" Doe yelled, howling with laughter and dropping his drink and making Cruz madder. Doe and Cruz were always fucking with each other.

"Ya'll Puerto Rican or something?" I asked.

"Both took Spanish since 6th grade, "Angel explained.

"What the fuck did you do that for?!" Cruz yelled at Jay.

"Don't call me no *faggot*, son!" Jay yelled, getting heated again.

"You little bitch-ass nigga; I oughta pop your stupid ass right now-"Cruz reached under his shirt but Lucky grabbed his arm.

"Cruz, don't do no stupid shit like that right now," Lucky snapped. "Damn, you ain't fucked up or nothing. Suck that shit up."

Cruz shook his head. "Well if I can't pop his ass, I *should* beat that lil chump with my fucking belt," he grumbled.

The two men sat there glaring at each other. I thought the whole thing was funny so I waited to see what was going to happen, the only sounds to be heard were the mechanical music chimes from the rides and Doe trying to catch his breath from laughing.

After a few weird seconds Jay goes "You need to let me put some of my music with your words. "

"WHAT?" Jay yelled. He started ranting in Spanish. "*Este psicópata ha perdido su mente y quiere morir...* This psycho has lost his mind and he wants to die…"

UNTRUST Deszion Nasir

"Hold on," I told Cruz. This little nigga had balls and something in his eyes that reminded me of me when I was his age. Cruz stared at me like I'd lost *my* mind.

"I want to hear what he got." I said, shrugging. I turned to Jay and Angel. "Bring some work you done to the party at my house tomorrow, okay?"

Jay nodded. I looked at Angel. "You make sure he gets there, okay?"

She nodded. I tore my blues from her hazels and looked at Lucky. "You got my cd player, man?"

"Oh, yeah. You got my T.I. cd?" Lucky pulled the player from his back pocket and we traded.

"Ya'll sure are friendly not to be friends," Angel quipped. I kept my same face on and looked at Lucky.

"I know *I* wouldn't lend shit to someone I claimed I wasn't friends with." she went on, looking from Lucky to me and back again.

I gave Lucky a death glare but he never even flinched. "We don't gotta be friends to loan each other shit," he laughed, ignoring my face. Angel glanced at him and nodded. "C'mon, I'ma get you home, okay?" he said to her. "I'll see ya'll tomorrow," he strolled off with Angel and Jay, never looking back as usual. I'd never seen him look behind him, not never.

Doe shooed the twins away and stepped next to me. "What you gon do 'bout that nigga?" he asked.

"Nothing. Keep your enemies closer," I said. He nodded. "Get rid of them hoes. We got work to do."

Thirty minutes later me and Doe were riding deep into the boonies out Smithfield, through woods and pitch black darkness with no lights on. Didn't need them. We knew to drive south 3 miles, then east for 5. That's all the instructions we needed. We got to exactly 8 miles and saw a dull, gray, old Lincoln town car. The boy Lucky may be strange, but he was accurate. He's earned every bit of that 7 grand I'd crammed in that CD player. It was hollowed out on the inside, so to a nosey-ass onlooker, you'd never see how packed it

23

UNTRUST Deszion Nasir

was.

Me and Doe walked up to the trunk casually. I reached on top of the back right tire and pulled out a key, unlocked the trunk and looked down into the terrified, bloodied face of the punk Lucky found who'd been stealing from me. We stared down at him for a minute, then I reached down and snatched the tape off of his mouth. He yelled out then grew silent, shaking.

"You know why they call him Doe?" I asked the dude, whose name was Jerry, I think.

He shook his head, his eyes darting from me to Doe, who now had a dark look on his face. The joking bruah that everybody knew had been replaced by the killer nobody remembered cuz the only people who'd seen him like this had crossed over into hell.

"Take a guess, then." I told him. He kept looking from me to Doe, trying to see if we were serious. "Answer the question, nigga." I prompted.

"Uh... that... uh... it must not be a nickname if you're askin', so... is it cuz he gets mad dough?"

Doe made a loud buzzer sound. "Why do they always guess that first?" he demanded.

"I don't know, man," I said, shaking my head. "But that's the wrong answer. When somebody has a ball of dough they can shape it, mold it, make it into anything they want. But when you put that dough around some heat, it swells up, gets tougher. It ain't soft no more. And when you burn it? Man, that shit gets so hard it can break things because it's become as solid as a brick. My man here is heated right now. He can break up things," I said pointedly. As I was finishing my little speech Doe reached into the front passenger seat of the car and pulled out a big wooden bat. When Doe showed up behind the car with the bat, Jerry got so scared the nigga pissed on himself. I guess he was having flashbacks about the bat and Lucky swinging it.

"Now," I asked, "I have other shit to do tonight, so I'm only gonna ask you *one* time what you did with my 7g's."

24

"Uh, um…" his eyes kept going to the bat. "I spent it on my girl's house note. You know she just had the baby-"

"Man, I don't give a *fuck* about your scandalous bitch or your bastard, retarded-ass baby. If you *needed* something, you stupid muthafucka, you should have just asked me for it. And now your baby ain't gonna have no father growing up over a *petty-ass* 7 grand. What kind of role model are you, yo?"

Doe raised the bat to bring it down over Jerry's head but I grabbed his arm. "Hold up. By the way, did you ever wonder why Lucky was in your spot waiting for you when you got home today? Nobody broke in, did they?"

Jerry shook his head, confused.

Doe laughed and reached in his pocket with his free had. "Why would a nigga knock when your bitch gave me a key?" he laughed, licking his lips and tossing the keys in the trunk, bouncing them off of Jerry's forehead and watching his face go from confusion, to realization then rage. "She had some *aight* pussy, but I've had better."

I laughed. "Yeah, me too. Her head game was on *point* though."

"Yeah. Too bad we gotta go body that bitch after we leave here. Hey, maybe we can get her to break us off again before I snap her neck." Doe suggested.

"I'd rather stick a gun to her head and make her suck my dick."

"You a sick fuck, Blue." Doe shook his head at me, then turned back to Jerry, who was doing his damndest to break free of his chains. "Oh, my bad, my dude. I ain't mean to hold you up-" Doe raised the bat and smashed both Jerry's knees open with one blow. Next he hit him in the stomach, the side and then the face until his whole body was an unrecognizable, bloody, pulpy mess. I'd stepped back cuz I ain't want that shit on my clothes. Doe got off on that murder shit. His face was twisted all crazy and his breathing was erratic. As soon as he calmed down he wiped the sweat off his forehead, went to the backseat of the car and pulled out

UNTRUST Deszion Nasir

rubber gloves and a huge metal container. I watched as he poured acid over the whole trunk until there was no body left to discover, not even blinking at the sound of a grown man screaming like a monkey set on fire. Then he put the car in neutral and we pushed it over the edge of the cliff and into the James River. Once the car sank and the water stopped rippling, Doe belched loudly and scratched his elbow.

"So you wanna eat now or later?" Doe asked.

"Now. Cain't go into no restaurant smelling like smoke once we torch that nigga's spot."

"Man, fire takes too long. I'm tryna knock this pussy out in a couple hours." Doe complained, pulling out a custom red Desert Eagle.

I sighed. "Fine. Stop whining like a bitch. C'mon.

PART II-THE COOKOUT
JASMINE

"For the *last* time, Dejah, stop smoking that shit around me!" I screamed, but I might as well be talking to a wall. Dejah didn't even look at me as she took a huge puff of a blunt that smelled real suspect and blew it towards the ceiling of my baby blue Benz. "You tyrna give everybody a contact high, bitch?"

"You need one, your uptight ass," Dejah said, her Arabic accent crystal clear.

"Hey, everybody don't need the type of high you probably dishing out. NINA!!" I screamed out of the car window and honked my horn again. I hated being late unless where I was going required it. I glared back at Dejah, who was just staring out of the window and I shook my head. I had never met a girl who could do so much dumb shit to herself and still be so pretty. Dejah Sadaat was Egyptian and had that dark gold skin, huge dark cat eyes and had thick, shiny red hair that she's lightened to a fire engine color. She wasn't too big or too small anywhere and if she was an inch or so taller she'd be very well paid international supermodel like this slow ass girl I was still waiting on- "NINA!! DAMMIT!!" HONK HONK HONK- Where was I... oh, right. Dejah drank like a fish, smoked more weed than most dudes I know and I heard rumors that were most likely true that she did cocaine, too. But I guess when your parents were killed when you were a toddler and you were shifted around from family to family with your brother until ya'll ran away and joined a terrorist camp, got abused by those men for 3 years until you ran away to America and your brother was a certified psycho... you might pick a few bad habits up, too.

Her brother, Caesar, had been locked up for 2 years this time and was getting out today. We were supposed to be on the way to pick him up while Blue was getting his welcome

27

home party together but we were waiting on Nina to come out of her condo so we could go.

After what seemed like way too fucking long out she came, dressed like she was on the set of a photo shoot as usual. Don't get me wrong, I ain't no hater and ain't nobody more banging' than ya girl, but I just hated waiting. Probably because I was spoiled.

Nina came out of her condo head-to-toe in Chanel. I figure that because she'd just done a fashion show for Chanel in Beijing a week ago. Nina was 5'10" feet tall and slim with just enough curves everywhere to keep the designers happy and every little bit she had was damn near perfectly round, which kept the men of all races after her. She was Puerto Rican, black and white with smooth skin and long, glossy ebony-colored hair that hung down to her waist in layers. She was the type that had her body parts insured and whatnot. My whole crew of girls were the finest in the 7 cities and I had hand-selected them to be around me because they represented me well and we were all silver dollars together. But she was still slow.

"Did you bring the clothes?" I snapped without a hello. I didn't wanna hear no excuses about her lateness and she probably didn't have one anyway so why waste 10 more minutes of my life I'd never get back?

Nina tossed a big Armani bag on the other side of the backseat, slammed my door –"Bitch!"- and pulled out a mirror and her lip gloss.

I zoomed off, heated. Don't get me wrong. I wasn't always a bitch-well, the mean kind of bitch-but I had a lot on my mind the other two girls didn't know about. Seeing Caesar again had me *truly* fucked up on the inside.

First let me tell you about Caesar. He's a Pisces. Pisces are loners, paranoid and bad with money. But they are also very emotional and are very good at being able to see through bullshit in a way nobody else can. The can see into your soul and refuse to let you hide from it. When they love, they love harder than any other sign I know. But they're vengeful and have an awful temper. They can't just get "pissed off". They blow up *all* the way, *every* time. I'm a Scorpio. I'm selfish, jealous and conceited but I have a good heart underneath all the superficial shit. Deep inside where nobody can see I just want somebody to love who won't try to fuck me over; somebody who is on my level mentally and financially.

Caesar works for my brother, Blue, as his wildcard. Doe is the right-hand man, Lucky is the negotiator/enforcer-don't let his size fool you-Cruz is the bullet you can never avoid. Caesar is usually who Cruz calls after he locates whoever he needs to find. Caesar is 5'8" with dark brown eyes, dark reddish-brown hair and was a few shades lighter than his sister. Caesar was unstable but very thorough and Blue only called on him when he needed somebody gone quick and ugly.

Normally, I would never be within spitting distance of someone like that, but for some reason I was very drawn to him. Of course we both knew without saying it Blue wouldn't have liked that shit at all. So we ended up seeing each other for over a year behind his back. Nobody knew about it. Nobody. I learned that Caesar was very loving and just what I needed, but I love to be seen and as long as I was dealing with him we had to sneak, hide and stay in the house or a hotel out of town and eventually we started to argue. I wasn't staying in and he didn't like me going out without him because of the men that constantly tried to holler at me.

At its worst point, our relationship turned really bad when we got in an argument at my house and I tried to slap him. He shoved me off of him, my heel caught in the carpet and I fell down two flights of steps. To this day I don't remember *what* the fight was about, but I remember what happened after that. Caesar picked me up and drove me to the ER at 95 mph. Luckily Blue was in Ecuador so he never knew what happened and Caesar paid for the whole visit. That wasn't the bad part. The bad part was that that fall caused me to miscarry a baby I never knew I was pregnant with. The day I got home from the hospital, Caesar got me settled in the bed, silent tears in his eyes, kissed me on the face and left to get me some dinner. He got pulled over 2 miles from my house for speeding and I haven't seen him since. He jumped one of the cops, broke both the rookie's arms before his partner shot him in the leg. I couldn't ask Blue where he was locked up because then I'd have to answer why I wanted to know and Blue isn't stupid. The only way we got away with it that long was because he was in South America so much during that time setting up some deals.

So, long story short, beneath my divaness I was nervous as hell to see him again.

Dejah fell asleep 20 minutes into the ride and Nina was on the phone running her mouth in Spanish to whoever had an attention span so I really had the whole ride to myself and my thoughts. All I really had to think about was Caesar actually. I didn't work, Blue wouldn't let me. He was overprotective since we didn't have no parents and our only close relative was our brother Terrence who was locked up on Riker's for killing our father, Gemini Knight. Apparently Gemini was a son-of-a-bitch that beat the shit out of our mother who won't shit herself cuz she was engaged to Gemini's best-friend when she fucked our daddy. She had us, then gave us up. Nobody has heard from her since and me and Blue spent our whole life in the system. That's why Blue is so...twisted, I guess. I don't want to talk bad about my brother because he has done everything for me, but...well, you'll see.

Anyway, when we got to Greensville Correctional Center, Dejah went in to get her brother. My mind was all over the place until I heard Nina go "Dayum, that's Dejah's brother?!"

I looked up. Dressed in the Armani suit Nina had brought him along with the matching shoes and shades, Caesar looked more like a famous producer that a felon who just got released from prison on a parole violation.

I didn't say anything, just watched him come up to the car. He leaned down in my window and said "What's good Jasmine Silk?" He used to always call me by my first and middle name right before we... did the grown up, so I knew were his heads were at.

Nobody else knew that so I just smiled and threw my attitude up. "Are you gonna stay out of jail this time, nigga? I hope you got some bills in them pockets to pay me back from all the damn gas I had to spend for coming up here and feeding these greedy-ass bitches."

He just smirked and peered in the car at Nina. "So are you the greedy bitch I need to thank for this outfit?" he asked her, looking her over. I glanced in the mirror and saw her smile despite herself. Attention whore.

Nina, who couldn't help herself, smiled and stuck her hand out like he was supposed to kiss it or something. "I'm Nina."

Caesar smiled at her but didn't take her hand. "No disrespect, baby but I been on lock over a year. The next female I touch I'm fucking."

Nina raised an eyebrow and looked at me. She was trying not to smile though. I seen that shit.

The whole ride back Dejah was talking Caesar's head off but he fell asleep 35 minutes into the ride. When we got back to me and Blue's spot I woke Caesar up and managed to get him into one of the guest rooms where I left him to take a shower and take a nap before Blue got back from wherever he was that kept him from going to get his boy himself. I hoped he didn't take long. People were already starting to arrive. Doe's dark red Excursion was parked out front. Hmm... I don't have nothing else to do at the moment... think I'ma go fuck with him...

31

DOE

On the average day, people look at me and see a fly ass nigga. On the average day, people don't take me seriously. Everybody thinks I'm just a party nigga who gets high and fucks a bunch of bitches. They think I'm Blue's bitch. On the average day nobody knows that when I met Blue and Jasmine in the 7th grade, Blue was just Scorpion Knight, a tall, lanky, funny-eyed nigga that stayed in the group home with his weird-ass sister who never took her hair out of its ponytail. Both of them were wearing raggedy clothes that were too short for their long arms and legs. I saw kids picking on them and I stood up for them. Maybe because I thought they were different and I liked different. When I was in school I was always the popular class clown that had all the little girls chasing after me cuz I was tall, dressed in the tightest gear, had the brand new kicks weeks before everyone else did. My family was paid, yeah, but as soon as I was old enough to push a lawn mower I was working, getting my *own* paper. I stacked *all* that money and only spent the money my parents gave me. Eventually I got real tight with Blue and started buying him and Jasmine clothes and shoes and taking Jasmine to my aunt's hair shop on Mallory Street out Phoebus where we lived at. Then Blue grew into his body and all the girls started getting on that nigga. Jasmine was the same way with the niggas. Blue was smart as hell, so between my status, his brains and just the strength of who the fuck we were, when Blue decided to skip selling weed and go straight from guns to executions, the success seemed to happen overnight and we ain't stopped rolling since. We are partners and brothers. We've done shit together that will never let us get into heaven. We've killed mothers children, pregnant chicks, kids and the dog too. Since we'd never get in heaven might as well make sure we get a window seat in hell…Too far gone to stop now… even though sometimes I wanted too. But on the average day, don't nobody know that.

UNTRUST Deszion Nasir

On a day like today, I'm sitting in my truck while broads are waiting for me in Blue's backyard. I see them peeking around the corner at me. But man, it was too easy to fuck them scandalous bitches. A nigga ain't had to work for no pussy for *years*. Everything and everybody I wanted I had or could get by blinking. That's why I continue to do the shit for Blue that I do. Yeah, it was fucked up, but in my demented brain it kept me busy. I owned two businesses at 26 that pretty much ran themselves. I needed something else, somebody else in my life. I was tired of tired of these damn parties, but I had to be there for my man. My mind drifted to Jasmine's car pulling up. I wanted to go greet my dude, but he looked dead on his feet so I decided to leave him alone for now. I lit some purple haze and leaned back in my seat. As soon as I closed my eyes good I felt my car door open. I knew who it was before I even opened my eyes because out of all the topnotch broads I've dealt with, none of them had the money to buy the perfume I smelled but one.

"What, Jasmine?" I asked, irritated, knowing she just came in here to fuck with me. Jas was one of those women who had so much they had no need to achieve anything else so they just decided to fuck with random people until they lost their minds. Just so she could have something to do.

"*Damn*, I'm just seeing how you were," she said in her fake sweet voice. Don't misjudge her, now, Jas had a sweet side, but she kept it hidden because she refused to be seen as weak. I knew her, though. Knew her well.

"I'm good," I said coolly, not opening my eyes.

"So… why you not in there welcoming your boy back?" she demanded like she was personally offended.

"He looked tired. I'ma let the man get his rest before it gets jumping over here," I explained, belching in her face and yawning myself.

"You nasty sum-ma-ma bitch-" She slapped my arm. "… Okay, cool, but that don't mean you cain't come speak to the rest of us, do it?" she asked.

"Who is 'us?'"

UNTRUST Deszion Nasir

"Me, Dejah and Nina."

I opened one eye, looked at her to see if she was serious, then waved her away. "Man, ya'll see me every damn day. Fuck outta here wit that shit, Jas."

Even in the brief silence I could hear her wheels turning in that swole head of hers.

"Well, you know that girl Angel is coming."

"So? She ain't coming to see me."

"Sherita is coming, too."

"Who?"

"Sherita, that girl from Brazil who makes those custom shirts in the mall. She was just featured in a show Nina did that I went to."

I laughed. "Got a new member in the bitch squad?"

Jasmine slapped my arm again. "I mean, you know how I am. She's a top-notch bitch like myself and my girls, and I respect her hustle, you know? She could benefit from being around people I know."

I shook my head. Jasmine collected her friends the way kids collected baseball cards. Only the most unique, top of the line ones would do. True, Jas might be looking out for the girl, but I knew in her heart, this chick would somehow make her look good or she wouldn't be dealing with her in no type of way. Her latest stick girl, Minya Ngyuen, was this black and Asian chick that was just as fly as the rest of them and owned the new hair salon Jasmine and Nina went to. No doubt she'd be here cuz I had seen her in a few clubs and she didn't seem the type to miss a party. Or turn down a drink…

"You know what? I think I'm a bounce for a minute," I told Jasmine, sitting up and sticking my keys in the ignition.

"What? Where are you going?"

"Why do you give a fuck?"

"I *don't*. I'm just asking."

"Well, why you 'just asking,' then? Since when do you give a shit about who I fuck or where I go?"

"Ain't nobody say *shit* about fucking so you must be on your way to knock the bottom out of some stank-ass pussy-

UNTRUST Deszion Nasir

bitch you fucking with," she snapped.

"You got some shit with you, damn!" I exclaimed, getting frustrated. "How do you know I ain't gotta work?" I did. A senator was tired of paying off his ex-mistress. He was up for re-election and she'd made one threat too many. He wanted her done quick and clean. Lucky would normally handle that kind of job, but right now he was busy dangling a dude off the roof off the Marriott, a first-class trip to hell sponsored by his battered wife.

"Look, nigga, *I'm* not fucking you; I just wanna know where you going when you 'posed to be here for your boy-" Jasmine was still talking.

"*Your* boy." I snapped, pissed off now.

"What you mean, 'my boy?'" Jasmine sat back, rolling her neck. I wasn't gonna bring the shit up, but fuck it.

"Oh, he ain't your boy no more? Did he stop being your boy *before* or *after* he pushed your ass down the stairs?"

She didn't say shit. Just like that, she was on the defense. But I wasn't done yet.

"Oh, you ain't got shit to say now? You don't got no more smart-ass questions, nosy ass? You don't even wanna know how I know that shit?"

Jasmine's eyes teared up, but I knew she'd never shed one. Bitches like her never cried.

"I was there, mami. I was about to knock on your door when I heard ya'll yelling and then I saw him push you down when I looked in the living room window. Then I saw his ass running down the steps to get you, apologizing and shit. Then you told him shut the fuck up and take you to the hospital because you were bleeding and your stomach was hurting." With every word I spoke, she started watering up more. I don't know how she was holding all that water in.

I let her sit in silence for a minute before I said "I ain't gonna ask you no questions cuz I really don't wanna know the answers. But I *am* leaving right now because I cain't look *that* nigga in the face right now. Okay? When I get my head together I'll be back. Is that okay with you or do you have another muthafuckin question for me?"

Jasmine shook her head. She was done. Or so I thought.

"Can you get out my truck now? Please?"

Jasmine cracked the door open and was halfway out before she turned to me and half grinned. "That happened at like, 3 in the morning. What were you doing here at 3 a.m.? Blue was out of the country."

I just shook my head at her and put my car in reverse. "Conceited ass..." I muttered as she closed the door. I wasn't fin to answer that question. It ain't like she really *gave* a fuck anyway.

CAESAR

There're too many people this damn house, man. I just woke up from a 2 hour nap and looked out the window. There were a million muthafuckaz I'd never met before walking around out there like fucking cattle.. Most of these people didn't come here to welcome me home cuz they didn't know who the fuck I was. They just knew *about* me. I know what the fuck people said about me. I know I was being called a psycho, a terrorist Blue had scooped up from Egypt to kill for him in exchange for American technology; hmm, what else, what else... oh yeah that I was a radical Muslim and I dyed my hair blood red cause I was obsessed with killing infidels. There was more, but nobody has that kind of time. Fuck them.

Was I a killer? Yes. Was I crazy? Probably. A terrorist? Never that. I was the last option. If *I* had to show up Doe wasn't that far behind, cuz everybody knows that Doe gets rid of fucked-up bodies. He used to do what I do now, but the weapon business got so big Doe was needed to handle other things. The biggest change came when the police started buying from Blue. Now, they don't know who they are getting the shit from- Blue ain't never been stupid and will do no face work with them-but they think he's one of "The Big Man's " -code for "rich white guy"-workers so they stay off of his businesses out of fear. That's fine with Blue. It wouldn't mean anything if they thought it was him, anyway. All his businesses and houses had been raided a couple of years ago in broad daylight and when they couldn't even find a cigarette butt anywhere they were looking stupid, especially when Blue sued them successfully for 1 and a half million dollars (he stuck 1 million in a sweeper account and every year it doubles, he gave the other half a million to his son's mother and told her to see if she could buy a damn clue with it.)

Where was I in the middle of all that? In the shadows,

37

where I belonged.

I didn't wanna do the shit I did, but all I knew was death and murder. Me and Dejah were born in Egypt but we were raised in Afghanistan for years until we were shipped out to America. No child should see the shit we had to see, man. I seen my only friends brainwashed into thinking they should kill themselves for a greater good and watched them murder hundreds of their own people and soldiers. Yes, I ended up in a terrorist camp as a young teen, but they didn't hype me up to kill myself. I was too valuable as a killer. I didn't want to do it but I needed to eat, shit. Dejah needed clothes, food and female shit.

Dejah was always more beautiful than any girl I had ever seen. And more beautiful than any girl the men in the compound had seen, apparently, cuz they were always touching on her until one man raped her and she severed his penis with her teeth. They'd never seen such a temper or such a hair color on a female. She got beat for talking back to men but it never stopped her mouth. The leaders said she was possessed after one of the men tried to touch her after the rape and Dejah sliced his face from ear to ear and he bled to death. I had to snatch her and run in the middle of the night when I found out they were going to kill her. It took all the money I had stolen to buy a ride with a stranger to the airport. Nobody wanted to help me at first, they knew what I was and wanted no part of the fall out if we got caught. The last dude saw Dejah hiding in the bushes. She was barely 11, chain smoking and crying. He watched her kill a cigarette after 3 pulls, toss it and pull out another for 2 minutes before his face softened and he let us ride under his truck. Dejah's hair came undone and we had a hell of a time keeping it from getting caught up in shit. She had never cut her hair and would rather have died before she did. (Our mother was the only woman we or anyone else we knew that had that same red hair and since she was dead Dejah swore she'd never cut her hair).

The airport is a very unorganized place and it was easy to get around security and on a plane. We hid in the back

UNTRUST Deszion Nasir

area with the luggage until a flight attendant came back there and found us sleep. She made me eat her nasty-ass pussy right there in front of my little sister and then after I went and threw up in the bathroom she let us have seats on the plane where we slept the whole ride. The plane landed in Norfolk, Virginia and we hitched a ride until we got to Hampton. The guy let us off in a section of the city called Phoebus: 249 Chamberlin Rd. with no luggage, no money and no English skills at all. He dropped us right in front of a candy-apple red Mercedes, which was parked next to a dark blue Hummer. Two men were leaning on the Hummer and smoking Newports and talking to a couple of kids. They were both giants.

"Who ya'll lookin for?" The one in the Rocawear sweat suit asked. I didn't know what he was saying so I just stared at him. The other one with him studied us for a minute when we didn't answer.

"They ain't looking for nobody," he said, flicking his cigarette to the asphalt. He stood up and came over to us. "You don't speak no English, do you?" he asked. I just shook my head at him, pushing Dejah behind me. He grinned and called a female's name from the open door of the center. She was short, dark as hell and beautiful. She looked like an islander and she looked at us, then the tall teen. He said something I only recognized as yet a different language –I found out later it was patois- and she stared talking to me in a few different languages until she said something in Arabic and my eyes lit up. That woman was Siovahn Effe' Baptiste, the mother of Azzure' Knight, the only son of Scorpion Knight, (Blue)-who was the teen in front of us. Of course, the other guy was Doe, and just like that, Blue took us in. He told me later he did it cuz he saw something in my eyes worth saving, but that's some bullshit. He saw a killer. He saw an opportunity. I don't hate him because nobody else ever gave us shit to this day, but I'm not stupid. I know what I was... and I know what I am now.

I was busy feeling sorry for myself when the door

UNTRUST Deszion Nasir

opened and a nigga walked in. I thought it was Pharell from The Neptunes at first and I had to look again. Behind him was a short, chocolate version of him but she had gold eyes that had the same emotion in them mine did: stress. That caught my attention. We caught each other's gaze for only a few seconds before I heard Jasmine's feet coming. I never knew how a woman so tall kept her feet so pretty and never took those damn heels off.

"Why did you come in that door?" she demanded of the kid.

"Cuz it's the door I *opened*," the kid said to Jas like she was slow. I smiled despite myself and Jasmine made her cold eyes small.

"Everybody out in the back. Don't nobody come in the house."

"*You* in here,"

"*I* live here."

"Shit, I don't know that. You might just be a sexy-ass thief or something. Don't try to push up on me to keep me from calling the police, neither," he said loudly. I burst out laughing and Jas was trying to keep a smile in.

"Okay, well, you didn't know the rules but normally you gotta let somebody know when you need to come inside," she said, putting her hands on her hips and flipping her hair over her shoulders.

"Shiiiit, I'll be damned if you catch *me* asking another mafucka to piss," the kid laughed, walking through the house like he lived there. Jasmine was still standing there as we listened to him piss with the door open, then flush and come back down the hall, walking past Jas. He saw Cruz sanding by the DJ table outside and walked out the back screen door and right past Jasmine without another word.

Jasmine's crew was in the hallway, doing a weak-ass job of pretending they weren't listening. She glared at them with her brother's look and they backed into the back part of the house. Then she glanced at me, then turned to the girl.

"Angel, right?" she asked.

"Yeah."

"You can come on back here. Blue isn't here yet and I don't want you out there by yourself. Them niggaz would attack you," she said, crossing her arms. Angel looked at me for some reason. I just shrugged and grinned.

"That's Caesar. It's his party but be careful, he bites. A lot," she added, glaring at me. I watched as she damn near drug Angel away from me. I saw that phat ass anyway. I *also* seen the way she looked at me. Blue better watch his self.

SIOVAHN

I was in a dream. In my dream was the only man that had ever made me smile. We were on the beach in my home town of Ocho Rios, Jamaica, and while I lay back in my itty-bitty bikini I watched his caramel body coming up out of the water with a mini-me version of him, complete with the smooth skin and the eyes that had gotten my attention in the first place. Once I met my dream, I never had to want for anything. Once I got pregnant, I never had to even create something even in my imagination. That was his gift. He could always read my mind. He turned my Honda into a customized Benz. I wasn't even thinking about that car; I was just looking through a catalogue and he saw me pause on a page that was featuring one. I said "Oh, that's a cute car," and I had one 2 days later. He took me out of the cramped 2 bedroom apartment out Lincoln Park and moved me into a four bedroom condo by the water over by Hampton University. I had a minimum of 5 thousand dollars deposited in my bank account every Wednesday, rain, shine or holiday, since the day I told him I was pregnant...up from 2500 since a week after we met. It just sat in the bank, really, cuz I had a safe at home that he put money in every time he came to see his son. He bought all his clothes, all our furniture and paid all our bills, so all I had to do was go shopping and go to the gym. The only thing he ever asked me to do was "Stay tight. My son is gonna use you to learn what a woman should be, so you have to be perfect all the time, so he don't get caught up by no raggedy-ass broad out here."

I sighed, opened my eyes, and was staring at the back of what my dream had turned into. All the financial things had remained the same...but everything else was different now. I watched him sliding his pants on, then picking up his $250,000 watch-one of many-and sliding it on carefully. I saw the towel he just took a shower with folded neatly on the

UNTRUST Deszion Nasir

top of the hamper. He was so neat it was frightening. He took his shirt off a hanger and slipped it on, sending a burst of his Boucheron cologne my way. How many guys hung their shirts up before sex? I mean, *really*. I was staring at him smiling until his phone rang. It wasn't the business phone; it had a different ring. It wasn't the one that he kept for me to contact him either...it was what I called his "bullshit phone," because whenever it rang, to me, it always sounded like some bullshit was going on the other end. I frowned and sighed loudly, falling back on the bed. He ignored me and answered.

"Yeah... hey..." I didn't see it, but I *heard* him smile. And that pissed me off. Blue rarely smiled, and if he was smiling over the phone...I told you: this was some bullshit. "Yeah, I know I'm late, but I'm on the way now... I got caught up doing something for my son's mother... yeah, you know how it is... what you wearing?... damn, that sounds sexy as hell... shit let me hurry up then... naw, naw, I got you... I got a present for you too when I get there... don't worry about it... well I'ma *get* to know you, but I bet you gonna love it anyway... yeah, aight... I can't drive if you say stuff like that over the phone... I might get in my own way... naw YOU nasty... hahaha... Yeah, I'm coming, don't go nowhere..." Blue hung up, ran his eyes over to mine as I stared at him open-mouthed. "What you got your face all twisted up for?"

"I *know* you ain't talking to no bitch right up in my face like that after we just made love, Blue." I snapped, hand on my hip, the other holding the sheet up.

"Naw, I'd never do that... but we were *fucking*, so what's the problem?" Blue asked, shrugging.

"What?!"

"Vahni please. You know what's up. You a whole lot of things, but I never called you stupid. Chill out. You know how we do." He waved me away like I was a gnat and checked his waves out in my mirror.

"Why would you even come *over* here to be with me if you got some bitch waiting for you? She must not be too tight." I laughed, even though I knew Blue never messed with

43

broke-down chicks. The response was a combination of my broken heart and bruised ego.

"Oh, don't get it twisted. She fine as hell. She's flyer than you, actually. But *you* called *me* over here. Don't I always come when you call me? You wanted to fuck, I fucked you, and now I got other shit to do." He looked at me through the mirror at my gaping mouth and tears. "See, this is why we ain't work out. You too damn emotional. We not together, ain't *been* together and you know it. What, Vahni? You want some more dick? Some more money, what? What you want that I never gave you? You think I be having time to run over here every time you get horny? I *know* you don't need no damn money, but if you want some, I don't never question you. What else you think I'm supposed to do that will stop you from *bitching* all the damn time? You want me to leave you alone? You sick of me? I can bounce and never come back. You'll still get your money and you know I got Azzure'... so, what's good? You want me to take me and my new 'bitch' and bounce?"

I wiped my tears away and sat up as straight as I could, as proudly as I could, as I listened to a man that was about to leave me to meet another woman while his cum was still running out of my body. "Just go, Blue." I managed. He shrugged.

"Cool. Take my son shopping, I seen some kid with the same shoes he had on this morning." He tossed a stack of money at me and he walked out. I got up, ran to the window, and saw him on his business phone, talking rapidly. I had the window up, so I heard him speaking in Portuguese, one of few languages I didn't understand. I wanted to throw that money at his head for making me feel like a hooker, but I knew what he would do to me if I did. I thought back to the last time I'd opened my mouth when he'd pissed me off...

Blue had come to my house in the middle of the night with Doe, a huge bag slung over Doe's shoulders. When I heard the door open I sat up, panicked. My son was at his grandmother's house in Ocho Rios for the summer, and I

44

knew nobody else had a key but Blue. I was panicked because Blue knew that and because I heard more than one voice, I knew this wasn't a social visit.

I jumped up and ran in the living room. "Oh, my God," I got out when I saw the bag slung onto my new carpet. Blood was dripping out of the bag and forever staining my carpet and hardwood floors.

"What the fuck did you bring that here for?!" I screamed. Blue's immediate response was to backhand me so hard I flew over the top of the couch, landing on my side. I came down hard on my arm. As usual, Doe just shook his head and went into my kitchen, grabbing some bleach, trash bags and some other equipment. He never defended me or helped Blue when he smacked me around.

Moaning, I climbed to my feet and looked on in horror as Doe unzipped the bag and he and Blue pulled a broken up, ripped up body out of the bag. I got sick instantly and ran into the bathroom and threw up. Nobody came to check on me. I mean, I figured no one would, but it would have been nice, you know?

So, I splash some water on my face and when I get back to the living room, Doe's pulled out this little electric chain saw and is slicing this body up like a turkey. As he separates each piece, Blue is stuffing them in different bags. I know he's planning on taking the body pieces and getting rid of them in different areas in different ways. That's his MO.

"Why...did you have to bring that here?" I asked, making sure I was far enough away from him to avoid another blow.

"Bitch, please. You think I would have come here to listen to your fuckin mouth if I had a choice? Nigga tried to get at us around the corner from her, near where Lucky stay at. Had to get rid of him fast. I'll replace all your little foo-foo shit, Siovahn. Shut that shit up. I paid for all this shit anyway. Those drapes, that stereo...the drawers on your ass..." he came over to me and shoved me toward the kitchen. "Go find something else to do besides stare at me, shit." he

45

snapped as his phone rang. He turned his back on me, answered the call, and after a few seconds, he walked over to my door and pulled it open. 5 men rushed into the apartment, grabbed the bags Doe had filled and disappeared. As soon as they exited, 5 more rushed in and within minutes, had stripped my whole living room. It took them less than ten minutes to scrub the room down and 5 more to put down new carpet and furniture. Blue and Doe left right after them, not saying another word to me...

Now, I shook my head to clear those bad memories and went to my mirror that covered an entire wall in my room. Looked at myself. I was a little thick, but I was juicy, that's what Blue always used to call me. Azzure' thought that was my name for 2 years when he was younger. I had a juicy butt, thighs and breasts, not to mention lips that were only found in my homeland. My hair was asymmetrically bobbed, always perfect, as well as my nails and toes. I was a bad bitch, and I don't care *what* Blue said, won't no female badder than me. Nowhere. Blue thought I was stupid. I know Caesar's coming home party was today. He must have that bitch he was talking to meeting him there. I would cuss Jasmine out later for not calling me and telling me what the fuck was going on. Naw, better yet, I'd tell her in person. I went to my overflowing closet and pulled out a custom Gucci jumpsuit that barely covered my ass and had no sleeves. I was going to that party and show him and that imitation of me he was dealing with who the bad bitch really was.

ANGEL

I knew when Blue got to the house way before I saw him. All I heard was the rumbling of a bass line and the ground shaking, and all the females started running to the front of the house like they were on a reality dating show or something. I went to the door and saw a brand new Crayon blue Hummer pulling up. I was wondering if I should go outside too when I heard Jasmine say behind me, "Groupies. You'd think Blue had a record deal or something."

"He got something better than a record deal," Nina chimed in. "He's got money and a big dick." We all broke out in laughter and Jas glared at Nina. "Oh, come on Jas. You know bitches talk. He may be *your* brother, but he sure as hell ain't mines."

Jasmine shook her head at her girl and patted me on the shoulder. "Don't sweat them thirsty-ass hoes. He invited *you*. Watch and see how he do..."

I turned back to the door and watched Blue move through the sea of women and men eager to get a hug, dap, or simply a greeting. The grin never left his face, but he never stopped moving, either. His eyes met mine, and I got a chill when a smile broke out on his face. About 40 pairs of green-eyed hate hit me hard from the females, but I just smiled back at him as he came up the steps, towering over me. I'd forgotten how tall he was and how short I was. "Damn, you wasn't lying... you look..." he shook his head at my strapless Dereon jean jumper and wrapped me in a huge bear hug, swallowing me up in his huge arms. "Come on," he said, leaving his arm around my shoulder and leading me inside, closing the door on the people outside.

"Caesar!" he yelled, and moments later, the red-haired guy who was staring at me earlier came from out of the kitchen area, holding a half-empty Heineken in one hand and a fresh one in the other. Blue grabbed him in a one-armed man hug, never taking his arm from around me, so it looked

47

for a minute like a group hug. They started talking in what I think was Arabic so I didn't know what was being said, but they were both smiling.

They were interrupted by a knock on the door and someone cursing loudly in English mixed with what sounded like something originally from Asia. Jasmine opened the door and a short girl walked in, pushing a man's arm away from her. "Fucking vultures...every time I come over here it's the same shit..." Her face changed and a beautiful smile popped up when she saw Jasmine. "Hey, Diva."

"Hey, sweetie." Jasmine pilled her inside and glared at the men outside. "What the fuck is *wrong* wit ya'll? Grabbing on bitches and shit. Get the fuck away from my door and get to the back. Ya'll know better, and if you don't you probably wasn't invited anyway, you stanking-ass bastards." Jasmine slammed the door to the men's laughter and shaking heads, but they began walking to the back yard as ordered.

The girl was obviously black and Asian. She had slanted eyes, but they were bigger and barely seen under her thick eyelashes. She obviously got the hair from her black side; it was kinky. It was curlier than mine and in a huge mass of dark brown with red, gold and orange streaks running through it. It sounds terrible but the way it was done made her hair look like 3D art. She had on what looked like a kimono that was cut off right under her breasts and a pair of matching short shorts in a solid white pattern.

"Ya'll this is Minya Ngyuen, the girl that does Nina's hair at her shop out Virginia Beach." Jasmine spoke up. The other girls who had been in the room with Minya all spoke. The introductions went around. Sherita was the Brazilian chick with her own independent line of custom made shirts and pants. She was about my height with wavy blond hair, dark tan skin and huge breasts that went with her curves. Nina was as tall as Jasmine and thin but still had a curvy appearance. Her skin was a perfect tannish-cream color and her hair hung in glossy black locks down to her shoulder blades. She looked like a picture in a magazine. I knew she was a highly paid high fashion model that had just returned from a Baby Phat show in Milan and was now on a two month break in between jobs. Then there was that evil-looking girl, Déjà, who was so pretty but her face stayed balled up. Her face was almost as red as her hair as she glared at Blue. She'd been looking at him like he shit in her cornflakes since he walked in the door. Jasmine saw her glaring at him and gave her a hard look that made her turn away and light a blunt that smelled suspect to my experienced nose. It was too tangy to just be weed.

The smile dropped from Blue's face as the smoke reached him. "Put that shit out," he said in a quiet yell, obviously trying to control a quick-rising temper.

"Nigga *fuck* you," she tossed back, but when she looked at the face Blue gave her-one I couldn't see-she turned as pale as death. Without another word she took the blunt and stubbed it out in a nearby ash tray. She rake her heavy hair back off her face and walked outside, never once speaking to her brother, I noticed. I glanced at him, but he was looking at me with this real intense look on his face. I couldn't even look away from it until I felt Blue gently nudging me the way Déjà had gone.

"Come on, let's get you something to eat," he said, his voice softer. He slid the glass doors open to the huge back yard, where tables and chairs were set up strategically all over the deck, grass, and around the club-sized speakers and the DJ table, where my brother Jay was now dominating while the hired DJ stood to the side, nodding and smiling with his arms crossed. That little Dominican guy Jai was standing on one of the tables *getting'* it. It was like he was already a celebrity, but I must admit, he was damn good. Even the people who couldn't speak Spanish (as he was switching languages back and forth) were excited and jumping around like he was. I could tell they were impressed by my brother's skills, but I already knew the boy was talented. Blue stopped for a second to watch him, smiling. Then he led me over to a table under a tree that no one was around. The tables weren't run of the mill wood, neither. They were actually covered with tablecloths and what not, and the chairs were foldable but very plush and comfortable. I sat down at one, but Blue quickly pulled me in his lap, nuzzling my neck.

"Damn, you smell sweet, what is that?" he asked me like we were the only people outside.

"Bath and Body works, Twilight Woods, that's all," I told him, shrugging and smiling. Blue glanced at a guy sitting next to him, who got up and walked away with a nod. "You gettin' real comfortable with me, ain't you?" I asked.

"I want to be around you," he said, smiling those eyes at me again. "I gotta get you comfortable around me, too." he added, squeezing one of my thighs.

"You fast..." I scolded.

"Naw, never that..I just don't waste time. You the finest thing I've seen in a minute and I love dark women like you. I know dudes tryna get at you and I ain't even mad, but my job is to let you know off *top* why I need us to be together, so I can't be bullshitting with the games little boys play. I don't deal with people not on my level and I don't deal with people not worth my time."

"You met me yesterday." I pointed out.

"Yeah but you didn't even know who I am, so you ain't after no paper, position, none of that. That don't happen to me every day, so I not even gonna play around with you. I want *you* to be with me cuz you already *know* that I'm a good nigga to the people who're good to me. I think you can make a good wifey and I KNOW nobody else can make you feel like I will. So why not start now, right? Why fuck around?"

I was stunned, obviously. Of course, there was something else to this because no one is that perfect, but...why not? I could ride with this for now. Don't act like you wouldn't. I leaned over and kissed him lightly and he sat back, smiling. He pulled me back against him and I relaxed on his huge chest.

When Jai-who Blue called by his last name, Cruz-got finished, he left Jay at the DJ table and came over to us. Just then, the tall guy with the huge arms and red hair, Doe, came strolling out of the house and was surrounded by the sac chasers. He seemed to love it and it took him several minutes of kisses, promises to call and half-ass reasons why he didn't come by or whatever, to get to our table.

"You and that *slutitis* disease of yours," Cruz said to him, smirking.

"Nigga, go make me a quesadilla and shut the fuck up. You *wish* you could get the pussy I get," Doe said, taking Jai's drink off the table and taking a big gulp. He immediately started coughing and his eyes watered as Jai burst out laughing. "Gatdayum! You gotta let somebody know when you be making that Dominican moonshine... *shit...*"

"Naw, I don't want none of the pussy you got; I'm allergic to hoes." Cruz went on, still taunting Doe.

"That's why you start sneezing every time I come from round ya mom's spot, huh?" Doe tossed back, and Cruz immediately broke into a Spanish-filled rage, knocking Doe's beer off the table while Caesar laughed and Blue shuffled a stack of cards, shaking his head. I was just staring at everything, looking brand-new and trying not to look shocked.

A few minutes later, I was sitting in Blue's lap looking at his cards when Jasmine and her friends came strolling past the table. Caesar's face changed and he reached out and grabbed Minya's hand as she passed. She acted like she was going to keep walking, but her eyes sparkled up. "Oh, you gon be all in my face in the house but you cain't speak outside?" he asked her.

"Whatever, C," Jasmine answered for Minya, rolling her eyes. "Don't nobody got time for your bullshit,"

"Yeah, especially not you and *your* dusty-ass pussy, huh?" Caesar shot back at her.

"*Oooo,*" came a few voices from around the table. Blue winced and shook his head, Jasmine's eyes flashed a dark purple and she picked up a plate of food and hurled it at

51

Caesar's face. He ducked and the food went all over a slightly tipsy Minya, who screamed out and dropped her pink-tinted drink.

"*Fuck* you, C, you psycho muthafucka! Fuck *you!*" she kept screaming as Minya was yelling "What the fuck, Jas?!" Doe was laughing louder than the women were shouting and Blue was ignoring them, nuzzling the side of my neck. I was horrified, but he whispered in my ear that this kind of stuff happened every time he had a cookout and not to worry about it, so I tried to relax. I jumped out of the way as Jasmine kicked Minya in the side and she fell on the table, cursing, squealing and yelling in Japanese.

I *did* see Lucky emerge from the porch just then, and for some reason, I felt relieved. Maybe because as long as I'd known Lucky he was always the one who could squash stuff like this. He held true to form. He zoomed in on the arguing, shook his head and shoved people out of the way to get to us. "Minya, shut up and go with Caesar. C, take her in the house and get her cleaned up or something."

"Don't put that bitch in MY shit!" Jasmine hollered, still trying to throw things at C. Lucky reached in his pocket and threw a few hundreds at C. "Go get her something to wear and take her out to eat or something. Party over for you two."

"But it's *my* party!" C yelled, laughing. Lucky gave him a dark look and C sucked his teeth and got up, tugging Minya away. "Pickup some rubbers before you get home, nigga," Lucky called, watching Minya whisper in Caesar's ear and nearly trip over herself.

Lucky grabbed Jasmine, who'd never stopped yelling, but she snatched away from him. Being that she was almost a foot taller than him, it wasn't hard, but he grabbed her arm and snatched her down in a chair. "Chill the fuck out," he snapped in a low voice. Jasmine sucked her teeth and looked in Caesar's direction, but Lucky grabbed her face and turned it to him. "I said chill the fuck out and I *meant* that shit," he said, his green eyes, boring holes into her blue ones. Jasmine kept her pissed off expression, but she shut up. "Good,"

52

UNTRUST Deszion Nasir

Lucky said, nodding and standing up. "Good. Now if I can put my *keys* down before someone else gets in fight, I'll go get me a drink. Don't *you* move," he said to Jasmine sternly, flicking a potato chip out of her blue-black mane. He finally looked over at me and paused. I couldn't read the expression in his eyes at seeing me in Blue's lap, but it made me a little uncomfortable. "What's good, Angel? Where's Jay?"

I pointed, and he nodded and walked off, leaving Jasmine's eyes on me.

Jasmine's other girls were still stuck on pause, not knowing what to do. Nina, who had been talking to someone and hadn't been with the group, came strolling over now, shot Jasmine a look and kept walking past the table. When she got near Cruz, who had been on the phone the whole incident, the scent of her perfume snaked into his nose and he looked up, mid-conversation. He made eye contact with Nina and ended the phone call without saying good bye. He called out to Nina in Spanish, *"¿Lo que es bueno, mamacita?* What's good, mamma?"* and she answered back (without stopping),

"¿Por qué no me siga y averigüe, papi? Why don't you follow me and find out, papi?"* Jai broke out in a huge grin and he hopped up from the table.

"Aw, come one, man. All ya'll cain't just keep getting up from the table before we start *playing*," Doe complained. "No matter *how* bad these broads are." he added, sneaking a glance at me and winking.

Jai made a face. "I can play with you *culos* any day. I wanna play with that-" he nodded in the direction Nina's twitching behind was moving-"today." With that, he grinned a smile with his mouth full of many white teeth, threw his cards down, and trotted off after Nina's scent.

Doe threw down his cards in disgust. He looked at me again, and, seeing that Blue wasn't paying him any particular attention to him, gave me another grin, sitting back in his chair. I tried to ignore him, but I felt him staring at me. I got a chill on my back, and I looked behind me when Blue sneezed and saw C leaving with Minya. He was staring at me, too. Then I saw Lucky watching C and Doe looking at me. And he wasn't smiling.

UNTRUST Deszion Nasir

BLUE

It had been 30 minutes since the big blowout between Caesar and Jasmine. I know you wondering why I didn't get in the middle of that shit. What for? All C and Jas did was argue for whatever reason. By the morning, Jas would be in the kitchen, cooking breakfast for everybody, making another hair appointment with Minya, so why worry about it? That's the way my sister is. She's evil cuz she's pretty and she can get away with that dumb shit. But she's a Scorpio, and you know Scorpio women are crazy. And dramatic. And selfish. So I let her do what she do.

I was busy anyway. I was dealing with the candy bar in my lap when all of a sudden I heard a lot of noise coming from my house. I looked up and saw Siovahn storming out of the back door, her Jamaican attitude tight and pissed off, as usual. She was looking around, searching for me. When she saw me, and saw Angel on my lap, her eyes turned red and she started pushing people out of the way to get to us. I sighed. Every damn time I had a party...

"Awww *shit*..." Doe said loudly. Angel had noticed her entrance too, glanced at her and glanced at me calmly, an eyebrow raised.

"Who is that?"

"That's Siovahn, my son's mother," I said, watching her reaction.

"Did you invite her?"

"Naw, cuz she don't know how to act. She crazy, but don't worry about her. I got you." I assured her.

"Naw, *I* got me," she said confidently, tossing her hair behind her. I looked up and saw Jay trying to break through the gathering crowd to get to us.

"Tell your brother that, then. He tryna get over here to protect you." I told her.

"Oh, he's not tryna protect *me*," Angel smirked, her eyes

UNTRUST Deszion Nasir

on Siovahn.

Seconds later, Siovahn was standing in front of us. "Oh, so this the new bitch you fuckin' around on me with?" she snapped, hands on her hips.

Angel laughed. "You dressed up pretty cute to fight," she commented in that soft, calm voice she had, brushing lint off Siovahn's outfit.

"Bitch, *fuck* you," Siovahn snapped, picking up a glass of Sprite and tossing it at Angel. The crowd gasped, but Angel didn't move. She just raked her hair back, reached in her pocket and pulled out a rubber band, pulling her long hair back in a ponytail. Siovahn was obviously unsure what to do because she expected Angel to swing on her. What she did was use a napkin to wipe the Sprite off her face and kissed me on the mouth. "I see why you dropped her ass off at the pound. Strays don't never know how to act, especially when they about to be put to sleep." she laughed. Doe burst out laughing and I did too.

"Oh, see, that's yo black *ass*-" was all Siovahn got out before I blinked. While I was blinking, Angel grabbed a full bottle of Heineken and brought it down across Siovahn's face so hard the bottle exploded and Siovahn was on the ground, her face opened up. The men jumped out of the way and the women screamed as Angel clenched the now broken handle and took a swipe at Siovahn again, slicing her chest. Siovahn screamed and managed to roll out of the way, knocking the bottle from Angel's hand, but just as fast, a butterfly knife came out of Angel's pocket. She flipped it open and opened up a gash on Siovahn's back through her new outfit.

"*That* bitch crazy!" Doe yelled. I decided that Siovahn dead in my back yard wouldn't be a good look, so I got up and picked up Angel off of Siovahn. Or at least I tried to, anyway. This broad was slippery as fuck. She actually slipped right out of my grip and jumped on Siovahn's back again, taking the two of them down over a table, and started whaling on her again. Siovahn wasn't even fighting back anymore. Angel was whooping her *ass*, snatching her hair out-Siovahn don't

56

have no weave by the way-blood all over her fists.

Jay eventually got over to them, pushed me out of the way, snatched Angel's knife and tossed it in the woods and grabbed Angel by the legs and drug her off of Siovahn, still swinging and kicking like she was possessed. He damn near tossed her at me and yelled "Pin her legs down! Don't grab her arms, you can't hold onto her." I turned Angel on her stomach in the grass and held her legs down. Jay snatched Siovahn up. She was tore the *fuck* up, clothes half gone, and blood was everywhere. He tried to steady her and pulled off his shirt to try and stop the blood from getting everywhere. Jay said he was going to run Siovahn to the ER.

"Don't worry about her saying shit to the police," I called.

"I'm *not*. *She* started it," Jay called back, damn near carrying Siovahn around the side of the house. Siovahn wasn't trying to be big and bad no more and was damn near running as she tripped and stumbled. The one heel she had left was sinking in the grass. Angel managed to grab the other one that had fallen off her foot and chucked it at Siovahn's head right as she rounded the corner. We didn't see her hit the ground, but we heard the clunk on Siovahn's head and saw her go down. Everybody who wasn't standing with their mouths open burst out laughing.

I nodded and looked at Angel. Her back was heaving and she was panting, but she seemed to be calming down after that last parting shot.

"Can you get off me, please?" she got out. I let her go and she turned over.

"Damn, girl, you a fuckin sociopath," I said to her, half-joking.

Angel's face was indifferent as she straightened her clothes. "That's what they tell me,"

I was about to laugh, but the look on her face was serious, and left me deep in thought. Common sense told me not to even start nothing up with a crazy broad like that...but the business side of my brain told me to hold onto her...she

UNTRUST Deszion Nasir

could be valuable in more ways than one. Besides, everybody knows crazy pussy is the best kind.

JAY

I sat up and stopped snoring when I heard my name being called. It took me a minute to remember I was in the ER at Sentara Careplex. The nurse staring down at me shook my memory to the right and I stood up.

"Miss Baptiste wants to see you," she said.

I rubbed my stiff neck and stood up, wondering what I was still doing here with the woman who tried to kick my sister's ass. Actually, I knew what I was doing. Damage control. I wasn't gonna kiss Siovahn's ass, but my sister had enough trauma in her life and no extra space to catch a charge behind some bullshit. I had tried to comfort her and at least get her a little cleaned up before she got to a hospital. She had stained up the inside of my car, too, dammit.

But when I got back to the girl's room, *man*, I couldn't help feeling sorry for the girl. She was *fucked up*, yo. I sighed as she looked up at me. She had stitches, bandages, and a look in her eyes like the patients on that show *House*. You know, all lost and pitiful.

"How you feelin'?" I asked, for lack of anything better to say.

Her face bawled up like she wanted to cuss me out, then she surprised me by breaking down crying. Shit. I don't deal with this shit... "Um..."

She just cried louder until I sat down on the edge of the bed beside her and she grabbed my arm, getting snot and tears all over my arm. "I feel *so* stupid... Why do I let him keep playing me like that? He don't give a *fuck* about me, he never did... I'm just a damn... nanny for his son..."

I tried to pry my arm away from her without snatching it away and running out the door. I wanted to say, "Shorty, I'm only 16. I don't care about that shit..." but instead I said "Look, I don't really know you or him or nothing, but I mean, if that's how you feel, you gotta be the one who makes the

UNTRUST Deszion Nasir

choice to stop fuckin' with him. If you keep putting yourself in this situation ain't nobody for you to be mad at but you."

"That's my son father, though..."

"So? So, cuz ya'll got a kid it's okay to let him take you through all that shit? You too pretty for that bullshit... ay, concentrate on your kid and you, you know? You can find another nigga and he can take care of his self, for real..." Wanting to do something, I reached over and handed her a tissue from the table beside the bed.

"Thanks," she sniffed, blew her nose and sat back. It got quiet for a minute.

I couldn't help myself. "Yo, my sister fucked you up," I laughed, grinning at her.

She scowled at me. "That crazy bitch is your sister?"

"Yeah, but don't get mad, shawty; you had that ass-whoopin' coming. You know you shouldn't have ran up on a broad you didn't know,"

Siovahn's face actually broke down and a smile crept out. "I guess I earned that, huh?"

I nodded, still grinning.

"Well, I learned my lesson. About her, and about Blue, I guess."

"Then that's what you take from this situation, then. You a soldier, right? Take that lesson you just learned and move on with your life."

"Oh, yeah? And what about your sister?"

I shrugged. "Angel ain't trippin' on that shit. You know how many fights that girl done got into?"

"At least one more than me,..." Siovahn said, shaking her head and looking around the hospital room.

I smirked. "She don't carry stuff like that around. Leave her alone and the whole thing will be like it never happened, trust me."

Siovahn sighed, sat back and looked at me. "How old are you?"

"16."

"Why did Blue send you with me?"

I felt myself tense up. "I'm not a kid, I'm not a pet. He didn't send me nowhere. I go where I want to go. I ain't one of his bitches."

"Not yet," she said, a wise look in her eyes.

"Not *never*. Don't underestimate me, ma."

She shook her head at me, now looking at me pitifully. "Why are you even *hanging* with them?"

"I'm not *hanging with them*. We got invited to a cook out and I'm just trying to get some studio time. I did my homework. I know he owns a recording studio out by the Coliseum Mall."

Siovahn smirked now. "And you think that's all he do? Run a studio or whatever?"

"Not my business what else he do."

"Oh, it's your business. If you gettin' tied up with him, everything he do is your business."

"So...what, you gonna tell me all the man's business now?"

Siovahn paused, looked around. "He's not worried about you hearing anything, obviously, or he-or one of his boys- would have been here. I know Blue thinks I'm stupid, but I'm not. I *do* give a fuck about people, and since you the only person who tried to help me, now I give a fuck about you."

I scratched my neck and shrugged, crossing my arms. "Tell me then. What is it, drugs?"

Siovahn took a gulp from her water beside her bed. "Blue never got involved in drugs. He always said drugs were sloppy and had a 100% failure rate. Nobody retires from the drug game. Blue runs guns and shit to and from different countries. That's his short money."

"Short money?"

"Yeah, that brings in a few million a year."

"Damn, what's long money?"

Siovahn looked me in the eye. "Murder."

I blinked. "What?"

Siovahn glanced around the room, as if suddenly nervous she mentioned that. She lowered her voice and sat up, moving the IV tubes out of her way. "Murder for hire. That's the big money. He has his contacts that nobody knows about all over. If he takes a job, depending on who he needs to get to, he sends one of his boys after them. Lucky does the quick and clean kills, you know, gets rid of people the client wants out of the way in a hurry. Like witnesses. Jai goes after the people that need to be sniffed out, or whatever. People undercover or something like that. Caesar used to be the one that did the messy kills, you know, the ones where somebody wanted to send a message or make a point about stuff. Doe takes care of the bodies...covers up shit. But he does crazy shit to them... If one of the guys is busy or, like, Blue got too many cases, Doe will take one, but nobody wants that cuz Doe is crazy and he be on that shit like that cat Jigsaw in the *Saw* movies." Siovahn shuddered like she was trying to shake a memory to the left.

I sat back, trying to process all that madness she'd just thrown at me. These cats weren't that much older than me. This was some deep shit.

"All them businesses Blue owns is just how he cleans the money up. I mean, they make money too, but not nowhere near what he makes doing the other stuff... So, make your own decision. He *will* make you famous. He *will* put money in your pocket. He *will* make all your dreams come true. But don't *never* play yourself and think he's doing it for you. The devil never makes a deal for nothing. He wants you for something. He wants your *soul*, Jay. And he'll get it."

Okay...

"What makes you so sure I'm not smarter than that?" I asked her instead of smacking her in the face with the Bible on the night stand.

Siovahn turned and looked out of the window. "Because he's the Devil. And the only person smarter than the Devil is God."

UNTRUST Deszion Nasir

PART III-VU
JASMINE

The weekend after the incident at the cookout, I was out Virginia Beach at Minya's shop, getting my hair done and listening to her go on and on about Caesar and how fine he was and how funny he was and how she loved bad boys, blah, blah, blah. Whatever. I tried to ignore her because she was the only person who could keep my hair tight the way I wanted it. I was taking a break from the wild look and I was having her flat iron it. Thing was, most people could never get my hair silky straight without putting a bunch of shit in it, and Minya did it and only put one kind of product in my hair. When my hair was straight it touched the top of my butt, and that would look good with the outfit I was planning to wear out that weekend.

We were sitting there talking shit when the door swung open and Lucky walked in. All the chit chat in the shop stopped for a second and all the females looked at him. Lucky swung his green eyes around at the sudden silence, then looked at me.

"What you doing all the way out here?" I asked him, enjoying how uncomfortable I knew he really was.

"Nothing... I was just driving up this way and I seen your car..." he shrugged and rubbed the back of his head, taking the inside of the shop in.

"So... what, you were checking on me or something?" I asked, smiling.

He just grinned at me. "Or something," he said. He nodded at Minya. "That looks good on her," he said, motioning towards my hair.

"Thanks... hey, tell your boy Caesar to call me," Minya said, reaching over me to grab a business card off her stand and handed it to Lucky. He took it, smirked, and stuck it in his pocket. "*Aight*, " he said, his tone clearly meaning "It's

63

UNTRUST Deszion Nasir

your funeral." He looked back at me again, running his eyes up and down me. "Look, J, can I holla at you for a second?" he asked quietly. I don't know why, cuz nobody else in the shop was talking.

I raked my hair out of my face. "Um, sure, I guess you can get a minute. I'm done, right?" I asked Minya. She smirked and took the cape from around my neck. Lucky held the door open for me and I stepped outside, feeling his eyes on me. I walked a few feet away from the big glass window in front of the store and turned to Lucky, the wind whipping my hair in my face. "So... what? What is it?' I asked, taking a mirror out of my bag to see if the wind was tearing up my hair.

Lucky reached up and took the mirror out of my hands. "You look beautiful, stop it."

"I know that, give me my shit," I snapped, almost laughing. I tried to snatch it back. He held it out of my reach. "You came all the way out here to tell me I was beautiful?"

"Naw, I told you, I was just passing by and saw your car. But I wanted to talk to you anyway and it's a lot easier when you're not focusing on yourself."

I put my hands on my hips. "Well, say what you got to say so I can get out of this wind, pay Minya and go on about my business."

Lucky licked his lips. "What are you doing Saturday?"

"Why?" I demanded, twisting my neck.

He shrugged. "Just wondered what you were doing. I got a taste for some Island food and I remember you like it to, so... I just wondered if you wanted to go chill or something...you know?"

I stared at him. "Are you asking me out or something?" I asked, amazed.

"Or something," he said, grinning. "You too high-maintenance for a cat like me, but we been knowing each other for years and the only thing I really know about you is that you like Jamaican food... so... what's good? You tryna roll with me or what?"

I thought about it for a second. Of course, I was surprised. Lucky'd never spoken more than a couple of paragraphs to me since I'd known him. The Jamaican food comment was made over a year ago, so that told me he remembered that little thing from that long ago. He also had to remember that I was a bitch. And he knew I wasn't no hoe or nothing, so...what was this nigga's motivation? I had to admit, Lucky was fine, but that's not no secret... Might as well. It's not like I had anything else to do... except-

"Well, I'm supposed to be picking my cousin Millay up from the airport."

"Ya'll got a cousin?"

"Oh, nobody told you yet? Blue was looking some stuff up about our dad...you know he's into all that-" I waved my hand in the air.

Lucky nodded. "-uh-huh-"

"-and he found out the only other person he could come up with that had shared DNA with us was this guy in Hawaii, somebody with the last name Padilla. He's got the blue eyes and everything. He never heard of Gemini, but when Blue sent him a picture, he sent a picture of him and his daughter. And check this: the guy don't know his parents, neither. He spent most of his life in the system, just like Gemini."

"Ya'll match huh?"

"Yeah, it's crazy... don't ask how Blue got DNA samples..."

"I don't want to know; that ain't none of my business... but look, don't worry about that... I'll get somebody to get her..."

"Eating dinner is gonna take that long?"

"Maybe I have some stops to make first..." Lucky said.

"Stops like what?"

"You know, little shit. There's a movie theater and a mall over there..."

I nodded, grinning. "I'm too much for you."

"*I'm* too much for *you*," he tossed back. His phone

65

UNTRUST Deszion Nasir

started ringing. "Just give me a day, Jas."

"Okay... *one* day," I told him as he backed up towards his car. I watched him leave and went back inside to everyone staring at me. I sucked my teeth. "Stop hating." Everyone started laughing. I paid Minya and was sitting around in her chair talking to her while she was doing another client when an orange Aston Martin pulled up to Minya's shop. That car isn't sold anywhere around here so it had everyone's attention.

"Damn, who's car is that?" a girl under the dryer yelled.

Minya turned her smiles to the window, and when her eyes landed on the car, her smile faded and she almost looked...scared. I didn't say nothing, but I watched her as the driver got out and heading straight for the shop. He opened the door, and I saw he was a few inches taller than Minya, same skin, same slanted eyes, and his hair was nappy as hell in an Eric Benet type 'fro, all twisted out, wild yet tame looking. He smelled like money and had a huge smile on his face. I could barely see it due to all the lights bouncing off the diamonds and jewelry he had on. His eyes searched the room and landed on me. He stopped walking.

"Minya, you don't answer your phone calls," he said to her, but looked at me. I just raised an eyebrow at him and flipped my hair over my shoulder, turning back toward the mirror.

"Is that your brother, girl?" her client asked, hopefully, I think.

"Yes. Girls, this is Vu." Minya said simply, turning back to her client, her face tight.

"I never knew you had a brother, girl," Minya's client said to her, turning her body fully toward Vu. He was fine, so I understood it, but I wasn't as easily impressed because I saw fine men all the time. I guess if you weren't used to being around beautiful people you'd over react when you were, like this chick here.

"I've been out of the country," Vu said smoothly, showing off a row of halogen white teeth. "I live in Tokyo."

UNTRUST Deszion Nasir

"Really?!"

"Tisha, you know that's where I'm from; I've told you that a hundred times. Hold your head still before you get burnt," Minya told her, turning her chair away.

There was some tittering and then silence. Vu turned his attention back to me. "Did my sister do that to your hair?" he asked, reaching out and lifting a lock of my hair.

I slapped his hand away. "Minya, get your peoples," I snapped, standing up. Vu just grinned at me as I tossed her payment on her counter and picked my purse up to leave. These other broke down broads may need this fool's attention but I sure as hell didn't. Minya stuffed the money in her pocket and gave her brother a pleading look as he stood up like he was going to follow me, but he ignored her and followed me out of the door.

"Prissy bitch," I heard a jealous female in the waiting area mutter. I simply turned to her and said "Prissy bitch that you wish your man would stop tryna holler at," and exited the building to her rolling her neck and standing up, but she knew better than to bring her stupid ass outside.

"Hey... hey Beautiful," Vu called after me. I didn't stop my stride and tweaked my car alarm off and had opened my door by the time he'd caught up with me.

"Look, you seem nice or whatever, but I'm not interested and I know you're not selling anything so don't waste your time. Those look like nice shoes so don't scuff them up walking on these rocks out in this driveway," I told him.

"Oh, that's how it is?" he asked, leaning against another car and still smiling at me, although his smile was tighter.

"That's how it's always been."

"Maybe you *are* a prissy bitch, then," he said.

"Nigga, please. Take that shit back to those common bitches back in there," I said, waving him off. He didn't faze me at all. "I don't got nothing for you."

"You awfully stuck on yourself, no matter how pretty you are."

I climbed in my car. "I'm not pretty, I'm gorgeous,

which is why you followed me all the way out *here* after I paid you no mind in *there*. I'm too good for you," I told him, slamming my car door. I started my car and backed out of the parking lot. When I looked to my left and saw him still standing there, he was still staring at me. He was still smiling, but the smile was different...colder...like he hated me or something. And it wasn't just because I had turned him down. It was like,...like we had beef or something. I ignored him, shook the memory to the other side of my mind, then pulled off to look for something to wear out with Lucky.

VU (In Japanese)

I went back inside the shop, took a look at Minya and walked towards the back of the salon where I knew her office was. I heard her say something to the girl in her chair then she followed me, closing the door to her office. "Nice place," I told her, crossing my arms. "How's the money?"

"Pretty good, actually, I make-"

"What's going on with that bitch's brother?" I cut in, not really caring about the little change she was making here. This was a business visit and she knew it.

Minya pushed her hair out of her eyes. "I can't get to him," she said finally, shrugging and keeping her eyes on the floor.

"What do you mean, 'you can't get to him?' What the fuck have you been doing the last few months, Minya? Playing? This isn't a damn game. I'm not trying to be in America any longer than I have to."

"These guys are harder to crack than you thought."

"You mean harder to crack than *you* thought," I cut her off.

She sighed. "Look, he's hooked on some little black girl. I'm not his type, obviously, but I *did* manage to get in good with one of his closest boys."

"Who?"

"Caesar."

"The little crazy one?"

"Yes."

"That just got out of jail?"

"Yes..."

I shook my head at her. "That's the best you can do? Get a towel head on parole? I thought you were better than that..."

"Look, I'm doing my best-"

"Blue is your best. If not Blue, than that guy Armando."

UNTRUST Deszion Nasir

"He's a whore. I'd make no difference to him."

"I don't want you to marry him-" Minya shook her head and waved her hand in my face, cutting me off.

"If he fucks with 3-5 girls a day, and I end up being one of them, I wouldn't stand out, he would tell me nothing and he'd treat me like all the rest of them throwaway bitches. If I bond with the one that's an *outcast*, he'll trust me faster and confide more in me," Minya said, getting annoyed with me.

I stopped and thought for a minute. "You might be right... but listen to me. Get this shit moving; I'm wasting enough time over here. This shouldn't be taking this long. I have other business to attend to."

Minya sighed, glanced toward the front of the shop. "Vu, something about this don't feel right... maybe you should let this go..."

"I will NEVER let this shit go, and you shouldn't either!" I yelled, then lowered my voice. "Don't get caught up in this shit... cuz we're not staying here. Do what the fuck you're supposed to do so I can do what the fuck I'm supposed to do and we can go home." I commanded. She nodded and stormed out of her office, but I already knew I'd have to step the game up. I couldn't risk coming this far and have her nerves or whatever mess this up. I wanted this shit over. I rubbed my eyes because I was tired from flying back and forth to Japan. I checked myself out in a mirror hanging from the wall to make sure I didn't slide my contacts out of place. Then I left the shop and started making plans of my own.

UNTRUST Deszion Nasir

DOE

I checked my watch as I stood inside Newport News' International Airport, waiting at Southwest's gate 5a for - I looked down at the name on the card I had- Millay Padilla's plane to land. Of course the fuckin' plane was late... that's why I didn't do too many favors for people. But Lucky never asked me for nothing, so the least I could do was go pick this girl up so he could bump his head against that Amazon wall named Jasmine. More power to him... I could *never* deal with her all the time unless she went mute or something....

While I waited I saw parents with their children being reunited with other family and thought back on how my life was heading, or where it wasn't headed. Weapons running. Murder. My life was not one suited for no wife or kids. Not that I'd make a good daddy to nobody no way. I would have laughed if the thought hadn't been so sad. I think in the back of my head I wanted a kid one day, but I had no idea how to change a diaper or nothing. The only thing I knew how to do was take care of myself. That took up enough of my time...

I shook them thoughts off as someone announced that the plane I was waiting on was landing. Finally. I stood up and rubbed my eyes, growing tired of four days with no sleep. I'd just made a run to Jersey and I'd hit the ground running. A woman had paid for her husband and his mistress-her sister- to get knocked off. Her man had gotten her sister pregnant and she paid thousands to knock off both of them and make sure the baby never saw the sun. Women were vindictive creatures. She was gonna take the insurance money and move to the Cayman Islands with her lover. I don't think she cared so much about being betrayed as she did about the scandal getting out. She was a judge.

I yawned as the people started coming around the corner of the security checkpoint. My yawn turned to a dropped jaw as I recognized Millay Padilla right away.

She was almost as tall as Jasmine, for one. I could see

UNTRUST Deszion Nasir

the blue eyes from where I was standing. Millay was a French vanilla complexion with the same blue black hair, only hers hung in a black curtain down her back like she'd never had it cut before. She was thick as all *hell*. Using my expert senses about the female body, I guessed her measurements to be 40DDD-28-44. Gatdayum. I closed my mouth and went up to her.

"Millay?" I asked her.

She turned those eyes on me and smiled. "Are you Scorpion?"

I almost laughed. "Naw, no I'm not. I know your cousins real well, though. They got delayed and asked me to come and get you cuz they didn't know how long they were gonna be."

"Oh... okay." Millay looked around the airport, that lost-tourist look in her eyes.

"Let me guess, first time on a plane?"

"1st time off the island *period*," she said, finally focusing on me.

"Oh, for real?"

"Yeah, for real. I don't know where my stuff is or anything..."

I grinned at her. "I know where it is." I motioned for her to walk ahead of me while I picked up her carry-on luggage. I got so caught up looking at that juicy, huge, round... basketball behind her I tripped over her bags and found myself face down on the carpet, little kids laughing at me. A very un-like me thing to do.

I quickly picked myself up, ignored her smile, and led her to get her luggage. She talked about the trip and Hawaii while I tried not to stare at her body. None of the other men we passed-of whatever race-did 2 shits worth of a job trying not to look at her, some cats were bumping into stuff, people and tripping just like I had done. Millay was either used to it or she really ain't have no idea of the effect she was having on men.

When we got outside the airport and she saw my truck,

UNTRUST Deszion Nasir

her eyes got wide. "Is this your car?"

"Yeah," I said, smiling.

"Wow...it's beautiful..." she almost whispered, running her hands across it. When she did, the wind whipped across her face and played with her hair.

"So are you," I told her, just standing there and admiring her for a minute. She turned to me and smiled again.

I studied her for a minute, then looked at my watch again. "Hungry?"

LUCKY

Saturday night came and I was outside Island P Cafe' before Jasmine got there. Not that I expected anything different, like her being on time for anything. I knew how she was. I was actually counting on her being late. once I pulled up, I noticed a familiar face in the back of the line. It was a cat that was on a contract I'd had for almost a week. He was supposed to testify against his boy in a Fed case in a few days. He'd been hiding out, but I guess he thought it was safe to go out. Negative.

I waited until he broke line and left his girl to go smoke a cigarette while they were waiting in the long line. I stayed behind the cars and nobody saw me slip behind the building. I could have done him while he had his back turned, but that ain't me. I believe if you man enough to take a life, be man enough to face your victim when you do it. So I let him suck on the nicotine dick one last time before he turned around and jumped, seeing me stand there.

"Shit, man, you scared me, nigga," he said, trying to hide his irritation. He tossed the butt in the grass and I could see his wheels spinning in his head, tryna figure out if I was friend or foe. I was neither. I was just a neutral party.

"Sorry 'bout that. Had to take a piss, man," I told him, unzipping my pants and peeing on the wall.

Dude relaxed, figuring a cat pissing won't no threat. "Yeah, we been in that long-ass line like 3 minutes already." He turned his back and stuffed his lighter in his pocket. By the time he looked up I had a gun trained on him. He froze.

"What-?" he stammered.

"You remember what your momma would tell you when you were a kid? Don't run with scissors; don't chew with your mouth open... shit like that?"

The guy nodded, clearly scared and confused at the same time.

UNTRUST Deszion Nasir

"What was that other one?" I snapped my fingers a few times, then smiled. "I remember now. Don't be a tattletale. Are you a tattletale, Shawn?"

Shawn turned pale as death, immediately knowing this was about him testifying in court. He tried to reach for his waist, but before his hand got there, my bullet was exiting his brain and sinking into the concrete in the back of the club. I put my gun away and strolled back around the side. The line was even longer now and nobody was paying me any attention.

Back to Jasmine. Why was I bothering with her? Cuz I'd always had a thing for her. I loved women taller than me and I loved taming the rough ones. Jasmine was one of the most beautiful females I'd ever seen but I'd sat in the cut and waited. You couldn't tame a wild animal by rushing at it. It'd bite your head off. You had to ease into it, track it and observe it, make it come to you. Once it got close to you, you could pet it. Was I worried about her brother? *Hell* no. Blue didn't intimidate me the way he did a lot of other people because I used to be just like him almost ten years ago, and I was only two years older than him. I didn't kiss his ass nor did I need him. I guess the reason I put up with this shit was because karma had caught up with me and I had to roll with the punches or get knocked the fuck out.

I saw Jasmine's unique car pull into the lot and I stopped reminiscing and stood up straighter. I didn't go over to greet her, cuz I knew that's what she was used to. I let her get out and look around for me. When she spotted me, she stood there and waited, but I just nodded at her. I saw a flash of annoyance in her eyes and almost laughed.

The men all around me stopped what they were doing and stared. Under the stars and street lights, Jasmine's diamonds flashed brightly and the dress she had on had all our pants tight around the balls. Jasmine looked like a thick-ass version of that singer Amerie with longer legs and was a shade or so a darker caramel color, which had many a man talking amongst themselves, asking if that's who she was.

75

Jasmine walked up to me, looked me up and down and didn't say anything. "That's a nice outfit to wear out to eat with a friend," I said to her, running my eyes up and down her body.

"Yeah, well, since we're just friends it never hurts to be on the lookout for that special one, does it?" she said in her usual sarcastic tone, but her voice was softer. I stood closer to her. "I don't share my friends," I told her. "Do that on your own time."

She crossed her arms in front of her and I knew I had her ass on the defensive. Satisfied, I turned and led her into the restaurant, breezing past the long line outside easily. The people who worked here knew who I was even if the other patrons didn't. I pretended to ignore the girlfriend of Shawn, who was clearly pissed and peering down to the end of the line, looking for her man. I'd bet she was the reason he'd come out of hiding. Chicks will do it to you every time…

Inside, I got us seat by the huge indoor aquarium and slid in next to her. "Um, don't you want to sit across from me?" she asked, scooting over slightly.

"No," I told her, sliding closer to her. She shook her head at me and opened the menu, probably to put some space in between us. I took the menu out of her hands. I had her cornered now so she couldn't get away from me. Time to put the game face on and step this up. "I know what you want," I told her, waving the waitress over.

"Oh really?"

"Yeah, really... Miss, let me get an order of Curry chicken, no onions, extra curry, rice and peas with some gravy from the chicken on it, a salad with lettuce tomatoes and cucumbers only on it, light Italian dressing and some fried plantains but sprinkle some cinnamon and sugar on them and a bottle of Hypnotiq." I recited. Jasmine blinked, frozen as I smiled to myself. "Bring me two orders of that, as a matter of fact. But bring me a Coke."

"No Heineken?" Jasmine managed.

"You don't like guys who drink around you when it's just

the two of you," I told her after the waitress left.

"Oh, so you think you know me, then, huh?" she asked.

"Jas, I know everything about you." I told her truthfully.

"Whatever."

"I know your favorite color is yellow but you never wear it because it don't go good with your skin tone; your favorite music is anything by Mint Condition but you tell everyone you like Lil Kim cuz she's a mean bitch just like you but you never bought one of her albums. I know you want a dog but you're allergic to them; I know you're actually the older twin by 10 minutes but you never correct Blue about it...I could go on and on, love."

Jasmine stared at me. "What, are you stalking me?"

I laughed. "Just observant. That's my job."

She raked her hair back. "It is, isn't it? So is this work for you? You been sent to check up on me?"

"Naw, Jas. This is all pleasure for me."

"Why? Why me?"

"Why *not* you? Why do I have to have an ulterior motive other than I just wanna be around you a little more than I have, get to know you a little better than I do?" I asked her, playing with the ring on her left middle finger.

"You can't handle me," she said again, smiling at me. This time it was a real smile, though, and that shit tugged at my insides. I caught myself to keep the situation under control.

"Let me try," I told her, putting my arm around the back of her seat. She leaned in a little closer to me.

"What if you fail?" she whispered in my ear.

"I've only done that once in my life," I said back, my lips brushing her ear. "I didn't like it, so I never did it again."

"So... what do you want me to do?" she asked, turning her face towards me.

"Let me try," I repeated, sliding my arm under her hair so I could hang it around her neck and pull her to me. I think she actually kissed me 1st. I don't really remember, but what I do remember is that she didn't let me go until our food came.

"Here you go, guys," the waitress said loudly, breaking up the moment and grinning down at us. Jasmine jumped and I just grinned, wiping her lip gloss off of my mouth with a napkin. I tossed the napkin to the side and waited for Jasmine to start eating before I did.

It was quiet for a few minute, then she goes "You kissed me."

That ain't how I remember it going down but I let it go. "You let me."

"Yeah, I did," she said, her mouth full of salad.

"Did you like it?" I asked her, taking a big gulp of soda.

"It was nice," she admitted, still not looking at me.

"Then... what's the problem?" I asked her.

"Nothing," she said instantly. "I just...if this doesn't work out-"

"It will."

"But it might not-"

"It won't if you start out this thing talking about it not working out..." I told her seriously. She didn't say anything and I slid my hand under the table to where her dress had slid up high on her thigh and put my hand on her bare skin right under the edge of the dress. "Don't worry about all that other shit and let me take care of everything, okay? Relax, love."

Jasmine studied me for a moment, then she finally smiled and nodded, picking her fork back up. She seemed to relax, and started talking about everything that popped into her head. I perked up when she said "I met Minya's brother today."

"Oh yeah?"

"Yeah."

"I didn't know she had a brother."

"Me either. She never talks about him. And she *damn* sure wasn't happy to see him. He was all in my face like he knew me, you know how cats be. Acting like I'm posed to be impressed he driving an Aston Martin. I gave him the 'Nigga please' speech and left, but Nina had called me after I left and told me right after I left Minya and her brother went in her office and started arguing."

"About what?" I asked, pretending to be nonchalant, but my radar had clicked on as soon as she said Minya had a brother.

Jasmine shrugged. "I don't know, Nina said it was all in Chinese, but when he left he was pissed as hell and Nina said that Minya looked like she'd been crying."

"Did you catch his name?"

"Vu."

"Same last name as hers?"

"I don't know, Lucky, why? You know him?" she asked, getting annoyed that my attention didn't seem to be on her for a second.

"Just asking, baby." I held my hands up and backed off. But that shit didn't sound right to me. Something about that whole situation had me uneasy. First, Minya pops up in the crew, she gets up with Caesar as soon as she meets him. She tried to play up to Blue when she first started coming around, but Blue ain't into no girls other than real dark girls, so she moves right on to Caesar. Now her brother shows up and all of a sudden he's on Jasmine that hard? I made a mental note to check that cat out as soon as I got a chance.

"Since we're asking questions," Jasmine went on, breaking me out of my thoughts, "let me ask you a few."

"Go ahead. What you wanna know?"

She leaned forward. "I wanna know if you used to fuck around with Dejah," she asked, point blank.

My response was to set my glass down on the table. I sighed.

"I'm not tryna judge you or nothing, it's your business, but if you did, don't you think I should know that?"

"Dejah is hung up on your brother. She don't think nobody knows that, though."

"Nigga, don't change the subject. Did you fuck or fuck *with* Dejah? It's a simple-ass question." Jasmine snapped, doing that neck-rolling crap.

79

I folded my hands in front of me and leaned forward, looking her dead in the eye so she could see how serious I was. "First off, don't ever talk to me like one of these ignorant-ass little faggots you used to dealing with. 2nd, *nothing* is ever a simple answer. 3rd... I *did* used to take company with Déjà for a second, but she got too much shit with her, so it never got nowhere."

"Well, what happened?"

"You know what happened," I told her, taking another bit of my food.

"If I knew, I wouldn't ask, Lucky."

"You know I used to smoke weed a lot, right?" I asked, and she nodded. "Well, I used to go over to the house when I was out her and Caesar's way in Buckroe and smoke with them, but when C got locked up I just kinda stopped, you know? But then she started calling me all the time. I just figured she was lonely, cuz, you know, she ain't never been without Caesar, so I would go over there and check on her, and she would always have a bag of that good shit...and you know how it goes when you get to smoking and it's late...anyways, one day I went over there and the blunt smelled funny. She was like naw, it's okay. I took one hit and almost fell out."

"Cocaine," Jasmine guessed.

"Yeah. She tried to deny it but I ain't never been stupid. I know Caesar used to do that shit with Jai until Blue found out and Jai quit, but you cain't tell Caesar nothing."

Jasmine's face changed up for a second, then softened back up. Hmm. I made a mental note of that response. "So, long story short, I told her I didn't get down like that and I wasn't rolling through there no more. I was like, you know, call me if you *need* something, but that's it."

"Do she still call you?"

"Naw, never. She did once one night, but when I picked up she ain't say nothing. I let it go...is that enough information?" I asked.

Jasmine shrugged. "It depends. Where are we going

80

after we leave here?"

"Where do you wanna go?" I asked her, scooting closer to her.

"Wherever you go."

BLUE

I heard two cars pulling up in my driveway.

"Sounds like your sister is back," Angel said, perched on top of my desk. I had seen her every day since the cookout. I had to keep my woman right under me and she didn't seem to mind that at all. She'd made herself at home right away and right now she was laying across my paperwork, playing with the buttons on my shirt while I was reading some invoices.

"Yeah, sounds like. Get up," I said to her. She got off my desk and told me she was going to get us a drink.

"Get me some JD," I called after her, watching her ass jiggle.

"I know, I know," she called back, not turning around. I smiled after her, straightened my shirt and headed to the front of the house, where I saw Jasmine coming in, hand and hand with Lucky. She tried to walk off, but he pulled her to him and kissed her before she pulled away and walked off down the hall, leaving him grinning at the door. He turned and saw me leaning against the doorway and kept his smile.

"Seriously?" I asked, lighting a Black.

"What, you don't think I can handle her?" Lucky asked.

"Naw. Actually, I think you'd be good for her." I said simply. "Just surprised. You know she's a lot of work." I would never trust my sister with nobody but Lucky and he knew it.

"Don't worry about her," Lucky waved his hand dismissively. "Look, I just came in to holla at you about something."

I made a motion for Lucky to follow me into the office. As I turned, I saw Angel coming back with our drinks. When she saw the serious looks on our faces she immediately turned and headed back into the kitchen. That girl came pre-programmed. I didn't have to teach her nothing.

Lucky walked into the office and closed the door behind him and sat down across from me. "You know that chick Minya, right?" he asked.

"The one that do Jas's hair, yeah," I nodded, recalling.

"Okay, well, you 'member how she was on you at first, then just jumped on Caesar, right?"

"Uh-huh," I said, waiting.

"Okay, how come Jas told me she got a brother? This nigga named Vu, who Minya *never* talks about. He lives in Hong Kong, drives this fly ass-whip-an Aston Martin- and when he gets to the shop he was all over Jas. Now, *that* ain't no new shit, but then after Jas leaves, Nina called and told her Minya and Vu get in this big-ass argument and she start crying and he leaves all pissed off."

Now most people wouldn't pay too much attention to that kind of conversation, but I knew what Lucky was trying to say: A chick shows up out of nowhere, seemingly perfectly tailored to blend in with Jasmine's crowd, gets in quick with one of my boys after trying to get up with *me*; then her brother shows up out of nowhere and comes at my sister just as hard. Shit smells a little strange to me, too.

"What's her brother's name?" I asked Lucky.

"Vu Ngyuen."

I wrote it down and nodded to Lucky. I had completely forgotten about Jasmine and Lucky left without getting a comment from me about it. Jas was the farthest thing from my mind as I ran through my mental files about how to find out about this guy. I thought back to a conversation I'd had with Angel earlier about how high-tech her brother Jay was. She'd left her phone on my desk so I just picked it up and got Jay's number.

"Yeah," he answered on the first ring.

"Jay, this is Blue," I started.

Jay was silent on the other end of the phone for a minute. "Okay."

"Listen. First, good looking out for me the other day at the cookout."

"I wasn't looking out for you. I wasn't tryna see my sister caught up in no bullshit."

UNTRUST Deszion Nasir

I felt a wave of irritation shoot through me, then it turned to something like respect. Had to respect the boy's words. He wasn't intimidated by me at all. I didn't know if that was because he didn't really know who I was or because he just didn't give a shit. Either way, I was going to have to throw something else on the table.

"Hey, you was pretty good at that DJing thing, too, man, I meant to tell you that. I was impressed."

"Impressed, huh...?"

"Yeah, man. What, you don't think you're that good?"

"Look, I'm a busy cat, so... what is it you want, Blue?"

I couldn't help but smile. "Oh, you think you sharp, huh?"

"Don't matter what I think. What do you want and what's in it for me?"

A hustler. A smart-ass, hustling kid. "Okay, skip the bull then. Your sister was talking bout how smart you were at computers and shit."

"If it has a wire or chip in it, I can do something with it. What do you want?" Jay asked again, having the nerve to sound irritated.

"I need you to find out who this guy is. He might be a potential problem for me."

"What do I get for that info?"

"Can you do it?"

"Nigga, *you* called *me*."

Damn. "Look, if you get me something I can use, I'll shoot you a couple thousand."

"Seven to ten grand."

"Boy, you only 16."

"And you're 25 and getting help from a kid. 7-10 or I hang up."

"How about 5 and studio time?"

"How about 7-10 and studio time?"

"You going the wrong way."

"Am I? All *you* gotta do is hang up. Pay me no mind. You agree to what I said and you got more info than you want in under an hour."

I was smiling at this point. This kid had game. It wouldn't hurt to see if he was able to deliver what he promised. "I'll call you back in 2 hours."

"Name?"

"Vu Ngyuen. Sister named Minya." I spelled it for Jay, along with the name of Minya's shop and he hung up in my ear. I sat back in my chair, thinking. Angel and her brother might be worth more to me than I first thought. I made a mental note to thank Lucky later.

40 minutes later, my cell phone rang. It was Jay's number. Did I give him my cell number? "Vu Ngyuen, 28 years old, born in Hong Kong, Japan on February 23. Raised by a mother until she was killed when Vu was 10, sister was 7. No address for either of them until Vu got started working for a big businessman in Hong Kong. I guess the boys a genius. v The boy is paid out of the ass, owns 12 homes all over the world, but none in the US. He never comes here, seems to hate Americans but speaks fluent English. His passport says he's been in town for three days today. Minya has been here almost a year in Virginia Beach." Jay went on and rattled off various businesses that Vu owned or owned a piece of. Even though he never came to the US, he had a lot of money circulating here. The boy had most def earned what he wanted. The only thing he didn't have was a hotel reservation, for Vu, which he said probably meant he was staying with someone he knew. My guess was that it wasn't his sister. Not with her messing with Caesar. She didn't seem to like her brother too much for some reason and probably didn't want her man around her brother, especially not one like Vu. Unless she was a plant and was trying to get in good with Caesar before they ran up on him or something. I didn't have enough background info to come to a solid conclusion yet and that fucked with me. "It'll take me longer to get some more stuff for you," Jay told me. He then gave me a bank routing number and an account number to wire his money to him and hung up.

85

UNTRUST Deszion Nasir

Who the fuck was this nigga and what did he want with me? I don't know no fuckin' people from Hong Kong. Stuff like this was too much to be a coincidence. I didn't like not knowing what was going on around me. I had to fix this shit here. Quick.

PART IV-INTERFERENCE
ANGEL

"This is some *bullshit*,"

"Shut up, Doe."

"It is, though. This is some *bullshit* and why I gotta be the one stuck babysitting you so we can both end up in fuckin jail?"

I took a deep breath and closed my eyes for a second.

"Look," I said, trying to control my temper and keeping my voice even. "For real? I don't give a fuck if you stay or not. I *definitely* don't need you here, complaining, whining, and in general just getting on my *fucking* nerves. I don't need you to do this job here. So as far as I'm concerned, you can either shut the fuck up or simply leave."

Doe raised an eyebrow at me, smirking. I rolled my eyes at him and turned back to the dark parking lot, studying what was moving and what wasn't.

"How you gonna get in the car anyway with no equipment?"

"You don't know what I have." I snapped.

"I know what you *don't* have..."

"What, patience?" I fired back at him. I located the car I was looking for, a 2010 Benz, and pulled a small device out of my pocket.

"What is that, a cell phone? Get the fuck out of here," Doe laughed.

"You know what? How about *you* get the fuck out of here," I snapped, pulling a knife out of my pocket. I was tempted to shove it in Doe's throat.

Doe held his hands up in surrender. "My bad, you got it, you got it...shit..."

I shook my head at him. "This is not a cell phone, stupid. This is a universal electronic lock scrambler. If a car has electronic locks-like a keyless entry system, you know...it'll scan the codes until one of them pops the lock and disable the alarm system. This button here turns the alarm back on." I said, pointing.

"Where'd you get some high-tech shit like that?"

I rolled my eyes. "Jay. Ya'll have *no* idea how smart that boy is, do you?"

"I guess not," Doe said, sitting back thoughtfully.

I shook my head and got out, tired of talking to him. I had work to do. It was bullshit work, but I'd prove I could roll with the big boys, even if it meant doing this grunt work. I'd been on Blue's back for awhile now, trying to get him to give me something substantial to do. I was never gonna be content with just being his eye candy. I was too intelligent for that and got bored way to easy to simply play wifey.

With no effort at all, I was in the Benz and crouched down in the back seat in a few seconds. When the business guy in a suit got in his car, he never saw me, but he damn sure felt me slice his throat from ear to ear. I knew how severe the vocal cords just right so he couldn't even *try* to scream. Like I figured, he grabbed his throat instead of trying to grab me. I took the briefcase he'd slung in the back seat and everything in the glove compartment box and was back in the car with Doe in under two minutes without a drop of blood on me. There were no fingerprints to buff out and we were out of there in no time.

Doe didn't say anything until we were far away.

"What happened to you when you were younger?" he finally asked, glancing at me sideways.

"What you mean?" I laughed, wiping my knife off.

"Naw, straight talk. Females ain't killers like that unless something done happened to him. What, you watch a boyfriend die or something?"

I refused to admit that I didn't know, so I turned and stared out of the window, silent until Doe tapped me and handed me a blunt.

"Ay, I'm sorry, okay? I won't trying to bring up no old shit or nothing," he said to me.

"This is your apology?" I asked, taking the blunt and

examining it.

"Hey, that's that sour *diesel*, ma. You'll forgive me after you get it in your system," he laughed.

I shook my head and lit it up. He wasn't playing. In five minutes I was so high I didn't remember how I got home. The only thing I remembered was Doe telling me to quit playing and stop before I started something. When I woke up hours later, I was on my bed at home with a passion mark on my chest. Panicked, I made sure I was still dressed. I was, so I laid there, trying to decide what to do. I didn't want to call Doe and ask what happened; I damn sure didn't want to call Blue, so I did nothing. I just sucked it up and put some ice on the mark and prayed I hadn't done anything too stupid.

DEJAH

I was laying outside in my back yard where the sun was the brightest, trying to stay peaceful. I had my hair up, in a white, might-as-well-be-naked bikini that nobody was around to appreciate, trying to add a few shades to my light gold color. I'd always wanted to be darker, especially since I'd lightened my red hair to a golden blonde color a few days ago. Darker skin made me stand out more. I was busy being mad about that black-ass little girl Blue'd been hanging around with. I mean, I'm that bitch and it was like all my creep niggas had new bitches now. Blue had that crazy chick and Lucky... I don't know what was going on with him but he never was available no more, so he must've had a new girl, too. Now my brother was spending all that time with that Asian bitch so where did that leave me? Alone... again.

I was busy feeling sorry for myself when I felt a shadow cover me. I opened my eyes and saw Blue's huge figure looming over me, just watching me. I was excited as hell because I knew he knew where the good-good was, but I'd never act that excited to see him, especially since he hadn't been breaking his neck to get back with me lately.

"You blocking my sun," I said coolly.

"I'm saving your life. You gonna get sun cancer," Blue said smoothly.

I sucked my teeth. "You won't be at my funeral so don't worry about it."

"C'mon, Déjà, don't act like that," Blue said, sitting down beside me on my hammock. It creaked, but I knew it wouldn't break because we'd had sex on it a lot of times. He took my sunglasses off of my face and brushed my hair out of my face. I shuddered, but I wasn't going to make it that easy for him.

"So...where's your new chick?" I asked, looking around. "What, is she taking a nap or something and you snuck out to

90

see me?"

Blue's eyes flashed and I got nervous for a second, but the anger disappeared as quickly as it came. "You think I really came over here to talk about her?"

"I don't know *what* you came over here for... since you never come over here no more," I said, rolling on my stomach.

Blue responded by reaching over and unhooking my bikini top. He ran his hands over my back and I stopped playing mad and straddled him. I kissed his neck and his ears and slipped one hand under his shirt and rubbed his ear with the other one. I heard him grunt cuz I knew that his ears were his hot spot. I undid his belt and slipped my hands in his pants, whispering in his ear "I bet that black-ass bitch can't suck it like I can."

I guess that was the wrong thing to say. I felt Blue's heat freeze and he picked me up and tossed me on the grass, where I bounced and rolled, sending a sharp pain up my side. "You never know when to shut your damn mouth, do you?" he yelled, standing up. He brushed some grass off of him and started walking to the back door of the patio.

I got up and ran up behind Blue, ignoring my side, and tried to slip my arms around his waist, but he shoved me off of him and went into the house.

I followed behind him and slammed the door. "Nigga don't walk away from me!" I yelled, furious.

"*Bitch*, you done smoked one too many dirty blunts. Get the fuck away from me. I'ma get me a *drink* and get the *fuck* out of here. I *knew* I never should have even come over here to deal with your stupid shit, Déjà."

"Bitch? Oh, I'm a *bitch* now?!" I yelled, feeling my face get hotter.

"Get the fuck away from me, Déjà," Blue said, a definite warning in his voice, but I was too far gone at this point. Yeah, I was a little high from some weed I'd been smoking earlier, so I had a serious case of the fuck-its.

"Oh, you wasn't saying that when I was sucking your

nasty little dick, was you?" I screamed, picking up a liter bottle full of E&J and threw it at his head before I realized what I'd done. It hit him in the back of the head and he staggered into the wall of the kitchen. He whirled around and his whole face had changed. His eyes turned a dark purple and he straightened up, taking off his coat as he did so. I knew what was coming next and I looked around frantically for an exit, but Blue was blocking the only door out of the room. When I looked back at him he was stepping toward me quickly.

"Blue *stop*!" I screamed as he rushed me like we were on a football field and he knocked me to the ground. I hit my head against the table and before I could curl up in pain he was on top of me.

"Crazy bitch!" he screamed, so angry he was spitting all over me. "You want this dick that bad? Huh, you dirty sand nigga?!" he yelled, snatching my bikini bottom clean off my body. I was scared to death now, trying to fight him off me. I even tried to bite him but he just punched me in the face hard enough for me to immediately taste blood in my mouth. Blue climbed on me and pulled his dick out of his pants. Every time I screamed he hit me in the face again. I kept fighting while drifting in and out of consciousness, but when he managed to pry my legs open and force that oversized monster in me, I snapped to and screamed out again. "Stop, Blue!" I kept yelling as I felt myself being ripped apart by his force.

"Naw, bitch, that's what you wanted right? Right?" He kept yelling back, fucking me like he hated me. He probably did. I was through trying to fight him but I reached out and grabbed the leg of a bar stool and tried to bring it down on his head, moving through the pain and his grunts. He grabbed it mid-air, threw it across the room.

"Oh, you wanna play rough?" he yelled. "I *got* you," He backed out of me flipped me over and rammed himself into me that way. I screamed and thought I was about to die from the pain because he didn't enter the same hole he'd just been

92

UNTRUST Deszion Nasir

in and I was helpless to do anything about it. It hurt so bad I couldn't even keep screaming. I just laid there, crying and trying to stay conscious while he yelled for me to shut up. I could feel blood running down my legs. Eventually he pulled out and stood up. I could barely turn over, and as soon as I did, Blue shot his load right in my face, laughing at me.

"Dumb-ass coke-head bitch," he yelled, grabbing a bottle of gin and pouring it all over me before pulling his pants up. He threw the now empty bottle right at my head. The pain from what he'd done, pouring the gin on all my cuts and bruises and now the hit in the head with the bottle sent me into unconsciousness for a few minutes. While I floated in and out of this new nightmare I saw him looking around, breathing hard. He bent down and felt for a pulse. When he got one, he stood up and went into the kitchen and I heard him washing his hands and cleaning himself up. As soon as he turned the water off his phone rang. He let it ring a few times before answering.

"Yeah," he said, his voice back to normal. "Hey, baby… what you doin'?...oh, yeah?...well finish that up... I'm about to take a shower and come get you...don't worry about where we goin," he said, laughing. He looked over at me and saw me stirring. He walked over to me and stood over me. He hung the phone up and stared down at me for a second. "You tell anybody shit and I'll *kill* your stupid ass," he said, grabbing me by the neck. I couldn't even answer him, he had such a tight grip on my neck. He threw me down. "Don't nobody want none of that dope-head pussy no way. I better not catch nothin from your dirty ass or I'll *fuck* you up," he said, right before he stood up and kicked me in the face. I tried to scream but everything went black.

When I finally woke up, it was nearly dark outside. The first thing that hit me right after the pain was the smell of shit. I looked down and saw that I'd defecated on myself. I pulled myself up, starting to cry all over again, but even that hurt, so I sucked it up and drug myself-literally-upstairs to the bathroom and crawled into the shower. It must have taken 30 minutes. I curled up in a ball in the back of the tub and just sat underneath the running water until I was finished crying and stood up to clean all the dirt, grass, liquor and semen off of me and out of my hair. I washed my hair and douched until my insides were burning and sore to the point I couldn't take it anymore. When the water ran cold I got out and numbly walked back to my room. I looked around until my eyes landed on the jewelry box on my dresser. I automatically went to it and pulled out my baggies of weed and cocaine. I wasn't even tryna to deal with the weed so I poured the bag of cocaine on my dresser and started separating it into lines. I snorted up a whole pack and whipped out my reserve pack, doing the only thing I knew to get rid of my horror movie life memories. I bent over and snorted until my nose started bleeding. When I saw blood dripping on the dresser, mixing with the cocaine I tried to stand up, but I was so fucked up I fell on the floor and passed out again.

This time when I woke up, it was pitch dark outside. I was still naked, so I was freezing and now I had been rewarded with a migraine headache, a lump on my left temple where I'd hit my head on the dresser, and a dull, hollow ache in the rest of my body. I walked/crawled to the full-length mirror, grabbed the edge of my bed post and managed to pull myself to my feet. I studied myself, taking in the cuts and bruises, some I hadn't noticed until now. I stared at the damage done to my body, touching the bruises on the girl in the mirror, and watching tear slide down her battered face, once pretty under the bruises and cuts that would leave scars and destroy the pretty forever. The realization of what had happened and the fact that I would have scars to remind me of it until I died made me so upset I got nauseous. I didn't make it all the way to the toilet before all the liquor and my grief came up. I lay on the cold floor, dry-heaving, until I could get up again. I just rinsed my mouth out because I didn't have the strength to brush my teeth. I just wanted to lay down and die. It's not like nobody would know I was dead, at least not for a week or so. That fact made me feel even worse. The closest room to me was Caesar's, so I went in, intending to pass out on his unused bed. In a daze, I pulled on a long t-shirt he had draped across the couch in his room. I looked on his wall and saw the shelves where I knew he had some kind of gun stashed. I watched as my hand reached out to the shelves, felt around the top shelf and felt my hand slide over cold metal. I pulled my hand out and saw I'd grabbed one of Caesar's 9s he kept all over different parts of the house. I stared at it, knowing it was loaded. His guns were always loaded.

With the gun in my hand in plain sight, I let my legs carry me out of the house and down the street to the deserted sand at Buckroe Beach, barefoot and wearing only a t-shirt. I stared out at the water for awhile, thinking, sitting Indian-style in the cool sand. My brother didn't give a shit. All he was worried about was his new little girlfriend. Lucky didn't give a shit. Jasmine, my supposed best friend, hadn't called me since the cookout. And Blue? Just thinking about him sent my emotions into overdrive. I heard a roaring in my ears that was overpowering the calming sounds of the ocean. I tried to shake it out like I had a tick, but it wouldn't go away. I finally stood up, and like I was watching myself, I walked down to the edge of the beach, put the gun in my mouth, tasting my salty tears and the tang of the steel. I pulled the trigger and I heard the gun go off... but I wasn't dead. I don't think. When my eyes refocused I saw the earth was tilted at an odd angle. I realized I was laid flat out on my back. I looked to my left by the water and saw the gun lying in the sand. I turned my head to the right and saw a man on his knees, panting. He had a helmet on and I saw a motorcycle lying on its side by the sand, one of the wheels still spinning.

I laid there staring at him, mind still foggy, trying to figure out who he was and where the hell he'd come from. He sat up, pulled off his helmet and tossed it on the sand beside him.

"Are you alright?" he asked, panting and looking into my eyes. I couldn't quite place his accent, or his nationality. He looked mixed.

"I just tried to kill myself. Do you think I'm alright?" I asked, lips trembling and I started crying again. "Aw, shit, baby, don't cry. Damn..." he said, pulling his leather biker gloves off and hugging me to him. Even though I didn't know him, the fact that a stranger cared more than my family and friends just made me cry harder. He didn't even complain. He just held me and rubbed my back until I was out of tears.

We sat in silence for awhile, me feeling comfortable with him, until he pulled back and looked me in the eye. "Now...I know you don't know me or nothing, but ...it might you feel a lot better if you talk about it...I mean, I ain't no shrink or nothing...but you *way* too beautiful to be out here trying to hurt yourself."

I wiped my eyes and pushed my hair off of my face.

He narrowed his eyes and frowned as his eyes landed on my bruised face. "Yo, somebody been hitting on you?!" he demanded, squeezing his hands into fists for a moment, then releasing them.

"He did a little more than hit me," I muttered, touching the side of my face where I felt a lump beginning to swell up. I started having flash backs, seeing Blue's fist coming at me, felt the pain between my legs and started crying again. The guy looked like he didn't know what to do. He sighed and said "Look, I don't know you, you don't know me, but whoever did this to you? He ain't *shit*, ma. Listen..." he rubbed his hand over his huge curly fro. The thought I remember having was wondering how he got all that hair under a helmet. "Let me put you in a hotel or something for a few days. I don't gotta stay there or nothing. Just...I have this thing about punk-ass boys putting their hands on women. If you don't want to, that's cool...just...I'm just making a suggestion, you know?"

I stared at him. I weighed my options. I don't know if he was real or going to kill me later, but I didn't really care at the moment, so I agreed. He helped me up and picked his bike up. I got on the back and he rode me to the house.

96

While I got some things from the house, he looked around the torn up house at the glass and blood, and frowned. He took out his cell phone and began snapping pictures, saying I might need those for evidence. "Let's hurry up and get you the fuck out of here," he muttered, glancing at the pictures and calendars I had all around the house.

When I was ready to go, I got ready to walk out the door and stopped. "You know what? I haven't even asked your name and you've been so ...great. I'm Déjà."

He grinned at me, showing off the whitest, most even set of teeth I'd ever seen. "I'm Vu."

BLUE

Two weeks later was Zure's birthday party. He wanted a skating party so I rented out the whole building at Sparetimes bowling Center off Mercury Blvd. and Armistead Ave. Besides Zure's classmates I had all my boys there and Angel and Jas. Caesar was laid up with Minya somewhere and Jai brought Nina, who looked nervous around all the kids and stayed up under Jai, whispering in Spanish and talking to Jas. One poor kid had been skating in Nina's direction when he looked like he was going to fall. Instead of reaching out to help him, Nina backed up and let the boy fall and slide across the floor like he was Wyle E. Coyote.

When I walked in with Angel, Siovahn looked at her for a long minute. Angel ignored her and I guess Siovahn decided to let it go. Probably a good idea. The scars from her beat down were still visible.

I'd told my boys about the Vu situation and told them to pay attention to what was going on around them. Jay had showed up with a backpack on his back full of stuff he said was "non-essentially important." Whatever.

In the middle of the party, me and Angel were leaned up against the front counter, talking about going to some comedy show this weekend, when Siovahn decided to show her ass after all. She walked past us and accidentally-on-purpose spilled Sunkist on Angel's shoe. Before she could fake an apology Angel shoved her from behind and Siovahn ended up flat on her face on top of the cup. All the kids, including Zure', burst out laughing, Doe's laughter among the loudest.

"Vahni, damn," I snapped, snatching her up off the floor.

"That was a damn accident! I cain't believe you even *brought* that bitch up here and now you lettin' her disrespect-"

I grabbed her by the arm, pulled her out of our son's line of sight and slammed her against the wall that separated the

UNTRUST Deszion Nasir

alleys from the arcade so hard her teeth rattled.

"If you *ever* raise your voice to me like that again I'll smack your fuckin head off your shoulders, *first* off," I growled at her in a low voice so the kids couldn't hear. I glanced around and saw Zure' heading in our direction, but Angel scooped him up and started tickling him, carrying him in the other direction. She glanced at me a second and I nodded at her. Good girl.

"I don't want that bitch around my son." Siovahn hissed.

"The only bitch around your son is *you*," I told her, slamming her against the wall again.

"*Stop*, Blue!" she hissed. She tried to push me off of her but I grabbed her head and banged it against the wall with the effort of plucking paper across a table. She cried out, grabbed her head and sank to the floor. I picked her up by her hair and pinned her against the wall. "Oh, now you wanna put your hands on me? You want me to *fuck* you up in here, don't you?" I demanded, a little louder.

"No, Blue," she whimpered, all the smart-assedness gone out of her.

"'No, Blue,' *what*?'" I growled, squeezing her esophagus like a ketchup packet.

"No, Blue, I don't want you to fuck me up." she gasped, her eyes going in and out of focus. " I'm sorry. I cain't help it. You know how I feel about you-"

I let her go and she slid to the carpet, gasping, shaking and crying silent tears. When she stood up I smacked her upside her head and she screamed out again. Then I grabbed her by the throat. "Shut your stupid ass up. Don't *nobody* give a fuck how you feel, *bitch*. You know what the deal is. All I give a damn about is my *son*, not *you*, nor your damn *feelings*. That shit's your own fault. You knew from the beginning what you was getting into, so however you feel is *your* problem, not mines. But I tell you this: you ever show your ass again like that around my son and I will fuckin *kill* you, you got me?" She coughed and nodded. I let her go and she fell against the wall, gasping. Just looking at her made me sick. "Get your dumb ass up and go fix yourself up in the bathroom. You supposed to look perfect around him at *all* times. I *told* you that. Get your shit together." She scampered to her feet and hurried off to the bathroom. I shook my head after her. Jamaican women were supposed to be strong and smart. How the hell was she supposed to pass that part of her heritage off to my son acting stupid like she did? Damn...I had to do everything.

I was so mad I had to go outside for a few minutes. I don't normally smoke, but it was either that or shoot somebody, so I pulled a Newport out and lit it, the tip lighting up the darkness in the parking lot. Doe and Jai came outside a few seconds later after noticing I hadn't come back to take my turn on the lane.

"Yo, you aight?" Doe asked, scratching his upper arm. He'd just gotten another tattoo, I think.

"Yeah, man, you know how baby mommas be," I sighed.

"No, I don't. You know I got a vasectomy at 18. What the hell *I* look like with a kid? You think I want problems like the ones you got?" he laughed.

I shook my head and smiled.

"Blue?"

I turned and saw Angel coming out of the building, Jasmine and Nina behind her. Nina went over to Jai and took a pull of the blunt he was lighting up. Jasmine crossed her arms at the sight of me smoking. I sighed and rubbed the straight out on the side of the building.

"You need to get this *soap opera* bullshit under control," she snapped. "Siovahn in there sniffling and shit. I had to tell Zure' she had a cold cuz she acting all dramatic like she cain't hear the boy talking to her."

"Go back inside," I said to Jasmine carefully. I didn't raise my voice but she understood my tone: Don't fuck with me right now. She sucked her teeth and turned to Nina. "Nina," she called impatiently. Nina sighed loudly and whispered something in Jai's ear that made him grin so hard it looked like his face was going to pop off. He said something back and she went off with Jasmine, giggling.

"You and Hollywood getting along, huh?" Doe asked Jai. "What the hell is she always whispering about?"

"Aw, man. Niña es mi amor'," Jai responded. "Whatever she tell me for *my* ears, yo."

"Look, I done told you about speaking that Taco Bell shit around me. Do you see me draggin' around a cart full of oranges, nigga?" "

"Ay, *fuck* you."

"Naw, fuck *you* Esay. Take that shit back across the border, chalupa-nigga."

"I already told you I'm not Mexican. Why you try to piss me off, mayne?"

"What's the damn difference?" Doe demanded loudly.

"What's the damn diff-is that a serious question?"

Then the two started arguing again, as usual. I shook my head at them and turned back to Angel, who had been waiting patiently for my attention. Her smile calmed me down and I pulled her to me. She pulled the cigarette I re-lit out of my mouth and tossed it on the ground in a puddle of water from the rain of last night. I kissed her on top of her head and sighed.

"You okay?" she asked me, picking a piece of lint off of my shoulder.

"Yeah...I guess. Just get tired of the ghetto shit, you know?"

"Yeah,"

"Look, I'm good, I just need to get my head straight for a minute. Go ahead and go back inside and I'll be there in a few minutes."

"You sure?" she asked, rubbing the side of my face and staring in my eyes, trying to see inside my head. I ain't have the heart to tell her that window had been blacked out years ago.

I nodded, and she gave me one last look before heading back inside, rolling her eyes at Doe and Jai.

I was watching them for a few minutes, letting their

UNTRUST Deszion Nasir

stupid shit entertain me for a while, when all of a sudden I heard something in the distance.

"Hey, ya'll shut the fuck up for a minute," I yelled, and when they saw me listening, they started listening, too.

"Motorcycles," Doe said. Normally, that wouldn't be no big deal. What was a big deal was that there sounded like there were a lot of them. And around here, the motorcycle groups came out on Sunday, and they also never came out this way. Anyone growing up in Hampton knew this.

Doe trotted over to the door and yelled inside the building for Lucky. By the time he did that, I could see them coming at us from off the main street. There was only one way in and one way out of Sparetimes' parking lot, cuz it sat back in the cut behind some other businesses, so even if I was in the business of running there'd be nowhere to go. I saw them reaching under their jackets and I automatically pulled a 9mm out of my pants and started firing. I guess they didn't think I'd be armed at my son's birthday party. Another sign that whoever these bitches were hadn't done their homework.

The bikes broke formation and scattered, trying to surround us. That shit wasn't happening. I know what came after that. Doe made it to his truck and grabbed both of his sawed-off shot guns and started blasting niggas off their shit. I had knocked off a few by then. At this point, Lucky came running out of the door. All he did was aim and shoot, from the same position, and he hit everyone he aimed for. That cat's aim was phenomenal. Always had been.

Of course, they were firing back, but they were missing. I figured they didn't think we'd come as hard as we did and it had knocked them off their game plan. I looked to my left and saw one rider staying back from the others, like he was waiting for something. I'd bet anything that he was waiting to get at *me*. Taking my eyes off the rest of them for that one second almost cost me. One of the riders came right at me, gun aimed, but crazy-ass Jai came out of nowhere and jumped on the biker like a stuntman. The biker swerved and then crashed into a Dodge Ram. His bike flew to the left, he flew

UNTRUST Deszion Nasir

to the right. Before he could get his head together Jai had his hands around the guy's helmet and snapped his neck. He tossed the body to the side and brushed his shirt off, looking around for another target, his eyes glazed over with the rush a seasoned killer gets from stealing souls.

I suddenly felt what I knew was a bullet sink into my right arm. But I also felt it exit, which meant I'd live. I stumbled, then turned and kicked the wheel of the biker who shot me. His bike fell over and he flew off of it and hit the wall of the bowling alley. A bullet to his head wiped my worries of him away.

There was only one biker left at this point, and it was the punk laying up in the cut while all his boys got fucked up. He was coming right at me and dodging the shots being sent at him like he was in *The Matrix*. Just as I braced myself and raised my gun, something silver flew out of the night air and sunk into his shoulder. He swerved, grabbed his arm and immediately turned and retreated, barely staying on the bike, dropping his gun. I watched it slide under a Dodge Charger and out of his reach. I also heard what sounded like a silencer firing and saw something attach itself to the rider's bike before he disappeared around the corner, a coward in flight. I looked to see where the help had come from and saw Angel standing behind Lucky, clutching 2 kitchen knives in her hand and Jay was next to her, holding some type of gun. I was in too much pain to show my amazement. It was time to work.

"Doe, get them bodies out of here. Jai, call them cats Scoot and Marcus to come pick these bikes up. Angel, go in my glove compartment and pay off the owner so I won't hear no shit from him. Give him like 10 grand or whatever I got in there. Jay…what did you do to that man bike?"

"Tracker launcher with a shock-lock attachment." Jay said, smiling and holding the thing up. "If he even *finds* it and tries to take it off the bike, it'll shock his ass. I'm the only one who can remove it."

"What, you Inspector Gadget or something?"

UNTRUST Deszion Nasir

Jay just smirked, stuck that thing back in his bag of tricks. Angel came over to me to see about my arm. I snatched away from her out of reflex and she shoved me in the back.

"If you *want* me here, let me *be* here. Don't push me away or I'm out. You can do this shit on your own," she screamed at me, her eyes hot.

"Hold up, hold up, who the fuck are you yelling at?" I demanded, getting pissed. I didn't give a damn *how* fine she was, she wasn't gonna scream on me in front of my people. "You fucked up if you thinking I need *you*,"

"Nigga, *you* got it fucked up if you think you *don't*," she snapped back. I took a step toward her and she pulled one of those knives out and pointed in my direction, blade up, clenched tight in a child-sized fist.

"Nigga, I wish you *would*," she growled, her eyes going someplace else. Everybody froze and Doe went "Aw, *shit*. now..."

"Blue, I don't know you that well yet, but what I *do* know is that I would do anything for you cuz I'm that type of female. I *think* you'd do the same for me... but you gotta learn *real* fast that while I will do whatever for you, I won't let you do whatever *to* me. Either I'm your equal or I ain't shit to you. And if we ain't shit, you can get it *just* like that nigga with a blade in him."

Silence. Part of me was done with her mouth and she had to know I could kill her whenever I felt like it. But the fact that she was willing to put herself out there like that...I had to give her some points for that, whether I wanted to admit it or not. Angel was staring me down, daring me to do something. I walked up to her, she didn't flinch. I stared her in the eye, reached out and took the knife out her hand slowly. Her eyes watered up and I sighed. She wiped her eyes while everyone stared at each other. "You need to go to the hospital," she said quietly. "I'ma go in, pay the owner, you know... tell everyone you had a little accident... and I'll take you to the hospital..." she said, heading back in the

UNTRUST Deszion Nasir

building.

After a stunned silence, Doe got on the phone like I told him and nobody spoke on the incident. We all just handled our business as usual. Except Jai.

"Am I the only person that saw that shit?!" he yelled.

"Cruz," I said in a warning tone. He shook his head and let it go. I took off my messed up shirt and put it over where I'd got shot, the pain starting to sink in. I walked over to Lucky, who was standing next to Jay. "You two get together and find some shit on this motherfucker Vu. Now." They nodded and walked off together. Then I waved Doe over. "I got them finding shit out on that chink nigga." Doe nodded. "But you know there's one person who knows the most about that cat."

Doe nodded, his eyes grim. "Minya."

DOE

Blue left the emergency room of Sentara Hospital as soon as the nurse wrapped his arm up. As usual, he gave a false name and went straight to the cashier's window in the hospital and paid the entire bill so there'd be no paper trail. I was still tripping off the way the cashier's eyes bugged out when Blue pulled 2g's out of his pocket, tossed it at her and didn't wait for the change before he was walking out of the hospital. We drove to Minya's spot out Virginia Beach after Angel refused to get taken home. We didn't call Caesar to let him know we were on the way over there or nothing. All three of us walked up to the door of her 4 bedroom house off Lynnhaven Blvd. and I kicked the door open. I heard the alarm go off and seconds later, we saw Caesar peering over the upstairs balcony, clutching a .45. Minya appeared behind him seconds later, wearing only a pair of see-through panties that let us know she had a piercing in a formerly private place. Both of them were sweaty and I could smell the delightful fragrance of freshly tapped ass in the air. I reached up and snatched the alarm box off the wall, silencing it.

"What the fuck is wrong wit ya'll?!" Caesar yelled, his face pissed off and shocked. Blue headed right for the stairs, ignoring Minya's nakedness and pushing past Caesar. He lifted his ham-sized fist and punched Minya dead in her mouth. She barely got a scream out as she fell back against the wall and slid down on her ass to the white carpet.

"What the fuck-?!" Caesar yelled, trying to go at Blue, but I ran up the stairs and grabbed him.

"Chill, C. Some niggaz on bikes just ran up on us at Zure's birthday party and tried to body *all* our asses, son."

"What?" Caesar stopped short, looked at me, then Blue, who had his eyes trained on Minya, watching for her response. Right now she was trying to stop her mouth from bleeding. She got up and ran-well, stumbled- in the bathroom

UNTRUST Deszion Nasir

for something to catch the bloody leak in her mouth.

Caesar then noticed the bandages on Blue's arm. "You got hit?" he demanded.

"Yeah, I got hit, and *this* bitch know who did it." Blue yelled, his voice making the house shake. Angel put her hand on his chest to calm him. He shut his mouth and started pacing the hall like a caged animal, glaring at Minya, who was creeping out of the bathroom, wiping her mouth, her scared eyes on Blue.

"Hold up, hold up... *what*?!" Caesar asked again, confused as all hell.

"Did you know ya girl had a brother?" I asked, in a calmer tone of voice. Calm but serious enough for C to know I wasn't kidding.

C frowned and looked at Minya. "So...?"

Now we were all looking at her. She took the wet cloth off her mouth and swallowed, her eyes not the eyes of someone innocent.

"Her bitch-ass brother tried to kill us tonight, man."

C turned and faced Minya. "Why would her brother try to kill you?" he asked me, but looked at her, his eyes darkening.

"That's what we came over here to find out."

Minya opened her mouth, but nothing came out. Blue sprung into action. He snatched Minya up by her hair, ignoring her screaming, and drug her into her bedroom. He threw her on the bed, pulled out his 9mm and stuck it in her mouth, gagging her.

"I'ma ask you some questions. If you answer wrong, I'll blow your *fucking* head off. Simple rules, chink bitch."

Minya nodded, snot and tears raining down the side of her face.

"Is your brother named Vu?"

She nodded, her eyes terrified.

"Is he trying to kill me?"

She glanced at Caesar. Blue cocked the gun. "Pay attention to the muthafucka with the gun!" he yelled.

Minya swung her eyes back to Blue and nodded slowly.

Blue took a deep breath, trying to calm himself. "When I take this gun out of your mouth, the only thing I want you to tell me is why." He pulled the gun out of Minya's mouth.

She coughed out "Your... your father."

I watched as I saw a look I'd never seen before cross Blue's face: confusion. Nobody *ever* spoke about Blue's pops.

"My what?"

"Your father...Vu... I..." Minya looked more scared now than when Blue shoved that gun down her throat.

"My father *what*?!" Blue yelled.

Shaking, Minya reached up and stuck her finger in her eye. She slid a contact off her eyes...and when she moved her contact, the brown moved. She took off the other brown contact and looked at Blue. He dropped his arm and stood straight up. Minya was staring back at us with the same blue eyes that Jasmine and Blue had.

"Oh, shit," I said, getting what was going on. Sort of.

"Your father... he's our father," Minya began, shaking like she was freezing. "Gemini came to Japan over twenty years ago for business or something and met our mother. Of course, her family hated him but she wouldn't leave him alone, so they threw her out on the street and disowned her. She went to your father's hotel room, but he laughed at her and put her out in the rain in the middle of the night. She was still homeless when she found out she was pregnant. Your father left and my mom had Vu in an alley. She eventually moved in with her aunt, who never told her father where she was. He would have beat the hell of my mother for disgracing the family. My mother tracked Blue down when he came back a couple of years later, and he acted like he was sorry, but that was just so he could fuck her again. She woke up and he had checked out of the hotel, not paying the bill. My mother went to jail for that shit and behind them finding heroin in the closet. Vu got sent to a foster home. Two weeks later she threw up in her cell and found out she was pregnant again. She had me while she was locked up. Blue never tried to see either of us. We both ended up in the same orphanage, but as soon as Vu got old enough to join the group he's in, he took me and we ran away, grew up on the street or staying with a member of the group."

Nobody said nothing. You couldn't even say the girl was lying.

Blue was trying to put pieces together. "Okay, so my pops was a fucked up nigga. Everybody know that. They also know the nigga been dead for years. So again," he said, raising the gun to her face. "Why is your bitch-ass brother trying to kill *me*?"

Minya was crying now. "Because your father destroyed our damn life! My mother *died* in jail. We never saw her after she got arrested. I don't remember her at all! I've never even seen a picture if her!"

"What the fuck do that have to do with me? I never saw the mutherfucker either, or my ho-ass momma!"

"I *know* that! But Vu..." she shook her head. "He's stuck on this revenge shit. He wants everything about Gemini gone. That means he wants *you* dead, *Jasmine* dead, and the other one who killed him dead too. "

"Then tell him to stick a gun up his own ass and pull the trigger cuz he's that niggas kid, too, right?!"

"He won't listen to me! He sent me up here to get in good with ya'll yeah, but I don't have the heart he does. I actually like ya'll-I didn't want to do this-"

"Bitch *please*. If you *gave* a fuck about me or Jas you wouldn't have let this nigga try to kill me and my son. Sloppy-ass rice eating muthafucka. You lookin for sympathy from me? Well *fuck* you, bitch. You *both* gonna die." Blue put the gun to her head and she screamed. I grabbed his arm, stopping him, but he snatched away from me and looked at me like I was crazy.

"Look, you heated right now but listen. You can kill her and get your hands dirty, but that won't get you to that dude. You need to get that nigga like he tried to get you. Straight

UNTRUST Deszion Nasir

up." I told him.

Blue took in my words and his face started to return to normal. He looked at Minya, then at me, nodding finally. He put his arm down and walked over to the big picture window in Minya's bedroom. "You my sister, huh?" he asked, not looking around.

"Yes," Minya said in a small voice.

"Just for the record, that don't mean shit to me. Neither do them tears. You'll never be shit to me, you *or* your bitch-ass brother. But I won't kill you. Not right now. "

"You can tell us where Vu is." I said.

Blue shook his head. "I wouldn't trust *shit* that bitch said to me right now. I'll find that nigga on my own..."

"So what do we do with her?"

Blue looked at her finally. "Nothing. Nothing right now."

"You ain't worried she gonna say shit to Vu?" I asked.

Blue shook his head. "No." With that, he turned and walked out of her room, down the stairs and out of the house.

I finally looked at Caesar, who hadn't moved the entire time. He was *mad* pissed off. I knew he was diggin' this broad or he wouldn't be so mad. Minya looked at him, too. "C, I...I really care-" she touched C and I cringed, knowing what was coming next. Caesar snapped to life and punched Minya dead in the face. She flew over the bed and was laid out on the floor, snoring. C stood over her, spat on her, then grabbed his clothes and stormed out. I heard his motorcycle revving up and then tearing down the street.

As usual, I was left behind for cleanup. I sighed, went to the back of my truck, and got out the cleaning supplies. I left Minya on the floor as l cleaned up the rage her brother and C had left behind.

PART V-UNREASONABLE BEHAVIOR
SIOVAHN (sha-VON)

I slammed my phone closed, pissed. I'd called Blue seven times and he hadn't answered once. I even left him messages, and I wasn't yelling or nothing. I was being nice and he still was ignoring me. I can't believe he was still mad about what had happened at the bowling alley. He'd gone outside and never came back. Neither had his boys, which was weird. But all them cats were weird. Except Jay. I smiled to myself as I thought back to the past week. Jay had called me a couple of times to check on me. It was so cute, with him being 5 years younger than me, but he acted like a grown man. Yeah, I invited him over a couple of times. He didn't show the 1st time. He said he was caught up in the studio. Yeah, Blue had sucked him in his world by giving the boys studio time, even pulling Timbaland in to produce their album they were working on. But me being me, as soon as I healed up I took a drive over to the studio. It was real late, and I only saw Jay's car outside, so I parked and walked up to the main door, buzzing to let Jay know I was down there. There was a long silent moment, then I heard Jay go "What?"

"It's me," I said, lifting my hand up to make sure my hair was in place.

"Me who?" Jay demanded, irritated. I hesitated because he sounded like Blue for a second.

"Siovahn."

Silence. Then the door buzzed. I smiled and went inside. When I got up to the studio, Jay was bent over all those knobs, concentrating. I watched him for a minute.

"Did you want something?" he asked, finally turning around and glancing at me. He looked me up and down, taking in my low-cut dress that plunged in the front to my belly button and hugged my ass, clung to my thighs. His eyes landed on my 6 inch matching sandals, then traveled back up to my face.

UNTRUST Deszion Nasir

"I wanted to see you," I said simply, smiling.

"Oh yeah?" he asked, leaning against the boards and crossing his arms. I had to admit, he carried himself like a grown man. He was tall, too, so the only reason I would think he was young was because he'd told me so.

"Yeah; you act like I'm supposed to give you a deep answer or something...but ..." I shrugged, drifting off.

Jay scratched his chin. "You look nice," he said, almost like an accusation. "You do all that for me?"

"Yes," I said, smiling and walking over to him. "You like?" I asked, even though he'd just told me I looked nice. He nodded. I took hold of his arms and pulled them down, put them around me and wrapped my hands around his neck, stroking the back of his head. He didn't back away, like I'd thought he'd do. He looked into my eyes.

"If you trying to piss your baby daddy off, I'm not that dude," he told me, sliding his hands up and down my bare back.

"I'm not, and I really don't want to talk about him," I told Jay, kissing his neck and face. He pushed me up against the wall suddenly and stuck his tongue down my throat. I kissed him back and tried to control myself behind that aggressiveness. It didn't work to well and a few minutes later we slid down on the floor of the studio...

I shook my head at the memory and looked around, realizing I was still sitting in my car at Military Circle Mall. I gathered my purse and headed into the mall, determined to do some retail therapy. I had to sort out the fact that I'd been turned out by a teenager. I tossed my hair out of my eyes and headed into the mall like I was on a mission. I frequented that mall all the time, so every time I came in, representatives from all the stores made sure they spoke to me. I felt important, which is the feeling I wanted, which is also why I shopped so much. I went straight to Victoria's Secret and examined the new, cute items that the salesgirl said they'd just got in. I spent about 600 hundred in there on lingerie and scented lotions, shower gels and whatnot, then I headed to

112

Papaya, another one of my favorite stores. I was looking at a cute dress when I felt someone watching me.

I looked up and saw this *fine*-ass guy grinning at me from a kiosk outside Papaya. It looked like he'd been trying on some sunglasses. The guy running the kiosk was trying to convince him that the shades he was looking at were real Gucci shades, but he wasn't paying dude no attention. He was staring right at me. I thought about Jay for a hot second, but *shiiit*. Jay could be my young boy. This could be my new *man*. I smiled back at him and that was all the encouragement he needed. He put the shades down, waited for a young mom to walk past him with her baseball team of kids, and came into the store. I met him at the entrance.

"What's good, beautiful?" he asked, his voice clam and even.

"You tell me. You were staring at me," I answered, smiling my best smile at him. He licked his lips and smiled wider. "Yes, I was. I can't help it... damn..." he said, shaking his head.

I laughed, loving the attention. It had been awhile since I'd gotten some...attention that is.

He ran his hand over his freshly braided hair and looked over his shoulder for a second. Then he turned those eyes back on me. "You know... I know you don't know me, but...can I buy you lunch or something?"

I shrugged. "I don't know, I was in the middle of shopping. I shop pretty hard and I was trying to narrow down what I was gonna buy... if I leave now stuff might not be here later..." I explained. The guy reached in his pocket and pulled out a Black Card.

"Get all of it."

I raised an eyebrow and watched as he paid for all my stuff and took my bags from the sales girl. "Can we eat now?"

What could I say? We went to the Cheesecake Factory. I followed him there in my car and we sat down and talked for three hours, me telling him about how I grew up in Jamaica

113

and him telling me about the places he'd traveled. His favorite place to vacation was Italy. He laughed and told me how he loved to go there and watch the faces of the Italians who stared at him when he toured different places and spoke the native languages. "They don't get too many tourists that look like me," he said.

"I bet," I told him.

We ended up spending the whole day together, and part of the night, too. We wound up at the Funny Bone, a comedy club. We had a few drinks and dinner and I was having the best time, and told him so.

"Yeah, me too, " he said, smiling at me. "You gonna let me take you out again tomorrow, right?" he asked.

I started to nod, then stopped. "Well, my son is with his grandmother. I'll have him back tomorrow." I explained.

"You have a son?" he asked, smiling wider.

"Yeah, he's 7." I pulled out a picture and showed him.

"Damn... blue eyes?" he asked, surprised. "Wow... what nationality is his dad?"

"I don't really know... I don't like to talk about him, though." I said quickly.

"Oh, my bad. Didn't mean to make you upset. I won't say nothing else about him. I want tonight to end on a good note." he insisted, smiling again, taking my hand.

He paid, leaving a huge tip and he walked me back out to my car. He gave me his number and a kiss on my forehead. "Call me in the morning. Maybe I can take you to breakfast or something after your son goes to school."

"Okay," I said, opening my car door. He leaned over it and kissed me on the mouth, slow and sweet. "I'll call you when I get up."

"Cool."

"Good night, Vu."

Vu flashed those teeth at me again. "Goodnight."

DEJAH

It'd been a whole month since I'd left the hell house in Buckroe. Vu had taken me to stay with him in his house in Kingsmill, Williamsburg. It was huge, bigger than Blue's, and it was beautiful. Vu had like, 6 servants in this big house just to take care of him, and he never made a mess like talking about it, so it seemed a waste. In that respect he was kind of like Blue and that was a little weird. He didn't *act* like Blue though. Vu had breakfast with me every morning and made sure the cook made all the things I liked for lunch and dinner, being that he wasn't there most of the time. After breakfast he always asked me if I wanted anything and then he left until real late at night. Same routine, day after day. Every so often he would wake me up when he got home and we would sit up and talk. He listened as I opened up to him about my life and my history and the drama I'd gone through with Blue. He always paid attention to what I said and he would always shake his head and say something like, "I know a guy like that...and I hate him with everything in me." Then his eyes would change and he'd start muttering to himself in Japanese. But a few moments later he'd be back to his smiling self and then say good night.

Vu really didn't have any rules to the house. He wouldn't let me leave for at least 3 weeks so I could detoxify and it was terrible. I'd never been through anything so bad in my life, and I'd been through some serious shit. After I dealt with all of that, Vu just told me I could stay until I got my head together, no pressure, no rent or anything. I eventually ended up sleeping with him a few days ago, but he didn't pressure me, I came after him. That's when he told me he didn't want me around Blue anymore. "You need to stay on the path you're on," He tried to reason with me, "and if you go around him or his boys again, you'll lose your temper and all your progress'll be shot to hell."

UNTRUST Deszion Nasir

"But what about my brother, though?" I asked him, sad. Vu cleared his throat and sighed. "Look, I'm not trying to be an asshole or nothing, but... you've been here for weeks. How many times has he called you?"

I sat back on my bed and sighed. It was true. So I agreed. But after being cooped up in the house for what seemed like forever, I was bored to death, so I got in one of Vu's cars he never drove and went to Coldstone creamery in Hampton. I had a craving for white chocolate mango ice cream with pecans in it. I wanted it so bad I was licking all over the spoon before I could even get out of the store. I ignored the men who were pretending not to be staring at me in front of their women. Since I'd stopped messing with the cocaine and weed cocktails, I'd filled out more, and my skin had gotten its glow back laying around by Vu's pool. But I wasn't interested in any of them at the moment, so I just brushed past them and walked outside.

I had pulled out my keys and was looking for the car so I could point the alarm thingy at it and have it started by the time I got to it when I saw them coming out of McFadden's, a restaurant right beside the ice cream store. I spotted Lucky first. Lucky had always caught my attention first, no matter who was around him. Then I saw him hold the door open for someone. When I saw Jasmine come out smiling and Lucky putting his arm around her, looking so confident and happy, I almost threw up. Then nausea was replaced with rage. All me and Lucky ever did was hang out at my house and smoke weed. He never took me nowhere when we were hanging out. I mean, true, when I gave him a dirty blunt and forgot to tell him he freaked out and stopped calling me, but it wasn't that serious. The blunt wasn't laced that hard. She's not even his type! Lucky is a mellow-type of guy. He hates loud, dramatic, bubble-headed bitches like Jas. What the fuck? Had I been gone that long??

I had almost called Lucky over a hundred times since I'd been gone, just to hear his voice. I knew he'd understand what was going on and keep quiet about where I was while I got my head together. But because I didn't want to put Lucky in a position where he'd have to choose between me and work and possibly endanger himself, I hung up every time.

I was trying to decide what move to make when the door swung open again and I saw Blue step out, holding the door open for Angel. I instantly flattened myself against the door, almost out of sight and felt myself hyperventilating. I hoped nobody decided to come out of Coldstone right then. When they walked a little further out, I could see how straight and proud Blue stood, looking down at Angel all proud and shit as other people in the parking lot turned and stared at Angel and Jas. Old jealousy ripped through my chest and things in front of me began to flash. Before I realized what was going on, I had pulled the same .22 I'd tried to shoot myself with out of my purse and was aiming at Blue's head. I remembered the sound of the gunshot and Blue jerking forward. I blinked, and when I opened my eyes Angel was coming at me like a killer bee, working that dress like it was a pair of army fatigues. Before I could raise the gun again Angel tackled me. My head slammed against the concrete and I saw stars. My vision cleared partially and I looked to the left. The gun was sliding under a car. When I looked up, Angel had her fist doubled up, her face twisted, hair falling on the sides of her face like curtains. She pulled that fist back and everything went black as she punched me dead in the face.

WHACK!

"Wake up, *bitch*."

Sharp, severe pain woke me up. When my eyes adjusted to my new surroundings, I saw Angel standing over me, holding a gun by the barrel. She'd pistol-whipped me awake. My eyes darted around and I realized I was lying on a hotel bed, although I couldn't tell which hotel. I was guessing it was the one across the street since I had apparently been unconscious. Not thinking about anything but being in front of this bitch I balled up my fist, but she whipped the gun and

117

pointed it in my face, smiling. "I said 'wake up', not 'move.'"

I swallowed. "Angel, you don't-"

And that little monster hit me in the mouth again. She hit harder than some men I knew, and trust me, I'd been slapped around by a few.

"You ain't allowed to talk. Every time you open your mouth, I hit you in it. Are those instructions simple enough or do you need another hands-on demonstration?" she asked me.

"Blue-"

CRACK!

"Slow learner, huh?"

I just glared at her, hating her. It was obvious Blue had told her not to let me speak. Gee, I wonder why, the bastard... As mad as I was, I knew I had no wins right now, so I had no choice but to sit back and wait.

The wait wasn't long. A few minutes later, the door opened Blue, Lucky and Doe came in the room. I immediately panicked because I saw Doe. Why? If you've been paying attention, you'd remember that 1. Doe wasn't at McFadden's and 2. Doe was the one people called to handle bodies. I almost shit on myself. All three of them had the same combo of looks on their faces: rage, disbelief and fury.

Blue looked into my face and smirked at my busted lip I'd gotten from Angel. "Still don't know how to shut that mouth unless a dick's in it, huh?" he asked. I just tried to will him dead.

He picked Angel up with one arm. Her face shifted into one of happiness, then he winced. She wiggled down and rolled up his sleeve, where I saw his arm/shoulder area bandaged up. I must have grazed his arm. Angel turned to me and I saw her fury returning. "You tried to kill him?" she yelled like she wasn't just there. "You tried to kill my man, you towel-head bitch?" she yelled, pointing the gun at me again and firing. It had a silencer on it so all I heard was a PSST! as a bullet flew past me and sank into a wall. The only reason she didn't hit me was because Blue moved her hand at the last second.

"Stop!" Blue snapped, snatching the gun from her.

"*Fuck* that dirty bitch!" Angel yelled, lunging at me. I grabbed a lamp off the nightstand and swung it at her. She ducked like a Marine, grabbed the clock radio off the stand and flung it at me in a flash. I barely had time to put my arm up to protect my face and the clock caught the top of my head. When I lowered my arm Lucky was dragging the psycho into the adjoining room connected to this one.

Panting, I looked at Blue, who wasn't smiling anymore. He was cold and calm again. He pulled his sleeve down and sat on the edge of the bed, never taking his ice eyes off of mine.

"Where you been, Dejah?" he asked like we were old friends but keeping that cold look on his face.

"None of your fuckin' business!" I screamed at him.

Blue nodded, then glanced at Doe, who ever so calmly, pulled a Berretta out of his jacket and pointed it at me. "You know I ain't one for repeating myself," Blue said, "But seeing as how you might not be thinking straight just yet, I'll let you change your answer. But just this once," he added, throwing a smile on his face. Lucky re-entered the room just then, minus Angel.

I swallowed. "I've been staying with a friend."

Blue shook his head. "A bitch like you don't got no friends, Dejah. At least none that I know of. So that tells me one of two things: either you lying or you done found a new friend recently. Due to your current situation, I don't think you lying, so let's go down road number two and you tell me the name of your new friend," he said, like he was talking to a two-year-old.

I opened my mouth, but nothing came out. I was trying to figure out why he was so concerned with this and not me trying to kill him.

"What friend?!" Doe yelled, growing impatient. I jumped a foot off the bed. I had never heard Doe yell and his voice shook the walls, the vibrations adding to the ones coming from my trembling body. I was scared now, my anger being replaced by a dark reality.

"You don't know him-" I tried to spare Vu from one of Blue's tantrums, but when Doe shoved the gun in my mouth it told me this was *way* past the point of me having any control over the situation or Vu's fate. "Vu, his name's Vu," I choked out.

With my answer, Doe withdrew the gun from my throat and got this…disgusted look on his face. He looked at Blue, who gave him a look of "I told you so," then shook his head at me.

I was surprised again when Lucky was the one who yelled out "How could you do some *stupid* shit like that?! How could you get up with that bitch-ass cat and lead him right to us? Over some high-school shit, Dejah?!"

"What the hell are you talking about?" I yelled back, confused as hell. "High school? This nigga raped me and beat my ass, Lucky!" I screamed, pointing at Blue. I know he'd told me not to say anything, but the way things were looking, I didn't have anything to lose right now. Maybe I could play the sympathy card and buy myself a few more hours on this earth.

That temporary feeling of hope left me when Doe waved me away. "Aw…save that shit, Dejah. We seen the tape."

Tape? What tape? "Tape? What tape?" I demanded, my blood running cold and looking from man to man.

Blue pulled a tape off the top of the television I hadn't noticed at first. "She don't know nothing about the cameras or she wouldn't have shown her ass like she did," he told Doe and Lucky.

"Cameras?" I repeated, sounding like a retarded puppet.

Instead of answering, Blue slid the tape in the player. I stared on in horror as me and Blue came up on the screen. It was that horrible day I'd been trying to forget. There I was, tanning in my white bikini, then there was Blue coming up, and sitting next to me. Then I was sitting in his lap, to him shoving me off walking in the house and me following behind

120

UNTRUST Deszion Nasir

him. There weren't cameras inside the house, but you could see through the open curtains how I threw a bottle at him. Then he disappeared from view. I was wondering why he would let people see his attack on me, but I should have known better. The video was seamlessly cut to the point of Blue walking out and talking on his cell phone. His whole attack had been edited out.

At this point Blue picked the remote up and fast forwarded to where I left out the house with a gun in my hand and hit play when I pulled up in front of the house with Vu. We walked into the house and through that same window you could see Vu taking pictures of the house with his cell phone. When I went upstairs, you could see Vu peering around to make sure I was out of sight before he dialed a number and started going through every drawer in the house, quickly digging through planners and examining a calendar on the wall. He took more pictures of that and was done before I came back downstairs. Blue hit fast forward again and later on that night I saw about 6 motorcycles like the one Vu drove pull up on my grass like the swat team. They swarmed the house like SWAT and ransacked the whole house, Vu standing at the door, giving orders and pointing. Then Vu and another Asian guy walked over to the calendar and pointed to the day I had circled, Zure's birthday party. Vu got on the phone again, and after about 7 minutes, they straightened the house up like maids, wiped prints off of everything and left as fast as they came. That's when Blue hit the stop button and I knew by the silence in the room I was fucked. Once again I had been played by a man wanting to use me for something. You'd think by now I have learned...and me shooting at Blue damn sure wasn't helping the situation. I knew there was nothing I could say or do at this point.

"Where is he?" Doe demanded, but Blue interrupted him.

"I don't want to hear nothing that comes out of that lying ho's mouth." he said.

121

"But you *know* she knows where that nigga rest at," Doe complained.

"Of course she knows. And Vu knows she knows. He also knows she's a dumb emotional bitch who was destined to act up after a while and most likely run her fucking mouth. I ain't walking into no damn traps set up by her little boyfriend. *Fuck* that. She over there lookin all bewildered and shit. If she was dumb enough to get tricked into helping this cat then that's on her. But as for that nigga? I'll find him on my own."

Lucky nodded, seeing Blue's point of view.

"Oh, one more thing. You fuckin that dude, right?"

I didn't answer.

"Yeah, I know. I know you, girl. I bet you fucked him last night, right?"

I just wiped a tear away from my eye and tried to look as dignified as I could with a busted lip and a gun pointed at me.

"It's cool... that actually works out for me. He played you, ma, and he thought he was gonna play me. You know why I'm glad you fucked him? Cuz now you've got his DNA on   you..."
Blue pulled out another gun. "Picked this up off one of your boyfriends boys when they tried to kill us the other night. So... with his DNA in you and his boy's DNA on this gun... your boy 'bout to find us *and* the cops on his ass."

He saw the confused look on my face and smiled. "Oh, you wanna know what the cops gonna be on Vu's ass for?"

I glanced at Lucky, who stared at me with those traffic light eyes for a second before looking away and closing his eyes. I turned back to Blue as I heard him say "They gonna be on him for murder."

I didn't even hear the shot. I felt my head jerk back, my arms flail out, then my head landed on softness. Softness, then darkness...

UNTRUST Deszion Nasir

BLUE

I heard my doorbell ringing. I sighed and took a deep breath. I stood up from behind my desk and went to answer the door.

C stood there, his eyes wicked. I almost changed my mind because he already looked too far gone for what had in mind. You gotta be careful waving lighters around dynamite, you know. But this shit was just business. Everything was just business with me. I had to get Caesar all the way gone.

"What's up, man?" he asked, and not in the way of a greeting. "You called me from the house phone."

"I know."

"You never call me from the house phone for no routine shit." Caesar pointed out.

"I know."

"Stop saying 'I know.'"

Caesar glared at me suspiciously, and then walked past me into the living room. When he saw Lucky and Doe sitting there, not smiling and not saying nothing, he stopped.

"What happened to her?" he asked quietly, each word spoken carefully.

Silence. Caesar looked at Lucky, who looked away and sighed. He hadn't been down with what I had decided to do, but the man knew what had to be done. Regret, like guilt and mistakes, couldn't be tolerated at this stage of the game, and he knew that, so I knew he'd stay quiet. A conscience was the one infection I didn't have a cure for.

"What happened to her?!" Caesar screamed.

Doe stood up and handed C the tape I'd shown them in the hotel room. Caesar smacked it out of Doe's hand. "Do I look like I work at Blockbuster?!" he yelled. Doe shook his head, picked up the tape and put it in my in-wall television, where I grabbed the remote and showed C everything I'd shown them at the hotel, fast forwarding past the same parts.

UNTRUST Deszion Nasir

C watched without moving, except for clenching his jaw and fists through the whole thing.

"Two days ago, we was out at McFadden's and Dejah tried to kill me, man. She shot me in the arm and everything. She got away, and because she didn't do what that nigga sent her to do... " I trailed off and handed C a picture. He hesitated, then took the picture. "Somebody sent this to the barber shop on Mercury off Armistead." The picture was one of Dejah tied up to the hotel bed, a hole in her head, naked and sliced up. On the wall, written in his sister's blood, was a message:

"Some Egyptians are red
Some Scorpions are blue
I got this bitch
Next time it's gonna be you."

Doe is a sick muthafucka. Lucky refused to get his hands dirty with the mutilation and had left, taking Angel with him. He didn't want to see the picture or know anything about what we were going to do to Dejah's body. I left because I didn't want blood all over my clothes.

Caesar's hands started shaking as he stared at the picture. Then he dropped it and started pacing back and forth, muttering in Arabic, getting louder and louder until he was shouting and knocking shit off my shelves. He took off for the front door but I blocked him. "C, wait, man. I know you upset, man, but you cain't go out like-"

"Why would she fuck around with that muthafucka? Did he come after her on purpose to get at me?" Caesar demanded, cutting me off. I tried to step closer to him, pretending I was trying to calm him down.

"MOVE!!" he screamed, so mad spit was flying from his mouth. He was ready to go head up with me.

"I cain't do that," I told him, pretending to be concerned about him. His response was to shove me. He was as strong as men twice his size, but so was I. When he realized he couldn't push me out of the way, he whirled around and went to the back patio doors, but they only opened with a key from the inside or the outside. We were all trying to get him to calm down at that point, but he got frustrated, snatched out a gun and fired into my ceiling. We all fell back instantly. He yelled out "Fuck this!" and grabbed one of my end tables and hurled it through my glass patio doors. Then he kicked glass out of his way and broke out through the back like a wild animal. The next thing we heard was him burning rubber down the street. By the time we got to the front door and looked up the street, C was gone, leaving cars side-swiped and bikes crushed in his path.

"Dayum," Doe commented, shaking his head. *"That nigga is fucked up,"* he said, while Lucky bent down and picked up the picture Caesar had dropped. I saw his face ball up.

"No, nigga, *you* fucked up. Why did you do that to that girl like that? Damn," he snapped, disgusted.

"Lucky, come on. A nigga did what I had to do-" Doe started, grabbing Lucky's arm, but Lucky snatched away from him and held the picture in his face.

"No. You didn't have to go that fuckin' far, Doe. *Fuck naw,"*

"Nigga chill,"

"Naw, nigga, *you* chill. Fuck you-"he turned and threw the picture in my direction. "And fuck *you*, too." he snapped. He grabbed his keys and stormed out of the house.

Doe stood beside me and watched him leave, shaking his head after him. "You think that nigga C gonna bring Vu out in the open?"

"No question," I said, staring out at my peaceful neighborhood as neighbors came outside and started looking around. Then I laughed. "I might have to move, though."

PART VI-HAWIIAN FEVER

VU

"…**19** year-old female found brutally beat, raped and murdered in a Hampton Hotel 2 nights ago. Police have identified the woman as Dejah Sadaat, graduate of Phoebus High school and native of Cairo, Egypt. According to police and initial examinations, there was DNA left on Sadaat and on the gun found in the grass near the hotel. If you have any information call Hampton police or 1-800-lock-u-up…"

I sat straight up on my couch. I *knew* that girl was hard-headed. But hold on…that put me in a bad spot. No doubt it was going to be my DNA they found on Dejah. Another thought occurred to me and I snatched my phone up and called my man Shiro. "Did you ever get Manny's gun from the bowling alley incident?"

Shiro was half sleep, so I repeated what I'd said louder. "Um… naw, I didn't. I thought-" I slammed the phone down. That mutherfucker Blue. He'd become a bigger pain in my ass than I'd thought. I still hadn't been able to get an address or valid number on him. All his businesses had back up addresses that all went to P.O. boxes. Nothing personal was listed about him anywhere. The only person my boys got a trail on was Jai Cruz, but he drove like a maniac on that bike and nobody could even get close to him.

I tossed the phone across the room and broke it, pissed off that my sister had been right about these young boys being more trouble than I'd thought. I was sitting there fuming and re-calculating things in my head when my cell phone rang.

"What?"

It was one of my workers telling me I needed to get my ass out to Virginia Beach like yesterday.

"Why?" I demanded, rubbing my forehead as I knew this was about to be more bad news to add to my fresh headache.

"Minya's shop is on fire."

"*What*? Is she okay?"

"She ain't there.   Don't nobody know where she is…but…whoever did it left a message on the wall for you."

"How you know it's for me? What does it say?"

"I don't know what it says cuz it's written in Arabic. But your name is printed in English. We covered it up before the cops got here, but I took a picture of it-" I hung up on him.

Blue knew. He knew she was with me and he killed her. Dejah's brother must think I killed her and that's why he set the shop on fire. This whole situation was getting out of control real quick and for a second, I wondered if all this shit was really worth it. I was already under pressure by the other Triads to get back to Japan. They never approved of this trip in the first place. But this was about family and honor. I had to finish what I'd started. I grabbed my keys, jogged out to my bike and sped off to Virginia Beach.

B the time I got down there, news reporters, cops and firemen were everywhere. I called my boy to meet me across the way from where Minya's shop was. When he walked up, he was already holding his phone out, showing me a picture of the message on the wall spray painted in red. It roughly translated into:

Fire is red,

Your eyes are blue

I know who you are, Vu *Knight*

And you're going to die, too."

"What it say?" my boy was asking me, trying to peek over my shoulder like he hadn't seen it a few minutes ago.

I ignored him as my mind spun in different directions. There was only one person who could have told that nigga my eyes were blue, and couldn't nobody find her. Was she dead? If not, what the fuck was on that girl's mind? Didn't she know if I thought for even a second she was on the other team I'd kill her and not even think about it no more? Traitors could never be a part of the family. I would be doing her a favor by killing her.

127

UNTRUST Deszion Nasir

My man was till asking me questions. "Get away from here and don't do shit until I tell you," I told him. "You tell the others to keep looking for Minya." The tone of my voice didn't leave no room for arguing. He left and I left, too. I needed to think and I was hungry. I went to my normal spot, and IHOP out of Norfolk, and asked to be seated in the smoking section, as usual. I didn't smoke, but there was a table back in the cut where I could sit in and think. I'd been running on empty lately, running behind these kids and keeping up with Siovahn. She could fuck a man to sleep but she had a mouth like a water faucet. I could see why Blue dropped her. But I needed her, though, now more than ever in fact.

I went inside, got seated, and waited for my usual waitress. I had my eyes closed and was massaging my temples when I heard: "Can I get you a drink?"

"Large cranberry juice," I muttered.

"You want some Aleve with that?" She asked in a sweet voice tinted by an accent I was vaguely familiar with. I looked up and saw this Amazon staring down at me. She had smooth skin that had obviously been tanned with a color only the sun could give her. She was thick as all hell and had the strangest green hazel eyes. She was obviously from some island, I just couldn't tell which one yet.

She saw me staring and smiled harder. "I'm Millay and I'll be your server today. I wasn't trying to be smart, it just looked like you had a real bad headache," she told me, her voice light.

"Where's the regular girl?" I asked, looking around.

"Oh, Michelle? She's here… I just might have begged her to let me get your table," Millay said, flashing that smile at me again. When I just kept staring at her, she goes "Oh, I'm sorry… do you want me to get her for you…?" Her face dropped and she blushed, starting to back away. I reached out and grabbed her hand.

"No, no, you're good… I just never seen you before, you know…I'm a creature of habit," I said, grinning at her despite

128

my mood. If I needed a distraction it was now. Besides, Millay was fine as hell and I hadn't got any ass since I'd been in America. Well, I hadn't got any unplanned ass... you know... it's a difference...

She smiled widely. "I know. I bet you're going to order a Belgian waffle with a side of fruit, no meat, and double hash browns, right?"

I sat back and laughed. "Yeah, I guess you *have* been talking to Michelle," I said, taking off my hat and scratching my new cornrows. They itched.

"Not used to braids?"Millay guessed.

"No, not really... I usually just wear my hair out or pulled back. Just trying to fit in while I'm in the States," I told her.

"Why? Everyone here is screaming that they're individuals while imitating everyone else here. Who you *really* are gives you one up on everyone here," she told me. "Hey, I'll go put your order in," she said, suddenly remembering that she was at work. She walked off and I sat back and watched her, eased by her conversation and calm voice. She floated around the restaurant and came back with my cranberry juice. "Here you go," she sang, sitting it down on a napkin, something the other waitresses never did here. "Did you need anything else right now?" she asked, pulling her order pad back out.

I scratched my nose. "Yeah, get me your manager."

Millay's smile dropped and she paled. "My manager? I'm sorry... I didn't mean to... uh..."

I kept my face even. "Can you just go get him before my food gets here?" I asked her, banging the end of my straw on the table to make it bust through the wrapper.

Nervous, Millay nodded and went over to a white guy on the phone. He hung up, listened to her, and then looked over at me. "What did you do?" he mouthed. "Nothing, I swear," she mouthed back. He glared at her, then came over to me, Millay behind him, looking timid and shit.

"Is there a problem?" he asked.

"Nothing that can't be fixed," I told him, pulling out my wallet. "I don't like eating alone, so I was wondering if she could take a break," I said, pulling out 300 dollars and waving it in Millay's direction. The manager had snatched the money and told Millay to take a break before I could put my arm down.

Stunned, Millay watched him and turned to me.

"Sit down," I told her, nodding across from me. She sat, smiling nervously. "What are you so nervous for?" I asked, grinning. Her innocence was helping my mood.

"Because that doesn't happen everyday…never, for real…"

We sat there and talked for two hours. I fed her some of my food and we talked about Japan and where she was from, Hawaii. She told me she was here to go to school and didn't like it in Norfolk and that she was homesick. I felt her on that. It felt good to just have a normal conversation with a normal person, considering that I wasn't anywhere near normal and didn't deal with anyone who was. Eventually, I caught her boss staring in our direction. The morning crowd was coming in and I knew he needed her back, but didn't want to ask. I didn't want her to end up in trouble so I was like "Look, I'm really trying to hang out with you while I'm still here. You free tonight?"

Her face broke out into a huge smile. "I can get free…"

"Cool… what do you wanna do?"

"Dance, go to comedy clubs, play paintball…"

Negative, negative, negative. I'd be wide open to whatever.

"I'm really just trying to hang out with you without all the noise and guys trying to talk to you," I told her, giving her my best smile. "Tell you what. I gotta private jet. How about we just shoot over to the Florida Keys and have dinner on a private beach?"

Millay's eyes bugged out of her head. "Are you for real?"

"Yeah," I laughed. "You can pinch me if you want."

UNTRUST Deszion Nasir

Millay narrowed her eyes at me. "Are you a drug dealer or something?"

I almost spit out my juice tryna keep from laughing. "Where the hell did that come from?" I asked, wiping my mouth.

"You got a plane and all this money or whatever. Plus, you hanging out here. That's a checklist for dope boys."

"Naw, sorry to disappoint you, love. All my businesses are legit. I own a lot of property all over the world and run a lot of businesses because I worked hard. I had to, you know...nobody in this country or this world is gonna give you shit, even if you deserve it. As a matter of fact, if you deserve it that makes people even *more* determined to take it from you. If we don't never see each other again, always remember that." I told her seriously.

She nodded. I gave her a number to contact me with and told her to just be ready to leave around 6. I'd send a car to pick her up and take her to the airport. I could see that she wasn't sure she believed me, but I'd fix that. Good or bad, Vu Katsamura was not a man who broke a promise.

MILAY

As soon as I got off "work," I paid the manager the agreed upon 2 thousand dollars and gave the waitress 500 for letting me work her section until Vu showed up. The tracking device Jay's put on Vu's car showed that he came to this IHOP like clockwork. Today wasn't a normal day, but Blue figured he'd show up because of the fire, and then end up here. I got into my new pink Lexus-thanks, Blue-and zoomed off, dialing a number I knew by heart without having to take my eyes off of the road.

"Yeah." Just the sound of Doe's voice made me shiver.

"Hey baby," I purred, trying to sound all sexy.

"What's good, sexy? Everything straight?"

"You tell me. He paid the manager 300 dollars so I could sit down to talk to him while he ate and then he invited me to fly on his jet to the Florida Keys for dinner."

"Well, shit, can you blame him? Look at you, ma."

I blushed behind the wheel. Doe was always saying something sweet to me, like I should know how special or beautiful I was. Where I was from, everyone looked like me basically, but I had been getting so much attention in the States...

"So what do you want me to do tonight?" I asked him.

"Just be your beautiful self. Just keep him busy, you know... he's supposed to be this high-class cat, so he should treat you pretty nice. Just enjoy yourself."

"I wish I was going with you."

"Ay, check it. We'll do whatever you want, go wherever you want, once you get back."

I rubbed my eyes. These hazel contacts were making my eyes itch. "What about Sherita? She gonna let you travel like that?"

"What you askin' about her for?"

"Oh, what, she's not your little girlfriend? She texts you

132

a hundred times a day."

He didn't know I knew about that, but I'd heard that he'd been talking to her. He'd seen her at the cookout Blue'd had and she'd slipped him her number before she'd left that night.

"That don't make her my girl, that makes her persistent."

"Whatever, Doe."

"C'mon, baby…"

"Look, I'm not your baby. I'm your little secret, remember? You know if Blue knew our shit was more than business-"

"I don't work for Blue!" Doe snapped, then took a breath then calmed down quickly. I knew that kind of talk irked the hell out of him, but I couldn't help it. He was irking the hell out of me with all his beat-around-the-bush-talk.

"Then why don't you tell anybody about us?" I demanded.

"Can we talk about this later?" Doe asked.

"No, we cannot," I said sweetly, merging onto highway 64 traffic. "Look, I'm not stupid, Doe. I know you deal with other females. I just like being with you when I'm with you. I mean, I'm probably going back home soon anyway. I can't be gone forever, you know? Just don't play me like I'm stupid. I'm sweet, not stupid…"

"Naw, you cain't be, comin' from the family you come from… aight, Mimi, look… just be careful and we'll pick this up when we get back, ok? That cool with you?"

"Yeah, I guess…" I sighed.

"Aight, bye sexy."

"Bye," I said softly, then clicked the phone off. I was mad at myself for playing down how I felt about him and letting him get out of that so easy. I may get more attention than girls from the states, but I wasn't built as tough as them. I couldn't stand the thought of the guy I was dealing with being around other females. It was this damn business with Vu. If I could get this stupid shit out of the way, Doe'd have a lot more free time for me and Blue could loosen up before he backed up against a tree and sucked the bark off of it. It

133

seemed a simple fix to me. I'd just get in the air with Vu and blow his damn head off. Simple.

JAY

"Aight... they're getting on the jet now, Jay."

"Cool... hey I'm 'bout to hang up now, then."

"Hold up, son; we 'posed to keep communication going-
"

"I don't *need* you, though, fam. You gonna slow me up. Wait for a phone call." I hung up in Blue's boy's ear. Fuck Blue's directions. I was running this shit. If he knew what the fuck he was doing he wouldn't need me, would he? I put in the work; I take the risk, so I run this. He'd get what he wanted. Shit, he *should* be happy. I was saving him money by cutting off that extra dead weight. He'd thank a nigga later.

I was in the back of the truck of the gardener that took care of Vu's Kingsmill property with all my equipment along with the gardener's shit. The first thing I did was send out a signal that would block any satellite sensors that Vu might have up to detect any of my equipment. As soon as the gardener got within a certain distance of Vu's property, I activated a program I created myself that would let me hack into all his files, even if they were encrypted. He wouldn't be able to trace or tack the signal if it was detected anyway. Oh yeah, the kid is nice like that.

So while the gardener did his job, I was busy accessing all of Vu's business accounts and transferring them into different accounts, $100,000 of over 11 million going into the gardener's account for his cooperation. The money wouldn't show up missing for 12 hours. That was a big a window as I could give right now. I was working on one that would take 24 hours, but Blue said Millay wouldn't need that much time. I wasn't sure about that, but hey, his business. Whatever money was withdrawn during those 12 hours would then show up immediately as overdrawn, which would probably send his business buddies in Hong Kong and Tokyo into a fit thinking Vu had embezzled all their money. I couldn't get to his personal money cuz I didn't know where it was, but his business investments were public and much easier to get to. This would do more damage to him anyway.

I honestly think Blue was playing a dangerous game. I don't know what he knew about what happened to cats who fucked with Asians and their money, but I knew a lot. They wasn't gonna lie down and get fucked in the ass by Blue *or* Vu. Most likely they'd do a blackout and kill everyone in both they families, so my plan was to get this money and get me and my sister the hell away from these clowns.

PART VII-BROTHERS, SISTERS AND COUSINS

TERRENCE –TJ (Riker's Island)

"Jones!"

I opened one eye as a guard beat on my cell bars with his stick.

"What?!" I yelled. Everybody in this muthafucka knew better than to fuck with me during my nap time. The warden didn't even bother me during my nap. I got respect in here like that cuz I respect other niggaz rules. I don't fuck with nobody that don't need to be fucked with and they don't fuck with me. The new bitches always tried me cuz I was quiet and the biggest nigga on the cell block. They took me for a bitch, and everyone that tried me ended up screaming like a bitch. It usually only took one time. A lot of times once they got back from the hospital they didn't come back to my cell block, but if they did, it was like they had some kinda religious epiphany and they had a whole different attitude. The bullshit had died down lately and I was glad. I'd been in this bitch 9 years and I was up for parole. I won't trying to trick that shit up for nobody. Especially since I'd been here this long on some bullshit anyway. I'd done the whole world a favor by killing Gemini Knight and the world repaid me by locking my black ass up.

"Visitation, TJ."

A visit? I had just seen my retarded-ass lawyer yesterday. I sighed and stood up, wondering what he'd forgot to tell me this time.

I got into the cold, cramped small-ass private room where prisoners met with their lawyers, separate from regular visitation and waited. I hadn't had any other visits the whole time I'd been here. Probably because I wouldn't put anybody on my list. My sister Jasmine had tried to get me to put her on the list after she'd found me, but I told her I won't nobody

137

UNTRUST Deszion Nasir

she needed to know. She'd sent letters for a few months but stopped when I never wrote her back. She didn't understand I was doing her a favor. Nobody ever got that. They just labeled me anti-social or gave me some psycho-bullshit title.

I was nodding off in my chair when the door opened. When I saw who walked in, I reacted instantly. I picked up my chair and flung it at the muthafucka's head. He ducked and the chair exploded against the wall. I was on that bitch in a second and was choking the life out of him before the guards grabbed me. It took 4 of them to get me off of him. He was about as big as me, but my anger had made me stronger. The guards had me on the ground and were cuffing me when the guy yelled "Chill out, chill,…" and pried the guards off of me. "He don't know who I am."

When he spoke, I realized the voice was different. I blinked, and as the insanity left my eyes, I realized it couldn't be him. He was dead, I'd killed him, and if I hadn't, there was no way he could have gotten almost 20 years younger than when I killed him. I calmed down and the guards let me up after looking at him, but kept the cuffs on him.

"Who the fuck is you?" I demanded, narrowing my mom's green eyes at his blue ones.

"Take them cuffs off him," he commanded. The guards hesitated, especially when I yelled "WHO THE FUCK ARE YOU?!"

"Be easy. I'm your brother Scorpion Knight. Jasmine's twin brother." he said finally.

"Jasmine…?" I blinked few times. Jasmine had said she'd had a brother, but she'd never sent any pictures of either of them. Shit…this nigga looked exactly like… like –

"You look just like Gemini," I managed. When I relaxed the guards uncuffed me, but wouldn't leave the room. Scorpion waited until I sat down before he did.

"So I hear," he said dryly, brushing his collar off and sitting back in his chair.

"So… you're Blue," I said, more as a statement than a question.

UNTRUST Deszion Nasir

"Yeah."

"Shit... you gotta give me a second...*fuck*," I leaned forward and wiped my face with my hands.

"You good... I know seeing me is a shock, especially since I look like..."

"Hell *yeah* it's a shock..." I got myself together, then other shit started sinking in. "How did you get a legal visit? You not no lawyer, is you?"

Blue laughed. "*Hell* naw, not even close. I got a bunch of them, though."

"I'm not understanding you. You not a lawyer, but you got a lawyer visit. I don't got nobody on my visitation list. They real tight on the rules about visits up here."

Blue smirked. "Enough money can loosen anybody up," he said pointedly.

"Oh, you got it like that?"

"Fam, you got no idea how good I got it. And what *I* got, *you* got."

That sent my radar up. Something was wrong. If this nigga was *that* interested in his brother, he could have been through here a while ago. His dollars were obviously as long as hell, so what would make him wait until now to come through? And since Jasmine was the one who'd been writing me, why he ain't bring her? This nigga wanted something.

"What you want, man?" I asked in a tired voice, rubbing my eyes with my fingertips.

Blue grinned. "I wanted to meet you."

"Why? For what? What you want, nigga? I already gave you the two best things I got to offer. I killed that devil Gemini and I gave my life up so you wouldn't have to kill his ass and give up yours. I don't got nothing left for you. I don't got nothin' left for *me*."

Blue studied me for a minute before responding. I didn't like what I saw in his eyes. I saw nothing. No anger, happiness, sympathy, sadness, nothing. He was a shell covering something. In my eyes, he was worse than Gemini. Gemini was a conceited, selfish muthafucka and not only did

UNTRUST Deszion Nasir

everyone know it, he wore that title like a badge. He was proud not to give a shit and it showed. At least you know where you stood with him. This kid Blue was 100 percent in control of his emotions and his thoughts and that type of nigga ain't never nothing good. Never.

Blue reached into his pocket and pulled out a picture. He slid it across the table in my direction and sat back. I stared at it before I picked it up like it was poisonous. It might have been. I saw it was a picture of a female. I picked it up and saw a tall, female version of him in a few darker shades of brown. Her blue eyes stood out more than his because she was darker. She was the most beautiful thing I'd ever seen.

"This baby girl?" I asked Blue, already knowing the answer. "This Jasmine?"

Blue nodded.

I grinned despite myself. "How many cats you broke up over her?"

Blue finally showed some emotion and frowned. "Too fuckin many, trust me…" he said, shaking his head. "It don't help she think her shit don't stink, neither."

"Her shit *don't* stink, " I told him, still looking at the picture, chuckling.

Blue let me look at the picture another minute before he leaned forward on the table. "You're right. I do need something from you."

"What's that?"

"I need you to help me before somebody kills her."

I sat back in my cell after Blue left, thinking over everything he'd said.

"You don't even belong in here," he'd told me. "I checked up on your case. You don't got no priors. You killed a nigga who tried to kill your mother. The only reason you in here rotting' is because you had a raggedy-ass public defender. Fuck that nigga Gemini. Fuck this lame-ass life in here. You don't belong in here and I'ma have you out in a week, I *promise* you that. Shit, you an uncle. We got shit to do, you feel me?"

I just stared at him. Maybe he was crazy after all.

"Don't worry about shit when you get out. I already had the guest house set up-"

Guest house?

"-and I already copped you this gold Denali truck with gold rims and all that good shit. It'll be in your name by the time you get home-"

"I ain't got no license man. I'ma convicted felon, remember?"

"Oh, yeah... hold up..." Blue said like he'd just remembered something. He pulled some paperwork out of his pocket and handed it to me. I took it and looked it over. In short, my whole case had been dismissed.

While I sat there trying to process that, he went on talking like we were talking about the weather. "I had my lawyers working on your case for a minute. I didn't tell you until now cuz I didn't want to get your hopes up if it didn't work out."

"Hold up... you tellin' me... you tellin' me that next week I'm being *released?* I thought it was a parole hearing."

"Your case is dismissed. What you need parole for?" Blue asked, looking confused.

Was everything that simple to him? It sure as fuck seemed like it.

Before that could settle in, Blue was telling me some story about some nigga named Vu who was trying to kill all of Gemini's kids behind some shit he'd done to his mother. He broke down everything you already read about the situation, then explained what he wanted us to do, telling me he couldn't trust nobody else cuz nobody else understood how important this thing was. "This is family business." he'd stressed.

I agreed. But I didn't want no part of this shit. I didn't trust Blue anymore than I trusted Vu, but I damn sure wasn't

UNTRUST Deszion Nasir

about to sit up in this bitch any longer than I had to. So I
agreed to do what Blue wanted.

UNTRUST Deszion Nasir

MINYA

I hung up the phone and curled up on my hotel bed, crying. My shop was gone. A total loss. My dream. I know Vu said it was supposed to be a front business for getting in good with Jasmine, but Vu wasn't the only smart one in the family. I really put a lot of time, research and effort into this and this was something I'd planned on continuing while Vu went back to Japan. I was tired of the hectic life Vu led, but he was under the impression I was supposed to do whatever he wanted because he was the alpha male-the only male-in our family. My mind was much bigger than the box he'd always wanted me to be in. It must have been the black side of me that was refusing to just lie down and do whatever he wanted me to do.

But honestly, I knew this was going to happen. Since my shop didn't mean anything to anyone other than me, it was doomed to be a casualty in the war between my brothers.

And I'd seen poor Dejah's murder on the news, too. I don't know who killed her, but I know Vu had something to do with it. He's going way out of the blueprints we'd set in place before we came here and now it was like all he cared about was not letting Blue have one up on him. He hadn't mentioned our mother once since we'd gotten here. His mind was somewhere I didn't want to be and that (along with not wanting to be within spitting distance of Caesar) was the reason I disappeared and have been holed up in this hotel room for what felt like forever.

I couldn't keep hiding here, I knew. I knew what I was supposed to do and what I had to do and eventually I'd have to get myself together and do it.

I'd heard and read a lot of things about my father. I knew how heartless he was, but I also knew how strong he could be. His sons weren't the only ones who'd inherited that. Jas was the strongest female I knew, and I had to have

143

some of that in me, too.

I walked over to the balcony doors and let in some fresh air. I took a few deep breaths and headed for the shower. I got ready to help one brother and betray the other. At the end of the day, I'd probably be dead, but at least at the end of all this I'd be with my mother and she'd be proud of me.

MILLAY

"It's so pretty out here," I said, looking past our beachfront table to the water sparking under the moon, 6ft. away from our table.

"I'm feeling the view from right here," he said to me, smiling.

I'd blushed, something I'd been doing a lot since we got on the plane.

We'd just finished eating a dinner of Black Bass, Asparagus tips and red skin mashed potatoes after a spinach, pecan and tomato salad and now I was trying to force down the best pineapple upside down cake I'd ever had...and I'd had some good ones. He'd tried to get me to drink this expensive wine but I wasn't a drinker and tonight was definitely not the time to start.

"Okay, so... we talked a lot about my family," I told him, wiping my mouth, "but you haven't really said nothing about yours,"

Vu paused, mid chew, his eyes narrowing for a minute, then they looked normal again, although his voice changed.

"My mom died a long time ago," he said, sitting back and putting his fork down. "And I don't have no other family," he added, glancing at the water for a minute before his gaze finally settled back on me.

"I'm *so* sorry," I said sincerely.

He didn't say anything for a minute, then smiled at me again and stood up. He took me by the hand and we walked out to the water, neither of us saying nothing for awhile, then he reached over and picked up some of my hair, something he'd been doing a lot tonight. "Let's stay another day," he said suddenly, throwing me into a panic. In my surprised I jerked away from him. He held his position as my hair slipped from his fingers. The expression on his face at that moment was unreadable.

UNTRUST Deszion Nasir

"What? I can't stay," I said instantly, swallowing nervously. "I have to go back to work and I got class and everything," I explained, trying to calm down. I wrapped my arms around myself like I was chilly instead of terrified.

"C'mon, Millay. You think money would be a problem for me? And you can go to any school you want, anywhere you want." Vu told me, waving his arms toward the water, indicating he could give me anything in the world I wanted. I believed him, and being as naïve as I was, I would have jumped at the opportunity any other time.

"Naw, I'm not even that type of female. Besides, I don't even know you that well." I protested, calming down.

"But you knew me well enough to get on a jet with me?" Vu asked, looking a little pissed off.

I was trying to reason with him, because I had to get back to VA before those 12 hours ran out. Before dinner we'd went to this club on the beach so he was already half-twisted as it was. Thankfully, he finally calmed down.

"I guess I can't be mad at you for that," he muttered. "I might be crazy, right?"

I laughed, but uneasily. I checked my cell phone again. I'd been checking it off and on for awhile now, and V noticed it, but never said anything. After a little longer he started rubbing his eyes like all the liquor he'd drank was getting to him. "We better get you back, I guess."

"Yeah," I said, calm but grateful on the inside. "It seems like it's so much later than it is," I added, using that excuse as a reason for me continually checking my cell phone.

Vu just half-grinned at me and led me back to the plane. Before we re-boarded, Vu took my hand and pulled me to him. I wanted to run, but that would have looked strange, being that I was supposed to be as into him as he was into me. "Are you sure there's nothing I could do to change your mind?" he whispered in my ear, nuzzling my neck and kissing my shoulder. I could smell the alcohol on his breath. "I been looking for someone like you for years; someone sweet and innocent to keep me grounded from the crazy life I live," he

UNTRUST Deszion Nasir

said, his lips moving from my shoulders to my neck to my mouth. "I could make you so happy," he went on, pulling me tight against him and squeezing my sides.

"I know you could, baby," I managed. "I just don't move that fast where I'm from. Give me a little more time, that's all. What female wouldn't want to be with somebody like you? You're strong, sweet, fine as hell and all you want to do is take care of me. You think I'm trying to mess that up? I just want you to get to know me a little better so you won't think I'm n this for the money." That sounded good to me.

"I don't think that," Vu protested, letting me go and looking more than a little rejected and once again, I started feeling sorry for him and feeling bad for what I was doing to him. He just seemed like a lonely guy who'd been forced to make some hard choices in life. Most powerful men had been put in that position all the time, and it sounded like all he wanted was someone who appreciated all those choices. I felt like shit. I just didn't see the killer that Blue tried to paint in my mind of Vu. From the short time I'd known him, Blue seemed way more dangerous than Vu.

Once on the place, Vu poured himself a glass of guava juice and sat back in a seat across from mine, stretching out and sitting the glass on the little table. He opened his mouth to say something, and then his cell phone rang, making me jump. He smirked at me and answered in Japanese. I watched his facial expression, which never changed. He laughed at whatever was being said and I relaxed. He hung up after a few minutes, then stared at me a minute, then asked "Why you keep checking your phone so much?"

I shrugged. "It just seems so late," I said again, trying to play the whole thing off.

Vu nodded, rubbing his tired eyes as his liquor was starting to make them red, and he picked up his juice again. "It be that way sometimes," he said after he'd swallowed. "What cell phone company do you got?" he asked.

"Nextel."

UNTRUST Deszion Nasir

Vu nodded again. "That's why you so confused, I guess."

My brow wrinkled. "Confused? What am I confused about?"

"Well, you know the guy that just called me?"

I nodded, panic slightly rising in my chest like heartburn, but I sent it back down. At least I tried to...

"He told me Nextel's satellite malfunctioned and the whole system went down, crashed, or whatever. Whoever got Nextel is having problems right now,"

"Oh, for real?" I asked, the panic shooting the calm in my throat back up and out of my mouth, leaving me sounding terrified while I sat there with a calm look on my face.

"Yeah, your clock is like ...4 hours slow or something."

Panic became ice as I froze. I'd been here too long. Way to long. Vu sat his glass on the floor of the plane. As he did, I reached in my bag and pulled my gun out. By the time he looked up, I had it pointed in his face. He raised an eyebrow at me and sat back, stretching his arms out on the armrest and sighed. " So... I guess I don't got to ask about what happened to all my business accounts," he guessed. "He called to tell me about that, too." He looked way more hurt than he looked angry. I truly felt fucked up on the inside now. I wanted to just undo the whole thing, but I couldn't. I wasn't built to do this type of work and realized I'd made a terrible mistake by even getting involved in this.

"I didn't have nothing to do with the money," I said truthfully.

"But you knew about it," Vu insisted, still in that calm voice.

"I'm sorry," I said, breaking down, but I didn't lower the gun. I wasn't *that* stupid. "I don't want to be doing this, I swear," I cried. My tears were itching my face, but I needed both my hands on the gun right now, so I tried to ignore it.

Vu nodded, his lips curling under angrily. He squeezed the armrests in frustration, and I heard two pops. I didn't even feel anything, but I saw the two mini barrels of guns Vu

UNTRUST Deszion Nasir

had built into the seats retract back into their hidden position. That's when I felt the burning and looked down to see two red spots swelling up on my chest. I dropped my gun and slid out of my seat, feeling a sudden sting, then a burning in my chest. The itching feeling was replaced by a pain that I couldn't even begin to describe. I looked up in time to see Vu standing up over me. He studied me gasping for air for a moment, then he bent down, picked up my gun and put it to my right eye. "I would have changed your life, Millay. I could have loved you. What is it about this bastard Scorpion Knight that has all you beautiful women dying for him?" he said the last part as if he were asking himself. I couldn't answer because the room was starting to fade, as I was having trouble seeing. He bent over and kissed me on the head before he pulled the trigger one last time.

BLUE

Jasmine burst into my room 1st thing in the morning. I was still tired from the trip to see my brother and Angel's mission to wear me out and make up for our time apart. Every time I left, that girl tried to fuck me to death when I got back. It was like she was trying to make me too tired to go anywhere again. It worked, at least for a few hours. But of course, Jas won't worried about none of that. She paused on my side of the bed, looking down at me with her hands on her hips like she was disgusted. I was half-covered by the blanket and Angel wasn't covered at all. She walked around everywhere naked, so she didn't care about being exposed.

"What? *Shit*," I demanded, when I felt she'd been standing there a few seconds too long.

"I thought you said you hired *three* moving trucks for today," she snapped. Yeah, I was serious about what I'd said before. It was time to move. I had found a house out Buckroe on the water. It had 5 bedrooms, a guest house and a private beach and a big-ass indoor pool, even though it was beachfront property. A nigga liked to have options. Besides, in the winter the pool was heated and it was inside a clear dome. It all depended if I wanted a breeze or not. It was still too early in the morning for stupid-ass statements like that so I threw a plastic cup of ice at her. "I *did* order 3," I yelled, causing Angel to groan and roll over, not bothering to cover herself up. Didn't bother me. She hated wearing clothes as much as I liked her hating them.

Jasmine picked the cup back up and tossed it and the ice that didn't spill out back at me. It hit me and the ice bounced off Angel's ass. She jumped up, woke now. Ha. "Well, it's *four* trucks outside, and they out there arguing with each other. Go handle that." She stormed out, her heels clicking loudly.

"Why don't you do it if you out there already?" I yelled

UNTRUST Deszion Nasir

after hr. "You know you like bossing people around."

I heard Jasmine's heels pause. "Nigga, please, that's management and you know I'm a rest, dress and impress type of chick. The shit you talking about is work, and I don't do that menial shit. Get your pit bull in a skirt to do that, and get her to do that shit in a hurry because they right outside my window, " she tossed, her heels clicking away again as her voice trailed. A few seconds later I heard the door to her room slam. I glanced at angel and saw her fuming. Jasmine had a habit of making off the wall comments and coming out of her mouth wrong where Angel-or any female I dealt with-was concerned. Angel tolerated her and they got along most of the time, even hanging out on occasion, but I could tell her patience with my sister's mouth was wearing thin.

"Shiiiit," I groaned, sitting up and scrubbing my face with my palms. I hated when I had to go outside without shaving. I also hated ignorant-ass people and I wasn't in the mood to deal with this shit today. I threw on a t-shirt and some shorts I had draped over a chair and headed for the front door. Sure enough, there was an extra Mayflower truck outside and they were huddled together, pointing fingers and trying to make it look like they weren't arguing.

I got on the phone with Doe.

"What, man?" Doe snapped on the first ring. He sounded more pissed off than me, but he sounded awake.

I didn't give a fuck, however. "Nigga, I said three trucks, *not* four," I snapped.

"Muthafucka I *sent* you three. Don't call here yelling and shit cuz *you* cain't count."

"Why I see four trucks outside?"

"What?"

"Damn, we must both be fucked up. I'm blind and you deaf. You heard me, nigga. Or your shit is gettin' sloppy."

"MY shit is never sloppy, *nigga*. I got other shit to deal with. You see an extra truck, send his ass on his way. I don't got time for your petty shit this morning, yo-"

I hung up on him before I got more pissed off than I

already was. If he had've been anybody else I probably would have put a hole in his forehead. I shook it to the left and went outside to get this shit straight so I could get this moving thing going.

"What the fuck, man?" I demanded, not hiding my pissitivity. I was bigger than all of them, so that made it even worse for them. One of the guys swallowed and stepped toward me, volunteering to be the spokesperson for the group.

"Mr. Knight, I tried to tell him that we was the only cats on this job-"

"And I tried to tell him I'm not here for no pick up. I'm here on a delivery."

"I told you, dog. If there had been a delivery, Joe would have sent it with me on the way over here. You know he won't gonna tie up an extra truck if one was already coming over here," the first driver said heatedly. He looked at me as if he was waiting for me to agree with him. I just looked at the second driver, waiting to hear his answer to that.

"It was a fly delivery. It came in after ya'll left. Look, I just take orders, man. I don't give them."

"I never had anything set up to be delivered here," I told the guy.

He sighed. "The order wasn't set up by you, neither. Somebody sent you something."

"Who?" I demanded, crossing my arms and frowning.

"Uh," the guy took out a clipboard out and flipped a couple of sheets up. "An Armando Taylor."

That shit sounded suspect. I'd just talked to him, and he didn't sound like he was in the mood to play no jokes like that. When he pulled pranks and whatever, it wouldn't be this kind of level, and he especially wouldn't have it done at my house.

"Bring it here," I told him and his partner, who just looked happy to be somewhere working. "The rest of you start getting the furniture out of the dining room and living room. I want everything out of here and moved into the other house by sundown if ya'll want that bonus I talked with Joe about."

The two guys finally went and got a huge box out of the trunk. It must've been heavy cuz they were struggling with it.

They sat it on the grass in the middle of my yard and looked at me.

"Open that shit up," I instructed. If something was going to jump out and splatter or blow up, it wasn't gonna hit *my* black ass.

They looked at each other and the other movers paused, curious too. They got a couple of crowbars off the truck and pried the lid off the box. They peered in and immediately started screaming and falling over each other trying to get out of the way. I peered in and the shit even had me speechless.

Jasmine and Angel came running out of the house at the sound of grown men screaming. I unfroze to try and hold Jas back, but I wasn't fast enough. She dodged me and looked into the box, saw what I didn't want her to see and did what I didn't want her to do. She screamed her *ass* off. Jas had lungs like an opera singer and I'm sure everybody up, down and around our street heard her screaming. Angel ran over beside me and just stared with her mouth open at Millay's body, hacked up into big pieces. Her head was at the top of the pile, a hole where her right eye used to be. The large box was lined with plastic so the pool of blood at the bottom wouldn't leak out.

On top of the bloody pile was a clear plastic bag. Inside the plastic bag was a cell phone that had been ringing since the top came off, but of course, I'd been distracted by Millay's hacked-up body. The name clearly displayed on the screen was "Armando."

Angel recovered before I did. She grabbed my phone out of my shorts and started dialing, walking away from me and into the house.

"Close it up," I said, my voice scratchy. I was already trying to figure out how I'd explain this to my uncle. I might have to kill him. He had no other kids and no family or wife, so he wouldn't let this rest and would make a hell of a lot of

UNTRUST Deszion Nasir

more trouble for me...

The moving men continued to stand there, but I didn't have time for that shit. I was back.

"Close it up!" I said louder, but not loud enough to draw any more attention from the neighbors. Jasmine was still screaming, but she was always yelling at somebody so...

"Yo, I'm not touching that body, man... you can keep the money I got paid, for real," one guy said, shaking his head and stepping away from the body.

"I didn't ask you to touch it," I snapped as Angel came down the stairs with thick-looking manila envelopes. I nodded at her. That bitch was my second brain. She was bred to be mines from birth.

"There's 10 stacks in each one of these," she said, handing one to each driver quickly. "Ya'll that's supposed to be moving the shit in the house, just keep doing your jobs. The other two cats, ya'll put the top back on that box and help them other cats. Ya'll have an extra 5 g's in ya'll envelopes."

Each man hesitated, looking at the others to see what the other one was gonna do. In the end, niggas did what niggas do. They all took the money. I was good with it. It was Vu's money anyway.

Angel nodded. "Aight, now all of you give me your licenses."

They all froze.

"Come on, now. You think we was gonna put out that type of change without some kind of insurance on ya'll? Nigga, please," Angel smirked, holding out her hand.

"What if we give ya'll our info and tell anyway?" one guy asked. Everybody looked at him, and his partner's eyes bugged out and he took a few steps away from him.

I walked over to him and looked down at him. "Let me just cut the bullshit. Whether you take this money or not, I *got* you. Ain't nowhere you can run, hide, or be protected on this Earth that I can't find your monkey ass. The nigga that did this is new, and trust and believe he gon *wish* the only thing I did to him was cut him up and shove him in a box. He done fucked it up for his whole family. Kids, wifey, grandmamma and all the muthafuckaz in between is gonna die. Trust."

The guy was watching my blue eyes turn purple the way they did when I was about to snap. I know because that's what everyone did that got that close to my face when I was pissed (most of whom are soulless now). He swallowed. "Ay, yo, I ain't mean *me*. I mean these niggas I work with, you know... I know them and I figured I'd better ask what they thinking before they get us all fucked up..."

The other movers shook their heads at him, one muttering "Bitch-ass nigga..."

I smirked. "Good point. If this shit gets out, gets on the net or to the Feds, it won't matter who told. All ya'll niggas get a blackout."

"A what? What's that?" one guy asked while the others went pale.

"Man, a blackout is when a mafucka takes out your whole family at the same time, all ya family, friends, er'body. Aunts, uncles, cousins... man fuck *that* shit. 15 g's to forget shit? When we done I'm in the *wind*, nigga," exclaimed the guy who pried the crate open. "I got kids and shit..."

The other men seemed to snap to and within minutes they were doing their job. I finally turned back to Jas, who'd stopped screaming to watch the scene. As soon as my eyes fell on hers she went off.

"You did this!" she screamed.

"Jas-"

"No, don't say *shit* to me! Don't even *speak*! You had something to do with this! Whenever something happens like this happens you have something to do with it! You know that girl didn't have no business being all up in your bullshit! That's how you do your family? Your only family? Am I next?! Don't ask me to piss on you if you catch on *fire*, nigga! " she screamed, rushing me and slapping me so hard I could instantly feel her fingers burning my skin and knew her whole handprint was tattooed on my face.

UNTRUST Deszion Nasir

"Hey, chill out," Angel snapped, not liking me being touched.

Jasmine whirled on her. "Bitch, who are you talking to? You ain't no-fuckin-body! You just some rent-a-pussy my brother picked up from the carnival like a t-shirt. You think you the first? You think you gonna be the last? I *would* tell you to get on my level before you step to the queen, but your ghetto ass *cain't* get on my level. So shut the fuck up before I fling your little ass back to the projects, you broke-down Thelma from Good Times. Don't *let* the Prada fool you, *bitch*..."

Aw, man. Angel rushed Jasmine just as Lucky and Doe's cars screeched up. Angel swung on Jas, but Jas was too tall for her reach and she missed. Jas swooped back like she was in the Matrix and when Angel's arm flew past her, she stepped behind her and kicked her in the back, sending Angel flying onto the driveway, scraping up the side of her face. "*Now* what, *bitch*. Talk that shit now, *ho*," Jasmine screamed as I grabbed Angel to keep her from going after Jas. Lucky grabbed Jas and drug her into the house, still cursing and screaming.

"What are you grabbing *me* for?!" Angel yelled, her eyes wide open in shock. "*She* jumped on *me*!"

"What the fuck is wrong with you?" I yelled at Angel, taking her by the arm and shaking her. "That's my fuckin' sister and she just saw her only other relative cut up in a fuckin box!"

"And she slapped the shit out of you," Angel screamed like I didn't remember.

"And? So? You don't think I deserved that? I knew I shouldn't have let that girl deal with Vu. I been shot, Angel. More than once. That lil slap won't shit. You need to get yourself together."

"I'm not gonna let *nobody* put they hands on you," Angel fumed.

"Jasmine ain't nobody. She's my sister, and I ain't gonna let *nobody* put they hands on *her*. The last bitch that

UNTRUST Deszion Nasir

put her hands on Jas is at the bottom of the James River," I told her, staring into her eyes to make sure she got the point. She stopped struggling, but was still glaring at me, tears in her eyes, her hair full of gravel and her face bleeding from where it hit the ground.

"You need to remember where you fit. This shit here?" I waved around the yard. "This is family. This is not business. Save the Rambo shit for business or next time you might fuck around and take a swim ya damn self," I snapped.

Angel snatched away from me, her eyes dark.

Doe was standing over the crate, his face black with anger. He wasn't surprised, cuz I don't think anything surprised him no more, but you could tell he was upset.

Just when I took a deep breath, Jasmine came flying back out of the house, still in her heels, her little .22 pointed at Angel. "You think you the only bad bitch on the block? You ain't *shit*, bitch," she screamed, squeezing the trigger. Angel hit the gravel again, barely missing getting her shit split open. Jas let off two more shots before Lucky wrestled the gun from her and hugged her to him. It almost looked funny cuz he was shorter than her and she struggled against him, but she finally broke down and started crying again. Lucky glared at me, then led her in the house and closed the door. Even through the heavy door you could hear Jasmine start to scream again.

I went over to Angel to help her up, but she snatched away from me and went to her car.

"You can't leave right now."

"Fuck you *and* your bitch-ass twin, nigga."

I sighed, trying to look deep down inside myself and find a way to deal with this new level of stress. "If he found out about Millay, you don't got no idea what else he knows. You ain't safe nowhere but with me right now," I told her, trying not to back-hand her ass. She finally shut up and walked off to the back yard, glancing up and down the street as she did so. I'd have to watch her. I know she felt betrayed right now and as the old men at the barber shop said, "Any

157

UNTRUST Deszion Nasir

worm riled will turn on the apple,"

"What the fuck happened?" I snapped at Doe.

"Hold up, nigga, what you asking me for?" Doe snapped at me. "This was *your* shit. You know I ain't think this was a good idea. You just cain't accept the fact that your ass finally made a mistake. A big-ass mistake. And that fool probably gonna kill your kid and your stupid-ass baby momma next. Great parenting nigga."

"Muthafucka don't yell at me. You know who the fuck I am? *I* run this shit, not you! I ain't make no fucking mistake except putting your drunk-ass in charge of the shit. And don't think I didn't know you were fuckin that girl, ya dirty-dick nigga."

"Blue you can keep that shit. 'You know who the fuck I am?' and alla dat. That shit don't faze me cuz I DO know who the fuck you are. I know you the trick baby of a bitch that didn't give a shit if you lived or died and I know your pops was a bigger muthafucka than you. He didn't give a shit about you or nobody else but himself. I remember how broke down and hungry your bitch-ass was before I got to you and you started trying to be your daddy. Yeah, I looked up your pops. Gemini Knight. Biggest demon in the spirit of Hampton Roads. Fuck that nigga and fuck you, yo. You ain't made shit. I made YOU, nigga, not the other way around! You can tell muthafuckaz whatever you wanna tell em, but you and I know what's good. Jas knows and at least her ass is grateful. You should be, too. I'm your REAL DADDY, bitch-"

I snatched my 9 out and put it to Doe's temple a second before he had his Berretta to mine. He'd said too much. He knew shit I didn't and said shit he shouldn't say to a nigga like me. I was so mad I was shaking, trying to decide whether or not to off his bitch ass.

I guess he heard all the yelling, cuz Lucky came to the doorway and seen the two of us pointing guns at each other in broad daylight.

"Hey, hey!" he yelled, running down the stairs. "Are

158

UNTRUST Deszion Nasir

ya'll niggas insane? What the FUCK, man?"

Neither of us said nothing, not breaking eye contact.

"Oh, so ya'll gonna ignore a nigga?"

Still didn't say nothing.

Lucky snapped. He snatched both our guns, pimp-slapped the shit out of me with Doe's gun and smacked the shit out of Doe with my burner before he could react.

"You hear a nigga now?" Lucky yelled.

"Bitch are you crazy?" Doe yelled, taking a step to him.

Lucky pointed the gun at Doe, and the other at me simultaneously. "Naw, nigga, are you?"

Doe froze. It was silent outside and you could still hear Jas crying.

"You hear that?" Lucky demanded. "You hear that girl in there screaming and crying and shit? Millay is DEAD, muthafuckaz.. That naïve, beautiful girl is dead behind *ya'll* niggaz. This is BOTH ya'll fault. It was Blue's idea and Doe, you know how that girl felt about you. Everybody knew that shit. She'd do whatever you told her. And instead of focusing on that nigga Vu and the fact that he's gunning for you, you, me, Jas and everybody else in our camp now, ya'll out here squabbling like two *bitches*!" He smacked us again. "There, I just hit ya'll niggas twice. You gonna beat my ass now? Huh? Fuck *both* of ya'll niggaz." Lucky turned and threw both guns in the bushes on the side of the house. *"This* is why I don't fuck with ya'll like that no more. *This* is why I only deal with ya'll on some business shit. Now, I'ma ride with you right now cuz this punk Vu is tryna dead all of us, but after that, I'm DONE. I'm not fucking with ya'll, and if you fuck with me I'll put a bullet in both ya'll brains; and you know I can do it. Ain't nobody else got the aim I got, not neither one of you or nobody else. So don't try me." Lucky spit on the ground and walked off back into the house, leaving us standing there, staring. We'd never heard Lucky say that much at one time since we'd known him.

"He's serious," Doe said.

"I know," I said, spitting blood on the grass.

"Angel looked at you like she wanted to kill you,"

"I know."

A pause. "This shit is bad...real bad. You cain't fix this."

I looked up at the sky and the clouds floating above my head.

"I know."

BOOK 2

PART VIII-CHECK
PROLOGUE

Daron Saunders propped himself up on a bench at the Alley nightclub in Newport News. It had been a good night for him. He'd gotten 6 numbers, paid to chicks to give him head in the bathroom, and moved 2 ounces of heroin. He sipped on his 3rd Blue Motorcycle and was looking for his next score of the night when his eyes landed on a girl several people away from him. She was halfway across the floor, but Daron zoomed in on her and everyone else seemed to fade away. She was staring at him with amber eyes that kept shining a beautiful gold color when the lights hit them, accenting smooth, chocolate-dipped skin. Her shiny black hair was curly and bounced around her face as she danced. She was tiny in stature, but she had huge breasts and a bottom that looked drawn on. Daron wasn't the only man staring openly at her, but he was the only one she was staring back at. He sat his drink down and stood up straight as the DJ began to spin Snoop and The Dream's "*Gangsta Love*."

Daron licked his lips at her and grinned. She smiled back and made a motion for Daron to come to her. He abandoned his fresh drink instantly and pushed through the crowd to her.

"What's good?" he asked, speaking directly in her ear so he could hear her over the music.

"I saw you staring at me," she said, her silk voice making his dick hard instantly.

"You want me to apologize for that?"

"Naw, don't never apologize for something you not sorry for, boo," she told him, pressing her full backside up against his growing interest and wrapping her arms around his neck.

Daron wrapped his arm around her waist and they continued to dance for a few songs. When the music picked up, she started throwing it back at him. He let his hands roam her body, squeezing her soft flesh when she didn't protest his

UNTRUST Deszion Nasir

wandering hands. He ended up behind her again and was transfixed to the floor as she bent down and jiggled her chocolate soccer balls at him. Jamie Foxx's "I Don't Need It" was blasting and the club goers were so hype no one saw the sexy vixen reach in her stiletto ankle boot. When she straightened up, she turned, and, smiling at Daron, pulled him close to her to whisper in his ear. She slid her small hand down and latched onto his swollen pride like a pair of pliers as she held her face close to her ear. Nobody saw her take the long pin she had in her mouth and jam it in Daron's ear. Nobody saw him jerk. They just saw him drop to the floor. The girl jumped back and screamed like she didn't know what had happened. Security ran over, breaking through the stunned crowd, some people too drunk to realize something serious had happened. There was no blood to discover so while security was looking all perplexed she backed away like she was terrified.

She was almost to the door when a man grabbed her arm. "Yo, what happened to my brother?" he demanded, trying to snatch her back. He only got a glimpse of her golden eyes before he felt a sharp stinging sensation in his chest, then on his arm, heat, and then something fell on his foot. He looked down and saw a knife handle sticking out of his chest. Then he noticed the hand he'd grabbed the girl with was rolling off his shoe and into the crowd of partiers. He screamed an ear piercing wail that got everyone's attention. By the time he looked back up, all he saw was the girl's back. As he fell to his knees, the life leaking out of him, the last thing he focused on as she disappeared were a pair of angel wings tattooed on her back...

VU

"Japan? You want to take me to Japan?"

"Yeah, why not?" I asked Siovahn, shifting my cell phone to my other ear and trying to type on two computers on either side of me. Thanks to Blue and his stupid shit, my business partners were two seconds off putting a hit out on my ass. True, I may have underestimated them, but that was easily fixable. Blue didn't know I could have him wiped off the face of the earth with a phone call, but this was personal... this was about my family, and nothing is more sacred than family. Nothing. Those millions of dollars he'd lifted belonged to family and they wanted it back or they were gonna kill me.

"I mean... I don't even know you like that, Vu..."

"So how are you gonna get to know me if you don't spend time with me? How better a way can you learn all about me than seeing my home, life and family?" I asked her, trying to be persuading.

"Yeah, that's true... but my son..."

"Bring him with you," I said, making it seem like it was no big deal. My hands were already itching at the thought of snapping his little neck.

"Oooo, I don't know about that. His dad..." fear crept into Siovahn's voice and I tried not to snap and curse her out.

"Are you still with his father, Siovahn?"

"No. Hell no... never again," she said bitterly.

"Well fuck him, then. You don't have to tell him everything you do. We'll only be gone a few days. I own a jet, so u can't miss your flight," I laughed.

She finally laughed back. "Okay, aight... I'll go... shit, I *need* some attention..."

"Sure you do...can you be ready to go in 2 hours?"

"Whoa... you wanna go now??"

"Why not?"

164

UNTRUST Deszion Nasir

"Um... I gotta pack..." she stammered, caught off guard by my urgency, I guess. "Naw, naw...don't even worry about that. I got all that. Just be ready, baby. You gotta learn how a real man treats a woman, okay?"

"Okay," she said, excited. I gave her a few more instructions and hung up.

I sat back in my desk chair and smiled. Then I picked the phone back up and started making plans for my new guests...

BLUE

"So… I had some people take a couple of photos of Vu… memorize this face…" I was saying to my crew, sitting around in my office. I passed around some shots of Vu to everyone.

Jay took one, glanced at if for a second, then did a double take and frowned.

"What, you seen him before?" I asked, noticing his reaction.

"Gimmie a magnifying glass," Jay commanded, holding the pic up closer to him.

"What, you need your grown-up glasses?" Jai teased him.

"Get me a fucking magnifying glass!" Jay yelled, stunning everyone.

Doe, who was the closest to my desk, riffled around in my dresser till he found one and handed it off. Jay snatched it and began studying the picture. Then he flipped open his laptop and started typing, ignoring us.

I was used to his strange ways by now, so I went on with the meeting, discussing contracts I had just come across and congratulating Angel on her successful job at the club the other night. I had to kiss her ass for a week before she forgave me for going off on her after Jasmine shot at her. She was just tryna help and I screamed on her. Was I really sorry? Naw, but I also won't in the mood for no drama with no female right now. So I acted sorry, gave her a big money contract and she calmed down. At least I thought she did… I was in the middle of assigning Lucky a contract to erase a guy in the Witness Protection Program when Jay sat back.

"Blue," he interrupted me loudly.

"C'mon with that *bullshit*, man," I snapped. Jay could be a disrespectful nigga at times and it was getting on my nerves.

"Blue. You gotta bigger problem than that fuckin

166

UNTRUST Deszion Nasir

contract, yo."

Everyone sat up, looking at each other.

"You still trippin bout that nigga Vu?" Doe sucked through his teeth. "Fuck that punk, man."

Jay glared at Doe, then held his picture of Vu up. "You see those symbols on his neck?" he asked me. I looked at the pic, frowning, and everyone else followed my actions.

"Them symbols?"

"Yeah."

"So?"

"In Japanese, those symbols stand for 8-9-3."

"Uh huh…"

"In Japan, those numbers are pronounced *Ya-Ku-Za*. Yakuza."

As his words sunk in, I sat back in my chair, a bad feeling spreading through me. The others weren't catching on, but I was.

Jay spun his laptop around so we could all see it. "I cross-referenced Vu Ngyuen with Yakuza. I hacked in a site and found out his real name. It's Vu Katsamura. He's a member of the Japanese Yakuza."

"The what? What the hell is that?" Doe asked.

Jay glared at him. "The Japanese mafia."

Silence at the table. While we were all looking at each other, Jay continued. "The Yakuza make most of their money in the sex trade, but they make a lot of money in corporate extortion, too. Ya boy Vu is what's called a *sokaiya,* that means he gets all this info about corporate heads and the dirt they do… like info on their mistresses, tax evasion, shit like that. Then they go threaten management at the shareholders' meetings. Then, if the shareholders don't pay them what they want, he'll raise hell or publish all the info for the public to see. Most companies don't even fight them because they got their hands in everything in Japan, from hookers to the government. Here's the best part-Vu is part of the Yamaguchi-gumi clan, the biggest and oldest gang of the Yakuzas. They been around since 1612."

UNTRUST Deszion Nasir

"Shit,"

"Yeah, shit indeed. So, whatever you was gonna do to this cat… you might wanna tighten it up," Jay suggested.

"If this dude is so big and shit, why is he going through all this? Couldn't he just… have his crew fuck us up?" Jai demanded.

Jay looked at me.

"Because this isn't business," I said finally. "This shit is personal to him."

Jai sat back. "Yo, I'm getting a bad feeling about this shit, man…" he said, shaking his head.

"Yeah," I nodded. "Me too. Get out." Everyone got up and left, looking at each other.

The game wasn't over. The players had just changed.

PART IX-MATE
ANGEL

I was in my new apartment in uptown Hampton-thanks, Jay-dancing around on my new carpet to Mobb Deep when I heard a knock at my door.

I pushed a couple of boxes away from the door that hadn't been unpacked yet and pulled the door open. I stared straight ahead at a thick gold chain around someone's neck, and when I looked up, I looked into Doe's laughing chestnut eyes.

"Hey," I said, surprised to see him.

"Sup, lovely?" Doe asked, grinning and glancing behind me inside my apartment. "It's coming along, huh?" he asked, meaning my weak attempt at unpacking.

"Yeah," I guess," I shrugged.

"I can hear your stereo waaayyy in the parking lot, yo," he laughed.

"Oh, my bad," I laughed, walking over to the BOSE system and turning it down.

Doe stepped inside and closed the door.

"So...what chew want?" I asked, picking up a glass of iced tea off the coffee table and taking a big gulp.

Doe grinned and pulled out a bag of bright green weed.

"Oooo, gimmie gimmie-!" I reached out to snatch it and he held it up out of my reach.

Since the last time me and Doe had hung out, he'd show up about once a week with some new blend of plant to share. I'd asked him about the hickey on my body after the first time, but he was like, don't sweat it, he don't remember doing nothing and Blue probably gave it to me and I didn't remember. It was possible...but I figured it was better to just let it go. It hadn't happened again so I left it alone.

"C'mon, Doe, stop playing. I'm in a real good mood right now and you gon' fuck it up," I snapped.

"Your attitude ain't my problem," he laughed.

"Well, what *is* your problem?" I asked, jumping for the baggie, but he just held it out of my reach again.

"My problem is that I wanna know why you're always staring at me all the damn time," Doe said.

"Whatever." I sucked through my teeth, denying it.

"Whatever my *ass,* yo. Every time we somewhere, you always looking in my face, Angel. Somebody might see that and get the wrong idea. I mean, I know I'm a fly *nigga* and everything, but you know, that might cause unnecessary conflicts..." Doe grinned, smelling himself.

I stared at Doe for a second, then I stepped up to him and pressed my body against his. "You wouldn't know if I was looking at you unless you were lookin at me, would you?" I asked him. I could tell by his expression I'd thrown him off. I liked holding the reins of the conversation so I pushed it. "Does that bother you or something?" I asked, staring in his eyes and smiling.

"It don't bother me if it don't bother you," he said, the tone of his voice lower. "Just don't want your boy to get the wrong idea."

"Lately, he don't pay me enough attention to get any kind of idea at all,"

"Is that right?"

"Don't act like you haven't noticed," I teased. "I haven't had much to do lately..." I went on, grabbing the bottom of his shirt with my hands and pulling him toward me.

Doe stared me in the eye for a few seconds, then finally handed me the baggie. "Aight, you win. You got it," he said, backing down.

I smiled and walked over to the coffee table and pulled out my stuff to roll the weed up and make a blunt.

I felt Doe's eyes on me as I sat on the couch. "What?" I asked, licking the blunt closed.

"You got any plans on sharing that since you took the whole bag?" he asked.

"I don't know where your mouth's been," I joked,

UNTRUST Deszion Nasir

looking for my lighter.

Doe shook his head and passed me his gold one. I snatched it and lit up. After 3 hits I was feeling more agreeable and passed the blunt to Doe, who took 3 hits and almost inhaled the whole thing. He rolled 3 more and within 10 minutes had smoked 2 while I was still on my first one. I shook my head at him as he laid back on the couch.

Feeling good, I climbed over the couch toward Doe and blew him a shotgun. He stared me in the eye the whole time, then says, "I think I need to leave. You feelin' it a lil too much,"

"Give me one back and you can go," I told him, sliding my hands under his shirt.

Doe sighed, but he was smiling. It was like I couldn't help myself. Knowing I was about to seriously fuck up didn't stop my neglected feelings from latching onto a place where I felt wanted and not just... an employee messing with the boss.

Doe took one of his blunts and blew me a huge shotgun, then let his lips linger on mine. I hadn't been kissed that good in a longgg time. I automatically responded by locking my arms around his neck and he pulled me in his lap. I thought he was going to just... attack me, but he didn't. He kissed my neck, ran his big fingers through my hair, and kissed me all over my face. I pulled his shirt up and over his head, knocking his hat and du-rag on the floor. Under his cap he had a head of close-cropped red wavy hair and under his shirt he had a chiseled body with freckles scattered all over.

Suddenly, Doe stood up and picked me up like I was a baby. I thought he was gonna head for the bedroom, but instead he went into the bathroom and sat me down in the plush lounge chair I had in there. He went over to the bath tub and ran me a bubble bath. While it filled, he kissed me all over my neck, shoulders, arms, everywhere. By the time the tub was full and steaming I was naked and don't even remember him taking my clothes off. He placed me in the tub and washed my body, washed my hair, massaged my feet and

171

shoulders after reaching across the whole bathroom with his long arms and turned on the stereo, filling the bathroom with the sounds of Alicia Key's "Unthinkable." After my bath, he lifted me out of the tub, wrapped me in a towel and laid me on my bed, where he grabbed the virgin coconut oil I had by the bed and rubbed my whole body down, massaging every part of me with his huge hands until I'd drifted off in another life. In between the rubs I felt heat on my breasts, stomach, arms. I looked down and realized the heat was coming from Doe's lips. A few minutes later he stopped and I looked up into his eyes as he hovered over me.

"Angel," he started, "Once we do this, you know we can't take it back, right?" he asked, tracing the details of my face with his huge fingers.

I nodded. "I know," I said in someone else's voice, reaching up and playing connect the dots with the freckle on his chest.

"How you gonna act when you start feelin a nigga and you see me with another chick?" he asked me, looking into my eyes. "If it's gonna be drama, we can stop now. Cuz I don't need it, and neither do you,"

"I'll be fine… how YOU gonna act?"

"Like I BEEN acting, watchin the two of ya'll," he grinned, his smile wiggling the key in the lock to my heart.

"Isn't it too late to be having this conversation?" I asked, smiling back.

"Is it?" he asked, running his tongue across my lips.

"Yeah, it is," I told him, grabbing his tongue with my teeth and sucking it into my mouth. He stopped asking questions.

Now, don't misunderstand a girl. Blue was by no means a slouch in bed. He was a monster, actually. But what me and Blue were lacking-especially lately-was an emotional link that us women need so much. Blue was sexy and satisfying, but he wasn't passionate. But Doe sure as hell was. He didn't try to make me keep up with him, he wasn't performing, he just seemed to know exactly what I needed

UNTRUST Deszion Nasir

and he gave it to me every time he looked in my eyes, every time he called my name, every time he squeezed me as he moved his hands over my body, exploring...

"Shit-"

"Damn, baby-"

"I've been thinking bout this for a minute now-"

"I couldn't tell-"

"Yes you could-"

"Mmmm..."

"Oh, you like that?"

"I *love* that-"

"You taste good-"

"*Fuck-*"

There was so much heat and energy pulsating through the room I couldn't tell who was speaking. Doe moved on from the foreplay-which already had me twitching, and pushed my legs further apart and he brought his body tight against mine. He lifted his body slightly with one hand and used the other to guide himself into penetrate the liquid fire between my legs. I squeezed my eyes closed in anticipation of the fit, knowing that from the foreplay and knowing my stature it wasn't going to be an easy feat to accomplish. He stopped when he realized I'd tensed up.

"Hey," he whispered.

I opened my eyes and looked up at him, frozen with the tip of his dick kissing my 2nd set of lips.

"You gotta relax, love. I'm not gonna never do shit that hurts you, okay? That's some bullshit you been dealin with from other niggas. Ain't no pain in pleasure, it's all pleasure or the nigga ain't doin it right. He ain't taking the time to learn this perfect body and what it needs...fuck them sucka-ass niggas, you wit a *real* muthafucka now, you understand me?"

I nodded.

"Keep your eyes open. Focus on me," he instructed.

I nodded again and he kissed me again, his eyes open and locked on mine, as he slid himself inside me slowly. I

173

flinched, but did as he asked, using his eyes as a focal point to relax my muscles and undernourished emotions.

"That's how you do it, that's my girl," he said, sliding in until he'd gotten himself all the way inside me. He moaned and put an arm around my waist, gripping me as he pulled out halfway, then slid back inside, instantly causing my body to vibrate in pleasure. He kept the same slow pace, but pulled out a little more each time, pushing in a tiny bit more aggressively each time, letting my body learn him, learn how he flowed, how he moved, until he was pulling out to the tip and smoothly gliding back in at an intense, yet beautiful pace. Our eyes were still open and connected like tractor beams as Doe picked the pace up, his heavy chain dancing on my bouncing breasts. Mid-stroke he lifted the chain over his head and dropped it with a clunk on the floor. He took the same hand and squeezed it over my breasts, leaning down and running his tongue over my nipple before taking it into his mouth. I remember wondering if your breasts could have orgasms. I damn sure could feel the fire building up in the rest of me. Doe let my breasts go and, without pausing, sat up slightly. As the CD in the bathroom switched to Jamie Foxx's *Freakin Me*, Doe lifted one of my legs up, repositioning us slightly so he could enter me from a different angle. With Jamie and Marsha Ambrosia's voices in my ear, Doe's eyes on my eyes, and his fire stick inside of me, the combination of events along with the sudden increase of pleasure in my body caused my body to twitch violently involuntarily.

"Uh-uh… fight that shit, Angel," Doe told me in a heavy voice. "Look at me and fight that shit. You can control everything your body does if you focus. Don't lose control, focus on how you feel, how good it feels… you don't want it over yet, baby… fight that shit, ma." I nodded, dug my nails into his huge back. He reached down and lifted the other leg, put it over his shoulder with my other one, gripped my waist and went deeper. My hands fell back and grabbed the pillows as my back arched. "Look at me," he commanded when my

174

eyes tried to flutter closed. "Look at me baby, don't break that connection I'm creating," he got out, a bead of sweat dropping from his forehead and rolling down in between my breasts. I moaned loudly, over and over as his pace was increasing. Doe slowed, but didn't stop, as he let my legs go and carefully turned me over, making sure we stayed linked. He pushed my torso down snug against the bed and slipped his arm under my waist, lifting it slightly. He gripped it and pressed his body down and into mine, touching my stomach with his dick that way. I cried out and I felt his body on my back. He was breathing almost as hard as me as his mouth was next to my ear now. He kissed it, licked and sucked on my neck, then my lips as he slid his arms up and laced my fingers with his. He finally let me close my eyes when our fingers intertwined with each other. Every time he would thrust, he squeezed my fingers. I kept my arms straight out so he could have a stable gripping point and tried to push my ass up so he could keep hitting my G spot. *Mmm*, twerk that ass up, baby, just like that," he said, the smell of my own sex on his breath behind me. He let one of my hands go and slid it up my back and into the nape of my damp hair, where he grabbed it softly but firmly and forced my head to the side so he could run his long tongue down the length of my neck. Control gave way to passion as Doe's breathing staggered. He pulled us to the edge of the bed, where he put his feet on the floor, kept my position and put my legs on his chest, forcing me to bend myself in a U shape, my face still on the bed. I banged on the bed in sweet agony and started smacking pillows on the ground and tugging at sheets, crying out as I fought to hold my orgasm in. *"Fuck,"* he yelled. "You not gonna make me go back to regular style pussy are you?" he demanded. "I cain't go back to that regular shit after this shit," he said, panting.

"No, baby, never," I shook my head.

"That's my girl... that's my baby," he panted. He turned me over, picked me up and locked my legs around his waist. He gripped me by the ass firmly and bounced me up and

UNTRUST Deszion Nasir

down on his dick, causing me to scream out every time his dick slammed back into me. Still bouncing me, Doe slid the middle fingers of both his hands to my clit and stroked it with two fingers. I threw my head back, overwhelmed by the overstimulation as I held onto his neck for dear life. I leaned back so far I could feel my hair dancing on my ass. I pulled myself up and latched onto Doe's neck with my lips, sucking on it and his ear like I was starving. "*Aaaaaahh*," he grunted out. I took one hand and pinched his right nipple. He yelled out louder, curses mingled with his grunts and moans. He stumbled back and put me against my closet door. I reached up and grabbed the doorframe securely as he kept up a severe pace, obviously losing the control he wanted me to have. "Look at me, baby," he gasped. I opened my eyes and was shocked at the intensity in his eyes. Behind him, I could see us in the mirror, and it turned me on even more. "Look at me," he said again. I turned my vision back to his. "Don't look away from my face," he commanded, his voice straining. I nodded and felt him back away from the door. He carried me over to my dresser and backed me into it. I used my hands to prop myself up and created a crazy angle. When Doe pulled out and re-entered me from this angle, he bitch-slapped a new spot awake in my body that took my breath away. "Look at me, baby," he kept saying. But it got to be too difficult as my eyes glazed over. My whole body jerked like I was having a seizure and Doe gripped me tightly so I wouldn't fall. He never slowed down his pace as a new sensation of heat built up in my body, searching for an exit. It rushed around inside me in a fury until it soared down to my lower half and I felt pressure building up between my legs. My body seemed to be hit by a rolling ball of energy and I screamed. My mind flashed to a place I'd never been full of light, peace, love and heat; Doe's eyes in the background. I came out of the flash of lightning and realized I was shivering violently, damn near strangling Doe. I gasped for air like I'd been drowning. I managed to open my eyes as I felt something wet sliding down my thighs. I looked down and saw something white and creamy spilling out of me, over Doe's still relentless dick, onto our thighs and down his legs. Doe noticed me looking and said "Yeah, that was you, baby. You a squirter," he got out.

"I never did that before," I panted, aftershocks shaking me. That revelation seemed to kick him into high-gear and he brought us back to the bed and went at me full force until I felt him swelling, stretching me like a rubber band, the tension making me clutch him tighter until he shuddered and exploded, yelling like a warrior and letting me go to grab the bed so he wouldn't crush me with his body weight. His release caused me to lose it again, and although it was on a smaller scale than the first time, my body went weak from the physical and mental effort of coming twice, one orgasm right behind the other. My scream followed his like notes in a song and then it was over, ending in short bursts of air, twitches and moans that died down slowly...slowly, until all that was left was heavy breathing and the sounds of tender kisses being placed on various body parts.

When my mind recovered from my out of body experience, I looked over and up into Doe's face, which was turned to my large picture window as he stroked my head absently. He felt me looking at him and turned.

"What now?" I asked softly, smiling and half-joking.

Doe leaned down and kissed my forehead. "I don't know," he said simply.

I sighed, snuggled up under his huge arm and fell asleep, refusing to let reality and the realization of what we'd done sink in and ruin the magic of the experience. I think he nodded too, cuz he jerked the same time I did when I heard the banging on the door. I jumped slam out the bed and fell on the floor, landing on top of Doe's tossed boxers.

"Aw, *shit,*" he hissed. "Who the fuck is that?!" He immediately began getting dressed in the dark at lightning speed. He'd obviously been in this situation a few times.

Meanwhile, I was tip-toe running toward the door. Since it was dark in the apartment, I could peek out of the peep hole

UNTRUST Deszion Nasir

without fear of being seen. I was frozen on my toes as I saw the back of Caesar's head as he stared off downstairs. When he turned back to the door again, I could see the disturbed look on his face. It looked like he hadn't slept in days. I bet he hadn't.

As he knocked again, I ran silently back to my room, where Doe was re-tying his du-rag again.

"It's Caesar!"

"What the fuck is he doin' here?!" Doe hissed back.

"Angel!" we heard C yell from the hallway.

"I don't know! I haven't seen him since... you know-" I said, snatching on a pair of pajamas.

"Damn!" I gotta jump off the fuckin balcony," Doe cursed. I couldn't help but giggle at his pissed off expression.

"Oh, you think that's funny?" he asked, grinning. He snatched me to him and kissed me, grabbing me by the butt. Then he let me go and shook his head at me. "Go answer the door. And don't let him back in this room. We fucked that bed *up*," he motioned toward the destroyed sheets.

As Caesar started knocking again, I rushed over to the balcony with Doe and watched him peek over the balcony, shake his head, then hop over the side. I was only on the second floor, so when I heard him land with a grunt, I ran to the door.

"Who is it?" I asked like I was sleepy.

"It's... Caesar. It's me."

I let a long pause go by. "What are you doing here?"

I could hear his frustration through the door. "I know I said I wouldn't keep coming over here, but...I really need you right now."

I sighed. "Give me a minute, okay?"

Okay, stop looking at me like that. Maybe I didn't tell Doe the whole truth. I *might* have forgot to mention that I ran into Caesar one day when I was at MacArthur mall in Norfolk. We *may* have hung out in the food court for a few hours talking about our lives and our pasts. We *may* have realized we had a lot more in common than you'd think. I

178

may have told Caesar he could call me when he had those nightmares that kept him up at night. *Maybe* one or two times when he called he was in the parking lot of my apartment building and I told him to come up and chill out, get his mind right. And he *might* have fallen asleep over here a few times. We'd *never* done anything, but I knew what it was like to need someone to just…hold you and listen to you.

I ran back to the bedroom, snatched the messed up sheets off the bed and stuffed them in the closet. I threw another sheet on after spraying Febreeze all over the mattress and opening the window. I just tossed a fresh blanket on the bed, since if I was really asleep the bed would be messed up, sprayed some Bath and Body spray all over me like I'd had it on after bathing like normal, and ran to the front door.

Caesar came inside, dark circles under his eyes. "I ain't mean to keep coming here," he stated again…"but you know those dreams keep fucking me up. Something about this shit…whoever killed my sister…shit ain't adding up. Something smells fucked up…"

I swallowed and turned away, heading to the kitchen. "Did you take your medicine today?"

I heard Caesar suck through his teeth loudly. I took that as a no and went to make him a drink of JD and Coke on the rocks, a drink I knew would calm him down. When I handed it to him, he crushed it, then after the fourth drink he finally sat back, sighed and leaned back on my couch. "My bad, Angel…" he apologized again. I noticed he was slurring a little bit. " I just… I be feelin so lost without her…" he shook his head like he was trying to clear it. I made him another drink and handed it to him, sitting down beside him on the couch. He drank it slower than the others, but still downed it in a minute or so. I listened to him slur his words more, then I scooted closer to him, our legs touching.

"Well, you know you got me, Caesar," I told him, putting a hand on his arm.

"Yeah… I know, Angel. I got you sometimes."

"You got me all the time," I insisted.

UNTRUST Deszion Nasir

"Now see? That's the type of woman I need," he said, waving at me drunkenly. "I need a down-ass chick like you. *You* need a down-ass nigga like me... not that punk-ass nigga you got, man,"

My ears perked up. "What do you mean like I got?"

"Man... Blue don't give a fuck about you for *real*, Angel. You just eye candy. Every girl he fuck with is finer than the last one. Finer and crazier. You like a collector's item to him. *That* nigga don't love nobody but himself. You're property, like a pure bred red-nose pit bull or something. As soon as he puts you in enough fights, he'll retire you or put you down and you'll end up like Siovahn. You ain't nothin to him for real..." Caesar drawled bitterly, shaking his head.

"Has he said anything like that to you personally?" I asked calmly.

"Not in those exact words...shit like that don't change wit niggaz like Blue..." Caesar ranted on a few more minutes, then he started nodding o ff, drained emotionally and physically.

I know, I know. I'm a bitch. Or so you say. Did I get Caesar drunk on purpose? Sure I did. But not because I'm malicious. I'm smart. Everyone thought I was sweet little Angel with a bad temper, but I knew I was living in a man's world and the only way to get ahead in a man's world is by thinking like a man and acting like a woman. In order to find out what was going on around me, I had to get some inside help. And Caesar was a perfectly willing assistant. After I saw how easy Minya got to him, it wasn't that hard.

I helped Caesar up and walked him back to my room, laid him down on my bed. He'd sleep for a few hours, wake up in a better mood and forget what he'd told me.

"C'mere, lay down with me," C said, reaching up to pull me down on the bed with him.

"Are you gonna be good?" I asked sweetly.

"Yeah, yeah, I swear..." he nodded, his eyes closed. I let him pull me close to him. He kissed my forehead and was

UNTRUST Deszion Nasir

snoring 5 minutes later. I was just drifting off myself when I heard a faint ringing. I realized it was my cell phone and slipped out from under Caesar and tipped toward the ringing, which was coming from the kitchen counter where I always tossed my phone.

Doe was texting me, saying he left his hat and was coming back to get it. I looked around and saw it lying by the sliding glass doors to the balcony. I clicked on the light to see if he'd dropped anything else and that's when I heard the knocking at my door.

I strolled over to the door, shaking my head and smiling at Doe's playfulness. I looked out the peephole for his smile and was met with a blue eyeball staring back at me.

"I see you, baby, open up."

SHIT SHIT SHIT. It was Blue!

Panicked, I ran to the balcony and tossed Doe's hat off the edge. I closed the door to my room and ran back to the door and pulled it open.

"Hey, baby," Blue grinned. He held out a gift box. "I know it's late and I ain't been around lately, so, you know... I brought you this..."

"What is it?" I asked, trying not to throw up in anxiety.

"Something I ain't never gave another female," he said, smiling down at me, wrapping his arms around my waist and putting his face in my hair. "C'mon, let's go lay down, I'm tired as shit, baby-" he stepped past me into my apartment. I was about to break for the stairs, especially when Blue took a good look at me and goes "How'd you know I was coming, anyway? You all sexy and nekked and shit..."

Just then the glass doors to the building swung open and Doe strolled in, minus his trademark hat. He and Blue stared at each other. Doe never changed his expression, but Blue did. He looked from Doe to me and back to Doe. "Maybe it won't me you was waitin' on," he said, frowning. Doe acted like he didn't hear him.

"What?" I fronted.

Doe hung his phone up. "Nigga, damn. You tryna get

181

here so bad you cain't hear nobody calling you?" he laughed.

Blue just glared at him.

"I guess so. You not focused lately, man…"

"Where's your fucking hat?" Blue demanded.

"It blew off in the wind when I was tryna catch up to you, man."

"Bullshit, nigga. What's so important you didn't go get it? And how the fuck you know I was here?"

"Man, I seen you when you were leaving Wendy's. I turned and was following you and calling you, but you ain't answer your phone, man."

Blue pulled his phone out of his pocket. Even I could tell by the dark screen that it was turned off. Hmm. Blue never turned his phone off. Never…

"What's the damn emergency?" Blue demanded, still skeptical.

Doe paused before he answered. "Vu is at the airport."

"So?"

"He's getting on a private jet to Tokyo with 2 people… a woman and a little boy."

Blue froze and frowned. He pushed his phone on, muttering "I *know* that girl ain't *that* fuckin stupid," over and over again. He called a number four times, and all four times we could hear Siovahn's answering machine kick on, her accent loud and strong in the silent hallway. The last time he called, after the beep Blue went off in Patois, then after the machine cut him off he called back and went off again in Creole, a language I'd only heard him speak when he was furious. He told me before he never knew why he understood the language as a child, but he picked up on it and fine-tuned his knowledge from a Haitian chick he met in high school.. In a burst of fury, Blue threw the phone against the bricked hallway, smashing the phone into a million pieces.

"That nigga got my *son*? He touched my *son*?!" he screamed, his voice like a terrible clap of thunder that shook the whole building. I'd never heard Blue yell like that and I was scared to death. I tried to reach up and hold his arm to calm him down before my neighbors called the police. Blue responded by shoving me off of him against my door so hard my brain vibrated. While I waited for my focus to come back Doe pushed me behind him. "We'll get him back, man. If he was gonna hurt him he would have done it already. He's fucking with you,"

Blue snatched away from Doe. "Who told you this?" he demanded.

"Jay. He said he called you and left you a bunch of messages, but you never called him back so he called me. I remember you said you might be through here, so...I got lucky I guess."

Smoldering, Blue stormed down the stairs, whipping out another phone and screaming on whoever answered. He turned and pointed at Doe. "Nigga let's GO!" he yelled and threw the glass door to the building open so hard it cracked all the way across.

"Hat?" Doe hissed.

"Threw it over the balcony."

"What?!"

"I had to get rid of it!"

"What did Caesar want?"

"He's just stressed. He fell asleep."

"In your bed? You know that nigga sleep naked."

"What does Sherita sleep in?" I demanded. Doe paused. "Yeah, I know all about you and Miss Carnival," I whispered. Caesar sang like a bird when he was drunk. Doe finally smiled.

"Look, ain't nothin' happening with him. Go get your hat, get home to wifey, okay?"

Doe narrowed his eyes at me a second, then turned and headed down the stairs.

I closed and locked my door, then leaned against it, sighing in relief. That's when I realized I was still holding the little jewelry box Blue'd given me. I opened it and peered inside.

A key to his house.

UNTRUST Deszion Nasir

PART X-INITIATION
JAY

I was sitting in the back of Blue's truck, yawning. It was 3 in the morning and me, Blue, Doe, Lucky and Caesar were zooming towards Williamsburg. After the fight at the bowling alley, I'd learned that two of the guys on motorcycles hadn't died. Blue was originally going to let them live to be walking examples of what happened when you fucked with him, but after he found out Vu had taken his son to Tokyo, he'd snapped. First he was coming after Vu's boys, then he was coming after Minya. He figured that'd get his attention. Unfortunately for him and lucky for Minya, I couldn't get a fix on her. She'd vanished.

We pulled up to the fancy hospital, no disguises. While they went inside and handled their business, my job was to hack into the satellite and paralyze the security cameras and the system. I'd have to bounce a few signals and some other technical mumbo-jumbo... but in short, they'd have 8 minutes to do what they had to do before the satellite would re-direct itself and re-power back up.

When they pulled up at the hospital, Blue was busy slamming clips into guns and Doe was slinging sawed off shot guns and an AK over his shoulder. I felt Lucky press a 9mm in my hand. I looked at him quizzically, and he leaned over and whispered "You need to know what type of muthafuckaz you rolling with, lil nigga,"

A second later, Blue was climbing out of the truck, a dark look on his face I'd never seen before. There was no time to say that I thought I was supposed to stay in the car. As soon as Blue's door slammed I hit the activate button and I got a signal back that the security systems were down. "8 minutes," I called out. Lucky nodded, but Blue had already stepped into the ER and started firing. That's when all this shit became too real for a lil nigga. Blue put a bullet in every person in the ER, man woman or child, and Doe was picking off anybody trying to run. The shaken staff had their hands in the air.

While Lucky was shooting the security and cop that were in the back and storming through the ER taking out whoever he saw, Blue yelled out the name of the man he was looking for. The shaken staff member typed the name in, wincing at the screams and curses surrounding her.

Out of the corner of my eye, I saw a man's crouching under a corner table, pulling out a cell phone. Without thinking, I took my gun, shifted my mini-computer under one arm and pointed the gun at him with the other. The shot sent my arm flying back, but the man fell on his face and the phone slid from his dead hands. I went over and stomped on it. Blue glanced at me, a slight nod came from him, then he turned and put a shot in the receptionist's shoulder, telling her to HURRYTHEFUCKUP! She was too busy crying at that point so I went behind the counter, shoved her out of the way and pulled the info up myself. He was actually downstairs right now in the x-ray room. Blue stormed off and I followed him, hearing Doe and Lucky firing away and causing more death and destruction with every second. They had sealed off the ER with the emergency dividers so no one from beyond the ER could get in, not that they'd want to, being that everyone on this side was dead. Lucky stayed positioned at the main door and Doe was coming up the hall behind us, taking down strays that had avoided Blue's psychotic gunfire or had been too stupid to stay hidden. I saw Blue reach under his coat and pull out a DENEL PAW-20 "Neopup" handheld grenade launcher from South Africa. Didn't want to know how the hell he'd gotten a hold of that one. Blue kicked the doors to the x-ray wing open, positioning the launcher on his shoulder mid-stride. When he got to the room, he saw the light that said "X-ray in use," took one second to verify that the man on the table was who he was looking for, and before the staff could comprehend what was going on, Blue had fired the launcher through the window and into the room. The explosion took *my* skinny ass off my feet. I felt my body

185

UNTRUST Deszion Nasir

being peppered by the broken glass and the heat from the fire. My ears were still ringing when Doe snatched me up and damn near drug me back down the hall, over bodies, blood, screams and moans from the dying and the dead. By the time we left, the only sound was that of the sprinklers and fire alarms screeching. Everyone on our side of the emergency dividers was dead. By the time I'd processed what'd just happened, we were speeding off down the street, not a cop in sight. While Blue burned the asphalt off the highway, the others were busy reloading. I was tripping on how cool and calm these cats were. They weren't anything like they guys on the movies or like the kids in school who were fake gangsters. There was no yelling, no "Did you see how I *popped* that nigga?!" None of that. They were quiet and mechanical like they were just some cats in a carpool together.

The second guy was in a private convalescent home in Norfolk. It was smaller and easier to tap into. I stayed in the car this time as the other 3 stormed into the building, the grenade launcher once again doing its job and taking the door off the building. I sat and watched and listened to the screams, explosions and shots as windows exploded and people trying to escape were gunned down by Lucky's on-point shots. One shot, one kill. I could already tell who was shooting just by the style and sounds. A couple of minutes later a man was tossed out the front door, a cast on his arm and both legs. He was howling in pain and screaming in a language I couldn't understand. But whatever it was, Blue understood it and he yelled back in the man's native language. The man was shaking his head harder every time Blue's yells got louder. Blue finally snapped and gave his grenade launcher to Doe. Then he walked over to the man, bent down, grunted and tore the man's arm clean off his body, cast and all. I almost lost everything in my stomach as blood went everywhere. The screams that came from that dude won't like nothing I'd ever heard before. Blue reached down, put one huge hand on top of the man's head and twisted,

UNTRUST Deszion Nasir

snapping his neck with that one hand.   His limp body dropped, and Blue stood up. The men came back to the truck, same identical looks on their faces.

I didn't say a word as the men got inside the truck. Doe took all the weapons as the others started pulling off their blood-stained gear like they'd just come from the beach. That's when I realized that Siovahn hadn't been exaggerating. Blue's camp consisted of a bunch of psychos and I was stuck right in the middle of them. I *was* one of them now. And my sister was dating the ringleader. We were stuck in the middle of anarchy, and I had no idea how I was gonna get us out of it.

CRUZ(in Spanish)

"Alright, Blue… Okay… I got you… I said I *got* you! *Shit*!" I hung the phone up and groaned loudly, flopping back down on the bed. I felt 100lbs heavier with this new stress.

Blue's been yelling in my ear for the past 10 minutes. He'd been yelling so loud my Queen Nina had sucked through her teeth and jumped out of the bed and stormed out of the bedroom, taking her sweet Jolly Rancher smell with her.

I sighed and sat up, ready to go find Nina and get this upcoming argument over with. I found her slamming shit around in the kitchen. "What did he want?" she demanded, throwing her hands on her hips. She flipped her hair over her shoulders and I tried not to get distracted by how beautiful she was.

"Vu… he's got Azzure' and Siovahn in Tokyo."

"So? What that gotta do with you?" Nina snapped. She crossed her arms, waiting for the rest of the bad news.

"He wants me to go to Tokyo with him to get them back." I admitted.

"Tokyo." Nina spat.

I nodded slowly.

"If you go to Japan with that crazy muthafucka, you gonna die," she said with the assurance of a psychic.

"I'm not gonna die."

"Is this why he gave you a record deal? So he could use you for this bullshit?!"

Oh yeah. Blue had inked a deal with Timbaland for me and Jay to drop an album. I don't know when we were gonna have time to work on it-

"-No, baby-"

"Well Blue didn't get you that deal! *You* did! You and Jay. All he did was make a phone call-"

Nina went on and on, me trying to explain shit to her and

188

UNTRUST Deszion Nasir

her screaming and yelling until I got pissed off and started yelling. "Why are you fuckin trippin, Nina? You never complained about spending the money I make working for him." Oops.

Nina went at me, no Vaseline. "Muthafucka *no* you didn't. You think I need your little shit? Do you know who you *fucking* with?? Nigga, I don't need *your* fuckin money! I'm paid out the *ass*. I fuck with thousands of dollars a week. I go to more places in a month than you can dream about in a whole lifetime! If you think I'm with your little ass for the money *you* got it fucked up. And if you think I'm raising this baby by myself you got that fucked up too-"

"WHAT BABY?!" I screamed like a bitch. But Nina kept going like I hadn't said anything.

"-And if you leave me here pregnant and run off to Japan behind that nigga Blue I swear to God I won't be pregnant when you get back-" she broke off, mid-sentence, breathing hard.

"WHAT BABY?!" I yelled again. I dropped my phone and leaned against the kitchen counter, suddenly weak as hell.

"I'm pregnant, Jai. You knocked me the fuck up. And I'm not gonna have no baby by myself. I never even wanted kids. If you leave me here pregnant, I'm getting rid of it, I *promise* you."

"You gonna kill my baby, Nina?" I asked, trying to contain my anger.

"What you care for?? You gonna kill yourself anyway!"

"I was doin this shit when you met me, Nina!" I yelled.

"I wasn't pregnant when you met me, neither!" she screamed.

"FUCK!" I yelled in frustration, picking up the plasma TV and flinging it against the wall. It separated into a thousand pieces, the force of its separation causing Nina to scream and cover her face and run into my bedroom. I sighed, ran in the room after her and tried to stop her from throwing her stuff in one of her Vuitton bags as she hurriedly packed her stuff up.

189

"Where you goin?" I asked stupidly.

"You putting that nigga ahead of me? Let *him* fuck you, I'm out," she screeched.

I tried to take a step to her, but she grabbed her laptop off the nightstand and smashed it across my face. "Get off me!" she screamed. Caught off guard, I fell and tripped over the edge of my bed. I looked up at her as she stood over me, an evil look masking the sexy, sensual one I'd always seen. "You gonna find out how I feels for me to be gone. Me *and* your kid. Let your ass think about *that* before you go chasing after niggas like a *bitch*," she spat. She snatched her bag up, stepped over me and stormed out.

I closed my eyes for a second for so my eyes could refocus faster, then I jumped up and ran after her outside and down the stairs.

"Nina…Nina calm down-" I saw her snatch her keys out, drop them, snatch them back up. I didn't want her to wreck her car when she was all emotional and shit. She was a bad enough driver when she was in a good mood.

"*Fuck* you!" she screamed. Pissed that she wasn't responding to normal, reasonable-ass behavior, I snapped and the next thing I knew, we were screaming at each other in Spanish, me trying to grab her bag and her swinging at me, asking if I wanted my right eye to match up with my left. She finally got into the car and when I tried to open the door, she opened the window and threw the new phone I'd bought out of the window, hitting me in the face with it. By the time I'd put my arms down from trying to block the hit, she was tearing off down the street.

Ignoring all my neighbors and feeling like shit, I picked up the smashed phone, held my head up and walked back into my apartment where I could sit in the dark and figure out how to keep from killing her, my baby... and myself…

PART XI-BULLSHIT RADAR

JAY

"Ay, ma!" I yelled as I walked into the house. Nothing. Good. I needed to make some calls and I didn't need her or nobody else bothering me right now.

I went into my room, closed the door, and pulled out one of my new cell phones and called Siovahn. I knew her phone would get service in Japan, but she didn't answer. I left her a detailed message and prayed she had enough common sense to check her voicemail. Did Blue know what I was doing? Nah. Blue gets in his own way too much. I only tell him what I want him to know most of the time. Besides, I didn't need him pulling the plug on my new album cuz he thought I was bangin' out his kid's moms... even if I was. He wouldn't be able to comprehend the fact that all this shit was business. Chicks like Siovahn only understood two languages: big dicks and big wallets. I wasn't givin' her ass no money so I had to go another route to get her to follow simple ass instructions. Ya'll lookin' me like I'm crazy but his ass would thank me later.

I grabbed the house phone and called my grandmother's house next. I talked to her maybe..2x a month on the sneak, every other Wednesday night. She and my moms may hate each other, but I make it my business to check on her. I couldn't be that cold-hearted, especially since no one would tell me why they hated each other.

The phone rang twice and a nigga picked up. "Yo."

Yo? "Who the fuck is this?" I demanded.

"Who the fuck is *this*?" the guy demanded back.

"Mafucka, don't play no games with me, son. Where's my grandmom, nigga?" I yelled.

"Grandmom?? The fuck is *you* talkin about? All Belle's grands are right the fuck here, *nucca*-"

What the fuck?

"Yo, Theory, some punk ass nigga on the phone talking bout he Belle grandson, man" I heard the man who answered the phone yelling to someone in the distance.

Who the hell was Theory? I was getting more pissed off by the second. Suddenly, someone picked up.

"Ayo," an angry male shouted, "I don't know who you is, but my folks just had a stroke 3 days ago if I find out you playin on her fuckin phone-"

"Hold up, hold up... Willie Belle Carr had a stroke??" I interrupted.

Theory paused in the middle of his rage, knowing very few people knew my grandmother's full maiden name.

"Who is this?" he asked, in a calmer voice.

"Who is *this*?" I yelled, still pissed I couldn't get a straight answer out of nobody. "Nigga, stop playin around before I come and put 2 in you, yo."

"This Theory. Ant's brother."

"Who? Who brother?"

"Ant Lewis, man. Antoine."

I was still drawing a blank. "This is Jay Lewis."

"Man, I ain't never heard of you."

Something in me, an old whisper, pushed out "I'm Angel's brother."

Dead silence. All the other chatter in the room stopped, telling me I was on a speaker phone. That told they not only knew my sister, but they had to know the secret to her lost memory from years ago. I hadn't gone with Angel that summer, but something had fucked her up so bad she came home without a big chunk of her memory and a hell of a temper. Angel would cry in the middle of the night, have night tremors, and she never knew why. Her doctors just kept saying it was a symptom of suppressed memories.

I heard some background noise that sounded like I was being taken off speakerphone and the sound of a door opening and closing, followed by someone going downstairs. I could tell they were going down by the clunking sound their feet were making, instead of a climbing sound, you know

UNTRUST Deszion Nasir

what I mean...

"This is Angel's brother?" Theory asked again, his whole tone 180 degrees different.

"Yeah."

"Hold up... are you in VA?" he asked, changing the subject. "You the same Jay Lewis that got an album coming out with that Dominican cat Cruz? You did *Cruz Ship* with him?"

"Yeah, nigga, that's me," I snapped, irritated. I wasn't on that shit right now and I was pissed he was tryna throw me off like I was some kinda sucka or something. Secretly, I was hyped cats upstate had heard of me... but still-

"Damn, I never knew..."

"What you got to say about my sister, yo?"

"Aw, man, she told you? What she tell you?"

"You playing games and shit. Of course she told me," I fronted.

"Shit, look man... I wanted to apologize for how all that shit went down, but Belle told me to just leave it alone, man. She figured Angel would never get her memory back and everyone could move on, you know-"

"Well, she got it back and I'm ready to come down there and fuck *all* ya'll niggas up!" I yelled, going along with it.

"Ay, hold up! I was just *joking*, yo. I ain't never tell Ant to fuck her and I *damn* sure never told him to fuck her pregnant-"

Pregnant?! "I'm comin to murk both ya'll niggas-"

"Whoa, whoa, Gatdayum, nigga. All I said was that Ant and Angel won't really cousins. We was all drunk and we was always teasing the nigga about having a crush on his lil cousin and shit. The nigga was obsessed with her. I didn't know he would go back and tell her that shit or that she'd believe him. I'm sorry she snapped when she found out, I'm sorry my own brother tried to kill me behind that shit, but damn, man, I lost a brother, too. I ain't seen Lucky in like...5 years now-"

My whole world slammed on the brakes.

193

UNTRUST Deszion Nasir

"Who? You ain't seen who?"

"Lucky, Ant, Antoine. That green-eyed yellow mafucka tried to kill me and ran out of the house. Ain't nobody seen him since-"

I hung up. Traumatized. Fucked her pregnant? Lucky fucked my sister-his cousin-pregnant? Then he moved his monkey-ass to Virginia and hooked her up with Blue?? All the nightmares, the doctors, the tears, the fights, the blackouts...all of that hell had been behind that nigga Lucky??

I couldn't even try to describe the kind of rage and anger that flowed through my body, my veins, filling me with red-hot fury. It's no words for it, man. I walked straight into my room, damn near ripped my closet door off, whipped out my brand new chrome glock, then stormed out to my Mountaineer and screeched off, clipping a little Neon in the process. I had a green-eyed nigga I needed to see.

UNTRUST Deszion Nasir

LUCKY

I was in a good place right now. Jasmine was standing on my coffee table, in my new condo wearing nothin but a string with 20 grand worth of diamonds strung to it and some matching $30,000 matching heels. She had 4kt studs in her ears and her wild hair was twisted up in a bun with diamond chopsticks in her hair, holding it all together. Won't *shit* a skinny girl could do for me... She was dancing to that old jam "Oops," by Tweet and I was throwing $100s at her. Just a thing we did. Damn that girl could move...

By the end of the song Jasmine was sanding over me, a foot on either side of me as she peered down her long frame at me. I grabbed her by the thighs and pulled her down to me, kissing whatever exposed skin I could get my lips on. She was purring like a kitten and snatched my shirt off, snatched my belt out my pants, bit my nipple and was yanking on my jeans when there was a frantic banging on my door.

"*DAMMIT*!!" I yelled.

"Who the *fuck* is that?" Jasmine snapped, getting up immediately.

"Shit," I muttered. Once Jasmine's mood was broken, it was gone. I watched her diamonds, wrapped around a pissed-off disposition, jiggle down the hallway and into my room, where my door slammed hard enough to knock a picture off the wall.

The banging started again so I sighed and got up, ready to curse someone out. I cain't even lie and say I won't surprised to see Doe standing on my doorstep, looking crazy.

"What, nigga?" I demanded, not trying to hide my mood.

"Ay, I gotta talk to you, man,"

"Now??"

"Yeah, now-" Doe pressed, trying to walk past me and into the living room.

"Nigga, I'm *busy*."

195

UNTRUST Deszion Nasir

"No, you're not."

We both turned and saw Jasmine coming toward us, fully dressed, her keys in her hand.

"Aww," I moaned.

"Ohh…shit, my bad, man-" Doe stammered.

"It's cool," Jasmine cut him off and pushed him out of her way. Then she looked at me. "I'll be back in 2 hours. *2*." she repeated. She looked Doe up and down, rolled her eyes and walked off.

"Damn, it's like *that*?" Doe asked me, half-smiling.

"What do you want, man?" I snapped, walking back into the living room and snatching my shirt off the carpet and tugging it back on.

"Think I fucked up, man," Doe began. Normally I'd ignore this kind of dramatic shit from Doe, but he really had a fucked up look on his face, so, as usual, I put my personal shit to the side and took on my role as group shrink.

"What happened? What did you do?"

"Man… I done caught feelings for this chick, man.."

I sucked through my teeth. "That's it? So what? Playas can't play forever, cuz."

"Naw, you not understanding… it's more shit to it than that. I think-I *know* she feelin me back or whatever, but it's just the *nigga* she fuck with that's in the way of shit…" He trailed off, pacing my floor and taking his hat off, something he never ever did unless he was seriously fucked up about something.

"Her nigga? Since when you worry about another nigga? I'm missin' something, Doe. Shit, unless it's *Blue's* chick or something, you ain't *got* no problem," I laughed.

Doe kept pacing and rubbing his waves out of their pattern.

I laughed, reached out and playfully slapped his arm. "Hey, you hear me, man?"

"Yeah, I heard you."

I stopped laughing. "Why ain't you laughing, then?"

Kept walking. Glanced back at me, then kept walking.

UNTRUST Deszion Nasir

"*Doe.*" I was getting a sick feeling in my stomach.

"I know, I know, I know…"

I shot up off my couch. "Nigga are you *serious*? *Please* tell me you ain't go do no *stupid* shit like that-"

"I *told* you I fucked up-"

"AW, *HELL* NAW, NIGGA!!"

Now I was pacing with Doe. "Angel? *Please* tell me you talkin about Siovahn, man."

The look on his face told me he wasn't. "Man, I don't know *what* happened. We was just talkin and shit… we was blowing trees, man… I was over there yesterday and she just-she *threw* it at me, man…"

"Shit!" I flopped down on the couch and put my head in my hands.

"-but I'm sayin'; I'm *feelin* her, man. I don't know what it is with her… it's like… cain't even explain it, yo."

Unfortunately I knew exactly what he was talking about. What Doe was suffering from was the same thing that had caused a major breakdown in my life. Doe had more to lose than I did at this point, though: his life.

Oh hold up, he's still talking-

"-then Caesar came over and I had to jump off the balcony and shit-"

"C?!" This was getting worse by the second.

"Yeah, she he just need a friend or whatever, but I know that nigga… he tryna get at her too."

"*Fuck-*"

"Then I left my hat, and when I came back Blue was there. I played that shit off but-"

I had a headache. All I was tryna do was protect her…

"Can't believe you fuckin that girl, man"

"I didn't *fuck* her man… it wasn't like that-"

"Oh, come on, nigga. What? You 'made love?' Nigga, you don't even know what the damn difference is. *Dumb* nigga… look… I don't care *how* you feel about her, you gotta *dead* that shit," I snapped, slamming my fist into my hand. "Period. *Fuck* love. Blue'll body both a ya'll-"

197

UNTRUST Deszion Nasir

"Man, *fuck* that nigga-"

"See? Listen to you, man. We got big shit goin' on right now! We ain't got *time* for this shit. You don't have no fucking choice! This is *business* and you *know* this gon' fuck that up!"

Doe sighed loudly and I knew I'd gotten through to him. He opened his mouth to say something and-

BOOM!

Doe instantly reached for his Berretta and I went for mine under the couch. What stopped me was the sight of Jay rushing in, piece already pointing in my direction. It froze me for a second. A second too long cuz Jay jumped on me, hit me across the face with the gun and had it pressed against my throat within the next second. Just as fast, Doe-shocked but swift-had a gun to Jay's temple, but Jay acted like Doe wasn't even there.

"Yo, Jay! What you *doin*, man?!" Doe yelled, total confusion spread across his face like a heat rash.

"I need to talk to *Mr. Lewis* for a hot minute," Jay growled back, spit flying from his mouth. "Tell him we need to talk, *Ant*."

My blood froze up at the mention of my government name. Nobody in VA knew my name. Nobody.

"Who the fuck is Ant?" Doe hollered, still confused but not moving.

"Tell him, Lucky! Tell him who the *fuck* Ant really is, *nucca*!"

"Jay," I said calmly. "Let's just…chill for a second-"

"Nigga *FUCK* you!" Jay yelled, shoving the gun in my mouth.

"Hey, hey, *hey*!" Doe yelled, cocking his gun, but I held up my hands to tell him to back up.

"Lucky," Doe said, hesitating.

"*Mr. Lewis*!" Jay corrected him.

"Man, somebody better tell me what the fuck is going on *now*!" Doe shouted.

"You ready to talk, nigga?" Jay asked me. I nodded, and

198

UNTRUST Deszion Nasir

he yanked the gun out of my mouth, cutting my lip. Before I could get up he'd kicked me in the stomach. When I doubled over he finally backed off of me. He lowered his gun, but Doe didn't. Now Jay was the one pacing, his rage making him unable to sit or even stand still.

"Antoine Lewis is my real name," I started, wiping blood off of my mouth. "Angel and Jay are my cousins."

Doe looked even more confused.

"They obviously didn't know until recently. Who told you?"

"Theory. Called to talk to Belle and he answered."

"Who is Theory?" (Doe)

"My brother."

"This shit is retarded. Why would he be mad about finding out ya'll cousins?"

I took a deep breath and looked at Jay. He wanted to hear me say it out of my mouth.

"Because... when we were younger... somebody tricked me into thinking we won't fam and I ended up getting Angel pregnant."

"Say what?? You what??"

"And behind that, she had a nervous breakdown when I had to tell her the truth. It fucked her head up so bad she had to go into a psych ward and she lost the baby. She's had traumatic amnesia all these years, man. She don't remember none of it. She snaps and goes off on niggas like she does just like she did the day she found out. She tried to kill everyone in the house before she got detained and they carried her off to the hospital. She don't remember me at all." I turned to Jay. "I'm sorry, man, I put that on everything I love. I moved to VA to watch over her. I felt real fucked up about what I done, man. I hooked her up with Blue cuz I knew he'd protect her when I couldn't -"

Doe dropped his arm and turned his back, putting his hands on his head in disbelief.

Jay seemed to be having a sane moment, so I hurried up and broke down my side of the story, about how I really felt

UNTRUST Deszion Nasir

about Angel back then and how I almost killed my only brother behind that shit. I actually thought I *did* kill him and found out after I left he was still alive, but I never stopped having nightmares about that day. Never.

"Look," I said, bringing my speech to a close, "I can only imagine how you feelin right now, but you got too much goin' for you right now. Don't do like I did and trick up your life behind other people's mistakes. I'm tryna *fix* this shit, man,"

"You cain't *fix* this *shit*, man," Jay said, frustrated.

"She don't remember me, Jay. It's better off like this, man. I know this sounds crazy comin out of my mouth, but you gotta trust me, yo. I'm not gonna let nothin else happen to that girl. I owe that girl my life, man, and she don't even know it. If I had never left Gary, Indiana, I swear I'd be dead now. I cain't change the past, Jay. If I could I would, but I cain't..."

Silence filled the room. Doe was looking from me to Jay, trying to see if he was gonna have to get in the middle of us again. I know Jay was thinking about his upcoming album release, and the shit I was saying to him made sense. He finally walked over to the coffee table and snatched his keys from under it. They must have fallen out his pocket when he jumped on me. He straightened up. "You think my *sister's* crazy?" He shook his head and stuffed his gun in his waistband behind him, pulled his shirt back down over it. "*Let* somethin' else happen to my sister, your fault or not..." Jay snatched my door open and left, his anger and threat hanging in the air.

I sighed and walked over to my door to close it. Then I turned to Doe.

"Leave her alone, man. Can you do that one thing for me?" I said to him quietly.

"Lucky man... I ain't have no idea..."

"Can you DO that for me?" I repeated, a little louder.

Doe sighed, pulled his cap back on. He tucked his own gun away. "I'ma go...so you can...you look like you need to

UNTRUST Deszion Nasir

be by yourself and shit…"

I just nodded, my lips curled under. He left me with my thoughts. They tortured me until Jasmine returned and took my mind off almost losing my life.

PART XII-GET LOW

DOE

"Your phone's ringing."

"*Fuck* that phone."

"You gotta answer that. You gotta get that, baby."

Shit." I shifted Angel from her position pinned up against the wall, her arms up against mine, her legs folded up and around my waist.

Man, don't look at me like that. I know what just happened and what Lucky said, but shit. You know the situation, man. That shit with Lucky was mad crazy, but that ain't really have shit to do with me. Ya'll know I was lying. If you didn't, you ain't been paying attention in this book *or* the last one.

So I reached for the phone without letting her down off the wall or dropping her. I already knew I ain't gotta tell her to be quiet.

"Yeah," I said, shifting my voice back to normal. I'd become used to doing it now.

"You heard from Jay or Jai?" Blue demanded without a hello first.

"Naw, man," I responded, shifting Angel around. "I ain't heard from them niggas in a minute." I heard Blue curse under his breath.

"Their release party been moved up from 3 weeks to a few days."

"What? Who did that shit?"

"Timbaland. I don't got time for this shit. I got like, 12 jobs to do before I go to Tokyo and deal with this nigga Vu.

"You want me to put it together?" I asked, trying to hurry up and get him off the phone.

"All you gotta do is bring the people and get the flyers out, man. Timbaland got the rest."

UNTRUST Deszion Nasir

"You know who you talkin to, yo? All I *do* is party, man. Party and bust heads," I laughed. I talked for a few more minutes and hung up.

"So, I guess you won't get to see me for a few days," Angel said, biting my ear.

"I'm always around," I told her, laying her down on the carpet and grinning at her. "Even when you don't see me, I'm around."

CONTRACT TWO

"Marcus, don't be hitting on the girl like that-"

"Bitch, *shut* the fuck up."

"Daddy, stop pushing my *Mommy*!"

"Get the fuck off me! You a pain in the ass just like your dumb ass momma, and *damn* sure like your bitch-ass grandma." Marcus shoved his 5 yr. old daughter off of him. She hit the uncarpeted ground hard and burst into tears. Her 19 yr. old mother, Crystal, scooped her daughter up and rushed from the room, Crystal sending Marcus a look of pure hatred he didn't see.

Crystal had met Marcus 5 years ago when he was hanging around her high school, trying to get a young dumb girl. Crystal fit the profile, at 14 never wondering why a 20 yr old had to come to a high school to get girls. All she knew was that he had a nice car and he was fine. Within 3 months he had her pregnant, in 3 ½ months she had her first black eye, at 6 months she had two black eyes and a dislocated shoulder, and by age 19, she'd been beaten too many times to count. Crystal wasn't allowed to leave the house, drive the car, use the phone or even go to the grocery store unless Marcus was with her.

Her mother, a woman from downtown Newport News, had seen Marcus's type all her life and hated him the second she met him. However, by then Marcus had already had a hold on Crystal. Her mother had him arrested, but Crystal would not cooperate and the charges were soon dropped. Her reward for that was a trip to the ER to treat 2 broken ribs for opening her mouth in the first place. Crystal's mother had only one child and wasn't about to let Marcus take from her the only person who loved her.

"Where my fucking cigarettes, bitch?" Marcus screamed. Crystal came to the edge of the hall and pointed silently to the table by the door where a fresh pack was waiting for him. Marcus picked up a glass and threw it at Crystal's head in

204

UNTRUST Deszion Nasir

response. "Stop moving my shit around... you think I got time to be running behind your dumb shit?" Crystal disappeared back in the room as quietly as she'd come out. She hugged her daughter to her and curled up on the bed, tears falling in the young girl's soft hair. Crystal rubbed her baby's thin arms, massaging the faint cigarette burn marks until the girl fell asleep.

Marcus went on his porch and lit up, inhaling the crisp air of the fresh fall day. He smiled to himself. He had her trained, now. Just like his daddy had his momma trained. Put some act right on a bitch and she was yours forever.

Marcus was happily puffing away, watching the lady across the street jogging back to her house when suddenly she saw two of her in front of him. He blinked, shook his head and looked again. One...then two...Marcus realized his vision was blurring and all of sudden his head hurt.

"Wha the fu-?" he slurred, unable to speak properly. He hadn't eaten anything or drank nothin...the only thing he'd touched today was-He looked down at his cigarette, the smoke swirling around like it was teasing him. He turned to go back to the house, but the first step he took, his legs crumbled and he collapsed on the porch, banging his head on the concrete steps.

When Marcus came to, his head was killing him and he wasn't on his porch anymore. He was...well, he didn't know where he was, but he was crammed into some kind of metal container. It was oddly shaped and cold.

"Hey!" Marcus yelled, hearing footsteps on the outside of the curved metal walls. He banged on the sides, frantic. He could hear someone walking close to him. The steps finally stopped somewhere above him. Suddenly, a door opened above him and the sunlight burned his eyes. He covered his face until his eyes adjusted and looked up into an unblinking pair of dark eyes. He had no idea what nationality the man was, but he looked...middle eastern or something. He was short and muscular with reddish brown hair and wore a crazy expression on his face.

UNTRUST Deszion Nasir

"Oh, you woke now," the young man said, his voice clearly Arabic-heavy.

"What the fuck's happening? Who is you?" Marcus asked, too terrified to play hard.

"Nobody cares who I am. But let's talk about who *you* are," the man said, reaching down and picking up a pair of thick work gloves. He put them on as he spoke. "You a nigga that like to beat females and little girls. That who you is, man?"

Marcus flashed between fear and anger. That stupid bitch Crystal. If he got out of here he'd kill her. "Man, that girl is a hoe, man," he lied. "She gave me VD and then had another kid by another man and shit...she hit me first, too. Don't believe shit she say."

The man smirked. "I *never* believe shit a woman tell, me, my friend. Women are liars."

Marcus relaxed. "Fuck *yeah* they are, yo..."

The guy bent down and picked something up with his gloved hands. It was a folder, and he dropped it into the metal container with Marcus. "I only believe what I see. What you see there, Marcus?"

Marcus scrambled to get the folders contents together. They were pictures of Crystal's many bruises, injuries, burns and black eyes. There were also pictures of his daughter's cigarette burns and doctor's reports for both of the females that dated back years. Marcus began shaking.

The man nodded, like that was the response he was waiting on. Before Marcus could think up a lie, the man had closed the top again. Right as he did, Marcus caught sight of a tattoo on the man's neck that read "CAESAR."

He could hear Caesar moving around near him. "You know what you're in?" he called. "It's called a Brazen Bull. The Greeks used it as a way to punish people. It was used for either torture or death. You know how it works?"

Marcus didn't get to answer. He heard a *Ting*! *Ting*! sound, then a whooshing sound, then it began to get warm inside the bull. Marcus looked around frantically and saw the bottom of the bull begin to turn red as it grew hot quickly. "Oh shit!"

"They made these things out of brass," Caesar went on. "Then they heated them from the bottom. I don't really have time for all that so I'm just using a blow torch." Marcus began to scream in pain as the brass quickly began to scorch his skin. He tried to back away, but there was nowhere for him to go. He was literally being roasted alive.

The interesting thing about the Brazen Bull's design was the way it was built. It was hollow brass, and it was built with special tubes that made the person inside's screams sound like a raging bull to anyone standing near it on the outside. While Marcus was inside the metal oven, he kept screaming from being cooked alive every time his skin touched any part of the sweltering metal. After a couple of minutes he had 3rd degree burns all over his body. Whenever his skin touched his metal coffin, part of his skin was left clinging to the bull's belly, sizzling and adding the stench of charred flesh to the heated smell of death.

"You think your little girl felt like you do right now? When you burned her with those fuckin cigarettes, nigga?" Caesar yelled, kicking the bull. When he kicked it, it threw Marcus off and he fell on his face. His shirt had been removed so the whole front of his body and face were sticking to the metal. He pulled away and screamed in agony as his skin separated from his charred flesh and he watched blood pour from his body, sizzling and stinking. He choked on his own blood and the lack of oxygen.

As Marcus laid there, the life force evaporating from his body, he couldn't help being shocked that his girl had done this to him. She hadn't. Her mother, tired of the way Marcus had been treating her, had paid Blue's hefty fee for having Marcus erased. She knew her daughter would never leave Marcus, so she told her daughter she wouldn't worry her about him anymore. As a peace offering, she'd even brought Marcus his favorite pack of cigarettes and left them on the table near the door...

UNTRUST Deszion Nasir

JAI

"Damn," I muttered. I had tried every door and called every number, but nobody was at the studio. I really needed to get some stress off my chest and out of my head and the best way for me to do that was in front of a microphone. I used to do cocaine to get rid of stress. Blue found me years ago when I tried to rob him for some money to get a fix. He beat my ass, but I made him work for it. It took him and Doe a week to find me. After they whooped my ass he told me he had a way out of the life I was living. I was a junkie so whatever he was offering I wanted to take. I had already lost my family in NY behind my addiction and was driven out here by a cousin when I was passed out and left at the bus station. My family was *that* sick of me. Blue took me to his house and got me off the drugs and turned me into the cat I was today. But working for him was a new stress. And when I was stressed, all I knew was sniffing powder. Now I had music as an outlet... but I couldn't get to it.

Nina. Death. Baby. Death. Blue. Death. Music. I looked down at my palms and saw them sweating. I used one of my slippery hands and took out my phone. I dialed a familiar number without looking and called my closest relative...my only one left that would have anything to do with me. Her name was Sirron and she lived in Washington Heights in Manhattan, where I was born.

"*¿Qué demonios quiere?* What the hell do you want?" she snapped as a hello. Her rough words didn't match her kiddie voice.

"Sirron."

"*¿Quién carajo es esto?* Who the fuck is this?"

"Sirron. I hate your fuckin mouth."

"Jai? *Jai.* What the fuck-I mean...where you been, *culo?*

"*Lo siento, lo siento prima...* Look. I need you right

208

now. Can you talk?"

"What's wrong?!"

"I'm stressed out, Sirron. It's too much going on in my life right now. My girl is gonna kill my seed if I go on this job with Blue. If I don't go with him, he'd gonna kill me, probably-"

"You still running around with that nut Blue?"

"What else am I gonna do, Sirron? I got that record deal, but until it drops and I'm big enough not to need him no more-"

"You willing to be his bitch," Sirron snapped, finishing my sentence in her own way. "Have you...you ain't been messing with that stuff again, have you?"

"No, no...you know I don't do that no more..."

"Uh-huh-"

"Sirron-"

She cut me off. "I'm coming out there. I'll fly out there tomorrow."

"No, no, hold up-"

"I'll be flying in tomorrow. I don't like the way you sound. Just make sure you have some gas in your car to come pick me up when I call you."

"Don't have a car. I got like, 4 motorcycles, though."

"How you gonna pick me and all my stuff up on that? I know you got a friend that can get you up here. If I have to catch a cab from Norfolk to Hampton I'm gonna fuck you up."

Click.

I stared at the phone and sighed. One part of me was happy she was coming, but the other part was nervous. Sirron was a Cruz, and my family wasn't known for blending well with people in Virginia. We all had the same shit in common: we didn't give a fuck, we were all short, and we were all loud. She was gonna get in trouble if she came up here.

I sighed, called Nina and left another message. I had called over 30 times and I could still get a message through, that meant she was at least listening to my messages. That

UNTRUST Deszion Nasir

was good. Her mailbox only held 15 messages. She wasn't done with me yet. I still had time to make stuff right.

Doe called me just then, telling me Blue had gotten word our release party had been moved up and to get in contact with Jay and let him know.

"Why don't you just call him?" I asked.

"Don't got time to play hide and seek with Jay, Cruz. Call him yourself." *Click.*

What the hell was all that about? Something was happening in the group right under my nose.

PART XIII-OVERLOAD
JAY

"...can you just do what I asked you to do without playing 20 questions? Don't you trust me?" I asked, frustrated.

"Yeah..." the person on the other end said finally.

"Then just do everything I told you to do and nothing I didn't, okay?"

A pause. "What?"

"Dammit-nothin. I'll call you later."

I hung up and tried not to throw the phone out of the window. Slow people were always the hardest to help... My phone rang again almost instantly and I sighed and clicked it on.

"Yeah."

"Whassup, man. Ay, look. Doe said we gotta, um, promote this release party and have it ready to do in 3 days instead of 3 weeks and I need you to run me to the airport sometime tomorrow to pick up my lil cuz who flying in from New York and Nina pregnant, man, and she told me if I go with Blue to Tokyo she gonna kill my seed, man-"

I hung the phone up. I stood up, went to the bathroom and popped a few Tylenol before Jai got a chance to call me back. He was talking in broken English and Spanish at the same time, so it took a minute to process everything that was falling out of his mouth. Once he ran out of words my mind went into hyper speed and I told him "Okay, look. Don't worry about Tokyo, I got you. I'll get you out of it."

"How??"

"Don't worry about that. Just tell ya girl you don't have to go and let me deal with that. I gotta switch some stuff around, but I'll run you out to pick your cousin up."

"Man..." Jai said, doubt in his voice.

"Look, if you ain't got no faith in your boy, why you

even call me? Give me 24 hours, man."

"Okay, you right…thanks, man."

"Yeah." I hung up and groaned. There was too much shit in my lap right now, man. Why did I do it? To prove to myself that I could. The only way to grow stronger was to exercise, put more and more weight on my shoulders until I could handle the pressure. I won't even lie, I'd look at Blue and think to myself I could handle his spot. But this shit had stopped being fun a minute ago. I spent the rest of the day driving all over the spirit of Hampton Roads, making arrangements to have the release party at Blakely's nightclub in Chesapeake. It was the only club big enough in the area to hold all the people I was trying to get to come to this party. I was so busy running around that day and the next that I didn't realize I hadn't eaten until my stomach was rumbling louder than my truck when I was on the way to pick Jai's cousin up. I had been reflecting on my conversation with Blue the other day. It took some convincing, but I told Blue that everybody couldn't just up and run off to Tokyo. Someone had to stay behind, and it to be someone pretty high up in rank. I didn't mention anything about Nina being pregnant cuz I knew in the end he wouldn't really give a shit and in actuality, it might make the situation worse cuz Blue'd figure Jai'd be too distracted by having a pregnant girlfriend to pay enough attention to running shit properly.

I told Cruz about Blue's agreement to let him stay behind. Jai stared at me. "What did you promise him to agree to that?"

I laughed. "Nothin, man. I just gotta go with him in your place."

Jai's face grew dark. He sighed like I'd just told him I'd gotten the death penalty.

"I got this, man. Don't worry about it," I told him, sounding more confident than I was. Jai just shook his head and the rest of the ride to the airport was silent. When we pulled up to the front of the airport, I asked Jai what his problem was.

UNTRUST Deszion Nasir

"You act just like him now," he said, shaking his head.

"I'm just being me," I protested. Cruz shook his head. "I don't know if that make it better or worse," he muttered, getting out. Once outside the car, he made a phone call. A female answered real loud in Spanish, and a minute later a girl came walking out of the airport, going off. She was cursing out a sky cap who was toting her other luggage. The guy looked like it was taking everything in him to keep from slapping the girl in her mouth. She had her fingers all in the man's face, rolling her neck. He responded one time and she mushed him in the face. Another sky cap came out to assist and got caught up watching the tiny Latina's thick figure squeezed into a pair of skinny jeans that hugged every curve. Her top half was just as picture perfect as the bottom half. When she spun around to confront the other skycap, I could see a huge pair of dark eyes framed under a bunch of bouncy black hair that seemed to be as jumpy and pissed off as she was. She spun around so fast she threw the poor guy off and he backed away, tripping over one of her trunks. She waited for him to get up before slapping him in the face and shoving him back down on the ground. She had a lot of power in that little fist. She was shorter than Angel but a lot louder.

"Sirron!" Jai yelled, jumping out of the car and pulling her away from the poor kid who was picking himself up off the floor, sitting his Pepsi on the hood of my truck. She let Jai pull her off the guy, but as soon Jai turned his back to apologize, Sirron threw an open bag of chips at the first guy and grabbed Jai's soda and tossed it at the other guy. One guy snapped and jumped at her. Jai responded by punching him in the head. He went down smooth and silent. The other guy backed away, his hands up. Jai then turned on Sirron and started yelling at her. He ended up picking her up and tossing her into my backseat, where she proceeded to keep screaming, her high-pitched voice grating on my ears.

"Ay, ay!" I yelled finally. "This car is sound proof. He cain't hear you but I *damn* sure can and I ain't tryna listen to all that. You gotta bring *that* shit *way* down, yo."

UNTRUST Deszion Nasir

"Who the fuck is you?" she demanded, her accent stronger than Jai's.

"You don't know who picked you up?"

"You know what? I can tell right off the top you gonna get on my fuckin nerves," Sirron snapped.

"Can you tell that I don't give a fuck?"

"You would if I wanted you too,"

I laughed. I was tired physically, drained emotionally and low on gas. I didn't need this shit. "You funny. Don't you know I'll make your happy ass walk from here?"

"Nigga please."

She was trying me. I got out of my truck. While Jai was calming down the skycaps' boss, I opened my back door, grabbed Sirron-"Get your fuckin hands off me-" and flung her little ass across the sidewalk. She whirl winded her arms to keep herself from falling but ended up on her back anyway. I got back in my truck and screeched off. Let her evil ass walk back to Hampton. If I never saw her again I'd be good.

TERRENCE (TJ)

My mother's green eyes stared back at me from the big mirror in the too-big bathroom in the too-big room Blue had me staying in. I stared at my head that had my mom's bright red hair trying to grow out of my scalp. The brain under the scalp was still spinning from my current situation.

The ghost of my father had walked into Riker's Island, gotten me unlocked years early, then brought me back to VA, not to face my own demons, but to fight his. There was more to this than he was telling me, but it was cool, cuz there was more to this than he knew, too.

8 years ago, I took a trip to New York with my best friends and this fine ass chick I'd been trying to get at. She was a few months older than me and she had my nose *wide* open, man. People started staring at us all the time from the second we touched NY dirt and we figured it was cuz she was so pretty. We got invited to a club and realized the owner of the club wanted to meet us. We went and came face to face with a hard truth. Her name was Jasmine and her father was Gemini. Her father was my father. Since I look exactly like my mother he knew who I was. When he told us who we were to each other Jasmine was fucked up. My mother, who'd always told me her husband was my father, flew out to NY and tried to get me to come home but I wasn't having it. She broke down and told me the truth but I was so mad I went AWOL and refused to come back to VA. In the middle of all that shit one bad decision led to another and all of my friends ended up murdered at the hands of someone who we'd never even met. Jas barely made it back to VA alive, and I never saw her again till she wrote me in prison. My mother and stepfather came to NY to warn me of why mom'd left my father and how dangerous he was, but I refused to see the truth until my mother's life was in danger. I made a final decision that cost me my freedom and I ended up in prison.

215

UNTRUST Deszion Nasir

For some unspoken reason, me and Jas never told Blue that we knew each other. I don't know why she didn't, maybe she was scared for me, but I know why I never said anything. Blue was too much like the nigga who'd ruined my life. I had a long time to get over that shit in prison, and I almost had, and since Blue didn't know who I was, I figured he could start making the shit up to me our father fucked up by getting me the fuck out of prison. That don't mean I trusted his ass. I'd never trust a Knight.

But what I *did* know was that Blue was tryna play me like a straight clown-ass boy. Throwing a car in my face. I didn't buy it. Giving me a fancy home to live in. I didn't pick shit out in here. Took me to Majik City. I didn't pay none of them broads a dime. I may have been locked down, but one thing you learn in prison is how to control your dick. Either that or turn homo… What was I gonna do with some rent-a-pussy? I got drunk as hell, though…

So anyways, I don't trust this nigga, but I was gonna ride it out.

I got up and washed my face to shake off a hangover when I heard a knock on my door. I pushed the button to the intercom-"Yeah-"

"It's me."

A second later, my door swung open and Jas walked in. She had her hair pulled back in ponytail and had on a simple pair of jean shorts and a light green Applejacks tee-shirt. She had two armfuls of shopping bags with her that she dumped on my bed.

"I picked some stuff up for you," she panted, straightening up, looking proud of herself. While I went over to her, I felt her eyes on me. When I turned to her, she darted her eyes to my dresser, where I had a pic on my dresser. She walked over to it and picked it up. "Who is this?"

I cleared my throat. "My parents… and yours…"

Jasmine brought the picture to her, frowning as she studied the man who looked just like Blue except for the long scar going across the length of his face, partially hidden by a

UNTRUST Deszion Nasir

wild mane of wavy black, pretty much like a shorter version of the madness usually flying wild on top of Jas's head... I saw her face darken at the memory. He was older when we'd seen him, but he looked pretty much the same, and her arm trembled. He had his arm around a short female with bright red hair. She was standing next to a dark-skinned male of average height that was hugging a shapely, tall girl with a huge smile and a long mane of dark hair that complimented her dark brown skin.

"That's... that's my mother?"

I nodded. "Her name was Jari."

Jasmine stared at the pic, unmoving until Blue came in the room."Why she crying?" he demanded, frowning.

Jasmine handed him the pic. Blue took it and studied it. "Who is this?"

"Our parents."

The only reaction Blue had, if you can call it that, was a slight flash in his eyes. He tossed the pic on the counter. "*Fuck* that nigga. And fuck *her* too. It's they fault we in this fuckin mess we in now." He stormed out of the room, slamming a door a few seconds later.

"*Fuck that muthafucka!!!!*" I heard him yell a second later, followed by a huge crash. Jasmine jumped as something else really big crashed into a wall.

Jasmine looked at me. "You coming to Jai and Jay's release party?" she asked, trying to change the subject.

"Naw,"

"Oh, come *on*, TJ, you been stuck in here, I want you to meet everybody..." Jasmine whined. I really wasn't into parties or clubs...but I couldn't sit up in this house all day. Something told me I'd better have some fun while I can...

UNTRUST Deszion Nasir

CAESAR

I rolled over, not surprised to see the sun going down again. I had been in the bed for 3 days, drunk, funky and high. My sister was dead, my girl would be, too, when I found where she was hiding. And my mind was wrong. All wrong.

Since I'd been too lazy to get more liquor from downstairs last night, I'd sobered up and was thinking about these situations. You didn't grow up in a terrorist camp and not learn to pay attention to minor details. Something about this whole thing smelled wrong, man. I got up to pee and replayed details in my head. I already knew Blue and Dejah didn't get along for some reason, but it ain't sound right that she would throw everyone else-including me-under the bus cuz he pissed her off. And when I saw that video of Vu and them cats going through the house? Who ransacks the house of someone who's cooperating? Wouldn't the person tell you where to look? I always trusted my instincts, and mine told me something was wrong with Blue's story.

I sat up, the dull feeling in my body telling me I needed to eat. I ignored it and threw on some sweatpants, a half-clean wifebeater and grabbed my helmet off my dresser. I knew Blue was probably gone cuz Jai and Jay's release party was tonight. That was cool. Him not being there was actually gonna work out for me...

Blue's security didn't give me no hassle about being in the house when he wasn't there. They never did. They were as scared of me as they were of Blue. I knew I'd have free range of the house. I went straight to Blue's office. I looked around at the sterility of the room. It looked unused. My eyes landed on the bookshelves where Blue kept the video tapes of the various places her had cameras all around the 7 cities. Didn't count on finding nothin interesting there. I walked to Doe's desk, felt around the bottom and side,

UNTRUST Deszion Nasir

knocking on it until I hears a hollow sound and the wood vibrated under my knuckles. I got down on one knee and examined the wood until I saw–barely- a tiny crack in the wood. I pulled a my keys out, which had a mini LCD light on them for when I was trying to get in my house and forgotten to turn the porch light on…which was all the time. I held the little light against the crack until a small glint of metal lit up. That's where the lock was on the trap Blue had obviously installed in the desk. I pulled a razor blade out of my wallet- I had a weapon of some sort everywhere-stuck it in the crack so the crack'd be more visible, then pulled my lock pick tools out. I figured Blue'd have something locked I needed to get to, so I planned ahead and followed my instincts again. It took me a couple of minutes to do it, but I got the door open by forcing the small metal slide up just enough to pop the door open . I put my tools away, wiped my sweaty hands and looked inside. First thing I saw were huge stacks of money, all in $100 stacks. I frowned and leaned further in. I pulled out a vacuum sealed bag of $100,000 bills. That shocked me, cuz I know for a fact the US stopped printing those way back in 1935 and they were never released into the public. They were to be used strictly for Fed transactions…then something else caught my eye. Under all the money, some guns, paper work and other crap were two unlabeled tapes. One had a yellow sticker on it, the other had nothing on it. Heart pounding, I pulled them both out. I stuck the one with the sticker on it in first. It was the same video Blue had shown me of Dejah fighting him, then Vu running up in the house. I took it out and put the other one in….

That tape was just like the other one… but it was obviously unedited. I saw everything. I saw Blue beat and rape my sister. I watched everything he did to her while I was out fucking around with Minya. I saw him leave her screaming on the ground in pain. I saw the camera switch to a camera on the beach he had planted somewhere, saw Dejah try to kill herself, then saw someone who I guessed was Vu stop her from killing herself.

UNTRUST Deszion Nasir

I watched the whole thing, then I stood up and snatched it out. Now, any other day, seeing shit like that would make burn this whole house down. But instead, I found a blank tape, made a copy of the unedited one Blue had, then put everything back the way it was. I buffed my finger prints off of everything and left, knowing Blue didn't keep cameras in his office for security reasons. I checked my watch. I had a party to go get ready for.

PART XIV-BLAKELEY'S, BULLETS AND BETRAYAL
DOE (Blakeley's Night Club, Chesapeake VA)

I inhaled the crisp fall night air and smiled. Man, this night was the kind of night a cat like me was built for. Before all the murder was a kid who loved to go to house parties, loved to show people that I could dance better than Crazy Legs or any other break dancer from my childhood/teen years. Sigh...

Me and Sherita pulled up in front of the club in a mint green stretch Hummer limo. When our car stopped in front of the cub, we could see that the line was wrapped around the building to get in. Jay had done a good job of promoting this thing.

Beside me, Sherita was like "Oh my God... all these people are never gonna fit in here,"

"Good," I said. "If the spot is too big, people will be like 'Oh, this event ain't shit, ain't nobody here...' now, if you take the same number of people and put them in a smaller building, there's more excitement to get in cuz everyone ain't gonna fit." She nodded, understanding.

Our whole camp was supposed to be wearing mint green and rolling in different style limos. When we got out, I saw that Jay had arranged Phoebus High School's band to start playing when the green limos came up. They started playing The Clipse's song "Kinda Like a Big Deal," my favorite song.

When we entered the club, the first thing you'd say is "Where the hell is the club?" In the front of the building is the little sports lounge/restaurant. But once you walk to the back of the lounge, there's a door that leads down some stairs. The whole club then opens up into 2 levels. On the 1st level is the dance floor. It was surrounded by tables chairs, a long bar on one end and VIP on the other. On either side of the VIP were the two cages females danced in to try and get the attention of the DJ and various ballers in the VIP. Upstairs were pool

221

tables, more tables and chairs, another bar and the DJ booth. They were all set up on the edges of the building and the wooden rails let the DJ and others look down at the first floor. The VIP section had been roped off entirely for our group's use. Everyone in our camp was there except for Angel and Blue. Figures. They were most likely gonna show up when they'd get the most attention.

Speaking of attention, even though most of it usually came to me, I checked how damn near all of it was going the Sherita tonight. But that was cool for me. I had to be with a dime at a big event or people would wonder what was wrong with me. Security did a double-take at my face and quickly moved out of the way of the VIP entrance.

I looked to one side of the section and saw Caesar in a corner by himself, nursing what my nose guessed to be a glass of Patron. I could smell it from over here.

"What's good, C?" I asked. "Good to see you out and shit," I sat at his table. He was dressed sharp as hell, but he looked... off... more off than usual. I guessed he was still stressing over his sister.

"Ain't *shit* good," C snapped, throwing his glass back and emptying it in a breath. He waved his glass at a waitress hovering near VIP and tossed her a $20. "Get me another one," he told her. She took the dub and hauled ass. C had that look on her face like he was gonna start throwing chairs. Hmm...

I turned to my left and saw Lucky sitting at the table with Jasmine. She was talking a new hole in his head, but Lucky was staring off into space with his arm around her. Lucky was always on point, 24-7. He had to still be distracted behind that shit that'd gone down at his house when I was over there the other day...

I looked next to Jas and saw Nina, who looked a little pale and tired. You could barely tell under her clothes and makeup, but I could see the fatigue on her face. Besides, Nina was a runway model. Partying came with her job description

UNTRUST Deszion Nasir

. There was a weird vibe up here in VIP tonight, but I was off the damn clock. I ordered me and Sherita 4 Incredible Hulks-ya know I had to match the green. Now, I'm a drinker, so those 2 drinks didn't do shit for me. Sherita was buzzing already, so I got up and went into the crowd as DJ Fontz from 103 Jamz was mixing Big Boi's song "Shutterbug." I was getting dap and flirts and all kinds of attention right now, and I was in my element. Unfortunately, I was too close to the bar. A little known fact was that I wasn't too good drunk up, but I'd been so stressed I wasn't on it like I should have been. I was on the floor getting it-don't get it twisted, a nigga got Chris Brown moves-when someone buys me a Zombie: dark rum, white rum, brandy, lime/pineapple juice. Bad move. After that, I got an Adios Muthafucka: vodka/rum/tequila/gin/blue Curacao/sour mix & 7 up. Now, for most cats they'd be out on their asses by then. I was a big guy, so I was almost there. I was feelin like Superman now, so I went and got an Unholy Trinity. *That* was my fuckin downfall. If *you* drink like *I* do, I know you reading this and shaking your head…you *know* what's finna happen. If you don't drink like I do, let me let you in on what that drink is: 1 part Bacardi 151, 1 part Stroh rum-which is 80% alcohol, and 1 part Everclear, which is the strongest liquor you can buy. It's 198 proof and can be pretty much classified as gasoline. I know cuz I used it in a lawnmower before. To say I was *fucked* up was a huugge understatement. In the middle of my fuckery I saw Blue and Angel walk in the club. Angel had on –barely had on- a white dress with no sleeves that looked like someone had smoothed a paint roller all over her body. The VIP was under Black lights, so she was literally glowing. Blue had on a white suit and enough ice to make a few people squint when the light hit them. I looked for Blue's infamous brother but didn't see him. I'd later found out he got a bad vibe and refused to come to the party. I could dig it. He ended up being smarter than all of us.

I pushed past all the people bouncing to Jamie Foxx's "Blame It" and made my way back to VIP. Sherita was looking super-pissed and stiff in her vinyl chair. Guess cuz I'd left her alone for about an hour. I ain't give a fuck-cuz I had the drunk-man-fuckits- and walked right past her. I went straight to Blue's table, walked right up to Angel, grabbed her by the neck and kissed her dead on her mouth.

All hell broke loose.

ANGEL

I felt Doe being snatched away from me, almost tearing my lips off in the process. I was in too much shock to do shit. I snapped to when I heard a crash and saw Doe lying in the middle of a broken table. Blue jumped over scattered chairs like he was Batman and landed on top of Doe. He grabbed him by the collar and snatched him up like he was a rag doll. Doe's no punk, but he was slithered, so his reflexes were fucked up.

"Did you fuck her?!" Blue was screaming, a fury exploding out of him like I'd never seen. It scared the pure-d shit out of me as I looked at Doe in horror, knowing he was so drunk he'd get me killed. Everyone was looking from me, to Doe, to Blue. Jasmine was standing up, her mouth open, waiting. Lucky was doing the same, and Caesar was still sitting, a strange look on his face.

"Chill out, nigga, I just *kissed* her," Doe slurred.

"DID. YOU. *FUCK*. HER??!" Blue yelled, his voice shaking the glasses on the nearby table.

"I just kissed her," Doe repeated, laughing. Blue brought his fist up to hit Doe. Lucky grabbed him, tryna clam him down. Blue spun around and turned the blow on Lucky, the impact sending him flying over the rail of the VIP. People screamed as Lucky tumbled to the ground, unable to prevent the fall. Jasmine screamed and Blue turned back to Doe, only to find Doe's Berretta in his face. He froze. "Chill out, my nigga," Doe said, sobering up a bit. He was still fucked up, but he had a gun, and Blue was unmoving.

In a crazed rage, Jasmine ran up and smashed a glass over Blue's head. "What did you hit him for?!" she screamed, referring to Lucky. Her Long Island Iced Tea poured all over Blue's jacket as he took a step forward to brace himself. She ran down the VIP steps and shoved people to the ground roughly as she reached where Lucky was

225

getting up. Jasmine tried to help him but he shoved her off of him. He turned and pointed up at Blue. "Nigga, *you* just fucked up," he snarled, then forcefully shoved his way out of the club, Jasmine running in her heels behind him. While everyone was watching this, no one saw Sherita growl out and jump on me, including myself. I fell against Blue and he crashed into Doe, sending the gun spinning under a table. She'd tackled me and had me on my back before I knew what was happening. She was pulling my hair and trying to choke me. She was bigger than me so I was struggling, but she obviously didn't know who she was fucking with. Bitches fighting on pure emotions were always the first to get rocked cuz they put all their points into attack and none into defense. I managed to snatch up a fork on the floor from the salad I ordered that'd fallen, and stabbed Sherita in the arm. She screamed and let me go. I scrambled up, crouched to attack her again, but security was on us by then. Sherita was pulled out of the club, fighting and screaming, and Doe was damn near carried out, stumbling and semi-conscious. Panting, Blue stood up, looking around at the crowd. They were obviously waiting for him to say or do something. He finally took off his coat, laid it across another table, and smiled at the crowd. "Well, ya'll muthafuckaz got ya money's worth, didn't you?" he yelled. The crowd burst out laughing as Blue shook his head. Waiters ran to clean up the mess and Blue took my arm and led me over to Caesar's table to get out of their way. "You okay?" he asked me, looking into my eyes.

I nodded, lying. "Blue... I didn't-"

Blue shook his head. "He drunk, baby. I'd probably do something like that, too. Look at you," he grinned.

I smiled, but my heart was pounding. I was in over my head.

After the party got back underway, someone came over to Blue and told him there were some problems backstage. Jay and Jai were arguing about something. Again. He sighed and got up. "I'll be back," he said to me, gulping the rest of his drink before straightening up.

UNTRUST Deszion Nasir

"I gotta go to the bathroom anyway," I said, looking down at my dress. "Gotta get this damn spot off my dress," I pointed where Sherita's madness had caused a drink to topple on me. Blue nodded. I waited till I couldn't see him before I got up. As soon as I stood, Caesar, who'd been in a social coffin the whole night, suddenly came to life. He reached out and grabbed my arm. I looked down at him, surprised.

"You goin' to the bathroom, right?" he asked me.

"Yeah, why?" I asked, looking into his eyes.

"Nothin… just… just stay in the front for awhile, okay?" he said, looking like he was regretting saying anything.

"Why?"

"Have I ever lied to you, Angel?" he asked. I shook my head. "Then just do it. Go on…" I was thinking hard, but as usual, I went with my head and decided to listen to him.

I headed straight for the parking lot to see if Doe had left. Apparently not. He'd made it to the side of his truck before he'd passed out. I sighed and went over to where security was trying to pick him up.

"Where is the girl who was with him?" I demanded.

"Oh, she hopped a cab. She was cussin' him out before he passed out. She just bounced on him." one burly guy said, struggling to hold Doe's dead weight. I sighed. Now what?

"Look," I said, pulling out $500. "I gotta go back inside. He ain't goin nowhere. Get him in the back of the truck and just make sure nobody fuck with him. You'll get $500 more after the show, okay?"

The security guard snatched the money. "Got it."

I sighed and hurried back into the club. I went to the bathroom to get the spot out my dress and went back down to the club area, and saw that a huge screen was being lifted behind DJ Fontz's head. It had previously been playing assorted videos. The crowd was screaming and the host was announcing that Cruz was about to perform his new single, "Cruz Ship," produced by Timbaland and new producer LJay. I looked around for Caesar but he was gone, his drink abandoned on the table. I walked over to examine the table and frowned when I saw some specks of white powder on the table. I put my finger in it and put it to my gums. My gums numbed up and that's when I knew it was cocaine. *Damn.*

CAESAR

I shook my head, clearing it as I stepped through the screaming crowd. I went into the bathroom, reached under the sink and pulled the assault rifle I'd duck taped under it off with a grunt. I stuck it inside my suit, concealing it with my jacket, and exited the bathroom. I had to push past the screaming fans to even get *out* of the bathroom. Cruz was onstage now, doing what he did best. Cruz was a performer. I saw Jay behind the sound table, pride on his face as he bobbed his head to his beats. I was shoving people out of the way and literally swimming through the crowd to the employee stairway. I slipped in the stairwell unnoticed and went upstairs, heart pounding from coke and anger. I came out behind the crowd swarmed around the upstairs stage. I looked around until I caught the attention of my boy that ran the big screen. We nodded at each other and I eased near him. He took the bag with the tape I lifted from Blue's and the 10 stacks I'd placed in it and disappeared. I went over to my secluded spot in a dark corner and waited.

UNTRUST Deszion Nasir

LUCKY

I was making my way to one of the side exits when something caught the corner of my vision. I wasn't into the show. I had too much shit on my mind about Angel, Blue, Caesar and Doe's drunk ass. For him to come at Angel like that, even drunk, was a bad sign. A sign that the nigga hadn't paid what I said about her no attention. I was blocking the music out, trying to decipher my next move, when suddenly a huge screen began lowering above Cruz's head. The crowd obviously thought it was part of the show, but it was clear by the look on Jay and Cruz's faces that they had no idea what was going on. I glanced over at Blue, who was watching with slightly narrowed eyes.

A minute later, a video came up on the screen. It was the video Blue had shown us of Dejah and all her shame, but this tape was different. It showed Blue and Dejah all over each other in her front yard. My eyes ricocheted to Angel, who'd just stepped back into VIP and was a few steps from Blue and their table. Her face was frozen, her eyes wide and unbelieving. Blue was a statue, but his eyes were dark.

The video continued to play, showing Blue and Dejah arguing, Dejah throw a bottle at her, and ultimately, his attack on her. I was stuck in shock mode. At this point, there was no music playing and everyone was watching either Blue or the screen. In the middle of all the silence, Blue sat his Black n Mild down in an ashtray, stood up, straightened his jacket calmly, all while everyone was either whispering or totally silent. In the middle of the amazement, Blue pulled out a .44 Magnum, pointed at the guy that ran the screen who was trying to hide, and fired. The bullet seemed to travel in slow motion as it flew above the partiers head and sank into the left eye of the terrified man. As he fell over the upstairs rail, he dropped a bag from his lifeless hands and a cloud of money spilled into the crowd, fluttering like death-covered

UNTRUST Deszion Nasir

butterflies. Nobody was sticking around to grab the money, though. As soon as the shot rang out, everyone began screaming and running, men shoving women out of the way and everyone trampling over anyone too drunk to get out of the way of the hysterical mob.

Jasmine screamed and I automatically shoved her down and yelled for her to get under the table. She came out of diva mode and crawled on those $100 tights under that $2000 dress like they were fatigues and tube socks.

Blue was scanning the crowd, no doubt looking for the traitor who'd turned on him. The behind the scenes guy obviously hadn't gotten a hold of that tape by himself. If I knew Blue-which I THOUGHT I did until just now-he'd have some shit like that hidden somewhere in his office. There were only a few people who had access to Blue's office, and all of them were in this building right now. It obviously wasn't me or Angel. She was still frozen in place, her mind trying to decide on how to respond to being betrayed, played and humiliated in public. Jay and Cruz loved their music more than anything else so you know they wouldn't do that shit in the middle of their 1st show. Cruz looked horrified and Jay was just staring, a blank look on his face that was trying to mask being highly pissed off. Doe wasn't on it enough to do no premeditated-type of shit like that. Even if he was, he'd never get pissy drunk before the event when he knew how Blue'd react. The only person left was –

Shit.

The second it all clicked, a bullet came shredding through the air and sliced right into the arm Blue'd been shot in a few week ago. He didn't fall, but the look on his face said he was in a shitload of pain. My senses kicked in and I zeroed in on where the bullet came from. Caesar was standing upstairs next to the Dj booth-who'd jumped over a pool table- his clothes blending with the video as he stood in front of the screen. He was holding a sniper rifle and glaring down at us. He was waiting for something, because if Caesar wanted to take Blue out, he could have killed him easily. He

UNTRUST Deszion Nasir

was a pureblood killer, born and raised in war and chaos. He hadn't missed; he was trying to get Blue's attention.

"You killed her, muthafucka!" Caesar screamed down at Blue, his rifle trained on Blue so he wouldn't have a chance to reach for anything he might have had stashed somewhere. Smart move. Blue knew Caesar had the advantage for the moment, so he was unmoving and silent, glaring up at Caesar, his blue eyes a deep purple, which meant Caesar would be on the top of Blue's to-do list until he killed him.

"You raped her, killed her, then told me that other nigga did it so I do the devil's work for you??? How you gon' do some shit like that to *me*?? To *me* nigga? You know how? Cuz you the fuckin Devil, man. Fuckin Lucifer in the muthafuckin flesh. Only the devil would do the shit you do, man. Only the devil would be sitting up in a fuckin *club* while the nigga that's tryna *kill* you got your son *and* your kid's momma in another country. You ain't *shit*, Blue. If I don't kill you, a swear fo- God I hope she do-" Caesar nodded at Angel. Caesar swayed a tiny bit, indicating he was high, and that was his undoing. Once Blue knew Caesar wasn't up to standard, his caution flew out the door and he dove under the table, but not before Caesar let off another round and hit Blue in the leg. Blue came up and fired at Caesar, who'd ducked behind the bar. Blue took advantage of that moment, tossed his gun and snatched his shotgun from under the plush bench he'd been sitting on. He snatched it up and blew a hole in the bar, sending wood, glass, liquor and olives everywhere. He braced himself for more shots, but there were none. The only sounds came from behind the bar where Jay and Cuz were, who were yelling Caesar's name over and over.

UNTRUST Deszion Nasir

JAY

"C! C!" Me and Jai were on the ground behind the bar when it exploded from Blue's shotgun blast. Me and Jai didn't have anything on us cuz we were performing, but even if we had, I don't know what I would have done with mine at the moment. My mind was already spinning from everything that had been going on the last few days and this was more than my 16 year old brain could handle. Sirron, Cruz's smart-ass cousin, wasn't helping anything. She's been backstage with us the whole time and she was screaming her head off as she looked down at Caesar's blood all over her once-snow white Gucci dress. Blood was all in her hair, on her face and shoes, just like it was on Cruz.

Nevertheless, I tried to shake the sound of the blast out of my head and realized that I had blood covering my shirt, too. For a minute I panicked, then I realized the blood belonged to Caesar. Jai was squatting next to him, pulling off his $1000 shirt and trying to slow down the blood breaking out of Caesar's body. Jai was talking to Caesar, trying to assure him that he'd be alright. Caesar was already coughing up blood and shaking his head.

"It's not shit left for me, man," he choked, faintly trying to shove Jai off of him. "Get off me before he come after you, too."

"Man, fuck that devil, C," Jai spit. "He lied to me and every nigga that was down for him. He snaked all of us when he snaked you, man. I'on know about no *other* niggas, but I ain't gonna be a part of that shit, man. That coulda been *my* sister he did that shit too... or..." Jai trailed off, glancing at his cousin, then at me while he tried to get Caesar's arms around his shoulders. He finally looked at me. "Yo, you gonna help me or what? Or do that devil put fear in your heart, too?"

I glanced down to where Blue was. He was gone... and

233

so was Angel. My 1st thought was to the safety of Angel, but I figured she could take care of herself as usual. I bent down to help Jai and we managed to drag Caesar to the stairwell, busting through the side door with people still screaming and running all around us. Sirron was shoving people down the stairs and out of the way like she was on a football field. She may have been small, but all those curves were hiding a lot of muscles, was the thought in my mind as she gave a security guard coming up the stairs a grunted shove and sent him tumbling back down and out of our way. As we're clearing the doorway, all of a sudden a noise burns out my hearing for a second, strong energy hits me from the back, I fall and then I go blind.

When I open my eyes again, I'm disoriented. Everything is blurry and all I see are lights flashing all around me. I slam my eyes shut when I realize my head is pounding and the back of my head is thumping. I try to force my eyes to focus and I realize I'm in the back of a car. It's MY car... I try to sit up and groan as pain kicks through my skull like it's trying to find a way out of my head. Whoever was driving glanced back at me as they sped through a red light. "Ay, you okay, man?" came Cruz's voice.

"What happened?" I managed, clutching my head. I felt something wet and pulled my hand to my face. Even in the dark with only streetlights lighting the car I could tell it was blood covering my fingers.

"Somebody tried to off us, man..." Cruz spit.

"Blue?" I asked. I looked to my side and saw Sirron rocking herself and staring out of the window, her eyes those of a person traumatized. Her shrill kiddie voice was silenced and she seemed not to hear anything me and Cruz were saying.

Cruz didn't answer, just bent a corner. I slid on my backseat and hit my head. The bump seemed to reconnect some memories. "Caesar..." I said, remembering the all the blood, some of it now mixing with my own on my shirt and hands.

UNTRUST Deszion Nasir

Cruz tightened his hands on the wheel and didn't answer.

"Fuck," I muttered, shaking my head. We drove around for awhile to let the area calm down. Cruz decided to stop by his house for a minute to clean me up before delivering me home to my mother's over-protectiveness. We pulled up to his condo and turned the car off. All the lights were off and I hesitated. He'd told me Nina was pregnant and I didn't think waking a pregnant woman up would be a good idea, especially looking how we did. Cruz wasn't tryna hear that so we got out. But even he seemed a little off kilter when he noticed all the lights off in the house. "Nina hates the dark," he told me. "Stay in the car, Sirron," he ordered. He ain't need to bother. That chick was in space right now.

Cruz jumped out of my car and ran up to the door. When he reached for the doorknob, that's when we saw that the lock had been smashed off the door. Cruz pulled out his piece and I followed his lead, a sick feeling rising from my toes to my throat. Cruz eased inside the house. Hearing nothing, he called out "Nina?"

His response was a faint sound and a whimper. Cruz took off toward the direction of the noise. He ran into the kitchen and froze. He dropped the gun and immediately fell to his knees, screaming in Spanish so fast I couldn't catch what he was saying. He started crawling and I ran up behind him. I froze at the sight of Nina laid out on the kitchen floor, beat all to hell, her hands wrapped around a knife that was sticking out of her stomach. She was gasping and rolling around in a pool of blood, her tears mixed with the bright red river surrounding her. I was standing there, my mouth hanging open, my young eyes inexperienced with this type of violence close up. All the fame, fortune and desire to maybe sit on Blue's throne came to a terrified pause as I watched one of the hardest cats I'd ever met crawl through his love's blood and the blood of his now dead child as he tried to cradle her in his arms. Nina was already drifting off, crying, her sad eyes on Cruz, asking without words why this had happened to her, placing a shaking hand over the knife in her abdomen.

235

UNTRUST Deszion Nasir

"Who did this, baby?!" Cruz cried, rocking her in his lap and wiping blood out of her eyes so he could see her angelic face clearer. Nina opened her mouth and moved her lips, but she coughed and all that came out was a spurt of blood that splattered on Cruz's face as he held her close to him. She took one last, painful breath and suddenly her body relaxed. Her arms slipped from around Cruz's arm and made a dull thud on the floor as she went where Cruz couldn't reach her. Her eyes were still open and stared up at Cruz's, lifeless.

Cruz rocked her for a second, apologizing over and over and telling her to take care of his daughter in heaven. Then his eyes went vacant and he stood up, laying Nina down gently as he did so. The silence in the house was the loudest thing I'd ever heard, man. Cruz got up and walked past me to the door. He pulled it open and stood by it, obviously waiting for me to leave.

"Cruz-"

Silence.

"C'mon, man... who did this to her? You gotta call somebody, yo-"

Cruz tightened one hand on the knob and the other around his gun. I took the hint and went outside to tell Sirron what had happened. I had to damn near shake her back to reality and when I did, she sprang out of the car and toward the house, screaming Cruz's name, but he had closed and locked the door. Sirron continued to peek in the window, bang and scream on the door for ten minutes before almost losing her voice and sliding down to her butt on the cold concrete porch. I walked over to her and sat down next to her, sighing. "What is he doin in there? " I asked.

"He was just sitting on the floor holding her," Sirron said, sniffling. But when I took a good look at her she wasn't crying. She was angry. "It's that devil that did this," she growled, her whole face contorting. I had to blink because she'd changed on me that fast. "That blue-eyed devil."

"Blue?"

"Look what he did to that girl! Look what he did to his

UNTRUST Deszion Nasir

own boy! He saw you and Jai *helping* that guy Caesar and he's making him pay for it. He must've come by while we were riding around, that sick muthafucka. Who stabs a pregnant woman in the stomach? There's a bunk bed in hell for him right under Satan," she snarled darkly, standing up and raking her now blood-stained black hair out of her face. "Go on, get out of here," she told me. "He'll be after you next. He already tried to shoot you."

Realization came down over me. "He's in love with my sister," I tried to explain, but Sirron reached out and slapped me across the face 2x. "Stupid, *puta*," she spat. "Where have you been the last 2 hours? He cares for *nobody*, he loves *no* one. He don't give a *fuck* about your sister's life and he *damn* sure don't give a fuck about yours. Leave me here so I can deal with Jai and his grief. A Cruz do what need to be done. *You* need to go do what you need to do for *your* family. Either *kill* that muthafucka or go shopping for a black suit. You'll either wear it to your sister's funeral or be lowered in it. "

ANGEL

I gritted my teeth as I hit another curb trying to steer Doe's huge red truck. I could barely see over the steering wheel let alone reach the pedals. I decided to run a red light instead of trying to stop and having an accident.

After Blue started shooting, I got the hell out of there. I was still stuck in overdrive and decided to sort out what I was going to do about everything after I was sure I wasn't about to die. One thing I knew for sure was that I wasn't gonna be riding home with him so I ran outside to Doe's truck. Of course, he was knocked out snoring so I climbed in-most likely showing everyone the candy box-and slammed the door. I stumbled to where Doe was and rummaged around until I found his keys and his wallet. I took a deep breath as I sat in the huge seat, started the beast and took off, sideswiping a Nissan in my path.

I ended up in Norfolk at the Courtyard Marriott off Newtown Rd. that was tucked back in a corner. I used one of Doe's fake IDs and got a room. It took me 30 minutes to drag his twisted ass into the room and nearly 10 more to get him on one of the twin beds. I called Jay multiple times but his mailbox was full, as usual. There was no way I was going home so I guess I'd just wait the night out and see how I felt in the morning.

Too tired to move, I forced myself to take a shower and put on one of the shirts I'd grabbed out of Doe's truck. I barely remember the shower and getting out, but falling asleep with a pillow wet with tears was something I'd remember for many dark nights to come.

The smell of fruit and coffee woke me up in the morning. The smell nudged me and caused me to open my eyes, but the painfully bright sunlight made me slam them shut again and let out a groan. They flew open again as the events from the night before came rushing back into my

UNTRUST Deszion Nasir

overtired brain. I sat up and looked around the room. On the small table sat a plate of fruit, croissants, link sausage, hash browns, strawberry jelly and a big pitcher of orange juice.

I stood up, stretched and looked around the room for Doe. I could look and see he wasn't in the bathroom cuz the door was open and the light was off. Had he bought me breakfast and left me stranded in Norfolk? Could my day get any worse?

I flopped back on the bed and got ready to call Jay again when the door swung open. I jumped up and stared into Doe's grinning face. He was carrying a bag from Mc Arthur mall and his face showed no signs of the drunk from last night, except for slightly red eyes.

"Hey, ma," he grinned. He walked over to me, kissed me on the forehead and sat the bag down on the bed next to me. He glanced at the small table. "Ain't you hungry?"

My mouth opened and closed. "Do you have any idea what happened last night?"

He shrugged. "I got fucked up and you brought me here. That's what I get for fucking with that Everclear," he laughed. "Eat your breakfast."

I just stared at him. "You not even gonna ask me why we in a fuckin hotel room?" I asked, throwing my hands up and letting them fall against me thighs in exasperation.

Doe sighed and sat down at the table in the chair opposite the one that had my breakfast in front of it. "Sit down, eat and talk to me."

I did as he asked, took a bite of food, then launched into everything Doe had missed-including his reckless-ass behavior in front of Blue. By the time I'd caught him up to the present, his habitual smirk was gone from his face. The room was dead silent for a few minutes, then he stood up and pulled out his keys and cell phone. He dialed a number and walked out of the hotel room without saying anything to me. A minute later I heard his voice soar in from under the 3rd floor balcony. He was talking in a serious tone of voice that I hadn't heard before. I peeked out of the open balcony doors and saw Doe chirp his alarm off of his truck and swing the barnyard doors on the back of the truck open. Balancing the iPhone on one shoulder, Doe rummaged around and pulled out a gun. He checked the clip, snatched the hammer back to make sure one was in the chamber, and stuffed it in his waist. He repeated this process three more times, each time putting a gun in a different, concealed place. He slammed the door closed and I disappeared from the balcony before he turned around. By the time Doe got back to the room I was sitting at the table with a mouth full of food like I had been there the whole time. What surprised me was that Doe seemed to be back to his old self, his smile back on his face.

"Is it good?" he asked, coming up behind me and massaging my shoulders. "I just got you shit I like to eat, you know…"

I put my fork down and turned to look up at Doe. "Did you hear anything I said? Blue *raped* Dejah, lied to us and we… we *killed* that girl! Now he's God-knows-where about to do God-knows-what to God-knows-who! What am I supposed to do now? I can't just walk away from all this, Doe. I can't go home cuz I don't want to see Blue, I can't reach my brother… and you're in here smiling like shit is cool!" I finished, throwing my plate against the wall in an overwhelming fit of emotion. Speaking all the drama out loud made everything painfully real and over-loaded my brain. I felt betrayed, stupid, hurt and so guilty for the part I'd played in all this. Blue had used me just like everyone had said he would. He obviously didn't give a fuck about me. He hadn't called me or even tried to look out for me when the shooting had gone down last night. The reality of the situation was too much. I felt it coming. I felt myself losing it and the room was turning a bright white. I was seconds from setting the room on fire when I felt Doe's arms around me. He picked me up off the chair and laid me back in the bed. He kicked his shoes off and got under the covers with me. He reached up and wiped something away from my face and that's when I realized I had tears streaming down my

UNTRUST Deszion Nasir

cheeks.

"How could he *do* some shit like that?" I demanded. I wasn't sure if I meant what he did to Dejah or the fact that he had obviously been cheating on me. That was why Dejah had always been looking at my ass sideways. I now strangely felt justified in dealing with Doe.

Doe wrapped his arms around me and I heard him sigh. "Blue is a grimy kinda nigga, Angel," he said, suddenly sounding tired and years older than he was.

"Why are you so calm about all this shit?? He got you right in the middle of all this shit. You should be angrier than me!" I yelled. I kept going off, but Doe's big arms and soothing ways eventually led me to break down and just cry everything out. Doe didn't say a word, just kept rubbing my back, my arms, until the tears stopped and left a hollow echo inside me. Doe squeezed me tighter and I tilted my head up and kissed him. He returned the kiss and turned me around and sat me in his lap. He put his thick fingers in my hair and pulled me to him, aggressively forcing my mouth open and grabbing my tongue with his lips. I reached for his shirt and tugged on it until it gave way in my hands. The only sounds in the room were of our breathing and buttons bouncing off the nightstand.

Red skin on midnight skin created a thin sheen of anxious sweat as clothes were ripped, tossed and pulled away from our bodies. Doe grabbed me by the hair and pulled my head back, dragging his tongue down my neck, making me shiver before he bit me, his hands rocking me back and forth in his lap. I could feel him swelling under me and our combined heat had the whole room on fire. My broken heart, overly sexual body and confused mind attached to Doe firmly and wouldn't let him go until I was sore, tired, and my hair had sweated into a frizzy mess. Wrapped in rented sheet glued to our bodies by our combined juices, Doe held me against his body, promising me he'd take care of everything.

"How?" I demanded, my voice soft but doubtful. "Doe this shit is bigger than you. We're already making shit worse

241

by being here now…"

Doe was quiet a second before he turned my hazel eyes up to his chestnut brown ones. "You and every other muthafucka out here is going to stop underestimating me. If I say I got it, I *got* it. It's more at stake than just this shit, Angel. We still got this nigga Vu to deal with. The shit Blue did was fucked up and the reaper's gonna get his pound from Blue for it, but right now this shit with Vu gotta be dealt with. I feel bad for Dejah. I feel bad for her brother. But they somewhere we can't get to now. Our world is *still* turnin, niggas is *still* tryna kill us, and in general shit gotta move forward, ma. I know you don't like hearing this shit, but it is what the fuck it is. As for you? You can chill here for a few days, get ya head right. Blue don't expect you to be around for a day or so. He knows he fucked up with wifey. I'ma take care of whatever you need till you decide what you wanna do."

"What I wanna do? I don't wanna be with that nigga!" I yelled. "I can't deal with that kind of nigga in my life! I thought you just said you was gonna take care of me," I demanded, panicking.

"Shh, fall back, ma. I feel what you saying and whatever, but I deal in reality. In reality, you cain't just 'leave' a nigga like Blue. Whether you think he gives a fuck about you or not, you his property and he ain't finna lay down for you getting all fly out ya mouth with him right now. That ain't gonna end well for you," Doe said pointedly.

Absorbing what he was saying, I asked "So, I'm supposed to ignore all this shit and just run back to him? What did you go to the car and get them guns for?" I asked, exposing my snooping.

"I ain't say that. What I'm saying is you gotta trust me right now. The guns is just for a couple days. Blue is gonna be looking for someone to take this shit out on when he's really brought it all on himself. I'll be dammed if I'm his release. He'll cool out. Play your position until this shit gets handled. You cain't get all emotional in this game, baby.

242

UNTRUST Deszion Nasir

Emotions can get yo ass killed. It got Dejah and Caesar fucked up, and if you don't snap yo shit back together, it's gonna get *you* killed, too."

UNTRUST Deszion Nasir

PART XV-TRUE COLORS

PROLOGUE II

Tarik and Samir Peterson were identical twins from Ridley Circle in downtown Newport News. They'd been tyrants from the second they burst out into the world. Their mother died giving birth to them and the body count had been adding up ever since. By the age of 10 they had become holy terrors. Between the two of them by the time they were 18 they had 7 bodies, 12 kidnappings and an assortment of rapes, robberies and other ignorant shit under their belts. The only reason they weren't dead was because people were scared of them. They were wards of the state, but after running away one too many times, no one reported them gone, just simply prayed they'd take their terrorist ways to another hood.

Today the two were walking from a party in Buckroe down to the beach where they'd parked their car. Cheap liquor and some raggedy weed had left them in the mood to bother somebody. It was about 2:30 a.m. when they came upon a guy walking by himself near the parking lot. He was tall, but looked like an easy target. He was all alone, apparently deep in thought, and they could see his jewels shining from up the street. The twins looked up at each other and both had the same thought: easy vic.

Samir slid his 9mm out of his pocket and motioned for Tarik to go around the cars so they could sneak up on the man. Their M.O. was to wait until their vic got to his car and jack his ride, too. And what a nice ride it was. They'd never seen a whip like that in their 20 years.

Samir waited until the guy pushed the remote starter on the huge vehicle before he put a gun to the man's head. "Lemme get them keys, nigga," he hissed in is gruff voice. The man paused, his back still turned.

"Give the shit up, muthafucka," Tarik said, walking out in front of the man. He raised his arm, pointing it at the man.

244

UNTRUST Deszion Nasir

The man had on blackout shades in the middle of the night, so the twins figured he had a hangover. There were always drunks hanging around the beach at night, which made Buckroe Beach's parking lot a great spot to hunt.

The man continued to stare at Tarik, not moving and ignoring Samir, who still had the gun to his head. Tarik became slightly unnerved and a warning bell dinged, but Samir quickly grew irate at being discarded. "Muthafucka I *know* you heard me," Samir shouted, pushing the man's head with the gun.

"If you not man enough to look me in my face when you tryna rob me, then, naw, playboy, I *don't* hear you," came the slow, calm and collected voice of the man.

"Man, *fuck* that Steven Seagal shit, yo. Tarik, *run* this nigga, man." Samir ordered, but Tarik wasn't moving. He was staring at the man who still hadn't shown any signs of fear. Once the man realized he had Tarik's full attention, he pulled off his glasses and stared back at him with cold, dark blue eyes that seemed to have violet flecks in them when the streetlights hit them. The voice was slightly familiar to Tarik…but the eyes were a dead giveaway. Tarik's wheels turned in his head as he took the eyes, added them to the voice and multiplied that to the area they were in, did some quick mental calculator work, and the sum he came up with sent him in to a time warp of fear and a black hole of panic.

"S-Samir-" he stuttered. It was too late by then. The blue-eyed man whipped his gloved hand out of his jacket pocket behind him and across Samir's arrogant face, the paper-thin scalpel he kept in his pockets easily separating Samir's flesh from his face, leaving a huge bloody hole where his cheek had once been. He figured if he had Tarik scared enough, he would hesitate to attack and he could focus on the bigger threat. Samir screamed like he'd caught the Holy Ghost and fell to the ground, dropping his gun as well as his gangsta attitude. Before the gun hit the ground the blue-eyed man had caught it and hurled it like a circus knife at Tarik. It hit him square in the nose, which made a loud cracking sound

245

as it cracked his maxilla, the bone connecting most of the face between eyes and mouth. The instant and unbearable pain sent Tarik to his knees, struggling to breathe. The man bent down beside Tarik and grabbed his head in his huge hands. "I'll go easy on you since you seem to be the smart one," he growled. He drug Tarik over to where Samir was writhing in pain and kicked him in the side, demanding him to look up at him. Samir did, pain clouding his vision and fear demanding his vision to get it together.

"Next time you decide to rob somebody, make sure your bitch-ass can actually do it," he snapped, then proceeded to jerk Tarik's head to the left. His neck was broken instantly and Samir watched as his brother's terrified eyes closed after staring at him for the last time. The man, just to make a point, then proceeded to twist Tarik's head all the way around with a grunt, breaking every bone in his path and ripping his neck open. He then threw the body to the side. The sight of his murdered brother caused Samir to vomit immediately, but in the middle of his stomach's protest he saw a pair of blood-covered hands reaching for him. He tried to roll under a car, but he was helpless as the man used one hand to grab the top of his jaw and the other to grab the bottom. His grip was too strong for Samir to try to bite him. Sensing what was about to happen, Samir thrashed wildly, but he couldn't prevent the man from pulling in opposite directions until Samir heard his jaw being forced apart and broken. He died trying to take a breath. The man picked both bodies up and tossed them in the back seat of a convertible next to his car. He grabbed a bottle of Everclear on the floor of the passenger side and poured it all over the car and on the bodies. He then snatched up a lighter in the cup holder and lit the car on fire, tossing the lighter and guns in for good measure. The blue-eyed man then calmly climbed into his crayon-blue truck and pulled off.

UNTRUST Deszion Nasir

SIOVAHN

Vu walked into my room, scaring the hell out of me. I mean, yeah, it was his house, *technically*, but he could've knocked. Vu was so light-footed I never knew where he was. I dropped my cell phone and prayed it wasn't broken. It would be the 5th time in a year I'd broken my phone.

"Sorry, baby, didn't mean to scare you," Vu grinned, his bright teeth blinding me as usual. "You ready to go shopping?"

Vu had been taking me and Azzure' shopping every day since we'd been here. Azzure' was having a ball and I felt like a queen. Vu was like something out of a fairy tale. He had the Triple C effect: He was clean, connected and cute. And the best part about it was that he treated me like he was lucky to be with me, not like I was lucky to be with him.

"Um, not quite. You know I haven't gotten used to the time zone here so I'm moving slow...Azzure' is still sleep," I laughed, brushing a stray hair out of my eyes.

Vu's eyes ran up and down my body slowly, taking in my peach silk bra and thong set. He closed my bedroom door and leaned against it, crossing his arms.

"What?" I asked.

He shrugged. "Nothing. Just looking at you. I shut the door cuz the help don't need to see you all exposed,"

"Exposed?" I laughed. "You act like I'd scare them or something, damn."

"You might. You scare me," he replied, grinning.

"How do I scare you?" I grinned.

"Cuz every time I get near you, I'm scared of that damn... it's like *fire*, man... you light my body up like a fuckin torch and I'm tryna be a gentleman about this so you don't think I'm just trying to fuck, but..." he shook his head.

"Are you serious?" I asked. "You've treated me like a little sister since I met you. I was starting to wonder if you

UNTRUST Deszion Nasir

was feelin me like that at all," I told him, setting my phone down inside an open drawer and sliding it closed.

"Naw, don't want you to think that... not at all," Vu said, sitting the bottled water in his hand down on the counter and stepping toward me. "Just trying to be a gentleman. You know we're kinda big on that over here," he told me, grinning and stepping into my space. He stood close to me and I could feel the heat coming off of his body.

"You don't have to be one all the time," I told him, looking up into his eyes. I'd never noticed it until now, but Vu's eyes had a strange tint to them. As I was trying to figure out what was so strange about them, Vu leaned forward and kissed me. Since I wasn't expecting it, it was actually a little awkward, but he got my attention and the next time he leaned forward I was prepared. This attempt was much better and actually sent a shockwave of pleasure through my body I hadn't expected to feel. I figured I was just gonna trick off of a guy who wanted an exotic chick to show off, like an accessory We had been here only a few days and that seemed to be what he was doing. But Vu wasn't carrying himself like he was all star struck or whatever. Not at all.

I don't know when Vu slipped his arms around my waist, but he was hugging me to him and running his hands down my back. He gripped my thighs and picked me up like I didn't weigh anything. He carried me over to the huge soft bed and instead of tossing me on it, he wrapped my legs around his waist and with me clinging to him, he climbed on the bed and laid me on my back, pressing himself on top of me. His gentle yet firm actions had me hot and it didn't take long for me to get his clothes off of him. I figured Vu was mixed because of his hair texture, but when I snatched those boxers down it was very clear what he was mixed *with*. Vu was kissing on me, rubbing, licking and sucking on me like he'd been in a sexual drought. But he wasn't acting like he was starving. He was more like...someone who'd had a craving for apple pie for months and now that he had it he was trying to enjoy it, savor it and relish every crumb. He

UNTRUST Deszion Nasir

wasn't rushing, he was trying to feel all of me and I definitely wanted to feel all of him. I was so overwhelmed by the sexual tension that was flaming between us I surprised myself and exploded before he did. This seemed to kick him into overdrive and he went harder and faster, gripping me tighter until I couldn't keep up with him or resist him and I came over and over. When I felt myself shaking and was ready to tell him to stop, he just ran his fingers through my hair, kissed my neck and stroked deeper and harder until I ended up somewhere I'd never been. I was so far gone I nearly missed the tension building up in him and by the time he was done he was on his own cuz I was totally in my own world at that point. A drop of sweat in my eye was actually what pulled me back down to Earth and I blinked to find Vu panting, his hair a tight sweaty mass of curls that had come out from being pulled back. He was supposed to get it braided later today-which was why it was loose- but he was going to have to wash it, now.

"You okay?" he asked me, noticing the glazed look in my eyes, I guessed. I just nodded and smiled. I reached up and wiped sweat off of his face and he smiled back. He laid down in the big bed beside me and pulled me to him. "So," he said seriously. "You know I'm gonna be real upset when you go home now, right?"

I smiled up at him, relishing this new feeling of feeling wanted and not just someone dealt with mechanically. "Oh yeah?"

"Are you kidding? I ain't never felt like that in my *life*, Siovahn." Vu told me.

"Me either," I admitted.

"Never?" he asked, grinning proudly.

"No, never, and stop smiling so hard," I teased, shoving him playfully. He laughed that golden laugh of his and pulled me to him, kissed my head, and cradled me in his arms.

"Okay…don't flip out or nothing, but…what am I gonna have to do to get you to stay here with me?"

I turned to him to see if he was serious. He looked like

he was. "Stay here? In Japan?"

"Yeah. I mean, what's stopping you from just saying 'Fuck it' and leaving all that bullshit behind?"

"Um, my son, first off," I began, laughing at the idea of moving across the world with Azzure'.

"What about him? I already got him a tutor for the whole time you're here so he won't behind. By the time you go back-if-you go back-he'll have a better education. His tutor was a professor at a New York prep school. C'mon, he'd learn so much by being here. He'd learn Japanese and have a *huge* advantage on other kids, especially other Black kids," he stressed. I didn't say anything because he was right. This was all moving too fast for me, though, but Vu was so persuasive I was actually considering it. Blue didn't give a fuck about me and as long as Azzure' was good, Blue wasn't really checking for him, either. I didn't have anything waiting for me back in America. Here, I had a man who was attentive, paid out the ass, and he was offering me a dream, my son a quality education and a chance to benefit from a great opportunity. "You don't gotta decide now," he said, seeing me so deep in thought. He slid his hand under the sheets and up my body, leaning over and kissing my neck, ready for another taste of me. I was so busy enjoying being worshipped and Vu was so busy doing the worshipping nobody was paying attention to the life-altering decisions and bullshit floating around in the room.

The next morning when the sun danced on my face, I rolled over and discovered that Vu was gone. I wasn't surprised, cuz Vu was like a vampire anyways, but I figured I'd show my appreciation by at least making him breakfast or something. He hadn't asked for anything from me since I'd been here and I didn't want to come off as some international sac-chaser.

As I made my way downstairs I could hear heated voices arguing in the south wing of Vu's house. I walked over that way on silent feet until I could hear the angry voices of Vu's business associates.

"….with this situation almost 2 months now," one man was declaring loudly. "You should have handled this by now. Our finances have had a horrible ripple because of this."

"I know," Vu said quietly.

The man continued as if Vu hadn't spoken. "We've stayed out of this until now because you asked us to do so. This is not the way the family handles business. We are not above you avenging your mother's death. What we are against is the way you have allowed this to affect your common sense. You should have killed Scorpion Knight when you had the chance. You used untrained people and lost your chance in your rush and anger and it has cost us a black eye. Do you know how it looks for a Yakuza to not be able to handle a petty American street hoodlum?! Especially one in your position? You are supposed to be a powerful member of the Yamaguchi-Gumi and this shit has the other families looking at us strange. "

Vu simply nodded, fire in his eyes but keeping his mouth closed.

"And to make matters worse, you bring the hoodlum's whore and his bastard here?! To Kobe for everyone to see? For what? You appear to be a *coward*, Katsamura. A coward who ran away from American trash and you are taunting him to bring him here on your own turf because you can't handle him on his! This whole thing is disgraceful. And it's ineffective. Am I correct in my assumption Scorpion has made no effort to retrieve his family?"

"You *are* correct…"

"And where is your sister? Where is Minya?"

Silence. The man ranting smacked Vu across the face. "Dishonorable child! Your sister has been drug into your bullshit and she is promised to Nakuyado Yodiriu! That was a crucial union for us! Do I need to ask if she's still pure from your misguided antics?"

Vu was still silent with a red hand print on his face. All the men were shaking their heads in disapproval.

"You are young, you are smart, but you are weak

UNTRUST Deszion Nasir

because you continue to think with your emotions and your penis. You have 1 week to get that whore out of this house and get your sister home. This situation with Scorpion is no longer in your hands." The men all stood and began to file out of the room.

I was so stuck on the conversation I didn't hide myself in time. The head man spotted me and stopped. The other men bowed slightly, but the main guy pursed his lips and stormed out of the house. They had no idea that I spoke fluent Japanese and had understood their whole conversation. Vu didn't either. He walked up to me, all smiles again, but I could tell he was visibly shaken. He offered to help me make breakfast and I accepted, but I couldn't help thinking it might be the last meal I had. Vu acted as if nothing was wrong and chatted with me like normal. When breakfast was ready I went to wake Azzure' and we sat down to eat. Vu seemed like he was in great spirits as we ate, and I found myself putting the angry Yakuza members in the back of my head.

Toward the end of the meal, however, I started to feel weird. First my stomach felt like I had cramps and I begun to have trouble breathing. That's when I noticed Vu wasn't eating, only drinking guava juice. It threw me into a wild panic and I looked over at Azzure', who was staring at me, puzzled. My one relief was that he seemed fine. Then again, he was eating cereal.

"Azzure', go on upstairs and get ready to go on that trip to the zoo I was telling you about," Vu said in his kid-friendly voice. Azzure's face lit up and he jumped up. He paused to look at me one last time. "You okay mom?' he asked.

I nodded, managing to smile instead of cry so I wouldn't scare him. He kissed me and ran off, making all the noise in the world.

"How could you?" I gasped, letting the tears fall. The room was already dimming.

"You're a liability," Vu shrugged.

"My... baby.."

"Your son will be sent to live with your mother in Ocho

252

UNTRUST Deszion Nasir

Rios," Vu said like it was nothing.

"But why?" I asked, having to use both hands to keep my head up.

Vu held up my phone and I froze. "The next time you try to pull a fucking scam on someone by making plans with your little juvenile buddies, make sure you lock your fucking phone." He tossed it on the table. It was true. Jay had been coaching me on how to get info and what to pay attention to. I had known what was up the day I'd flown out here. I thought I'd help Blue with this situation and he'd finally *finally* stop treating me like shit, but I guess I couldn't even do that right. My last thoughts were that I had wasted my whole life on a man that couldn't care less if I lived or died and not lived it for the one child who did.

UNTRUST Deszion Nasir

DOE

I stood in front of Blue's front door, rubbing the back of my neck wearily. I wasn't really ready to deal with this nigga right now, but this was something that had to be done. I glanced back at my truck at Angel, who was sitting in my passenger seat with her arms crossed. I pulled back my urge to run back to the car, throw her in the backseat and tear all of her clothes off, and knocked on the door instead.

A second later a terrified-looking security guard swung the door open. I'd be scared if I were him, too. Letting Caesar get a bead on Blue like that wasn't something that was gonna be easily fixed, man. Him and Blue's 2 other hired security had to be ready to shit their pants right about now. I walked past the guy without acknowledging him and headed for the back of the house. I knew Blue was back there from the sound of Madskillz floating from the back deck. When I stepped outside, though, I saw TJ relaxed at a table, reading a newspaper, a black n mild dangling from his mouth.

"Oh, my fault, man. Thought you was Blue," I said, giving him dap when he looked up at the sound of my feet on the rich wood.

"Shiiiit, not hardly," was his response. He dumped the ashes on the back of some junk mail and scooted his chair over so I could walk around him and sit down across from him.

"Where's Blue?" I asked. He'd told me he'd be downstairs, but I hadn't seen any other signs of life.

"He was out here, but his phone rang, so..." TJ shrugged, which either meant "I don't know where he went" or "I don't give a fuck where he went."

I nodded, yawning.

"You look tired, yo."TJ said, studying me with narrowed eyes.

"Yeah, man. Too much extra shit going on right now," I

agreed.

TJ stared at me a minute, giving me that same intense look Blue would, except with hazel green eyes, then folded his paper and leaned back in his seat. "Yeah, I heard about that shit at Blakeley's. Something told me not to fuck with that bullshit."

"You not stressed about what your brother done?"

TJ smirked. "My brother. Look, Doe, you seem like a laid-back typa nigga and so am I. So I think we understand each other. We both know Blue ain't about shit but money and power. Anyone in the way of either one is gonna end up just like Caesar and Dejah: fucked and tucked. I'm not stupid. I know Blue just got me here for this Superman shit he tryna do to Vu. He don't give a fuck about his kid or his kid's mom. And a nigga who don't give a shit about his kid *damn* sure don' give a shit about you. Blue goin after this cat just cuz for his rep, man. I'm goin' along with it for Jasmine. She's the only person left on this fuckin planet who gives a shit if I live or die, man. I cain't let Blue's bullshit get her killed. I been through that shit before behind a blue-eyed demon," TJ said, narrowing his eyes. I'm guessing he was referring to the drama that surrounded Gemini Knight. I wasn't gonna dwell on it, cuz Blue never wanted to talk about him, but TJ threw me off by changing the subject anyway.

"So who's the broad?" he asked, taking in another huge drag of his black.

"What broad?"

"The broad you stressing over," TJ explained. "I know that look, man."

I leaned back in my chair and sucked through my teeth. "Sherita? I ain't stressin that chick, man. She'll forgive me. I was kinda showin my ass at the club, man. She won't answer my calls but she ain't blocked my number, neither, so she'll forgive me."I grinned.

"I'm sure she will. I'm talking about the other one, though," TJ went on.

"What other one?"

UNTRUST Deszion Nasir

"The one that got you lookin all out of character. I been knowing you less than a month and I can see that shit. Whoever she is, you need to tighten that shit up. I can see the shit all over your face."

As soon as what TJ said processed in my brain, Blue came out onto the deck, his eyes cold and what looked like fatigue was settled on his face. His pile of problems were wearing on him, but he'd never show it anywhere other than in the confines of his house. I remembered what TJ had just said and got my face together instantly, not tyrna be caught slippin.

"What's good, man," Blue said, flopping in another chair at the table.

"That's what I came to find out," I said pointedly, glaring at Blue. The deception he'd shown me in Dejah's death wasn't lost on me, but I knew better than to come at him wrong. He wouldn't give a fuck anyway, so there was no point in even getting all pissy about it. Especially since he didn't seem to be trippin on me pushing up on his girl in his face at the club. He probably chucked it up to me feelin my liquor too much, like I tended to do from time to time.

"Man, this nigga got bad timing to fuck around and get his back blown open," Blue complained, surprising me. TJ shook his head, blew a cloud of smoke out of his mouth and I just stared. Blue completely skipped over his rape of Dejah and subsequent murder of her brother and launched straight into how the shit had affected *him*. Guess it was my fault for expecting him to act like a fuckin human being.

"Yeah, that *is* fucked up," I said, going along with that shit. "You heard about Nina, right?" I'd heard from my sources about her murder.

"Fuckin tragic," Blue said, no emotion in his voice.

"You heard from Jai?" I asked, studying his reaction.

"Naw. *He* need to pull his shit together cuz he costing me money. He done already missed two shows behind this shit."

I shook my head and TJ looked away.

"He lost his girl and his kid, man," I said, frowning at Blue.

"That bitch was a sac-chaser and the kid probably won't his noway. You know how them model typa chicks are, man...money is like crack to them, they'll do anything to get it," Blue waved me away. I sucked back what I wanted to say and took a deep breath.

"Whatever, man. That ain't what I rolled through to discuss with you no way..."

"What is it, man?" Blue being asked, sounding weary.

"I tracked your girl down," I told him. Blue and TJ looked up at me. I knew Blue had been waiting for Angel to call him, being used to a female coming after him. She hadn't. As hard as he was, Angel seemed to be the only person he had trouble controlling and I knew it bothered him. He wouldn't never admit it, though...

"Where is she?" he asked.

"Out in the truck." I nodded toward the front of the house.

Blue sighed. A sigh of relief, I think. "She pissed, ain't she?"

"Man, go see for yourself."

"I'm not tryna deal with no bullshit this morning, Doe."

"You want me to go tell her that? You don't think she got a reason to be pissed off, man?" I demanded.

"Look, Blue. She obviously ain't come over here to NOT forgive you, man. Suck that shit up and go talk to her," TJ said, sounding like an older brother. Blue looked at him, then me. I shrugged, and he finally stood up, sighed and headed for the front of the house, leaving me and TJ alone again.

TJ stared at me, blowing another smoke ring. He reminded me of Blue the way he looked at people like he could see through them.

"You a good friend," he said.

I shrugged. "I'm a good businessman. When a man is worrying about what his lady is doing, he's not worrying

257

UNTRUST Deszion Nasir

about his money," I pointed out.

"True piece," TJ agreed, nodding. He leaned back in his seat, his long legs dangling over the edge of the deck like mine were. "I didn't mean a good friend to *him*, though."

"Who you talkin bout?" I asked.

"Angel."

"Angel?"

TJ nodded. "Takes a big man to bring a woman he cares about back to her man so she can be safe from his bs." he said casually.

Now it was my turn to pull out a blunt and lean back in my chair. I lit it and looked at TJ. "Shit that obvious?"

TJ shook his head. "Naw, I notice shit others don't. How'd you get tied up in that crap, man? You seem smart enough to know better."

I just exhaled. "You don't know that girl, man. Just being around her makes niggaz act straight reckless, man."

"I'll pass," TJ laughed. "What about that Brazilian chick you was with?"

"Sherita? Man, I 'on know. She mad at me, but I was twisted, so, you know…she'll forgive me." I peered at him. "Why? She fine as all hell, ain't she?" I asked, catching the look in his eye.

TJ grinned silently.

"You want me to introduce ya'll? We never really hooked up or nothin, we just hung out a few times…"

"Naw, I'll pass again."

"Aight, but if you change her mind, she works in Patrick Henry Mall. She has a store in there."

TJ looked like he was thinking about it when Blue came back outside, his arm slug around Angel, looking more like himself than he did a few minutes ago. He dropped a kiss on Angel's forehead and said "We got some shit to work out. I'ma get with ya'll later," Blue said. Angel glanced at me for a second before she let Blue drag her away towards the west wing of the house.

I stood up, my work here now done.

UNTRUST Deszion Nasir

"Where you off to?" TJ asked.

"Gotta job to do. Jay found out where one of Vu's American contacts is and he wants me to go shake his ass by his ankles till some good info falls out his mouth."

TJ shook his head. "Ya'll niggaz crazy."

I scooped up my keys and glanced at where Blue and Angel had departed to. "That's what they tell me..."

I dapped TJ up and walked around the front of the house, not wanting to hear Blue trying to make up with Angel. I climbed into my car and went into work mode.

I got in the car and when I started it up, I put my "Zone song" on. I closed my eyes. This is the song I listened to before I went out for a job. "Power" by Kanye' West shot through my speakers and through my body as I felt the lover leave me and the killer take a choke hold on my soul. Angel faded away, Sherita faded away. Blue faded away. Niggas thought a killer just went out and blasted his gun. I skilled killer had to get his mind into damn near tunnel vision status to become immune to fuck ups and distractions. When I listened to the song 3 times I opened my eyes and the world was now tainted. Tainted with the need for me to remove someone from it. I put my car in gear and pulled off, my eyes not those of a normal man. I got on the highway and drove off to Virginia Beach, about an hour away from where I was. Jobs in Virginia Beach were always tricky. Virginia Beach is a huge city and a huge tourist spot, so police came down on you hard if they caught you fucking up their precious reputation. But I had a job to do. I drove out to an upper middle class neighborhood out around the Lynnhaven area and pulled up in front of the house after driving for a couple of minutes up a private road. There were people sitting around outside like they were having a cookout. I sighed. This job was a blackout. Blackouts meant put one in everything breathing: kids, momma, dogs. Dude picked a bad day to have a family gathering. I got out, no mask, four guns on me and two in my hand. A shotgun was strapped to my back.

UNTRUST Deszion Nasir

A man standing over the grill reacted first. He saw the guns and tried to yell something out in Japanese, but I raised the gun a sent a bullet searching for a home right through his head. He fell over on top of the grill, the stench of burning flesh clogging my nose quickly. By then I had put an end to the life of an old woman in a chair with a bullet, which exited her body and sank into the back of a little boy trying to crawl out of the way. He fell next to the pit bull that tried to run at me from the back of the porch that I'd laid down. I blocked the sight of the kid bleeding out of my mind and fired on a woman who was hiding behind a Lexus. My bullet sliced through both doors and made a clean, neat hole in her temple. As she fell the cell phone she had clutched in her hand flew out and under the car, sliding near my feet. I stomped it and pulled out the shotgun. I blew the front door off the hinges and walked inside. Two men, their women and another teenage boy were soon laid out in a path in front of me like human throw rugs. None of them were the man I was looking for.

Suddenly my spidey-sense lit up as I felt myself being watched. I reached inside my jacket and fired to my left through my coat. A man fell down the stairs, his 9mm tumbling to the ground a few ticks before he did. He was trying to grab his head and his leg, blood oozing out from both. *He* was the man I had come to see.

I stepped over the bodies in the now quiet house and snatched him up by the collar. "Get yo ass up," I barked, snatching him to his feet, not giving a shit about having just shot him in the leg. He begged and pleaded in Japanese but I just slapped him in the mouth with a gun. "I know you speak English, muthafucka, so knock the sucka shit off." I said, shaking him and throwing him on the kitchen table. He got a boost of courage and kicked the gun out of my hand, but another bullet in his other leg from the other gun in the other hand slowed him down. I banged his head on the back of the table. "VU. I want everything you got on him. Don't play stupid cuz if my people didn't have rock hard proof you roll

UNTRUST Deszion Nasir

with him I wouldn't be here." The man looked terrified, but I didn't know if it was because of me or the thought of turning on Vu. Either way I didn't give a fuck. I drug him off the table and out to the front of the house and forced him to look at all the bodies littering his front yard.

"You see this?" I growled. "This is all because of your punk-ass boss. Now, he got my man's kid and he got my man's baby momma. We might not know where he is, but we know where you're your boys are. 7 of them. What kind of leader brings his team into his personal bullshit then leaves ya'll to pick up the shit he dropped? You protecting a cat like that? He don't give a shit about you." I pulled out my cell phone as the man moaned and bled and sweated. "You tell me what I want to know and I'll call my boys and cancel the rest of the blackouts we got on your whole crew. It's up to you,..save Vu or save all your boys' families...and I'll make sure they all know you were the one that sent the grim reaper on their houses," I added, looking him in the eye. I could tell the heavy weight of that decision was weighing on his mind. He looked from me, to the phone, to the still bodies spread out all over the yard in front of his secluded property. The guy looked like he was gonna pass out, but he nodded. I hit the video button on the phone and held it up to his face.

"Wait. You gonna record me?" he asked, shaking.

"Well, I didn't bring a fuckin notebook, man. Just answer the questions I ask you!"

He nodded, flinching, and proceeded to answer every question I asked with detail. Satisfied, I saved the video, then dialed a number. When someone answered, I said "See you tomorrow," and hung up. That was my code for canceling the other hits.

I let the guy go and he collapsed in a fit of pain mixed with relief. He looked up at me pulling out a machete from inside my coat and his eyes grew wide. "What the hell, man??" he yelled. "I thought you weren't gonna kill me!"

"I said I wouldn't kill *them*. Your boys and their folks. And I'm not. Besides, your whole family is dead. What you got to live for?" I raised the shiny blade and while he let out a high-pitched scream I brought my hand down and sliced clean through his neck. I kicked his severed head off my new sneakers and wiped the blade on the dead man's shirt. Then I got back in my truck and went off to my next job...I didn't scrub the site cuz I was trying to leave a message. The 11 o'clock news stated they had no leads on another bizarre massacre. They never did.

PART XVI- HEART(LESS)
SHERITA

I sighed and clutched my phone as I got out of my car. I stuffed it in my back pocket so I could grab my work bag, sling it over my shoulder and close my door in one movement. As I walked away I tweaked the alarm button and headed into Patrick Henry Mall on my way to work. I had been in this shop only a short amount of time because the Coliseum Mall had shut down to rebuild a tourist area and I refused to pay the new rent for the new shops. I was a business woman and I had plenty of customers to keep that extra rent and still make good money.

Let me clear a few things up, being that nobody's been interested in my story till now. 1. I'm Brazilian *and* Black. 2. Yes, this is my real hair. 3. Yes, I tried to kick Angel's ass. 4. No, I have not tried to call Doe. I refused to be broken-hearted about his ass because I knew what I was dealing with when I went out with him. I seem to have a weakness for pretty boys, but you'd think at 25 I'd know a cup of hot piss over hot chocolate without having to drink the whole glass. I was more bitter than anything because I had been embarrassed in front of a ton of people.

I walked to my shop, ignoring the men who were always trying to get my attention. They were all either married, ugly, or a combination of the two. I came to work to work and had long ago stopped flirting with shop owners. I'd smile a lil at customers because most of them were males and they would buy more items if they thought it'd get them some pussy. It wouldn't.

I opened up shop and was arranging a new mannequin that had my latest creation on it: I customized Virginia Tech jersey with Michael Vick's face on the back. The jersey was official and I already knew it's sell for around $500 for maybe an hour's worth of work. Not bad. And I had 10 of them. They'd sell out in a few days once the word got around

UNTRUST Deszion Nasir

so by Friday I'd be a *minimum* of 5 grand richer. Not a bad week at all.

I had a Crissette Michelle CD playing while I was unpacking some supplies in the back of the store when I heard the little electronic *ding!* letting me know someone had entered the store. I stood up, wiped my hands on a work towel and glanced at myself in one of the dressing room mirrors. My gold hair was still bouncy and curly and my curves were tucked into my stretch True Religion jeans nicely. I don't care what anyone said. I *loved* being curvy. I was a borderline big girl, but with measurements of 36-29-42, I'd take that.

I threw on my "store smile" and headed out into the front. A tall man was standing in front of the jersey I'd just put out. He had his back to me and his hands in his pocket.

"That's a large, but I have bigger sizes in the back," I called out to him. He turned to see who was talking to him and I tripped over my own feet at how attractive he was. He rushed over to catch me from falling on my face. He was too slow to save me from that, but he used huge, strong hands to help me up off the floor. I looked up into dark green eyes and my own brown eyes ran across a head of bright red waves sitting on top of a light gold-complexioned face.

"Oh, my God, that *would* happen to me today," I muttered, turning fire-engine red. "Thank you."

"It's a small thing...can I get a damn *discount* on this *jersey*, though, damn..." he shook his head, grinning at me. His smile was familiar to me but I couldn't tell how. I *know* I'd remember seeing *him* before.

"No, I need the money to upgrade my health insurance, apparently," I said, brushing my hair out of my face. I leaned against the counter and smiled at him. He laughed and nodded.

"So, you made this?" he asked, nodding at the jersey.

"I designed everything in here," I said, nodding and trying not to sound too proud. Men never thought I did all these designs by myself. "Except for the shoes. My girl

Miko Makai specially designs the sneakers in here specifically for the outfits you see here."

The guy nodded, appreciation in his eyes. He walked over to examine some things on the side wall. I couldn't stop myself from staring at him so I busied myself behind the desk doing nothing. A few customers started flowing in so I was distracted enough, but he didn't leave and I felt his eyes one me whenever I wasn't looking at him. About 10 minutes later I helped all the other customers and turned to him, hands on my healthy hips, and tilted my head to the side. "You gonna buy something or are you gonna just stare at me all morning?"

He smiled that sexy smile again and said "If I buy something, *can* I stay and stare at you all morning?"

I couldn't help grinning back at him. "If you buy that jersey you can stay all day."

"Damn,"

I laughed.

"What about if I buy you lunch?"

My heart skipped. "It's only like, 11."

He shook his head. "Give a nigga a break, ma."

I studied him like I had a big decision to make, as if I weren't ready to scream "YES!"

"Tell you what. I usually don't leave for lunch cuz I miss customers, but if you go and get me something to eat, I'll eat it in here with you. Cool?"

He smiled. "You got that. What you want?"

"Chick-fil-a. Number 1 deluxe, extra pickles, 2 mayos, lemonade and a brownie." I recited.

"Okay," he laughed. "Anything else?"

"Isn't that enough?"

"What you mean?" his eyebrows knitted together.

"Stop playing. You cain't tell I like to eat?"

He smirked. "Oh, I can see that. And what I can see is why I came in here," he added.

I laughed again and he said he'd be right back and left. As he passed by a group of females, they all stopped and

UNTRUST Deszion Nasir

watched him depart, whispering and shaking their heads after him. One girl was fanning herself...

My day was looking up. By the time my mystery man returned, carrying two big bags, the smell of waffle fries made my stomach grumble. At this point, females were shamelessly staring at him in groups, some even with their men. He ignored all of them and brought me smiles and my lunch.

"You causing a scene," I told him, nodding behind him. He glanced over his shoulder at the girls, who smiled back, a few waving. He turned back to me without responding. "I didn't even see them. I was too busy tryna get back here," he said. I guess his snub pissed them off. He wasn't whispering. Most of the girls frowned up and walked off.

I usually have a problem eating in front of guys but for some reason I had no problem tearing into my sandwich. I hadn't eaten since lunch last night and I was starving. The steaming chicken sandwich was halfway gone before I realized the guy was just staring at me, enjoying me eating my food. He licked his lips without realizing he was doing it, then snapped to attention when he realized I was staring at him staring at me. We both kind of just laughed at each other.

"Okay, so," I paused, wiping my mouth with a napkin. "You can't just bring me lunch, watch me eat and not tell me your name. I haven't even asked."

He paused. "It's Terrence."

I paused. "Terrence. I'm not tryna seem rude but it's like I *know* you, but I *don't* know you. I'm just tryna figure out why you seem familiar to me..."

He leaned on the counter, glancing over his shoulder like he didn't want anyone to hear him. "You know my brother."

"Who's your brother?" I asked, hoping it wasn't an ex.

He hesitated for a second. "Blue."

Hearing that name made me snap up straight. "Blue's your brother?"

He nodded. That's why something was familiar about

UNTRUST Deszion Nasir

him. He had that same confident aurora about him Jas and Blue did, but none of the cockiness. It also meant if he knew Blue,...

"So I take it you know Doe, then," I said, flatly, suddenly losing my appetite.

"Not really. He comes by the house sometimes. I don't deal with him like that,..he did mention, however, that the two of you seem to have fallen out."

I tossed the food at him. "So you thought you'd come over here and pick up his leftovers? Are you fucking serious? Who *does* that?" I yelled. A few people walking past the shop slowed, but didn't stop and peered at us with accusatory faces.

"Hold on, ma. I *don't* do that. But I'd be lying if I said I thought he wasn't fucking stupid. I really just meant to come by and see if you were as fine in person as in the picture I saw of you in Jasmine's room. She talks about you too," he added. I felt my rage simmering down. I was so caught up in being pissed I had forgotten all about Jasmine. Seeing me calm down he went on. "I was just gonna look, you know, but I couldn't help it, I had to say something to you. I can go if you want, I'm not tryna bring no static to your place of business." He stood up tall and baked away from the counter, brushing French fries off of his cream sweater.

"No, no... wait.." I sighed, once again feeling stupid and guilty. "I'm sorry... Terrence?"

"Just TJ is cool."

"TJ. I guess you know I'm a little touchy about everyone in your camp right now, so... forgive me for trippin.."

"That's not my camp. I don't know none of them. Not even Blue. They don't know me, neither. The only one I'm tryna get to know right now is *you*," TJ said, coming back over to me and leaning on the counter, his green eyes locked on mine.

"You're not worried about drama?" I asked him.

"You think they worried about us with all that other shit

267

UNTRUST Deszion Nasir

going on in that house? Better yet, you think I care what them niggas think?"

I grinned, feeling my old powers returning. "I guess not."

TJ fed me one of his fries that I hadn't thrown. "So...when you get off work?"

BLUE

I glanced down at my watch again, pissed off. I glanced at Lucky beside me, who had his eyes narrowed. We were in Norfolk down by the docks, waiting on a shipment of fresh weapons from South Africa and my connect was 15 minutes late. Everyone knew I didn't tolerate tardiness at all. My time was money. A whole lot of fucking money. I had another pickup in an hour and I had to go way out to Newport News from here in traffic. Getting through the Hampton Roads Bridge Tunnel was gonna be hell on its own without this bullshit.

I'd had a long enough day just getting Lucky to calm down enough to even come out here. I'd overstepped at the club when I hit him and when I came through to his house, my sister'd cursed me out again and the only reason Lucky even spoke to me was to get Jasmine off of me. I apologized and he eventually sighed and nodded, a sign of his forgiveness. I wasn't scared of no nigga, but I was smart enough to know which ones were less of a headache when they were on your side. Lucky was one of them. I wasn't under the assumption we were cool or nothing. I just knew he wouldn't kill me right now.

I had just pulled out one of my work phones to curse someone out when I saw a raggedy Chevy pull up a few hundred feet away from us. It was the car we were waiting on, but because they were late I immediately pulled my gun out, sensing a problem. Lucky already had both of his out.

The car doors opened and my contact Makodo got out with a few of his sidekicks. All of them looked nervous.

"Ya'll late," I yelled, pulling the hammer back on my gun. From here I could see Makodo swallow and glance at his comrades.

"I know, Blue. It's not our fault. We've been in country for 3 hours but our boss called us back to the warehouse when

269

we were almost here. We-we have a problem, Blue."

"'We' or 'you?'" I demanded, tightening my finger around the trigger.

Makodo swallowed. "Our boss... he got a hold of a video... someone posted a video... you and a girl... you did... things to her... my boss says he won't do business with men who do what you did to a helpless female..."

My jaw clenched. "I already paid him." I said, my voice controlled.

Obviously terrified, Madoko reached inside the car and pulled a briefcase out. "He has returned your payment."

In my peripheral, I saw Lucky shaking his head, but he didn't say anything.

"It is not up to me," Madoko said. "I was not there so I cannot pass judgment. I am just the messenger."

I sighed. This shit was getting old real quick. I didn't give a fuck what random muthafuckaz thought of me cuz most of em were pussy-ass suckas who'd never step to my face and say shit. But this bullshit was fucking with my money now. The only thing I regret is killing Caesar. If I had left him alive I could make him suffer over and over for causing me all this damn headache.

"Are we cool?" Madoko asked, trying to decide if he was gonna live or die.

I thought about it, looked at Lucky, read his expression.

"No." I fired a shot and sent in through his left eye. It exited his head and sank into the neck of the man who'd been peeking from behind him. Madoko dropped, his man tried to scream and fell back into the raggedy car, and the other man tried to reach for his gun but Lucky dumped 3 in his head before he could reach his pocket.

Irritated, I walked over to the car, tossed Madoko's body to the side and me and Lucky searched the car and the trunk. My guns weren't there.

"Fuck!" I yelled.

"Chill out, Blue. Let's just get this other shit. We can get these shits from Dawnagi, remember?" Lucky said,

UNTRUST Deszion Nasir

mentioning another contact. I didn't like to deal with him cuz he was more expensive, but at this point had no choice. I already had orders in for the shit I was supposed to get today and the luxury of having things delivered when I wanted and saving money was gone.

Me and Lucky headed to the other contact spot. We made it in time, but the same funny-style shit was going on over there, as far as shit not smelling right. The cars were all there, but there was no life outside the house. No security, no cops, not even a stray cat. I had a sick feeling in my stomach, but me and Lucky eased our way inside the building anyway.

Everyone in the building had been killed. And I don't just mean shot up. I mean fuckin murdered. There was blood, brains, body parts and guts all over the place, like someone had opened these niggas up and used them like a salt shaker to spread shit all over the house. My weapons were gone again, too.

"This won't no muthafuckin coincidence," Lucky said, stuffing his gun back in his pants.

"Fuck naw."

"You think that nigga Vu is back?"

I shook my head. "No."

"Are you sure?"

"Yeah." I wasn't. I know I probably seem cold to ya'll, but I wasn't sweating Vu right now for a reason. If he was gonna kill Azzure' and Siovahn, he would have been done it and I would have *been* heard about it. I actually didn't know if he'd come back to America, but I didn't think he'd done this. As I glanced around at the wreckage of what used to be 10 lives, I recognized the chaotic order of the murders and pulled out my phone.

"Who you callin?" Lucky asked.

"Jay."

"For what?"

I glanced around at the bloody slaughter one more time before I answered him.

"You seen Cruz lately?"

SIRRON

The knocking on Cruz's door forced me out of the first sound sleep I'd had since I'd come to Virginia. I looked up, groggy from being passed out on my stomach on Cruz's couch and realized I couldn't see anything. Things became clearer and I realized it was my hair covering my face. I flipped it back and blinked sleep away. More banging on the door brought me to my feet. I glanced back at Cruz's closed door, knowing he wouldn't open it if the house was on fire. Ever since the coroner came and carried Nina's body away, Cruz had given his statement to police and shut himself up in the master bedroom. The media had been swarming for a minute because Nina was somewhat famous, but since Cruz refused to come to the door, answer the phone or even come out of his room to eat, the crowd eventually disbursed.

I glanced out of the peephole and into a pair of gold eyes. It was that kid Jay, the one I'd snapped on the other day. No one else from Cruz's clique had been by to see him. I figured they were just giving him space, but it had been almost a week now and I guess they figured it was time to check on their boy.

I quickly ran my fingers through my hair, trying to fix myself so I'd look half-way decent, sniffed under my arms—hmm… passable I guess, and pulled open the door. Jay was looking all fresh and crisp in a wintergreen shirt, hat and customized Fatheads. I felt like Cinderella before the magic in my raggedy t-shirt and a pair of Cruz's basketball shorts. I normally don't wear stuff like that cuz with my big chest I know I looked right chunky… but… it was just Jay, right?

"Hey," I said, trying not to yawn in his face and singe his eyebrows off with my breath.

"Hey," he nodded at me. He glanced behind me. "Is he up?"

I shrugged. "Nobody knows. He won't come out of

there."

"He ain't eat?"

"Naw, he ain't opened the door at all. Sometimes I hear music playin'. I guess he's lettin me know he's alive or whatever…but he has a bathroom in there, so he don't never need to open it, I guess."

Jay shook his head, his attitude suddenly of a man much older than 16.

"Can I come in?" he asked.

I glanced behind me at the messy house. God, he'd think I was trifling. There was shit all over the house, but it was basically cuz I was so drained from trying to keep myself together and field all the questions and traffic that came to the house. I know Cruz needed quiet so I was scared to run a vacuum or anything.

"It's not really a good time," I began apologetically.

"Damn, I can't even get a glass of water on my birthday?" Jay asked, those amber eyes flashing.

"Oh, damn, it's your birthday?" I asked, covering my mouth with my hand.

"Yeah, I'm almost old enough to buy cigarettes I'll never smoke," Jay joked.

I glanced behind me again and sighed. Fuck it. "Come on," I said, stepping aside.

Jay walked in and looked around briefly. Then he glanced at Cruz's closed door and walked back to it. Before I could say anything Jay turned the knob and opened the door. I ran back to the doorway, prepared for the worst.

It wasn't as bad as I thought. Cruz was stretched out on his bed, laying on his stomach, asleep. He stank to high hell, probably hadn't taken a shower in days. Jay walked over to him and shook his arm. When Cruz didn't respond, he shook him again. Then again. He glanced at me, worry in his eyes and rolled Cruz over. That's when I saw the white residue all over Cruz's nose.

I ran to the side of the bed and saw a CD cover dumped on the floor, white powder all over it and spilling onto the carpet. "Oh, God," I cried, grabbing Cruz's wrist for a pulse. I got a faint one. Jay was already kicking shit out of the way on Cruz's junky floor and preparing to drag him out of the room. "I gotta call 911." I said, frantically looking around for the house phone.

"We don't got time for that. Hospital is 5 minutes away. It'll take an ambulance 10 minutes to get here. Help me get him in my car," Jay grunted, dragging Cruz from the bed. I grabbed Cruz's feet and helped Jay get him into the backseat. I didn't bother with any shoes or putting a bra on. I just climbed in the backseat with my cousin and Jay took off for the hospital.

"What is he taking?" Jay demanded, running a light. I hesitated to tell him but Jay started yelling. "Sirron, stop fucking around, girl! What is it? Heroin, crack, what?"

"It's Coke," I admitted. "He had stopped a few years ago when he first moved from New York to here, but every now and then when he gets real stressed out he fucks with it again. This whole shit with Nina must've sent him over the edge..." I sucked my tears up, my Cruz pride refusing to let me scream and cry like my heart wanted to do over seeing Cruz like this. Neither me or Jay said what I knew both of us were thinking: Cruz had just tried to kill himself.

When we got to the hospital, Jay pulled up where the ambulances were supposed to park and started banging on the horn repeatedly. Some attendants ran outside instantly and surrounded the car.

"Cocaine overdose," Jay yelled, and the crew sprung into action. Less than a minute after we got there, Cruz was whisked away on a stretcher, Jay talking to a Hispanic nurse in Spanish.

I was left with the questions from the staff and I was ready to grab a scalpel and slice all of them 100 ways to hell until Jay popped back out from behind the swinging doors and grabbed me by the arm, dragging me through the heavy doors and into the room where they were working on Cruz.

"How long was he in his state? How long has he been

274

UNTRUST Deszion Nasir

on cocaine? How much did he take? What are his allergies, health problems..." They were bombarding me with a million and one questions but weren't answering any of mine.

Eventually they kicked us out of the room so they could work on Cruz and all we could do was wait. I wasn't very good at waiting and ended up pacing back and forth in the waiting room, barefoot until Jay stood up and came over to me. He put an arm around my shoulder and said "Walk with me."

"Walk with you where? We need to be here when the doctors come back out!"

"That won't be for at least an hour. They'll get him stabilized and move him to a room. They not gonna let us see him until then. You need some breakfast and some shoes," he added, looking down at my feet. I followed his gaze, looked at my bare feet, then around the room at the people who were staring at me like I might pull out a grenade any second and sighed. Jay took that as my surrender and I let him lead me out of the waiting room. He draped his arm over me while we were walking. Him touching me sent a chill through my body. I looked up at him with questions in my eyes.

"You were shaking," he said, not letting me go after seeing my expression but pulling me closer to him. I hadn't even realized it, but my whole body was twitching violently. Jay took me into the gift shop and found me some kid-sized slippers, the closest things to shoes he could find. He was paying for them and a couple more things for me he'd thrown on the counter-despite my protests-when an orderly pushing an old woman in a wheel chair did a double take.

"DJ LJAY!" he yelled, abandoning his task and letting the poor old lady crash into a lunch cart. He ran up to Jay and started going off about what had happened the other night and telling him how he escaped the shootout and all this extra bullshit that was drawing a lot attention our way. Jay was trying to push the cat away from him, pissed off that he was all in his ass in the middle of the hospital, but I saved him the trouble and smacked a new taste in dude's mouth.

275

UNTRUST Deszion Nasir

JAY

As the attendant's supervisor came running over, I pulled Sirron off him, tired of breaking up chick fights. He apologized to us for the man, and drug him off, fussing at him and running over to where the elderly woman was tilted over, trying to sit up on her own and cursing.

I looked over at Sirron, who was fuming and shaking her left hand, the one she slapped the orderly with.

"You got a shitty-ass temper, girl," I told her.

"Yeah, I've heard," she said, raking her hair out of her face and looking around. I walked her out to the hall and she realized we were right across the hall from the chapel. She surprised me when she reached out and took me hand. "Come pray with me, Jay?" she asked, her mood instantly switching back to one of a scared little girl. I was hesitant, but I couldn't look in those big brown eyes and tell her no. I hadn't been in a church since my father was killed. I'd spent a good deal of my life angry with God for allowing so many bad things to come into my life. I had since realized God didn't cause any of things, yet allowed them to happen for His own reasons, but I honestly didn't think He'd want to hear nothing I had to say because I'd ignored Him for so long. But I let Sirron drag me into the quiet room. She knelt down in front of the little altar and steepled her hands. I was feeling awkward but I folded my long legs down beside her and listened to her beg God for her cousin's life. I know we were supposed to be praying for Cruz, but I couldn't help silently throwing in some words for me and my sister, hoping we got out of this mess with our lives. When I finished, I felt peaceful, something I hadn't experienced for a long time. I looked up and saw Sirron sitting back on her heels, smiling softly at me.

"What?" I asked, not used to being stared at like that.

"Nothing…" Sirron climbed to her feet and pulled me to

UNTRUST Deszion Nasir

mine. We walked back to the waiting room slowly, her arms crossed, her head down.

"What you thinking about?" I asked her.

"You don't know Cruz real well, do you?" she asked me, glancing up at me.

I shrugged. "I 'on really know none of them cats like that, for real," I told her truthfully. "Started out as business and I kind of got caught up in everything..."

Sirron nodded. "Let me tell you something about my cousin. Cruz left New York because he had a hit on him. Years ago the kid you guys called Cruz was known around the hood as 'Jai the crackhead.' He had a real bad habit and he wasn't above kidnapping, trying to get ransom money for drugs."

"Damn,"

"Damn, indeed. Well, one of the cats he tried to rob was connected to a pretty ruthless organization and they came after him. Jai is damn near impossible to catch in a chase. He's always been like that, even when we was kids. After 2 months, the gang stopped trying to catch him and went to his mother's house and killed his mother, his sister, and his girlfriend, who happened to be pregnant with Jai's first child."

"Aw, damn," I muttered, my stomach turning over.

"Yeah... so... they killed everyone but me, cuz I was visiting my mother back in the Dominican Republic. When I came home and found out what happened, Jai had vanished. He eventually got in contact with me and told me he'd hitched a ride with this guy who was coming back to Virginia. Jai didn't really care where the guy was going, he just had to get out of NY. So, the guys get back here and by then the dude fed Jai and promised to get him in rehab. Jai was so grateful he decided to stay in VA and work for the guy. You get one guess as to who the guy was."

"Blue,"

Sirron nodded. "For Blue to kill Nina over this stupid shit, especially after he knew Jai'd already been through this

UNTRUST Deszion Nasir

before... it was like cutting out his heart. He specifically did that to destroy my cousin. He's the devil, Jay."

I was stunned and disgusted at the same time. Blue had too much control over lives he didn't give a shit about, including mine.

"I know me telling you all this is probably fucking you up, but you not like all of them, Jay," Sirron went on, stopping walking and grabbing my hand again. Her little hand was warm and it felt like I belonged in mine. I looked from our hands to her eyes. "You actually still have some of your soul left. You need to break away from them while you still have a life to live. Your sister is in deep, from what I hear and see. Now, I know you're probably gonna try to save her and end it trapped as deep as she is," Sirron sighed. "But I figured you should at least know what kind of people you're dealing with."

I smiled down at her. "You act like you give a fuck about a nigga or something," I told her. She just smiled. Sirron kept holding onto my hand and we went back into the waiting room. The attendant at the desk confirmed what I'd said earlier: there was no news yet. Sirron sighed and I led her outside to get some fresh air. While we were walking, we rounded the side of the building and were hit by a big burst of wind. It damn near blew Sirron back on her ass and I turned her back to the wind, laughing. She smiled up at me again, reached up, grabbed my collar, pulled me down to her level and kissed me hard. When she let me go, she laughed at what I'm positive was a shocked-ass look on my face.

"Happy birthday," she told me, reaching up and pushing my open mouth closed.

And even though I was spending my 17th birthday in a hospital, with some chick I barely knew, I didn't know where my sister was and my partner was almost dead in a cold room, I didn't wanna be anywhere else.

PART XVII-SNAP
CRUZ

When I opened my eyes it felt like I had died. The only reason I figured I was still alive was that if I was dead I always figured I wouldn't be in this much pain. I groaned and tried to move. Me moving around must have caught Sirron's attention, cuz the next thing I know she was standing over me, her eyes peering down at me. That's when I looked above her head and saw the florescent lights and not the ceiling fans that were in my room. I squinted my eyes at them and I realized I was in a hospital. The reason I was in a hospital came back to me. Instead of the feeling of sadness, I only felt dull and empty, like there was nothing inside of me. I stopped trying to move and laid back on the pillow, sighing painfully.

I heard more movement in the room and then Jay appeared, standing beside Sirron and looking down at me like he could see into my head. I tried to talk but when I opened my mouth, a weird ass noise came out. It sounded kinda like my voice, but like I'd been gargling barbed wire.

"Don't say nothing," Sirron instructed me, then ran out of the room and came back with a nurse and a doctor. They examined me and gave me the long version of what had happened. I tried to open my mouth again.

"Did you want to say something?" one doctor prodded. If I had been feeling better I would have spit in his eye. Instead, I looked over at Sirron and got out "You look like shit."

Everyone in the room laughed and relieved tears fell out of Sirron's eyes. She wiped them away before they streaked her chubby cheeks. "Don't you never do no stupid shit like that no more," she snapped, straightening up. I turned my head over to Jay and motioned with my hand for him to come here. He came and stood by my side.

"Sup, man?"

279

"Blue,…" I got out. Jay shook his head.

"Man, don't think ab-" something to his right caught his attention and he stopped talking. I followed his gaze and froze. Blue was standing in the doorway, holding a big ass basket of flowers like I was already dead. Angel was standing slightly behind him, peering into the room.

"What's good, big man? Heard you was doin bad, man," he said, smiling at me.

I forgot all about feeling empty as blinding rage ripped through me. A rush of adrenaline shot through me and I leapt from the bed, snatching needles out of my arm and knocking over equipment as I lunged for Blue. I tackled him and we both fell onto the used needle box, which crashed to the floor with us as we fell over onto the nurse, who screamed, pinned under Blue as I grabbed one of the used to needles and tried to stab him in the neck with it. The girls were screaming at us to stop and Jay was trying to break us up. He got tossed over the side of the bed, breaking up some more equipment.

Blue shoved me off of him. I hit my back on the edge of the bed, but I was so furious I ignored it, plus ignoring all the other pain in my body. I snatched up the portable blood pressure machine and hurled it at Blue's head. He ducked, and it clipped his head as it crashed through one of the glass walls. Other staff rushed in and held me and Blue apart. Sirron pushed through the crowd, saw Blue in the room and then she went at him full throttle. She grabbed a scalpel off the counter and stabbed Blue in the arm, drawing more blood. "You killed Nina you sonofabitch! You dirty, cold-hearted bitch!"

"What the fuck is she talking about?!" Blue yelled, shaking hospital security off of him like flies.

"You killed my baby, muthafucka! You gonna die for that! You hear me?! Fuck that nigga Vu, I'm the nigga you gotta worry about!" I yelled as the nurses strapped me down to the bed.

"Man, *fuck* you and that trick ass *bitch* of yours! That baby probably won't even yours noway. Guess you'll never

UNTRUST Deszion Nasir

get to see if it had my eyes or not, huh?" Blue laughed, wiping blood from his mouth.

My eyed widened and I yelled out like a trapped warrior, unable to free myself from being strapped down. I saw Angel's stricken face as she whirled on Blue. She slapped him across the face so hard she left a handprint on his face. "You fucked Nina too?!" she screamed.

"Who the *fuck* are you putting your hands on, bitch?" Blue roared, turning his fury on her. He back-handed her and she sailed out of the room on her ass, sliding down the hall. At that, Jay jumped into the fray again, pulling out a gun and firing a wild shot at Blue. He missed, but everyone got low, screaming. Blue ducked out of the room and Sirron was yelling for Jay to take Angel and run. I didn't see where Blue disappeared to but he wasn't stretched out on the floor so I figured once again he'd slithered his way out of another close call. But as security finally made it into the room and found no one, I knew it wouldn't be the end of me and Blue. That muthafucka had to die, and I was determined to be the one that finally put his snake-ass underground.

ANGEL

I hung my cell phone up when I saw Doe's truck pull up into the shopping center up the street from the hospital. After Blue'd attacked me I'd ran. The only thing that saved me from stabbing Blue with the knife in my pocket was the realization that security was running in our direction. I knew there weren't enough of them to detain everyone, so I'd snuck over to the emergency stairs exit and made my way downstairs and out an employee exit.

I was shaking from hurt and anger. My first instinct was to trash Blue's car, but the grown-up side of me picked another route and I pulled out my cell phone. I called Doe and he told me to keep walking away from the hospital until he called me back. When he did, I was nearly a mile away.

He pulled up in front of me and threw the passenger door open. He reached a hand out to pull me up into the truck, as I always had problems climbing into the huge vehicle with my short legs. As soon as my ass hit the seat Doe pulled off.

I broke down what had just happened and Doe's face contorted into a mask of anger. He didn't say anything until I was finished, then he shook his head, busting a right from Coliseum Dr. onto Mercury Blvd. "This shit is my fault, ma," he said, his eyes on the cars passing him with no signal.

"How is that shit your fault?" I demanded.

"I took you back to that motherfucker. I was just tryna get his head back in the fuckin' game so he wouldn't get all our asses murdered... some selfish shit," Doe muttered.

I sighed. "I'm grown. I could have said no. The only person who's at fault for how Blue acts is Blue," I recited, something I was determined to beat into everyone's heads, including mine.

I noticed Doe was getting on the I64 entrance that would take us 1st to the Hampton Roads Bridge Tunnel, then to Norfolk and Virginia Beach. "Where are you taking me?"

UNTRUST Deszion Nasir

Doe was silent a minute, then glanced at me, his eyes taking me in. "Home."

"You don't live this way."

Doe licked his lips. "There's a lot you don't know about me, Angel. There's a lot a whole lot of niggas don' know about me. One is that I own a house in Virginia Beach. "

"Does Blue know?"

"Naw, nobody does. I usually just stay at my condo out Hampton cuz I'm always there. Everybody be so focused on Blue that they don't realize he ain't the only nigga caked up. I keep telling ya'll, I don't work for Blue, we're partners. Who do you think put all the money into this shit at the beginning? A nigga never been broke. That don't mean I wasn't hungry, though. I was hungry for a fuckin life outside of the bullshit my parents wanted for me. I had to find my own damn way. But I'm not a cold-hearted businessman like Blue, and that's exactly what the fuck you need to be to be where we at. I don't have the overhead he does, though, cuz I'm not tryna be the boss. So all the cheddar I get belongs to me. I own 2 other homes. One in Miami and one in Aurora, Colorado."

"Colorado?"

"Don't sleep on Colorado. There's a lot of money there. I let everyone think I'm this big-for-nothing hired gun to stay under everyone's radar. I'm tryna keep it that way, too," he said, glancing at me a very serious look on his face.

"Who am I gonna tell?" I demanded.

"Your brother. You gotta keep everything I ever tell you close to your chest, Angel. You already know more about me than you need to."

"So why are you even doing this? Why not let me stay at another hotel or something?"

"Because the shit that nigga doin is reckless. I'm a killer, baby, born and raised. I was getting into shit my parents never knew about when I was still a shorty. He ain't making rational decisions right now and I'm not tryna get nobody I give a fuck about killed behind his dumb shit." He

UNTRUST Deszion Nasir

stopped talking.

Despite the situation, I smiled. "You give a fuck about a chick, huh?" I asked, leaning on the seat divider.

Doe's serious face changed and a grin escaped and danced around the freckles on his face. "You crazy, girl."

"But I'm right, though, ain't I?" I demanded, reaching over and sliding a hand up his huge arm.

"Quit playin, Angel," Doe said, some of the playfulness coming back into his voice.

I climbed over to his seat and sat in his lap, the huge seat making it possible for me to straddle him if I pulled my legs up and sat on them. I took his glasses off his face-he only wore them when he was driving- and kissed the side of his face while he tried to steer.

"You gonna get us in a car accident, girl," Doe said, but his right arm slipped around me, tightening around my waist as I bit his neck lightly. He grunted out his approval while trying to say in his lane. His hand slipped under my shirt and up my back. He unsnapped my bra and I wiggled out of it, unbuttoning my shirt and pulling his up so our skin could touch. He kissed me, keeping his eyes open so he could see around me. I could feel heat radiating off his whole body.

"You gonna make me think you in love or something," I warned him jokingly.

"What if I was?" he asked me, sliding his hand under my skirt and gripping the flesh that connected my thigh and my butt.

"Wait, what?" I asked, thrown off by his response.

"Come on, Angel. You think a nigga'd go through all this shit with you for some ass? You know I got a sea of pussy tryna drown me everywhere I go. Every time I *sneeze* I'm blowing horny bitches out the way. The shit I do for you I don't do for no other females," he insisted, sliding his fingers under the bands of my panties. "Long story, short, ma, I think I been in love wit your lil ass since I met you. I just ain't know it then."

I was so overwhelmed by what Doe'd just said I couldn't

UNTRUST Deszion Nasir

respond. When a man notoriously known for fucking and flinging women drops the "L" bomb, it was a big friggin deal. Sensing my surprise, Doe squeezed me tighter while he took an exit off the highway. Alicia Keys' "Butterflies" was bumping in the Bose speakers and I could tell Doe was having a harder time driving than he had been before. He finally pulled over on the side of a busy road. I realized we were still in Norfolk.

"I ain't gonna make it all the way home without being inside of you," Doe told me, putting the car in park.

"Doe, people can see us," I protested, trying to ignore how good his hands always felt on my body.

"No they can't," he said, pulling my shirt off of me. He was kinda right. He'd bought his truck out of state, so he had blackout windows. It was illegal in VA to have dark windows, but-

"Come on, Angel, you know you got love for this nigga," Doe rasped, reaching down and ripping my underwear off with little effort.

"Doe," I moaned as I felt him tugging on his belt buckle under me. He was kissing that spot behind my ear that had my left foot shaking.

"You know you love me, girl," he whispered, shifting around in his seat until he connected us and stole the breath from my body.

I wrapped my arms around his neck tightly as he slid me up and down.

"You want me to tell you that on the side of the road?" I asked, pushing his hat off of his head.

"I don't give a fuck about that shit. As long as you say it and mean that shit, that's all I give a fuck about," he said in between grunts. "Tell me, baby."

My eyes rolled in the back of my head. "I love you, Doe," I told him, meaning it with everything in me.

"Shit...say it again. Say it louder, Angel," he commanded, becoming more intense with his motions.

I did, and then I said it again and again. Still holding

onto me, Doe managed to crawl to the back of the truck where he proceeded to wear my ass out like he'd never done before. That truck was rocking so hard a complete idiot would know what was going on in here if he passed, but me and Doe were so far gone we didn't care. Doe finished with a mighty roar and almost tore my insides out. It took him a few minutes to be able to realize he had his full weight on me. He propped himself up on his elbows and looked down at me.

"Damn... you aight?"

I smiled at him while he wiped a tear out of my eyes. "You cryin and shit..."

"I'm just happy," I told him, leaning up and kissing him.

"You sure? You not just saying that cuz I broke ya back, are you?" he asked, grinning down at me, his dimples making him look like a teenager.

"No, stupid... I really meant that. I guess I just needed to say it, you know... to make it real."

Doe nodded. He looked me over like he was making sure he didn't break anything before he sat up. "Damn," he muttered, taking me in his arms and leaning back in the seat. "Got me out here acting like a fuckin kid and fuckin my money up," he shook his head playfully. I turned in his arms and kissed him, smiling. He returned the kiss for a little too long and seconds later, he was up again and we were back at it again. This time Doe damn near kicked out the side window on the truck. By the time we finally made it to Virginia Beach, I was totally drained.

Doe's house was beautiful. It wasn't as quite as big as Blue's, but it was on more land and it felt like people actually lived there, not like a big fancy museum where you couldn't touch nothing. You could tell Doe had grown up around nice things because even though his furniture and decorations weren't as high tech, they all matched perfectly and made the whole house seem rich and tasteful. He didn't have a cook, a maid or security. He did, however, have a Jack Russell terrier named Revelation who jumped on me the second she saw me and wouldn't let me out of her sight. Doe showed me around the house and took me to a gold and strawberry-colored guest bathroom so I could take a bath. While I was in the Jacuzzi-like tub surrounded in pink bubbles, Doe's slipped out, went to some kind of boutique and came back with a beautiful high-waisted pair of pants, a deep cut blouse the same color as my eyes and some matching amber ballerina flats, along with a satin bra and panty set.

"Where'd you get this?" I demanded over Revelation's barking, surprised as I saw it all lying on the bed when I came out of the bathroom in a huge towel. Doe had a "his and hers" bathroom that he admitted he never used. When he was home he just used the room downstairs. I was so touched, I dropped the towel. Doe licked his lips at me, walked over to the sound system and turned on a Jodeci CD. "Cry For You," filled the room like the group was there singing in our ears. Doe took his gear off, exposing that rock-hard body he kept hidden, and I laid him on his stomach. I massaged and kissed all the kinks out of his tight muscles and whispered words I'd had hidden in my brain for months in his ears while planting kisses all over his body. He finally turned me over and we were off on an hour trip this time. When we finally heard our stomachs protesting being mistreated and ignored, we cleaned up, got dressed, and Doe took me to Lynnhaven Mall to buy me all new things to have at his house. He didn't want me going back to my apartment in Hampton at all. Seemed like a good idea. Until we ran into one of the only people that could fuck up our perfect night.

TJ

"Oh, see, I like this," Sherita said, holding up a purple and black bustier set for me to look at. I could already see her body filling that outfit out and it was making my stomach growl. Me and Sherita had spoken everyday for the last couple of days since I came to her job. She finally had some free time so I picked her up and took her out to this mall so she could go to her favorite store, Torrid. This was the first time I'd been grateful to Blue. He'd given me a car and 50 stacks to hold me over until I decided what I wanted to do with myself upon my release from prison. Taking Sherita out was the first thing I'd done. I struggled with telling her about being in prison, but I figured it was too early to divulge all that info. Maybe I'd take it there once I saw where her head was at. If this didn't work out, I'd have less of a chance of her putting all my business in the street.

We were getting her some stuff and just talking when I saw Sherita's gaze land on something behind me. Whatever it was stole her smile and caused her to stop walking. I had been staring at her, so I didn't see what she'd seen. I turned my eyes in the direction hers were going in and saw the cause of her change in attitude.

About 30 people in front of us, Doe and Angel were walking this way, lost in their own world. Angel had her arm wrapped around Doe's waist and he had his heavy arm draped over her shoulder, pulling her curly-haired head against him and whispering in her ear and kissing on her like they were the only people in the building.

I sighed and realized I was about to end up in a real uncomfortable conversation. There wasn't even a point in trying to say anything to sway Sheritas's attention.

Doe was the one who felt eyes on him first. He looked up and around and after a few seconds his eyes landed on me and Sherita. He kept smiling, but when his met Sherita's you could faintly see the look of "Awww *shit*." in them. He

UNTRUST Deszion Nasir

slowed down and that's when Angel looked up. She didn't even pretend to be pleased at all. There was a Mexican standoff between the women while me and Doe-having previously talked about the two women- merely gave each other the "Whassup" nod.

Sherita opened her mouth first. "Look who's been downgraded to jump-off status," she hissed, crossing her arms, her shopping bags rattling.

Angel raised an eyebrow. "You talking 'bout jump-offs? What do we call you,? Left-over Lashay?"

"Whatever. I didn't have to fuck nobody to get attention."

Angel laughed. "Neither did I. You were at the club the other night, right? I was just sitting there minding my own business and *Doe* came to *me*."

"He was drunk."

"He's not now," Angel laughed.

"Like I said, I didn't fuck nobody to get here."

"Too bad for you," Angel tossed back, grinning. "And where exactly *are* you, anyway?"

Sherita lunged at Angel, but I grabbed her arm. "Be a lady," I told her.

Doe was holding onto Angel, who looked like she was ready to put Sherita 6 feet under. Doe leaned over and whispered something to her softly. Her whole face changed and she softened up immediately. She surprised me and Sherita both when she looked at us and said "I'm sorry, Sherita. I didn't have to take it there,"

Being that Sherita had started the fight at the club and the argument today, she looked taken back by the apology. Not knowing what else to say without looking like a bitch, she managed to say "No, I guess I'm sorry. It's not like me and Doe was all that serious, you know?"

I let out a breath. "Aight, now that we got that shit out of the way, I think we all need to sit down and talk," I said. The girls looked hesitant again, but Doe nodded. "Indeed, my man. C'mon, baby."

We all ended up at The Cheesecake Factory at a private table. The uneasiness was awkward for a minute, but Doe and Angel were so into each other there was no way to pretend the two of them didn't have it pretty bad for each other. At one point I leaned over to Sherita and whispered "You think we could end up like that one day?"

Sherita rolled her eyes. "Please, we'd be sooo much better than that."

I turned her face toward mine as Angel's phone rang. "How we ever gonna get there if you so hung up on what *they* doin?" I asked her. While Sherita was thinking of an answer, Angel put her finger to her ear to hear better. "WHAT? Where are ya'll at?... In Virginia Beach... long story... oh God..." Angel covered her mouth and Doe frowned, sensing the mood had been shot to hell. "Come up here... yeah, fine, bring her too... Come to Mount Trashmore Park when you pick her up...okay." Angel hung up and looked at all of our anxious faces. "That was Jay. Cruz went into cardiac arrest... someone broke into my apartment and set it on fire and went to Jay's house and smashed all of his equipment. Our mother is in Gary, Indiana for the family reunion so she's okay, but..." she shook her head. "Sirron done lost it. She passed out saying she was going to kill Blue. Jay's with her but he's gonna sneak her out of the hospital."

I saw Doe sit back and take his hat off from the new stress. "This shit is mad crazy, man. Blue's ass is gonna fuck around and kill all of us, fuck that nigga Vu. What we gonna do about your folks, man?" he asked, looking at me.

I sat my fork down and wiped my mouth before answering. "Kill him."

PART XVIII-CHECKMATE
BLUE

I sat in my office in the dark, waiting. I picked up my bottle of Jack Daniels and tried to take a swig from it, but I only got a couple of drops. I looked at the bottle and realized it was empty. It'd been empty since the last 3 times I'd tried to drink from it. I took my other hand and rubbed the blunt out I'd been smoking. If I was steady tryna drink from empty bottles it was time to put this shit out. I was sitting in the doorway to hell and being full up with liquor was just gonna make me catch on fire faster.

I was waiting on them to come for me. Who? Anyone who was gunning for me. In short, everybody. I knew them muthafuckaz was out there somewhere...

I looked down at the report sitting in front of me on my desk. The light from the moon pouring through my skylight was shining directly on the thick stack of paper, making it possible for me to read without turning on the light. I shouldn't have been surprised by what I was looking at, but I was.

A phone call from Jamaica had set my mood into fuckedupitis. Siovahn's mother had called me ranting, raving, cursing and threatening to put all kinds of voodoo shit on me because Siovahn had been killed in Japan. She had Azzure' and I'd never get him back. In all honesty, that worked out for me. I didn't have to deal with her stupid ass no more and Azzure' was most likely safer in Jamaica than here right now anyway. When it was safe for him to come home, nothing in heaven or hell could stop me from getting him. Nothing.

Niggaz didn't understand how my mind worked. I had to make the decisions other muthafuckaz ain't wanna make to keep shit moving and running. Nobody had the heart to do what the fuck I did. You can call me cold, evil, the Devil or what-the-fuck-ever, the King had to do what the fuck he had

291

to do to keep the kingdom running. Especially when all the kingdom's subjects had lost their fuckin minds.

Had I made all good decisions? Of course not. Everybody fucks up sometimes. Problem was, when you were on top, you're put there cuz you're expected to make the best decisions. When I fucked up, I caught the most hell.

I sighed and sat back, waiting for the papers in front of me to change. They didn't.

The silence in the house was fucking with me. Jasmine hadn't been back to the house since the club fight. I'd fired all my security after I'd gotten shot at, and TJ never made a sound when he was in the house. I didn't sweat him too much, though. He just got unlocked and you had to give the man time to enjoy being free for a minute before you got him back to work.

Oh, I hadn't forgotten about Vu's monkey ass. But I knew he was waiting on me to come after him. And trust and believe I WAS coming. But not when the fuck HE wanted me to. I knew Azzure' won't in no danger otherwise I would have heard from Vu's bitch ass by now. I know the mind games the nigga was playing. I was playing smart. No matter what other niggaz thought, I was smarter than every nigga around me. That's why I was on the top of all this shit. And it was true what the old heads say: it's lonely up here. I'd fucked up with my woman, she was gone, but I knew she still loved a nigga. I cain't worry about her, now. I just hope whatever she was doing now was worth it. I blame myself for that shit anyway. Tryna wife a crazy –ass broad like her…for tryna wife any bitch, period. Bitches take up too much work and too much energy. At least, that's what I was tellin myself when I heard someone moving around in my house. I froze in my chair.

The sound was coming from the far back end of the house. I quietly picked up a remote in my right hand and clutched the gun on my left with the other hand. I hit a button on the remote and my security cameras popped up. I searched around until I saw a figure staying against the wall in the

UNTRUST Deszion Nasir

shadows of my pool room. I couldn't tell who it was cuz whoever was sneaking in my house seemed to know I had cameras and was staying just out of range. I briefly wondered how the hell they got around my security system. Then I realized for someone to even be in my house told me a few things: 1. They'd been in my house before 2. They had some knowledge of electronics to be able to override my high-tech security system and 3. They wasn't scared of dying.

The person disappeared from my view and I stood up, pushing my chair back. They had to be coming back here. They knew I was back here. He wasn't even checking around in any other part of the house. Another thought went through me: My shit had been hacked into right under my fuckin nose.

I dropped down out of the sight of my camera, my survival mode switch flipping on. I grabbed the sawed-off strapped under my desk so now I had two guns on me. I crawled over into the shadows and waited for the intruder to come in the room. It was the only way in the room.

Suddenly, the hairs on the back of my neck stood up. Something flashed out of the corner of my eyes and told me to jump to my right. I did, and narrowly missed getting shot in the head. A bullet sank into the wall where my head used to be, the bullet coming so close to me it had skimmed by my face, leaving a stinging sensation across the left side of my face. By the time I'd rolled out of the way and fired back, the person who'd shot at me was gone and the door to my office was trying to be kicked down. My shotgun blast blew the door off the hinges, but I missed the intruder. Now aware that there were two of the muthafuckaz, I got up, kicked over my desk that I'd had bullet-proofed a few years ago for such an occasion. I drug it over in a corner and crouched down behind it, listening.

At first all I heard was my own breathing, so I closed my eyes to focus an extra sense on my hearing. Very, very faintly I heard movement. I put my cheek to the ground and felt light vibrations coming from somewhere near the door. Whoever was creeping in here was on their hand and knees. I

UNTRUST Deszion Nasir

could tell by the pattern of movement. I silently put my .45 in my left hand —one of the things the street taught me was to learn to shoot w/ both hands cuz an enemy don't care if you're left-handed or right-handed-and without moving any part of my body other than my arm, I kept my eyes closed and aimed the gun around the desk at a target I couldn't see. I fired once, and heard a body drop. Shots were immediately returned from another direction, I'm guessing the window where that sucka-ass muthafucka tried to get at me before. When they realized the desk was bulletproof, I heard them retreat. Shit won't gonna be that easy. I jumped up and ran after them, guns blazing. As soon as I rounded a corner I saw feet and an arm hurling something at me. Whatever it was broke when it hit the ground and exploded. I fell back on the ground and covered my eyes as fire rushed over my head. Their punk ass had gotten their partner and hauled ass, but he was lugging a corpse I figured. There was blood all over my carpet. I jumped back and ran to Jasmine's abandoned room, which was near the front of the house. I blew her windows open so I wouldn't have to stop and open it and jumped through it just as another explosion went off. I landed in the bushes and rolled on the cool grass of my front yard. I rolled like I was a Marine and sprung to my feet just in time to see a door slam and a car try to screech off. I got to my feet and took off for the car at top speed. I fired on the car until it swerved a few houses away and crashed into a light pole. I was ready to murder anything moving when I saw someone lifting a grenade launcher out of the broken back window. I got low as they fired, heard a WHOOSH! and turned on back to see my house go up in flames as the grenade blew my living room to hell. I covered my head as debris flew everywhere and landed all around me. By the time I could lift my head and I got to my feet, the crashed car was empty. As I stood there, panting, cut up and pissed off, all I could do was watch my brand new house burn to the fuckin ground.

By the time the fire department got there, the only thing left standing were my fire-proof safes and a few walls. I

294

wanted to kill everyone within spitting distance, but I couldn't. Wrapped in frozen, silent rage I had to sit there and answer a million fucking questions from 5-0 and firemen. I HAD to let them take me downtown to file a bullshit report just to keep the peace. After all, I was supposed to be a legit businessman and it'd look suspect as hell if I didn't report this shit. I didn't have a phone, key to my other spots or nothing on me. The chief asked was there anyone I wanted to call and the shit hit me: I couldn't call nobody. Anybody I knew could be behind this shit. Anybody. I got a cop to take me to get some money and spare keys and shit out of a safe. I'd come back here later to get my fire. All I had right now was the shit in my truck, which had been parked on the street and not in the driveway so it just had some scratches on it from the explosion. I ended up at the Courtyard Marriott for the night. As I sat in my bullshit rented room I plotted. I had memorized everything on the report I was reading before I got attacked.

So... everybody wanted to shit on a nigga now, huh? Muthafuckaz I feed tryna take *my* head? I had something for they asses. All of them. If I couldn't get the one who did it I'd kill all their unloyal asses. At least at the end of the day I'd know I'd gotten the right one...*fuck* family. It's all me, nigga. Always had been, and at the end of the day, it still would be... believe that...

JASMINE

"Lucky, talk to me."

"Jasmine, I already told you I don't have time for this shit right now."

"Why're you yelling? You cain't get your fuckin point across without yelling like a bitch?"

"Can you get yours across without turning into one?"

That stupid-ass question was responded to by an open-faced smack across the face. Lucky balled his fists up, curled his lips under, and walked away from me, slamming the front door as he left the apartment.

Frustrated and having no one to vent to, I fell back on the couch, smacking the magazines I'd been looking at onto the floor. Shit had been real stressful since the shooting at Blakeley's. Lucky wouldn't let me go back to the house. Fine, I get it. But a bitch like me needs shit. So if you expect me to treat this like it's my house, it needs to look like my house. Me and Lucky had been arguing for the last hour about why we needed new furniture and why we didn't. I wasn't used to being questioned by anyone so the conversation had turned real ugly real fast. Lucky eventually was like "Fuck it, I'm done talking about it," but of course the conversation wasn't over with until I decided I was finished talking about it... hence the argument you just walked in on.

I heard Lucky coming back inside and I braced myself for round 2 of the fight, but the look on his face and the way he was clutching his phone told me some more new bullshit was on the horizon.

"What is it now?" I demanded, rolling my blue eyes.

Lucky hesitated minute. "Sit down, Jas."

Ice shot through my veins. Everybody knows when someone tells you to sit down, shit was about to get real serious. I sat down, my nerves starting to get the best of me. "Is it Blue? What happened to him?"

UNTRUST Deszion Nasir

Something in the corner of Lucky's eyes flashed. "It's not Blue... Cruz went into cardiac arrest at the hospital, Jas."

"Oh, God...is he-is he dead?"

Lucky kept his composure, but he nodded. "Someone killed Nina, too."

"OH GOD!" I screamed. "The baby-" but I already knew the baby was dead. Nina wasn't far enough along for the baby to survive, even with the help of doctors. Through tears I looked up at Lucky and saw that there was more. "What else, Lucky?"

"Someone tried to kill your brother, baby. He got away... but they blew the house up. The house is gone and nobody knows where Blue is."

"He's... he's not dead?"

"No, nobody was killed... but his ass got in the wind. I'm sorry, love," Lucky came over to me and wiped my wet face.

I was shaken, but somehow not surprised. I always knew someone would come for my brother one day... I just never imagined I go down like this. I was ashamed to admit it, but I knew this day was coming and secretly I was just glad I hadn't been home to be a victim of Blue and his bullshit. I loved my brother but I also saw him for who he was and I knew karma would never let him keep killing and terrorizing people without coming to claim him. What he did to Dejah in that video still gave me nightmares.

"Who was that who just called you?" I asked, curious.

"Doe. He said someone called and he didn't recognize the number so he didn't answer. They left him a message with their voice distorted and after he heard it he tried to call it back but the operator was saying they couldn't accept the call."

"A payphone," I guessed.

"I'm thinking," Lucky agreed, nodding. "But what I *do* know is that Blue is gonna come after every nigga who he *thinks* is tryna do him dirty." Lucky went over to where he kept his guns locked up and started pulling assorted firearms

297

out.

"What, you think he's coming after you?" I asked, not wanting to believe that.

"Jas, I know that's your brother but check it: whoever got close enough to Blue to blow up his fucking house *had* to know how to get in his fucking house. Now, you know and I know it's only a few select muthafuckaz who been in ya'll house, let alone know how to get in... so my guess is that he's coming for every head he can get a bead on... and you know how often I'm wrong," Lucky added, slamming a clip in a gun.

I was well aware of how often Lucky was wrong about something-next to never.

Numb from the news, I let Lucky speed me along in packing some stuff up real quick as he proceeded to get me away from his house. He only grabbed a duffle bag full of money before he was dragging me to the door. As soon as the door opened a bullet whizzed past our heads and sank into the picture me and Lucky took at Sears mounted on the wall. I screamed and fell to the ground. I felt Lucky toss me back into the house and I landed on my side. Before the pain had a chance to register Lucky was throwing the bag and keys at me as he fired back out the front door.

"Go out the back!" he yelled, ducking behind a wall.

"I can't get to the car!" I screamed.

"My bike is in the back!"

"I can't drive a motorcycle!" I screeched.

"Then it's *muthafuckin* time to learn," Lucky yelled, scrambling for an assault rifle in his closet.

"Lucky-"

"Jas if you don't get your ass out of here and on that bike I'ma shoot you my *damn* self," Lucky yelled. I grabbed the bag and ran out of the back door of Lucky's condo, crying. I got the bike started and fell over the first time I tried to take off. Lucky had been trying to teach me but I'd only had a few lessons and none of them included riding on my own. But the sounds of gunshots and police sirens sent my mind into

UNTRUST Deszion Nasir

survival mode and I managed to get the bike up and moving. I was wobbly, but I got it together and pulled out onto the road. As I passed the front of Lucky's house I saw a familiar crayon-blue SUV parked behind a wall, the doors open. With my heart in my chest I pulled off onto the main street, leaving behind me the sounds of gunshots and the shouts and curses of the two men I loved the most.

DOE

There was silence in the living room of my apartment back in Hampton. I had gotten a call from a woman who *sounded* like Jasmine but she was screaming into the phone, all hysterical and shit. I ain't have no idea what in the hell she was talking about but I heard "Shooting" and "Blue" and told her to meet me at my apartment. After that uncomfortable-ass gathering at the Cheesecake Factory, we all had gone our separate ways with heavy hearts. Being a sitting duck wasn't a position I was used to playing and the shit wasn't sitting right with me. Hearing Jasmine screaming that Blue had tried to kill her and Lucky left me feeling even worse. Lucky had a hell of a point-blank range, and he never missed a shot, but he'd never had to go up against Blue before. The fact that he hadn't gotten in contact with anyone in a few hours pretty much told me what I needed to know as far as Lucky's status. A sick feeling had taken a new home in my gut.

"So, now what? We just sit around waiting for his ass to pick us off one-by-one?" Sirron snapped. She looked years older than normal. Actually, she usually looked about 14 so now she looked 25 or so, but to people who knew her, you could see she was drained and exhausted, her usual gold color ashy and pale-looking.

"You can't just run around trying to find his ass. If Blue don't wanna get found, he ain't gonna get found," Jasmine snapped, her frustration coming out loud and clear. "Who the hell *is* she, anyway?" Jasmine snapped to no one in particular.

Sirron's response was to lunge across my coffee table at Jasmine. She was already on edge and Jasmine's thoughtless attitude was just enough to set her off. She caught Jasmine in the face with her fist and her ring left a long scratch across Jasmine's previously unmarked face.

"Awww, *dayum*," Jay moaned a second before Jasmine

UNTRUST Deszion Nasir

screamed and tackled Sirron. Sirron happened to be sitting next to Angel and before she could jump out of the way, her hair had gotten snatched and she fell backwards on top of the other two women. The brawl was now a catfight.

As the three women rolled around on my floor, cursing, screaming and fighting, me and Jay looked at each other, both of us wondering whether to break the fight up or let them beat the hell out of each other so they'd all shut the fuck up. When they fell through my glass coffee table me and Jay broke it up.

"Hey, HEY!" Doe roared, his voice damn near cracking the windows. The three females quieted, but glared at each other from different corners of the room.

"Look, ya'll is emotional right now, so that's why ya'll acting like you don't got no fuckin home training," Doe said, glaring at each of them. "Nobody has time for this shit. We already talked about what we have to do and the first thing we gotta do is get the fuck out of this apartment. The only reason I let everyone come here is so we can all get on the same page. Are ya'll gonna keep clucking or are ya'll emotional asses gonna try and make it to sunrise?"

FINALE

Covered in blood, and insanely homicidal, Blue took his binoculars down from his face on the roof of a nearby building, his midnight blue eyes narrowed. His darkest side had come out and the demon was loose. Any semblance of normalcy was trapped in a titanium box as he tried to focus his kill shot on the people closest to him. The first person he got in his focus was Angel. His brain ricocheted back to the report he was reading before his house was blown up. He closed his eyes, but the data on the page never changed. It contained pictures and other data about Angel and Doe in various places, the most recent being at a mall. There was a picture of them fucking in Doe's truck, there were pics of Doe leaving Angel's apartment. Dates, places and times, all spelled out. Blue didn't know which of his snitches kept sending him shit but he figured it was someone scared to cross Doe. Contained in the same report were pics of Angel sitting at a table at a restaurant with TJ and Sherita. All of them were plotting on him, huh? They all figured they were smarter than him? Niggas seemed to always forget who ran shit in VA. It was cool. He'd lay all they asses down, wipe em out, start over. Maybe he'd move somewhere new and run shit there. He had the money, the connections and the balls for that kind of shit. But first things first...Blue squinted one eye to get a better shot...

BANG!

Doe vanished from Blue's sight.

Doe hit the ground instantly. Angel screamed and fell to the ground next to him, but he reached up and snatched her flat on the ground.

"Stay down!" he commanded. Everyone else was in the living room, screaming and asking what was going on.

Doe looked down at Angel, then himself. No one was bleeding. Doe looked up at the window. It wasn't broken.

UNTRUST Deszion Nasir

"Where the fuck did the shot come from?" he demanded.

Blue rolled on his back, clutching his hand. Blood was leaking out of the hole in his useless right hand. Blue looked up into the face of a ghost. The person who shot him grinned down at him. "You ain't the only nigga with a plan B, muthafucka."

BANG!

Clutching his favorite Berettas, Doe ran outside, guns drawn, ready to go up against Blue and all his madness. He'd yelled at Jay to stay inside with the girls. When he ran outside, what he saw on the top of the apartment building next to his made him freeze. He blinked a couple of times, then yelled for the other people to come outside. When they came out to where Doe was, they followed his astounded gaze. Sirron, the most surprised, fainted.

Blue was staring up into the bruised face of Cruz. He was beat up and obviously still in pain, but the hate in his eyes was overpowering any pain right now.

Blue was clutching his right arm, grimacing in pain from the second slug Cruz'd put in him.

"What was the first thing you taught me, man?" Cruz demanded. He was so furious he was drooling and shaking in anticipation of killing Blue. "Make sure your mark is dead before you celebrate? Ain't that assassin 101, nigga?"

"Cruz," Blue said in a controlled voice, clutching his arm like a broken wing. "I'm not the nigga who killed Nina, man."

"You a *fuckin* lie, nigga!" Cruz yelled. "Nobody would have a reason to kill her. Ain't nobody else got a heart as fucked up as yours! You killed my seed, yo!"

"Cruz!" Blue yelled. "I'm a whole lot of shit. You know I ain't perfect, nigga. But I would neva kill your seed, man." Blue took a staggered breath. He turned and looked around him. He finally noticed Doe and the others staring at him down in the parking lot. He frowned, grimaced, and tossed some folded papers at Cruz's feet. "Someone emailed

UNTRUST Deszion Nasir

me this shit this morning."

Suspicious, Cruz snatched the paper up, keeping his gun trained on Blue. He opened the paper and stared at it. What he saw didn't make sense to him. He looked down at his crew.

"Muthafucka!" he screamed, redirecting his gun at the person who'd murdered Nina.

All eyes followed the barrel of Cruz's gun to Angel. She narrowed her eyes but didn't flinch.

There was a stunned silence.

"Awww *shit*..." Doe yelled, his face unbelieving. "Are you fuckin *serious*?"

"What the fuck did you kill her for??" Cruz screamed, as Jay's face went from shock to horror.

Angel never took her eyes off Cruz. "After the shoot out, I had to drive Doe's truck. I had to get somewhere before I wrecked the SUV. I ran up on your house, Cruz. When I banged on the door, Nina came out cursing and screaming and shit about how I broke her sleep. I tried to tell her what happened and she went off talking all this shit about how all of us are beneath her and her man and she'd be sooo glad when we all killed each other off so she and her man could move on with their lives. I asked her did Cruz know she was talkin that shit and the bitch goes 'Hoe, I'm talking about *Blue*.' I fuckin snapped, grabbed a knife off the kitchen counter and *yes*, I *gutted* that bitch!" Angel screamed. "Then I took my ass back to the truck and left with Doe."

"That don't make no fuckin sense! Why would you let me take you *back* to Blue if you knew he was fucking Nina?" Doe yelled.

Angel narrowed her eyes at Blue. "To bug his house."

While Doe and Angel screamed on each other, Cruz was trying to come out of shock. He whirled on Blue a second too late. Blue kicked his foot out and kicked Cruz's legs from under him. Cruz waved his arms, but feel back, hitting his

UNTRUST Deszion Nasir

head on the edge of the building before toppling over it and landing with a sick thud on the freshly laid black tar of the parking lot. The way his neck was snapped made it clear he wouldn't be pulling another magic trick out of his ass.

"You blew up Blue's house?" Doe yelled at Angel, who still had her fire eyes on Blue.

"You muthafuckin right I blew that bitch up. I would have *killed* his monkey ass if this simple bitch here hadn't fucked around and got clipped-" Angel stepped to Sirron's prone figure and snatched up the hem of her shirt to reveal a bandage around her torso. "She had her own shit to get off on him because of how he carried Cruz."

"But that was you!" Doe yelled.

"She didn't know that," Angel shrugged, her eyes cold. "I *told* you you'd fucked up, nigga, didn't I?" Angel screamed up at Blue.

"ANGEL!" another voice screamed. Everyone turned and saw Lucky standing in shock to the side.

"You're not dead?" Angel's eyes bugged out.

"No, he's not, bitch" Jasmine spoke up, swinging a porch chair at Angel's head. The heavy wood connected with her skull and Angel was laid out. She spit on Angel and straightened up. "Gutter trash,"

Lucky stepped over to Angel and searched her, pulling out a burner phone. "This is where all the fuckin mysterious calls were coming from.," he snapped, disgusted.

"She played all your stupid asses!"Blue screamed from the roof. "As soon as a bitch open her mouth, fuck me and *all* the shit I did for ya'll! I expect that shit out of you Lucky. You feel sorry for her ass cuz you fucked her crazy. But *Doe*? You fuckin turn snake on my ass over some *pussy*?!"

"Hold up. Lucky you fucked Angel?" Jasmine demanded.

"Fucked her pregnant. And check this shit: that's his *cousin*, yo!" Blue yelled out. Now everyone was looking at Lucky. Jasmine went at Lucky with balled fists. While they were fighting, Angel, having never really lost consciousness, reached in her boot and pulled a gun out. She aimed it at Jasmine, knowing Jas was distracted. As she pulled the trigger, Blue yelled out and fired at the same time Angel did. Jasmine's long body dropped to her knees, a bullet hole in her temple. She glanced at Lucky with one last blue-eyed stare before she fell forward on him. A few feet away, Angel dropped her gun and fell to her side, the gun sliding away from her.

"Noooooo!!!!!" Jay screamed as he ran to his sister's side. He rolled her over and saw the lifeless look in her eyes. Shaking, he looked around, saw his sister's gun, snatched it up.

"JAY! DON'T DO IT!" Doe yelled, then paused when Jay turned the gun in Lucky. "Didn't I tell you if anything happened to her I'd *kill* you, nigga?"

Doe jumped in front of him. Lucky was still clutching Jas's lifeless body. "Jay, listen, little homie. I know you fucked up right now. I know it. This ain't the way to do it man. You the only one here who got a life after this, man…I ain't never begged nobody for shit, yo… but I'm beggin you now, man… get your *girl*-" He nodded at Sirron, "-and get the *fuck* out of here."

Jay's eyes bounced from Doe to Lucky to Blue and back to Doe again. After what seemed like forever he nodded. "I'm takin my sister," he said, his voice raw.

"Cool, man." Doe stepped back and watched as Jay drug Angel's body to his car. He put her in the back, then came and picked up Sirron, who was moaning and groaning and disoriented. He looked back at the death and bad choices behind him one last time before he jumped in the truck and screeched off, on lookers scared to move that had peeked out of their windows.

Lucky, Doe and Blue were left staring at each other. Lucky, tears on his face, looked up at Blue. "Look at her!" he yelled. "I told you your bullshit was gonna get her killed, man!" he said, looking back down at Jasmine.

"Oh, you ain't have nothing to do with this shit? Fucking

UNTRUST Deszion Nasir

a family member? Nigga *you* brought all this shit on yourself when *you* brought that crazy bitch to *me*!" Blue roared, trying to climb to his feet. "Nigga instead of screaming on me you *need* to take that gun and just suck that metal dick, yo!"

Lucky stared at Blue a minute, then just as Doe realized what was about to go down he yelled "Lucky!" but it was drowned out by one more blast as Lucky snatched a gun off the ground and opened his own face up with it, brain and bone going everywhere before his body fell on top of Jasmine's.

Police sirens were sounding in the distance. Blue and Doe looked at each other in a standoff. Neither was sure why, maybe there was a little of their brotherhood still lingering, but both turned and retreated, feeling enough blood had been shed for a lifetime. They never laid eyes on each other again.

UNTRUST Deszion Nasir

EPILOGUE
2 WEEKS LATER

Vu strolled through the corridor of his brand-new mansion, eager to see his sister. Minya had been located hiding out in Miami, scared for her life. She had finally broken down and called Vu, and he immediately had sent for her. He wanted to wring her neck, but she had to be brought back intact for her marriage to an important Yakuza official.

She looked beautiful as usual, and was the spitting image of their mother. As Vu hugged her to him, he could feel her shaking with emotion.

"Finally found your way home, huh?" he grinned. He had been furious all the way home from Okinawa after an important meeting with some businessmen.

Minya wasn't smiling and Vu realized her emotion wasn't joy. I was fear. Vu took a step back and finally looked around him in the great room where Minya'd been sitting.

Surrounding the large room, lined up around the walls, were the bodies of most of Vu's security. There was blood all over his freshly painted walls and inefficient fire arms were scattered all around, some men still clutching theirs.

"What-?" Vu began, then he noticed Minya looking over his head. Vu spun around and came face-to-face with his blue-eyed demon.

"What's up, Bro?" Blue asked, right before he took the gun in his hand and put two in Vu's chest. As he collapsed, he looked up and saw Minya standing over him, Blue beside her.

"I told you to leave it alone," Minya told him, glaring down at him. "You never listen to me, you never respect me or treated me like I mattered. You won't ever use me for *shit* again," she spat, right before she raised a .22 and closed her older brother's eyes forever.

9 WEEKS LATER

Blue was pushing his new Bentley through the streets of

UNTRUST Deszion Nasir

Atlanta where he'd relocated. He's set Minya up with a few shops here, knowing her skills as a stylist would make her a ton of money in a city full of women. Some chick he'd picked up downtown had her head in his lap, pleasing him on his way to the airport. He had no idea what her name was but she was damn good at what she was doing. He was trying to make his flight to Jamaica to go see Azzure', but the traffic was terrible.

"This shit's in the fuckin way, man," he said crossly.

"Don't worry, baby, I can keep your mind off traffic," the girl said, pausing to wipe her mouth and smile up at him.

Blue smirked down at her and grabbed her head to shove himself back in her mouth as the luxury car slowed under a bridge. Blue was settling to let her finish her job in the gridlocked traffic and had just closed his eyes when something heavy landed on the hood of the car. Blue's eyes snapped open and he was horrified to see a pair of feet and legs standing in front of his windshield. Blue instantly grabbed his groupie by the hair and snatched her in front of him as his windshield shattered and bullets sank into the screaming female. Blue hit the gas, rammed the car in front of him and sent the assailant flying off his car. Everyone around him immediately began screaming, running and abandoning their cars in an effort to retain their lives.

Tossing the girl's body off of him Blue reached under his seat for his glock. By the time his hands slid over it bullets were blowing the lock and handle off his car.

Blue fired out his window but he didn't see anyone. Suddenly someone jumped on the back of the car and leapt onto the roof, prompting Blue to simultaneously fire at the roof of the car. He obviously missed because a second later a huge hand reached in from on top of the car and grabbed him. Blue was totally knocked off his square by the force of the man holding onto him, never having experienced the feeling of being over-powered before. He was pulled through the open window and tossed on the asphalt, knocking the wind out of him and causing him to see stars as his head hit the

309

UNTRUST Deszion Nasir

ground hard, his back and scalp slicing open via the ground and broken glass.

When his eyes focused, Blue looked up in surprise into the green eyes of his brother, TJ.

"TJ?! What the *FUCK*, MAN?!" Blue yelled, grabbing his head. He looked at his hands at the blood, glass and debris covering his fingers. "Why you doin this?"

TJ spat blood out of his mouth. "Because you ain't never gonna stop," TJ growled. "I *told* you that you were just like Gemini, and all you done ever did was prove me right. I cain't ever sleep at night knowing another devil like him is walking around above ground."

"Come on, brother, I got you out of prison, man," Blue yelled, angry and hurting.

"And *I* told *ya'll* to leave me the fuck alone a *long* time ago. You shoulda listened to me, son. But instead you tried to carry me like a *chump*-ass nigga; thinking I was gonna kiss your maggot-ass just cuz you got me out of a place you agreed I never should have been in the *first* gatdayum place."

"My son, man," Blue started, but TJ hit Blue in the face with his gun, not buying the sudden change of heart bullshit.

"Oh, yeah, you *just* like your fucking daddy. He didn't give a *fuck* about his kids and neither do you. It's too late for *me*, it's too late for *you*, but *that* boy got a chance to do something with his damn life and I ain't gonna let *you* fuck that up for him." His face twisted into a gruesome smile, his voice a tortured, hoarse whisper. "And by the way, nigga…you remember when Jas went to NY when she was in high school? *I* know what the fuck you did, you faggot-ass nigga." Blue's eyes narrowed, then widened as the memories flowed back in his diseased brain. "I know *everything*. And so does she. But I ain't God. You get *no* redemption, *no* forgiveness from me, fuck-boy." His whole face twisted into the same mask of hate and evil their father carried.

"Fucking *bitch*-ass muthafucka. Gemini shoulda killed you when your fucking mother died," Blue spat in a different voice.

UNTRUST Deszion Nasir

TJ was silent for a minute. "He should have...but he didn't. When you get to hell, tell him Terrance said 'What's good?'"

With that, TJ pulled a knife from his jacket and snatched it across Blue's throat. Blue was a rabid animal, so he should have died like one: execution style. There would be no quick, merciful death from a bullet for him.

As Blue's blood spurted all over TJ and the highway, his cold eyes refused to close as his already soulless body transitioned from this life into his much deserved spot in hell.

The police had been called but unable to get to the scene due to traffic and new chaos. That gave TJ the opportunity to get back to where Sherita was waiting on a motorcycle. She quickly handed him a helmet and scooted back so TJ could climb on the bike and zoom them away to their future.

On a little island off of Oahu, Jay's cell phone vibrated. He quickly picked it up so he wouldn't wake up Sirron, who was asleep in his arms. The text message simply read "Gracias." Jay grinned, and turned his phone off. He kissed Sirron on top of her head. He looked at the edge of the water and waved at the woman trying to surf and her instructor, who was trying to keep her from drowning. He'd probably have an easier time of it if he'd stop rubbing his hands over her fresh tattoo that was hiding the bullet wound on her midnight skin.

Angel and Doe waved back.

UNTRUST Deszion Nasir

HERE'S A SNEAK PEAK AT *WICKED BLUES*, THE STORY OF WHAT STARTED IT ALL...
PROLOGUE
ST. MARTIN PARRISH, LOUISIANNA

A 16-yr. old girl ran through the muddy swamp water, clutching something in her arms. Fearfully, she glanced behind her, making sure her pirogue was still tied to the tree she'd hidden it behind. Her heart raced. It was still there. She didn't have much time before she was found. But if by some small chance she escaped, she'd need her pirogue. It bobbed against the swamp plants, almost seeming to be waving goodbye to her. She shivered, turned in the cold water and tramped through the marsh to drier land, her legs more tired than they'd ever been, her arms growing heavier by the second. She heard a dog barking across the swamps, and knew they were gaining on her. She ran for what seemed like hours, but was actually around 10 minutes, until a dim light shone through the night and gave her hope. She stumbled up to the raggedy door and pounded on it with one hand, clutching her other around what she had hidden inside her shabby coat.

A minute later, the door swung open and a middle aged woman with silver hair that made her look older despite the lack of wrinkles on her face was gazing down at her. Her face held no emotion or surprise to find a terrified girl shivering at her door.

"Please, Madame Touroux," the girl gasped. "Please help me. They gon' kill me."

"Who, child?"

"Monsieur Landry. "

UNTRUST Deszion Nasir

Madame Touroux looked down at the bundle in the girl's arms as it squirmed. She sighed and stepped back inside her house. The girl rushed inside gratefully. As Madame closed the door, the girl's hood fell away some and a heavy lock of silky, raven-colored hair fell into her ice-blue eyes. Madame sighed to herself.

"The pretty ones always cause all the trouble for me," she told the girl, picking her up by the arm and setting her down on an old settee. "Lemme see what the fuss about, child."

The girl slowly handed the bundle to Madame, who moved the rags used as a blanket from around it and looked down into the ice-blue eyes of a baby boy.
"
This here a beautiful one," Madame commented, smiling. She looked at the young girl closely. "You been in this kinda trouble before, ain't you?'

The girl lowered her blue eyes. "He took the last one…sent him off to some place, some island I never heard of. But I was to keep this one. He told me I could keep him and he'd let me leave…"

Madame sat back and sighed. Monsieur Landry was known for dabbling in between the creamy thighs of black Creole girls, much to the distress of his wife and the rest of New Orleans. A mayor mingling with black girls wasn't good for their image. According to the girl's tearful story, the mayor had returned to be with her, only she'd refused him because she was still hurt from him giving away her last baby, and he'd forced himself on her. He'd gotten her pregnant again, and was going to let the girl keep the baby and send her away, probably to make up for her forced impregnation, but his wife found out, so he'd made up a lie about the girl seducing him and getting him drunk. The punishment was to be the death

313

of her and her baby, so she'd fled to Madame, hoping the Cajun healer could do something to protect her baby.

"What about you, child?" Madame asked.

She shook her head tearfully. "I have to let them find me. They'll stop looking for the baby if they find me...I'll...tell them the baby fell in the swamp. They gon kill me eventually anyway. But this baby...he special. He cain't die like this."

Madame looked down at the silent baby. He seemed either oblivious or comfortable inside the chaos surrounding him. Something in his beautiful eyes scared her for a moment and she felt a terrible chill pass through her soul

"Has he cried since you ran?"

The girl shook her head in confusion. "No, ma'am. He don't never cry. Not ever. Not even when he came out of me."
"That be a bad sign, child. This child born out of evil. He got a bad cloud hangin over him when trouble don't bother him none. Might not be a good idea to let him reach that cloud and bring down his storms..."

"No! Please...it's not his fault...please...I lost one baby, I cain't let another be killed because of another person."

"He be *cursed*, girl. He'll never bring nobody nothing but pain. And his children...if they be born with these demon eyes, they be cursed, too. Cursed with beauty but no soul that *will* destroy the lives of all they love and who love them."

The girl was shaking, looking so beautifully small and terrified. "Is there something you can do??? Please..."

Madame sighed. "Sometimes...sometimes the curse can be broken by one of them who be born different."

UNTRUST Deszion Nasir

The girl looked confused.

"Them eyes, child. Them eyes is the heart of the curse. One gotta be born of him or you that don't have them blue eyes to break the curse. That mean the evil done ran its course. The one without the blue eyes can end it."

The sound of dogs in the distance grew louder. The girl looked at the door, then Madame in fear.

Madame finally sighed. "Come kiss your baby, girl. Come kiss him with all the love you gonna be able to give him. I do this for you. My sister goin to Virginia in 2 days. She gon' take this child to a home there. He be safe."

The girl wiped water from her eyes and came over to the baby. She raked her waist-length hair back and kissed the baby on his soft cheek. Then she hugged Madame and ran to the back door. She gave Madame one last look and fled into the night, her ebony hair vanishing behind her.

Madame closed the door and sat down on the settee. Only minutes passed before she heard barking, shouting, screaming, then gunshots. Then silence.
"It be done," Madame said, sadly, glancing down at the baby. She lifted a ragged shoelace tied around the baby's neck with an old leather strip attached. In scratched handwriting she read his name: "Gemini. It be done wit yo ma, but you only getting' started…"

WICKED BLUES…. COMING SOON… THE DEVIL IS PATIENT…

UNTRUST Deszion Nasir

AUTHOR'S COMMENTS:

Aw, man…do you think I'm crazy yet? If you do… good. If you don't… wait…

This book was written back in 2010, but it's not the first of its kind. Gemini, Blue's dad, had his story created first, and the few people who heard bits and pieces kept asking me about Gemini's kids, hence, this book and others were created. I made the decision to release them backwards to keep the readers in a constant state of "What in the world? This can't get any worse can it?" Suuurree it can… it came out of here *taps head*

God, thank you for the patience to get through these trying years and many… MANY obstacles it took to get me here personally and professionally before I decided to stop relying on anyone but You and do this project entirely on my own, for it wasn't until then that things began to move.

Destani, my genius writer and oldest daughter… you're right behind me, baby… *Phantoms* is gonna be big! Zion, thanks for being the big brother everyone wishes they had. Shamar… my intellectual… stay in your own world… it's beautiful there… Amani… you'll always be my hurricane of light and love. You all were so patient with me. To my family, Mom, James, Daddy…I love all of u…

To Chris, my bestie and my editor, it took us a minute but we did it! You're the only person who can critique me and not piss me off.   Vershorn, nobody can ask for a better test reader… you'll always have a special spot inside for that. Cary, ups and downs… you gave me the time and space to work this thang out and you'll always have a special spot for that. I'm not easy to deal with when I'm writing and I know it. To all the people who supported me online, u know I got ya'll… but all ya'll not getting free copies, sorry. Love you Lesa Jones! Sonja Simone Blade (cover model)??? GIRL YOU KNOW YOU BADDD!!!

REAL WOMEN VS. REAL MEN: THIS IS YA'LLs

UNTRUST Deszion Nasir

OFFICIAL SHOUT OUT!!!
To all the people who *pretended* to support me…this is your *pretend* shout out…(-_-)

Stay tuned for the next edition of "WHAT IN THE WORLD WAS GOING ON IN HER HEAD??"
Deszion Amani Nasir -2012

UNTRUST Deszion Nasir

Look out for these other titles by Deszion Amani Nasir

And Coming soon…